Gradchanted

MORGAN MATSON

Disney • HYPERION

Los Angeles New York

First Edition, March 2025
10 9 8 7 6 5 4 3 2 1
FAC-025438-24353
Printed in the United States of America

This book is set in Adobe Caslon/Monotype
Designed by Marci Senders
Library of Congress Control Number: 2024940679
ISBN 978-1-368-09742-0

Visit www.DisneyBooks.com

SUSTAINABLE
FORESTRY
INITIATIVE

Certified Sourcing

www.sfiprogram.org
SFI-01054

The SFI label applies to the text stock

For Sneha and Kate
In every loop, I choose the one where we're friends

Part One

At any time, press 1 to start the game over.
—*Excalibur!* video game manual, page 4

1

FRIDAY, JUNE 9TH

On the night that started everything—changed everything, really—I had no idea what was coming.

But that's always the way it goes, isn't it? We're just tossed along in the slipstream of time, moving forward, reacting as best we can. We never know what the most consequential nights of our lives will be, and we only get one chance to do it right.

Usually.

But that night, hours before things would start to change, I didn't know anything was out of the ordinary. I was just trying to get my dad to stop crying.

"Dad. Dad. Oscar?" I looked over his head at my other dad, Angelo, who shot me a look that clearly said *I know*. "Um. People are looking?"

We were at Otto, the fanciest restaurant in Harbor Cove, California. It was really nice—wood paneling and white tablecloths and a piano player by the bar who'd been going through a repertoire of pop songs with classical arrangements. Oscar had been trying to get a reservation for months, and when one cropped up two days after my graduation from Harbor Cove High, he'd jumped on it. I would have been fine going to the Mermaid Café, my favorite restaurant, but I was overruled. This meant that on the day of my actual graduation, we'd eaten pizza on the couch in front of a rom-com we all knew by heart—which, honestly, no notes.

My dad had been fine then, but now that we were all here, ostensibly celebrating, he'd been breaking down in tears every few bites.

"Oscar," Angelo said firmly, putting a glass of water in front of him. "Come on. Get it together. You're ruining Cass's night."

"You're not," I said quickly. "I'm just worried that your pasta is getting damp."

Oscar nodded, blew his nose into his napkin, and took a deep breath, running a hand over his now totally bald head. For a while there had been a few last remnants of hair around the back of his head, but finally even these had given up.

"There you go," Angelo said, rubbing his back. In contrast to Oscar, Angelo's hair was long and luxurious, swooping up and across his forehead, a perfect mix of salt and pepper.

"I'm just—so proud of you, Cass," Oscar said after drawing in a shaky breath. "Graduating with such high marks! Getting into Berkeley! And to do it with all our moves, so much disruption . . . it's really impressive, sweetie."

"It truly is," Angelo said, raising his wine glass to me. "We're both so proud."

I smiled at them and raised my own glass—filled with sparkling water—to clink theirs. "Thanks, Dad. Thanks, Pop."

Oscar wasn't exaggerating about moving a lot. My dads ran Issac & Issac, a house-flipping business. They'd scoop up an old property (usually one only they saw potential in), then renovate, redecorate, and sell it for a profit. Then they would find their next diamond in the rough—and we would move to wherever the next house was. And when that project was over, we'd move on again. I'd lived all over California, with sojourns in Washington, Nevada, and Arizona sprinkled in to keep things interesting. We'd only been in Harbor Cove for six months, making Harbor Cove High the sixteenth school I'd attended in my academic career.

Because of this, I'd learned a long time ago not to get too attached to anything—not school, or friends, or the Band of Brothers poster hanging on my bedroom wall. All of it was temporary, and soon we'd be moving on again, to the next town, the next project, the next fresh start. So when I'd started the second half of my senior year at a new school—not ideal—I'd resolved not to make any close friends; just keep things light and easy, since I'd be going to college in the fall anyway.

But then—I hadn't planned on Bryony.

The piano player finished her rendition of "Time After Time" to a light smattering of applause. She nodded before starting her take on "Blank Space." I watched her play, my eyes following her hands on the keys.

When I was younger, I'd really wanted to learn piano. My dads had gotten me a keyboard for Christmas the year I was twelve. We'd try and find new teachers with every new move, and I attempted to keep up via YouTube tutorials and videos. But I found it was hard to sustain any kind of momentum, to actually get better beyond learning the basics. So after a while, I just stopped practicing, and Angelo and Oscar tacitly stopped asking me about finding more teachers. I still had my keyboard, even though I hadn't taken it out of its case in years. I just slid it under my bed in every new place.

But whenever I saw a pianist, I liked to watch them play. I was always amazed at how they had such a limited number of notes and could still create such variations with them.

"So, are you excited about tonight?" Angelo asked, and I looked away from the piano player and back to my dads—relieved to see that Oscar seemed to be pulling himself together.

I nodded as I smiled at him across the table. "I really am."

Oscar sighed. "When I had my grad night party, do you know what we did?"

Angelo raised an eyebrow. "What?"

"Nothing! We literally did nothing. We certainly didn't go gallivanting off to Disneyland."

"I promise," I said, taking the last bite of my steak, "there will be no gallivanting."

"It does sound fun, though," Angelo said as he stole a piece of pasta off Oscar's plate. "Think we could pass for recent high school graduates?"

Both Oscar and I burst into laughter at the same time. "Sorry, Pop," I said, spearing a fry. "High school seniors only."

Harbor Cove was in Orange County, and we were only about half an hour away from Anaheim. So, our grad night celebration was taking place . . . at Disneyland.

I hadn't known this was a thing until we moved to Harbor Cove. I'd been to Disneyland several times with Oscar and Angelo, but when Bryony had first mentioned Disney Grad Nite, I'd assumed she was joking. A night to run around in a theme park after hours, with only other recent graduates? And we would get to be there all night and go on the rides as many times as we wanted, without long wait times? It seemed too wonderful to be possible.

But Bryony explained to me, her face serious, not only was it possible, it was a school tradition. Harbor Cove High had been doing Disney Grad Nite since it basically started in the 1960s. And since the administration knew how much HCH students looked forward to it, it was the way they kept the senior class in line. Too many participants in Senior Skip Day? No Grad Nite. Senior pranks getting out of hand? No Grad Nite. People misbehaved at prom? You guessed it. But we'd stayed on our best behavior all spring, which meant Grad Nite was happening—tonight, in just a few hours.

I couldn't stop myself from taking a peek at my phone to check the time. Even though I hadn't been looking forward to this for years, like my classmates, I was still beyond excited. I quickly opened up my phone and took a selfie of me smiling, then sent it to Bryony with the message

SEE YOU SOON YAY 🐻 🏰 🕯️ 🎓

I kept the camera on me for just a moment longer, making sure that I didn't have anything in my teeth. There I was—Cassandra Elle Issac, eighteen years and three months old. I was just a hair under 5'5", with green-brown eyes, freckles, and slightly crooked teeth, which seemed incredibly unfair, given how long I'd spent in braces in middle school. At various schools over the years, I'd tried out different versions of my name. My dads had called me Cassie when I was little. And for a while in elementary school, I changed it with every new move: Cassandra and Cassie and Casey and Sandra and Andra and Andie and Sandy and Sandie, then back to Cassandra again. But during one fifth grade math class, I'd realized that if I went by Cass Issac, my name made a loop—a combined-name palindrome. Since that day, I hadn't gone by anything else. I'd even gotten it monogrammed in a circle on the white purse that was currently resting at my feet. It had taken a *lot* of emails back and forth with the Etsy seller, explaining what I wanted, but in the end it had been worth it.

I smoothed down my hair, which had a mind of its own. It was light brown, long and curly, and it had taken me years, but I'd finally figured out how best to handle it so that it behaved at least half the time. I'd tried to thread the line tonight between a cute outfit and one that I could run around an amusement park in. So, I was in a short, flower-printed dress with three-quarter-length sleeves, my favorite embroidered sneakers, and a jean jacket in case it got cold.

"Cass?"

I set my phone down and glanced up. Both my dads were looking at me, our waitress hovering near the table. "Sorry," I said quickly. "What?"

"Are you done?" Oscar asked.

"All set," I said, laying my fork and knife across my plate. "Thanks so much." The waitress cleared our plates, and Angelo leaned forward across the table.

"I hope you have a great time," Angelo said, smiling at me. "Even if we can't tag along."

I laughed. "Thanks, Pop."

"You're just lucky, kid," Oscar said, sighing wistfully. "It's the kind of night that only comes around once. Make sure you take lots of pictures, okay?"

"And I'm happy you get to have this time with your friends," Angelo said, exchanging a look with Oscar. His smile had started to dim a little. "Especially since . . . well . . ."

I nodded, too, and looked down at the table. I'd expected that I'd be able to stay in Harbor Cove until I went to UC Berkeley in the fall. But three weeks ago, my dads had sat me down at the kitchen island. Oscar had turned his laptop around so I could see it—the next house they'd found to renovate. In retrospect, I really should have known this would happen. The Harbor Cove house was looking great—nearly done, the work moving fast, everything coming together. But I was still surprised as I stared at the pictures in front of me.

"It's in Oregon," Angelo said, sitting down on the stool next to me.

"Oregon?" I echoed, feeling my stomach drop. I had been hoping, vaguely, that maybe work on our current house would take us all the way through the summer. Or that their next project would be somewhere around here.

"Obviously, since this house hasn't sold yet, we'll be back a bit. But we really need to get started as soon as possible."

"We had hoped that maybe you could have the whole summer in Harbor Cove," Oscar said, exchanging an unhappy look with Angelo. "But we couldn't wait on this one."

"But you'll be able to see your friends when we come back to deal with the sale," Angelo added, sounding like someone trying very hard to find the bright side.

I nodded, turning all this over in my mind. I looked around the kitchen—it was absolutely perfect. The paint was fresh, the brass drawer pulls bright and shiny and scratch-free. And as I took it in, I realized that this was the best it would ever be. It could really only go downhill from here—it would get messy and stained and lived in. It would never look as good as it did right now. And all at once, my situation suddenly seemed very clear. Was there any sense in sticking around when there would only be diminishing returns? Wasn't the very best thing to do to leave when things were at their peak?

"It's okay," I said. "And I might not really be able to come back much. I'm sure I'll be busy with stuff in Oregon and getting ready for school. So, it's fine. I promise."

"Are you sure?" Oscar asked, his expression skeptical.

"Yes," I said quickly. I didn't want to dwell on this. I needed to keep looking forward—looking back would only make it that much harder. "I'm leaving for college in the fall anyway, and besides, I've only been here six months. It's not like I'm leaving a place I've been forever."

They both took a breath at the same time, like they were preparing to argue with me, when Oscar's phone rang with a permit update from the contractor, and they snapped back into work mode, and we all moved on.

So, we'd be flying to Oregon in the morning, to begin the whole process all over again—turning something that was just potential into something shiny and special and perfect.

"Don't worry about it," I said now as I folded my napkin and laid it across the table. I gave them both a big smile. "I promise I'm fine."

"You never told us how Bryony took it when you told her we were moving," Oscar said, giving me a sympathetic grimace. "Was she okay?"

"Did you tell her you could come back and visit?" Angelo asked. "And that she can come and visit us?"

I looked down and concentrated for a moment on smoothing out any wrinkles in my napkin. "Sure. I mean, she was sad, but she totally understood." I glanced up, relieved to see that the waitress was here and handing out dessert menus. I took mine and focused on it, like I was really having trouble deciding between the German chocolate cake and the mixed berry plate. Which, I mean, there wasn't even a question. Chocolate cake all the way. But the truth was . . . I hadn't actually told Bryony I was leaving.

I'd thought about it, of course. And it had been hard to keep it to myself, especially when she talked about summer plans—plans that she assumed I would be around for. But in the end, I'd decided a clean break was the best way to handle it.

I'd left too many friends behind over the years, and I'd had too many years of awkward texts and strained phone calls, in which you tried to connect with someone you'd once been *such* good friends with, and now could barely find anything to say to. I found it would retroactively wreck your memories of the friendship—like soon you would have trouble recalling why you'd even gotten along so well with them in the first place. And so, somewhere around ninth grade, I'd decided I was just going to go. This meant not telling people I was leaving but always making sure to slip away after a fun, great time. Leave at a peak, when everything was wonderful. This way, the memories were of the best of a friendship. It didn't slowly become a faint echo, a copy of a copy.

And sure, sometimes it got hard. Like leaving Washington. I knew the way things had ended there had not been ideal. And I could tell that I was really going to miss Harbor Cove and the friendship I'd built with Bryony. But this system had worked great for me for years—I wasn't going to change things at the last minute just because the end was always hard.

And so I'd decided that I would just concentrate tonight on making sure it was a fantastic night for us—so that I could depart on a real high note.

Oscar ordered an espresso, despite Angelo reminding him that it always kept him up all night. Feeling like staying up all night was just what I wanted, I got a latte. Angelo, telling both of us that we were playing with fire, got a mint tea, and we all ordered the chocolate cake. It was delicious, and I'd nearly finished mine when I asked, "Did you know German chocolate cake doesn't actually have anything to do with the country? It was invented by a man named Samuel German. The proper name is actually German's chocolate cake."

Oscar smiled at Angelo. "I knew we wouldn't be able to make it through dinner without a fact."

"What?" I said, laughing. "You know you love them." I'd been collecting facts since I was little and discovered that I had a real memory for retaining them. It had never come in handy until the year we were in Arizona, and my quiz bowl team went all the way to Nationals. But I liked always having something at my fingertips, something to say on a big variety of subjects and places. This calmed me down, somehow. And the first thing I usually did when we moved somewhere was to find out a couple of obscure facts about it. It made me feel a little less like a tourist, someone who was just passing through.

"I just feel bad for this German guy," Angelo said, reaching over to my plate to steal a bite. "They dropped the apostrophe and suddenly he's not getting any credit."

"That's how the cake crumbles?" I tried.

Oscar shook his head. "Quit while you're ahead, kid."

I took a breath to reply just as my phone lit up with a series of texts.

BRYONY:
Hey I'm early! Outside whenever you're done.

Say hi to A&O!

DISNEEEEEYYYYYYYY!!!!!!!

"I should get going," I said, taking the last bite of chocolate cake and setting my fork down. Bryony was driving us to Harbor Cove High, where we'd get the buses that would take us to Disneyland. And the fact she was here meant that the night was about to begin. I pushed back from the table and hugged Oscar, then Angelo. "Bryony's outside. She says hi. Thank you for dinner."

"Thank *you* for being the best daughter ever," Oscar said, starting to get misty again.

"Now he's going to be overwrought *and* overcaffeinated," Angelo said with a sigh. "It's not a good combination." Then he smiled at me. "But have a great time tonight, kid. You're back late, right?"

I nodded. "Grad Nite ends at two a.m.—so I'll probably be home around three or three thirty."

Angelo shook his head. "We'll definitely be asleep." He looked over at Oscar and sighed. "Well, I will be, at any rate."

"Have fun," Oscar said, wiping his eyes with his napkin. "See you in the morning!"

"Bye," I said, giving them both a wave. Then I shouldered my bag and hurried out the doors of the restaurant—where my best friend was waiting for me.

1

I had not meant to become best friends with Bryony Tsai.

It had been my intention not to be close friends with *anyone* at Harbor Cove. Not that I wanted to be enemies with anyone either—I just wanted to get through these last six months with very few attachments. And I was pretty sure flying solo was going to be easy to achieve. Who wanted to make a new friend the second semester of senior year? A friend they were just going to say goodbye to in six months? I'd figured everyone would be on the same page. I just hadn't planned on Bryony. Or the exploding sink.

I'd been at Harbor Cove a week, and my plan seemed like it was on track. I'd met some people to chat with in my classes and had been floating between various tables and spots at lunch. I was being friendly with everybody, but not getting too close with any one group.

It was after PE, and I was taking my time getting ready in the locker room. I'd had enough credits that I'd been able to test out of taking a language, which meant I had a free period next. So, while everyone else got dressed in a rush and hurried back to their next class, I hadn't been stressing about it. And I also thought I was alone in the locker room, so when I rounded the corner and saw a girl sitting on the floor, with her back against the lockers, I jumped in shock.

"Agh!" I yelped, then shook my head, trying to pull myself together and get my heart rate to calm down. "Sorry," I amended quickly. That didn't seem like a way anyone would want to be greeted. "I didn't know anyone else was here."

The girl looked up at me, and I could see that her face was tearstained and puffy—she'd clearly been crying. I was pretty sure I recognized her from our gym class. "I'm not s-supposed to be here," she said, wiping a tear away. She had dark brown hair with pink streaks threaded through it, and blunt, straight-across bangs. She was wearing a shirt that said, for some reason, LUCKY & CHARMED.

"Are you okay?" I asked, taking a step closer, worried that she was hurt. "Do you need help? Should I call someone?"

Our gym teacher had been scrolling through TikTok while we played volleyball, so I wasn't sure she'd be particularly helpful in this—or any—situation, but she *was* an adult, at least.

"No," the girl said. "It's okay. I'm just . . ." She drew in a shaky breath. "It's just been a really bad day."

I nodded, giving her a sympathetic grimace, even as I was aware I didn't want to be pulled too far into this, whatever it was. My whole plan for flying solo was contingent on not getting involved in people's personal drama. "Sorry about that," I said, taking a step back, heading toward the exit. Now that I knew this girl wasn't hurt—just having a crappy Friday—I wouldn't feel guilty about leaving. "That sucks. So . . ."

"Yeah," she went on. "My boyfriend broke up with me right before the holidays. And then I came back to school and found out that all my friends had taken his side. So, I'm basically closing out my senior year with no friends?" She gave a little incredulous laugh at that.

"Oh," I said, trying to ignore how this was hitting a little too close to home. "That really sucks. But . . ."

"And then this happened," she said, standing up and gesturing to her jeans.

My eyes widened as I stared at her. There was a huge, dark stain covering the front of them. "Did . . . um . . ."

"It was the sink!" she said, cracking a smile for the first time, maybe at my expression. "Everyone knows to avoid the last sink—water just explodes out of it. But I was so distracted I forgot. And now I can't go out like this."

"The *sink*?" I asked skeptically. I really didn't understand how a sink could have done that—it looked for all intents and purposes like she'd had an unfortunate accident.

She raised an eyebrow at me. "If you don't believe me, try it yourself."

I was about to tell her that I had to go, lie and say that I was late for class. But there was an unmistakable challenge in her tone, and I wasn't just going to back down from it. "Fine." I dropped my purse and walked over to the last sink. It looked like a normal sink to me. I was about to tell her so when I turned the knob for the cold water. A geyser immediately exploded out at me—hitting me right across the front of my cords. "Agh! What!" I yelped, shutting off the water and jumping back, sliding a little, and then struggling to regain my balance.

The girl was cracking up, bent double. "I told you," she managed. "The sink explodes!" She started laughing again, sliding down the locker to sit on the floor, her shoulders shaking.

"Why would anyone do that?" I asked. I was laughing now, too; I couldn't help it. There was something about this girl's laughter that made you want to laugh too, like singing along to a song you've always known. I looked in dismay at my reflection—and at the identical dark stain that was now across the front of my pants. "This is awful!"

"I guess we just live here now?" She was still laughing as she looked from me to her, and the identical terrible situation we were now in. "I'm Bryony, by the way. Bryony Tsai."

"Cass Issac," I said, coming over to join her.

"Are you new?"

"Yeah, we just moved here from San Luis Obispo."

Her eyes widened. "You moved second semester of senior year?"

"Yeah, but it's okay. It's . . ." I took a breath, about to rattle off all the excuses and lines I'd told myself about how it would be fine to have no friends, that I was okay starting over, yet again. But as I looked at Bryony's sympathetic expression, all those flimsy arguments collapsed. "It sucks," I said, sitting down next to her.

"It really does."

"And I'm really sorry about your breakup—and your friends being jerks." I shook my head. "That's awful."

"I mean, I guess better to find out now that they were kind of terrible? But I was just so blindsided. And now this happened," she said, gesturing down at herself.

"Well, I'm in the same boat."

"You could have just believed me," she said, starting to laugh again.

"Yeah, in retrospect that would have made a lot more sense," I agreed, laughing too.

We stayed in the locker room for the rest of the period—it took that long for our pants to dry. And by the end of it, when we walked out together and headed to lunch, sitting down and continuing our conversation without even having to talk about it, we were friends.

It was the last thing I'd been expecting—that I'd meet the best friend I'd ever had when I was determined not to make any friends at all. But Bryony and I had just gotten along, from that very first day.

And now, as I hurried out of the restaurant and saw her slightly dented white Jeep in the parking lot, I felt myself smile. I ran over to the passenger side and yanked open the door. "Hi, friend!" I yelled, as she jumped.

"*Oh* my god," she yelped, placing her hand on her chest. "You scared me!"

I laughed. "You were the one who texted me you were here."

"I know! I just didn't expect you to, like, apparate here."

"I hardly think that's what I did." I got into the car and immediately recognized what she was listening to. "*Cereal?*" I asked with a sigh.

Bryony grinned at me. "Well, naturally!" *Cereal* was the podcast Bryony was obsessed with. She'd been talking it up ever since we met, but I'd just never understood the appeal. It was just two friends sitting around, eating and rating different breakfast cereals while chatting. Bryony *loved* it and was always trying to get me to listen so we could talk about it. But honestly, I'd never understood the point. Why was I going to listen to total strangers gab over Lucky Charms? What was fun about that? But Bryony was a super fan—she'd gone to a bunch of their live shows, lived for the new episode drops, and even now, was wearing *Cereal* merch—a T-shirt that read IT'S BETTER WITH MILK! which was apparently one of the show's catchphrases. "How was the dinner? Did Oscar cry?"

"Delicious, and of course," I said, as I buckled my seat belt. I smiled across the car at her. "Are you so excited?"

"I'm *so excited*!" she practically yelled, and I laughed. "It's going to be the best night ever."

"It really is. Oscar was talking all about how he didn't do anything for his grad night. This just feels super special."

"It's going to be amazing," Bryony said as she put the car in reverse and backed out of the parking lot. "I've been hearing about it for forever, and now our turn is finally here."

"I can't wait. Angelo was telling me to take lots of pictures, to make sure and remember everything, because it's only going to come around once." I checked my phone—seven thirty. "Think we're okay on time?"

Bryony nodded. "We're good." Everyone was meeting at Harbor Cove High, in the parking lot by the soccer field, and then we'd drive over to the park. Grad Nite started at nine, so the buses were going to start leaving at eight. "You want to DJ?"

"Always." I scrolled through my songs, looking for her favorites, before stopping on Taylor Swift's "Long Live."

"Yes!" Bryony grinned at me and cranked the volume. "Perfect!" She started singing along to the song, her hand out the window, keeping time on the window frame.

As I looked at Bryony, I felt a little squeeze in my heart. I knew that this, tonight, would most likely be the last time we would ever hang out. But I quickly pushed this away, not wanting to deal with it just yet. Tonight was about having an amazing, once-in-a-lifetime experience. *Tomorrow* was for dealing with the future.

Bryony parked, and then without even talking about it, we ran over to the group of seniors gathered by the waiting school buses.

I waved as I passed Stella Griffin and her boyfriend, Reece Suarez. Stella and I had been in AP American History together, and I'd loved working on group projects with her—she was the most organized person I'd ever met. She gave me a smile as I passed, and then I hurried to join Bryony, who was already lined up.

She was standing next to Amy Caruso, who, as usual, was pretzeled around her boyfriend, Carlos Cabello. When I'd first arrived at Harbor Cove, Bryony had given me the scoop on them. They were usually just called AmyandCarlos, one word, since they were always together. It turned out they'd been dating since something like sixth grade, and you almost never saw them apart.

"Hey, you two," Bryony said, and they broke apart with what looked like real reluctance.

"Hey," Amy said. Carlos immediately nuzzled her neck, like even a few seconds not kissing was far too many to be borne. "You ready for this?"

I nodded. "I just had a latte. I'm good to stay up and ride all the rides." Bryony gave a very fake-sounding cough, and I felt my cheeks get hot. "Fine. All the rides that don't have big drops or go super fast." I could handle things like Soarin', and Radiator Springs Racers, but those were about my limit, and Bryony knew it. We'd been to Disneyland twice together since I'd moved to Harbor Cove and learned the true joy of living so close to the park.

"You had a *latte*?" I turned around to see Sheridan Williams standing behind us. He was wearing an eye mask pushed up on his forehead and a skeptical expression.

"Uh . . . yeah," I said, looking at Bryony and widening my eyes.

"Why do you have an eye mask?" she asked, as usual, reading my mind.

"So I can sleep on the bus," Sheridan said, like this was the most normal thing in the world. "It's why you shouldn't have caffeinated this early, Cass. I've timed this out, because I want to be at my peak energy level once we arrive. In addition to the rides, there's a DJ in Cars Land, a karaoke stage, and a live band. And I want to hit them all. I want to go without stopping until the moment we have to leave."

"Uh, sorry to barge in, but you should stop a *little* bit." This was Ms. Mulaney, who'd been my English teacher. She walked over to our group, and I smiled at her—I hadn't known she was going to be one of our chaperones. She was one of the very best teachers I'd ever had—and I had a very large sample size to pull from. She welcomed me into her class, which focused on Dickens and Austen. It had been one of the most interesting classes I'd ever taken, and unlike most of my teachers, she didn't seem to mind that I peppered my essays with more random facts than were probably *strictly* necessary.

"After all," Ms. Mulaney continued, "you have to pace yourself. This is the fifth Grad Nite I've chaperoned, and I've seen people try and go too hard . . . and then end up sleeping on a bench near the Ferris wheel at midnight."

"Well," Sheridan said, with a shrug, "we can just agree to disagree." He turned away and walked over to join Manny Ortega.

"You've chaperoned *five* grad nights?" I asked.

"Sure have."

"Wow." Bryony turned to me. "I feel like this is a sign from the universe. I should become a teacher, right?"

"It's fun," Ms. Mulaney said. "In addition to making sure you all behave, I get to go on the rides, too. And then when I've had enough of that, I can go to the lounge and do some work."

"But school's over," Bryony pointed out. "What work do you have?"

Ms. Mulaney glanced down at the canvas bag over her shoulder for just a moment, then shook her head. "Don't worry about it."

"What lounge?" I asked.

"It's for chaperones," Ms. Mulaney explained. "Stocked with snacks and coffee so we can try and stay awake."

"Mickey bars, too, right?" Carlos asked, raising an eyebrow.

Ms. Mulaney grinned. "I can neither confirm nor deny the presence of free ice cream," she said as she checked her watch and then walked away. "We're leaving soon," she called to us. "Get your things together!"

"Where did you hear that?" I asked Carlos, but he didn't respond—because he and Amy were back to making out again. I shrugged and pulled out my phone, and started scrolling through my social media apps. I stopped when I saw a story posted by Tabitha Keith, promoting her new makeup line.

Tabitha Keith, as the daughter of a movie star and a musician, had been famous practically since she was born. But now, as she was starting to get movie roles herself and was constantly having her picture taken while she got brunch or coffee, her profile had exploded. Her makeup line had just come out, a skincare line was in development, and she had been heavily rumored for a role in the newest superhero team-up movie.

"What?" Bryony asked, looking over. I tilted my phone screen so she could see it. "Oh, I was thinking about trying her new stuff," she said. "The really pink blush?"

"It's wild she's our age and has a makeup line," I said, as her next story started—this time she was washing her face in a bright-white bathroom and talking about how her skincare line was going to revolutionize clean beauty.

Bryony laughed. "I mean it's not like she had to raise money and develop it for years. I'm sure that she's just the face of it."

"Still," I said, then closed out my stories. It was very clear that Tabitha never had a bad-skin day—or probably any kind of bad day—in her life.

Bryony's phone beeped, and she pulled it out of her bag. Her eyes widened as she looked at it, and she grabbed my arm. "Cass! I just got an email from Mermaid Café! Did you get one, too?"

The Mermaid Café was the centerpiece of Bryony's summer plan. She had a whole vision for how the summer would unfold—we'd both get jobs, ideally with shifts together, at the Mermaid. She was hopeful that even with no food service experience, we could get hired as servers—but if not, she was willing to take a hostess position. In addition to getting to work together and make good tip money, she had *lots* of other plans. She wanted us to drive down to San Diego for their legendary fireworks display on the Fourth and was determined to spend every Friday at the beach. And she'd announced that we also *had* to take a long road trip before she started school at University of Washington and I went to Berkeley.

"Let me check," I murmured as I unlocked my phone, keeping my eyes averted. "Hmm . . ."

"They've received my application and they're processing it," she read, her voice going high and excited. "And if they're interested, they'll call this

23

week for an interview!" She leaned over to look at my phone. "Check your email. I'm sure you got the same one."

I checked my email, knowing full well that there wouldn't be anything there, but hoping I pulled off pretending there would be. "Nothing yet. But I'm sure I'll hear soon."

Bryony nodded, twisting her long, pink-streaked hair into a messy bun. "If you don't hear soon, I'd reach out to them. It's *really* important that we both get this job."

"Totally," I said, bending forward and letting my hair fall over my face, shielding it from view. I tucked my phone in my purse, taking a little more time than was strictly necessary, just trying to keep my face averted so Bryony wouldn't be able to read the truth on it.

Because the fact of the matter was, there was no way I was going to be getting an email from the Mermaid Café about my pending application there. I hadn't put in an application—after all, what would be the point?

My phone beeped, and I looked down at it in surprise. "Is that them?" Bryony asked.

I shook my head. "AirDrop." I squinted at the screen, then realized that the photos that had been sent to me—all of my classmate Renee Burrows making kissing faces—were most likely not intended for me.

"Renee?" I called, looking around. She was a few people behind us in line and raised an eyebrow.

"Yeah?"

"I think you meant to AirDrop Cassidy, right?" Cassidy Zeppes was standing by the front of the bus—everyone knew Renee had a huge crush on her.

"Oh," Renee said, turning a deep red. "Uh—sorry, Cass. Just saw the first few letters."

"It happens," I said easily, already rejecting the AirDrop. "No worries."

"Bryony! Cass!" I looked up and saw the Emmas coming toward us. The Emmas—Emma R., Emma J., and Emma Z.—were best friends who all shared a name. (Technically, Emma R. was an *Emily*, but she'd been allowed in anyway. She'd argued that Emma Stone, one of the pre-emma-nent representatives of their name, was technically also an Emily, which apparently had been enough to convince everyone.)

Bryony had told me that the Emmas had been really nice to her when she'd been dumped by her ex and then her whole former friend group. And even though they'd been really welcoming, the Emmas were their *own* unit, and had been ever since middle school, so it just wasn't the same. Bryony had always felt like she was just slightly outside the jokes and traditions, and when I'd come to town, she'd gone back to being a more casual friend of theirs. I hadn't spent a ton of time with the Emmas, but we'd always gotten along, and I smiled now as I saw them coming toward us.

"Hey, guys," Bryony said, giving them a smile. "Are you on our bus?"

Emma R. gave us both quick hugs, while Emma J. shook her head. "We're on bus one," she said, pointing to the front of the line. "We should get going."

"But we just wanted to say hi!" Emma R. said with a grin. "Aren't you so excited? It's going to be the best night ever, right?"

Emma Z. scoffed, and I glanced at her in surprise. Her face looked drawn, her eyes were puffy, and she stalked away to the first bus without a word, her head down and her shoulders hunched.

"What's going on with Emma?" I asked the other Emmas, looking after her in surprise. I wasn't super close with Emma Z., but she'd always been friendly.

"Oh," Emma R. said, dropping her voice. "She got some bad news today. She'd gotten this scholarship from the Harbor Club that was going to help her with a lot of college expenses—books and food and stuff? But she found out today that they're actually pulling it. They're over budget or something."

Bryony grimaced. "That's tough. Is she okay?"

"I think so," Emma J. said, but she looked after her friend, her forehead furrowed. "I'm going to go check."

She followed after Emma Z., and Emma R. pulled out her phone. "I meant to ask you two. Want to go see Band of Brothers in August? Tickets go on sale tomorrow."

"Of course," Bryony said. "Maybe not behind a pole this time?"

"I can't," I said with a shrug. "I won't be here."

"What do you mean?" Bryony asked, and a second too late, I realized what I'd done.

"I . . . Because school starts," I said, trying to will myself to think faster. "In August."

"This is the beginning," Emma R. said. "Like, August third or something." She looked at me with alarm. "Does Berkeley start that early? Now I'm not sad I didn't get in."

"Oh sorry—I just misunderstood," I said, pulling out my phone, pretending to be looking for something as I scrolled through it. "Let me check and I'll get back to you, okay?"

"Cool," Emma R. said. "Have to grab my bus, but see you there!"

She hurried off and Bryony turned to me. "You should be able to go, right? No school starts that early."

"No, totally," I agreed, still not meeting her eye. "I just got mixed up. Too bad about Emma Z., huh?"

"Seriously. That's so hard. To have the rug pulled out from under you at the last minute like that . . ."

I nodded, wanting to change the subject. This was veering dangerously close to what had happened to me with my dads' announcement, and that was the last thing I wanted to think about. "You know where that phrase comes from?"

Bryony grinned at me. "Is it fact time?"

I laughed. "It *is* fact time! So it's from the thirties. The older version, from the 1500s, was *cut the grass under my feet*."

Bryony thought about this, then shook her head. "I don't see that catching on."

"Me neither."

"Okay!" Ms. Mulaney was back and clapping her hands together. "Bus five, we're ready to rock and roll. Twenty minutes to the park, and even though you've all graduated and we technically have no sway over you any longer—please behave. Okay?"

We all nodded—I saw Manny Ortega give her a thumbs-up—and then Ms. Mulaney climbed on the bus. I turned to Bryony. "Ready?"

"*So* ready. Grab a spoon!"

I just looked at her. "Is that *Cereal*?"

She grinned at me. "You know it!"

I laughed, then gestured to the bus. "Let's go!"

1

O kay!" Ms. Mulaney said. She adjusted the tote bag on her shoulder and raised her voice "Can everyone hear me?"

I nodded, and so did Bryony, but Amy and Carlos were kissing again and—I had a feeling—not paying attention to anything except each other. We were lined up, along with the rest of the students from Harbor Cove High, outside the Grad Nite welcome tent. It turned out we weren't going in through the main gates. We'd come around a side entrance and seen a long line of other high schoolers—and their chaperones—going into the tent. It was huge and white, with WELCOME TO GRAD NITE printed on the side of it, the *G* in *Grad Nite* adorned with neon Mickey ears.

Maybe feeling like she'd gotten enough nods and muttered yeses, Ms. Mulaney continued. "Inside the tent, you'll have your bag searched and receive your wristband. Then you can enter the park. As a reminder, California Adventure is the only theme park you'll have access to. Please do not attempt to leave and go into Disneyland, because you will be escorted away by security and not able to return to the rest of your night."

"Wait," Manny Ortega said, raising his hand like we were still back in English class. "But then how do we go on Space Mountain?"

"Well—you don't," Ms. Mulaney said. "We're in California Adventure. You can put your hand down, Manny."

Bryony turned to me and shook her head. "It's like he didn't read any of the emails."

"I know."

"Grad Nite goes until two a.m., when you're going to make your way back over to the same door we will be going in. If you are not there, I will not be happy. If you have an emergency, find me or one of the cast members. Okay?" She looked around at all of us. And maybe sensing this, AmyandCarlos stopped furiously kissing and glanced over at her. "Great. I want you all to have a lot of fun and celebrate your accomplishments. But please keep in mind that tonight, you're still representatives of Harbor Cove High. I will expect you to uphold our school's good name. Any questions?"

"Yeah," Sheridan said, looking up from his phone. "Who's the celebrity that's here tonight?"

A murmur went through the crowd immediately, and I turned to Bryony, but she shook her head—she clearly didn't know what Sheridan was talking about either.

"Wait—like, a celebrity that's our age?" Manny asked, for some reason raising his hand again.

Ms. Mulaney shook her head. "I don't know what you're talking about. And, Manny, you really can put your hand down."

Sheridan held his phone up. "DitesMoi is saying that *it's extra starry right now at Disney's Grad Nite.*"

DitesMoi was a social media gossip site that I looked at much more than I would have admitted to. And while sometimes they were way off base, most of the time they were at least partially correct, which meant that there was a not-insignificant chance someone famous was going to be at Grad Nite with us.

"So, it's probably someone from LA, right?" Manny turned to me. "Cass, what do you know?"

I blinked at him, surprised. "Me? How would *I* know?"

"Didn't you go to school in LA?"

"Yeah, but, like, two years ago." When my dads had been flipping a craftsman-style bungalow, we'd lived in Raven Rock, a small suburb in the northeast corner of Los Angeles. It had not exactly been a celebrity magnet.

"So?" Sheridan took a step closer to me. "Can you find out?"

I took a breath, about to tell him no, since I wasn't in touch with anyone from my old schools, but then decided it wasn't worth going into it all. "It's probably just a rumor."

"Exactly," Ms. Mulaney said, clapping her hands together. "Why don't you all focus on having fun, and not who might or might not be here?" The rest of us nodded, even though Sheridan was still focusing down on his phone. She smiled at all of us. "Good. Now let's have a great night."

Everyone cheered, and the line moved forward. I could see the people in front of us seemed to be from a school in Santa Barbara. They were all wearing matching T-shirts that read SANTA BARBARA BUCCANEERS GRAD NITE, and I gave a silent thanks that we hadn't been required to dress in matching outfits.

I glanced over and saw Sheridan frantically scrolling through his phone. He caught my eye and gestured down to it. "If someone famous is here, I'm going to find out," he said. "They definitely would have posted it to their feed."

"Well—good luck." I mentally shuddered, just thinking about someone being able to go through my internet profile, dig through my past, find out stuff about me that I didn't want people to know.

But then, I kept a lower online footprint than most of my friends at school. Since I'd found it better to make a clean break whenever I left, I always started a new social media profile when I moved somewhere new. I liked it this way—it was a fresh start, and I didn't have to look at the happy pictures of all the people I'd had to leave behind. It also meant that I no longer could see any of my old friends, but I'd learned through experience it was better that way. It just hurt too much to see stories and posts and videos of everyone having fun without me, moving on, and eventually forgetting me. I knew it would happen anyway, and at least this way I didn't have to *see* it.

We moved up in the line, and Bryony looked over at me. "So, what were you thinking our plan should be? I know you want to go on Radiator Springs Racers, right?"

"Always." It was my very favorite ride in the whole park, and if I could ride it with a low wait time or even get to ride it *multiple* times, it would make my whole night.

"And I want to do the Spider-Man ride."

"Of course you do." Bryony had a not-so-secret crush on Tom Holland. "Anything beyond that?"

She shrugged happily. "I mean, I think we can just let the night unfold, right?"

I grinned at her. "Totally. It's going to be amazing no matter what we do."

We moved forward again in the line, reaching the cast members. In short order, our bags were checked and we'd both been given neon-green plastic bracelets with today's date and DISNEY GRAD NITE—SENIOR printed on them.

"There's a QR code on your wristband," the cast member closest to me said, pointing at it. "It has tonight's schedule, a map, everything you'll need."

"That's really cool," I said as Bryony and I walked out of the tent. We scanned our codes, and I felt my eyes open wide as I took in the sheer amount of information that had come up on my phone.

DISNEYLAND GRAD NITE!

Friday, June 9

9 p.m.–10 p.m. . . . . Bus drop-off. Arrival tent check-in. Welcome inside the park!

9:30 p.m. . . . . Club Candy Stage Karaoke Kickoff!

9:30 p.m.– 2 a.m. . . . . . Costumed characters available for photo ops (various locations).

10 p.m.–2 a.m. . . . . . . Pacific Wharf Paradise Garden—this is a quiet location for any guests who might need a break.

10:30 p.m.–11:30 p.m. . . Cars Land DJ spinning.

12:00 a.m. . . . . Main Stage: live performance by Eton Mess.

1:30 a.m. . . . . Last call for rides!

2:00 a.m. . . . . Event wrap. Please proceed to the exit and make your way to your bus.

Have a great night!

"Wow," I said as I read it, scrolling down on my phone, trying to take it all in. "Have you ever heard of this band?"

"Eton Mess," Bryony read off her own screen, then shrugged. "Nope. But I want to do all of this. And the rides. And get a lot of delicious snacks . . ." She shook her head. "So basically, we'll need a month to get through all this."

"Well, since we just have tonight, we better get cracking!"

Bryony shook her head at me as we started walking out of the tent. "Did you just say *get cracking*?"

"What?" I asked. "It's what Oscar always says."

She raised an eyebrow at me. "*Sure* he does."

I laughed at that and grabbed her arm, more than ready for our night to start. "Let's go!" Outside the tent, there was a step-and-repeat with DISNEYLAND GRAD NITE! printed on it, along with the silhouettes of people jumping for joy and tossing their mortarboards into the air. Beyond that, I could see two large wooden doors, propped open, with cast members on either side of them checking wristbands as people entered.

I felt myself smile as we got closer. I knew I was doing the right thing. Bryony and I would have one epic, fun night—and then I'd leave tomorrow, taking only amazing memories with me.

We hurried toward the door, and I flashed my wrist at the cast members, who nodded. Bryony was keeping pace next to me, bouncing on her toes the way she did when she got really excited. I grinned at her, knowing we were about to have an unforgettable experience.

And it was all going to be great.

I glanced up at the doorway for just a second, then straightened my shoulders as I walked forward and crossed through—and into this night that would only come once in a lifetime.

Or so I thought.

1

W ow." I stood just inside the park, stock-still, attempting to take in everything around me.

There was pop music playing from the speakers, and people were streaming past me, laughing and talking in groups. There was an energy I'd never experienced at Disney before—the feeling like we were starting an adventure, like anything could happen. It reminded me of a carnival—the lights against the darkness, the groups of friends running around together, the feeling that you were about to have a great time.

We'd entered the park near the Avengers Campus. Just to the left, I could see the Guardians drop ride. The park's lights were glowing brightly, and as I looked around, I realized that I hadn't ever been here in actual nighttime before. In the past, I'd stayed until dusk or late twilight. But it was properly dark now—we were here after the park was normally open and looking at all the lights glowing in the darkness, I could really appreciate what that meant.

The song changed to "2Night's the Night," the pop song by Band of Brothers that had been inescapable this spring. It had turned into a de facto graduation anthem, and someone sitting next to me had started blasting it on their phone at the ceremony the moment we were declared graduates, and everyone cheered and threw their mortarboards in the air. Right now, it was kicking into the chorus—the Powell brothers warbling, *We only have tonight/Let's dance until first light/Remember this night will never come around again.*

There were people streaming past all around us—friends walking in groups, people running past and yelling happily, couples walking hand in hand. But, I realized as I looked around, these were *all* teenagers. And while I saw this every day at school, of course, there was something surreal about seeing a huge group of my peers at an amusement park—with no parents in sight, no little kids, nobody pushing strollers, just the occasional adult chaperone peppered in.

In the swirl surrounding us—the lights, the laughter of the other kids, the song hitting the final chorus about how tonight would never be forgotten—there was an air of excitement and giddiness that was palpable. Like everyone there was taking the song's words to heart.

"Who's ready to have the best night ever?" Sheridan—looking very awake now—yelled this as he barreled past us. Presumably, he was heading toward the Cars Land DJ he'd been so excited about.

"Me! I am!" This was Manny, hurrying behind Sheridan and seeming to think that this rhetorical question needed an answer—but at least this time he didn't raise his hand. He stopped to take a selfie, directly in the middle of where everyone was walking, creating a bottleneck.

A group of kids I didn't recognize dashed through the wooden entrance door. A girl in a blue sweatshirt, running fast, dodged out of the way of Manny at the last minute—only to crash hard into Bryony, sending her stumbling and falling to the asphalt.

"Oops!" the girl said. She clapped her hand over her mouth, paused for only a second, then ran on, her friends following behind her. "You okay?" she yelled over her shoulder once she was too far away to have done anything about it if Bryony wasn't.

"Oh my god," I said, hurrying over to Bryony. I reached down to help her up, but it was Amy, surprising me, who got there first.

"Are you all right?" Amy asked, helping Bryony to her feet.

"Yeah," she said, wincing slightly as she stood up. "Did everyone see?"

Amy and I exchanged a look, then both collectively decided to lie to her. "No," we said at the same time, with exactly the same inflection.

"There's so much going on," I added, hoping that Bryony would buy this. She certainly didn't need to know about the people I'd seen filming it, undoubtedly for some collection of epic falls on TikTok.

"Totally," Amy agreed, bending down to pick up Bryony's cross-body purse from where it had fallen to the ground.

"That girl came out of nowhere," I said, looking back to the entrance. Manny had moved on—probably realizing that this was partially his fault, and not wanting to deal with the fallout. But I could see that we *were* kind of in the way. I gestured to a nearby stone bench, and Bryony nodded and headed over to sit down on it, still moving a little gingerly.

"Babe!" This was Carlos, calling to Amy from where he was standing nearby, clearly ready to get their night started. "Come on!"

"Just a second!" Amy snapped. It was such an unusual tone for her to take with anyone—but especially Carlos—that Bryony and I exchanged a loaded, silent *what-the-heck?* look.

"I'm really okay," Bryony said, giving her a smile. "Thanks, Amy."

Amy gave her a nod, then handed her back her purse before going to join Carlos. "Why didn't you help her?" I heard her ask as she joined him.

"Me?" Carlos asked, sounding baffled. "Why would I?"

"Why *wouldn't* you?" They headed off, their voices fading out and blending with the music—currently Carly Rae Jepsen.

"That was weird," I said, looking after them. Seeing Amy and Carlos arguing was like what I would imagine seeing the yeti was like. Technically possible, in theory, but you never expected to actually encounter it.

"So weird," Bryony agreed. "But they're AmyandCarlos. They'll be fine. They're going to get married and have a million kids, the way they told everyone they would back in seventh grade."

"Maybe the pressure of graduation is getting to them. They'll have to face what their relationship will be like without the bubble of school—you know, going their separate ways."

"Hey!"

I turned and saw the Emmas coming toward us, Emma R. carrying a blue plastic Disneyland bag. I was impressed that she'd already managed to buy something—we really hadn't been here that long. But clearly bus one had gotten the jump on us.

Emma R. was smiling and waving, but Emma J. and Emma Z. didn't look quite so happy. They seemed to be having an intense conversation, their heads bent together.

"Hey, guys," Bryony said, standing up from the bench. Emma J. and Emma Z. stopped talking quickly, Emma J. shaking her head as she moved a few steps over from Emma Z. It was surprising to see—like they were in a fight. First Carlos and Amy were bickering—and now the Emmas?

"Look!" Emma R. said, reaching into her bag. She pulled out what looked like regular Mickey ears—except they had a tiny mortarboard in the middle. "Isn't this *so cute*?"

"Wow," I said, leaning closer to look. It *really* was. I hadn't known they'd have graduation-specific merchandise tonight. Bryony and I had agreed ahead of time that we'd each get one souvenir. I'd been thinking I'd get a sweatshirt—from everything I'd heard, it was going to be chillier in Oregon—but this was making me rethink things.

"Oh man, I might need those," Bryony said, her eyes lighting up.

"We're debating what to do. Either the Incredicoaster or Soarin'," Emma R. said, scrolling through her phone. "There's, like, no line right now."

"Well, Cass doesn't really do roller coasters," Bryony said, glancing at me.

"It's okay." I wanted Bryony to have the best time tonight—I didn't want to stop her from having fun just because I suffered from motion sickness. "I can just wait . . ."

"Chip!" Emma Z. yelped, which didn't seem to fit with this conversation. I turned to look the way she was pointing, and my jaw dropped. A chipmunk was walking toward us. He was dressed in a graduation robe, complete with mortarboard on his furry head. There was a cast member walking with him, and he was waving to everyone as he passed. All around us, people had noticed him, too, and they were pulling out their phones to take pictures, or jogging along beside him as he walked, trying to get selfies. I looked closely, then turned back to her.

"It's Dale," I said.

"Um, he's wearing a robe," Emma Z. said. "How can you even tell?"

"Fun fact," I said, and I heard Bryony let out a laugh—she knew what was coming. "Dale has a red nose. But Chip's nose is black, like a chocolate chip. So that's how you can remember it." Emma Z. just stared at me, and I gave her a smile back. She *had* asked.

"I had no idea that the *characters* would be in graduation outfits!" Bryony said. "This is the best thing ever!"

"It really is," I agreed.

"So? Incredicoaster?" Emma R. asked, looking from me to Bryony. "You guys coming?"

"Maybe later," Bryony said. "I'll text you?"

"For sure," Emma R. said. The Emmas waved at us, then hurried away as a group, Emma R. putting on her new Mickey ears, the other two Emmas resuming their conversation, heads bent together.

"You want to find the Mickey ears, don't you?" I asked.

"I really do!" Bryony said immediately, and I laughed. We walked away from the entrance, scanning for souvenir kiosks. I didn't know which one Emma R. had gotten her ears at—but I figured most of them would have the same stuff.

We stopped at the first kiosk we saw. In addition to selling regular souvenirs, there was also graduation-specific stuff, like T-shirts and sweatshirts with GRAD NITE printed in collegiate font. There were also lots of variations of Mickey ears—but none with mortarboards.

"Do you see them?" Bryony asked.

I shook my head, then caught the attention of the cast member working the kiosk. "Hi—do you have the mouse ears with the graduation cap?"

The cast member—her name tag read SNEHA, SUGARLAND, TEXAS—shook her head. "Sorry. We're all sold out."

I blinked at this. "Already? Didn't Grad Nite just start?"

She shook her head. "Some of the schools do a day pass thing as well, so they can be here longer. Sorry." Maybe seeing the disappointment on Bryony's face, she added, "But I'm not the only one selling them. Other kiosks have them, too."

"Okay, thanks," Bryony said.

We walked away from the kiosk, both of us nodding respectfully at Thor as he passed and taking a moment to appreciate his resplendent hair. "Sorry about that," I said, glancing back at the kiosk. "We can keep trying, though."

"Do you think maybe Emma got the last pair?"

"I'm sure she didn't. But if so, we can bargain with her for it," I suggested. "Find out the thing she wants the most and dangle it in front of her."

Bryony laughed at that and looked around. "So, what do you want to do?"

"Whatever you want to do," I immediately countered. "Why don't we keep trying to track the ears down? And we can check out the rest of the park while we're at it."

"Sounds great."

"Which way?"

Bryony pointed to the left. "That way."

"Onward," I said, with a laugh, turning and heading in that direction, then stopping short when I realized I'd nearly crashed into a group of three coming toward me. "Oh—sorry," I said, moving along.

"Cass?" I heard someone call. I turned back, surprised, and looked more closely at the trio I'd almost bumped into. A second later, I realized two of them looked familiar.

"Reagan?" I asked. "Oh wow, hi!"

I hadn't seen Reagan Edwards in three years, but they still looked the same. And they were standing next to Zach . . . something, their friend that I hadn't known very well. The two of them were with a girl I didn't recognize, who was in Princess Leia Mickey ears. I'd met Reagan and Zach back when we'd lived in Raven Rock. Reagan happened to be in three of my classes, and we'd become fast friends.

Reagan was staring at me, their eyes wide. "It is you, right? Cass?"

Next to her, Zach did a literal double take. "Cass . . . Issac?"

The girl I didn't know gave a wave. "Hi, I'm McKenna."

"Hi there," I said, smiling at all of them. "It's so wild to run into you here!"

"How do you all know each other?" Bryony asked, looking around at us.

"We all went to school together in LA," I said easily. "Like, three years ago? This is so funny!" Just like that, I remembered what Sheridan had said and how he'd assumed I'd have some knowledge of the celebrity situation. "Hey, have you heard anything about someone famous being here tonight? One of our friends saw something on DitesMoi—"

"You never came to my birthday party," Reagan interrupted me.

"Your . . ."

"My *fifteenth* birthday party. It was my golden birthday, remember? I was turning fifteen on the fifteenth. You only get one of those."

I blinked at Reagan. Suddenly, I was clocking their tone—angry and clipped—and the fact that they didn't seem pleased to see me. Quite the opposite, in fact—their eyes were narrowed, their arms folded.

"Ohhh," McKenna said, looking at me with wide eyes. "You're *that* Cass?"

"I'm what?" I'd known a few weeks before it happened that I wouldn't be able to make it to Reagan's birthday party, since my dads had finished up the work on the craftsman and had found their new project, a home in Northern California. But Reagan had been so excited about their party, I hadn't wanted to bring down the day by telling them I was moving. Who wants to be bummed out on their birthday? So, I'd sent a text I couldn't make it once I knew the party would have started, and they would already be having a good time, my absence not missed. I was honestly shocked they remembered, three years later. "But I told you I wouldn't be able to come. I texted you—"

"But then you were just *gone*," Reagan said, talking over me. "Like, no explanation, nothing. And you never came back!"

"Well—I moved," I said slowly. "So . . . that makes it harder to swing by."

They just stared at me, and I caught Bryony's glance as she widened her eyes at me slightly, which I knew meant *Let's get out of here*. "But it was so great to see you," I said, already starting to edge away. "Such a funny coincidence."

In all the lead-up to tonight, I hadn't really thought much about the other schools that would be attending Grad Nite as well—much less that they might be one of my former schools. But it made sense that Raven Rock High was here—it was just an hour away from Disneyland on the freeway (more in traffic). For just a second, I thought about

Washington—and Bruce—and how messy things had gotten there when I left. But just as quickly, I pushed this thought out of my head, telling myself it would be fine. I couldn't imagine Evergreen High—Home of the Mustangs!—coming all the way to Disneyland for their grad night. It was one thing for Los Angeles–area high schools to do it. I'd even heard that schools in Vegas did the six-hour bus ride each way. But from outside Seattle? You'd have to get on a *plane*, which made the whole thing seem very unlikely. I started to breathe a little easier.

I backed away from the group, more than ready to move on from the weird energy of this interaction, when Reagan glared at me.

"You were supposed to bring churros."

"I . . . was?"

"To my *party*!" they sputtered, sounding increasingly incensed. "You promised me you'd bring some, and then you just bailed, and I never heard from you again or saw you. And we didn't have any churros."

"It kind of sucked," Zach chimed in.

"Well, um . . ." But before I could say more (I hadn't gotten so far as what) Reagan turned on their heel and stalked away, Zach following behind.

"Bye!" McKenna said cheerfully, then hurried to join them.

Once they were out of earshot, Bryony turned to me. "That was weird. Who cares that much about churros?"

"I guess they do?"

"I always forget you've lived all these other places. It just feels like we've always been friends."

I felt my heart squeeze a little at that but made myself smile. "I know." For just a moment, I considered telling her the truth—that I was leaving, that tonight was going to be our last hurrah. But that thought only lasted a second before I doubled down on my plan. Even if I wasn't moving to Oregon, we were going to college in different states. So we were always going to have to say goodbye, one way or another. All I could do was make sure we had one last epic night. "Come on," I said, starting to run. "Let's go check this out!"

The running didn't last long—I started getting a stitch in my side, and it was crowded enough that it wasn't the best idea—and plus, I found that moving too fast prevented me from really getting to take everything in. And I really wanted to, because it was *amazing*.

There was music booming from the speakers, everything was lit up with colored lights, and I literally gasped when we turned a corner and I saw Grizzly Peak, silhouetted against the sky—the perfect profile of a bear, lit up in blue. There were lots of places to take pictures—a big neon outline of Mickey ears with a graduation cap that you could pose in front of, or a fancy car in Hollywood Land with HAPPY GRADUATION painted on the trunk. We also saw characters in graduation robes posing for pictures, and the long lines of kids waiting for their turn.

Most of the people around me were strangers, but every now and then, I'd get a jolt as I saw someone I recognized from Harbor Cove. It was a pretty big school—there were five hundred seniors who'd graduated along with me—but you had some familiarity with a lot of people, even if you didn't necessarily know their names. And the effect was kind of disorienting, seeing familiar faces in a sea of strangers, like we were in a living *Where's Waldo?*

I was most impressed with seeing Hollywood Boulevard all lit up at night. The line of shops and illuminated palm trees, GRAD NITE projected on the cloud-painted backdrop—it all felt magical. Bryony liked the Club Candy that was nearby—cast members were handing out free mini packets of Skittles and M&M's, and once you entered through a tunnel of brightly colored rings, there was a stage with karaoke set up and a foosball table, everything cast in a cool purple light. We swung by Cars Land just briefly. We were there long enough to take in how bright the neon was against the night sky and realize that Sheridan hadn't been mistaken, because there was a DJ playing loud music while people danced and others just walked past, sometimes grooving a little as they went. There was just too much to see. We knew we were going to be coming back to all of this later, and we still had rides to go on, but right at that moment, it was like I couldn't take it all in fast enough.

The only negative at Grad Nite so far seemed to be a distinct lack of graduation Mickey ears. It didn't seem possible that Emma R. could have gotten the last pair—but every kiosk we stopped at no longer had them. I was starting to get worried that we wouldn't be able to find them anywhere, which would go against my goal of making sure Bryony had the best night ever.

We passed San Fransokyo Square, the Big Hero 6 area, with its mini Golden Gate Bridge made out of torii gates, and finally headed toward Pixar Pier. In front of where the Little Mermaid ride usually was, I saw there was now a stage set up. A nearby sign read, ETON MESS TAKES THE STAGE AT MIDNIGHT! Underneath this was a picture of four guys who looked around our age, wearing what appeared to be deconstructed prep school uniforms—button-down shirts, tiny ties, blazers, but everything either undone or very tight-fitting.

I saw Amy and Carlos walking toward us, next to each other but not too close, both of their arms folded. They were radiating an unmistakable post-fight energy. Bryony and I exchanged a look, then turned away at the same moment, both of us sensing that this was not a situation we wanted to get ourselves involved with. Were they still fighting about the fact that Carlos hadn't helped Bryony up? That seemed a bit extreme, especially since she hadn't minded.

"So where to now?" I asked, once I was sure that Amy and Carlos were out of earshot.

"Well . . ." Bryony looked down at her phone. "I definitely want to go on the Spider-Man ride at some point."

I nodded. "It makes sense that you'd want to see your boyfriend."

"I mean, I should *be* so lucky. But that's all the way back by the Avengers Campus."

"So, let's do something here." I looked around. We were near Pixar Pier, which meant we could see the water in front of us, reflecting the Ferris wheel, with its Mickey Mouse in the center, all lit up. Next to it was the Incredicoaster. At regular intervals, it whooshed past, and you could hear an "AAAGH!" as people went upside down in the loop.

"Swings?" I asked, nodding toward the Silly Symphony Swings. I'd been on it before and knew I could handle it. I didn't love it when it dipped down, but since the average age of the rider, on non–Grad Nites, seemed to be under six, this wasn't something I felt the need to mention to Bryony.

She nodded. "Sounds good."

We headed in that direction, just as I thought of something. "Oh, here's a fun fact," I said, turning back to her. "It's—"

I heard someone shout "Oi! Watch out!" But I had no idea that this was referring to me until a second later, when I crashed directly into someone. Someone who'd been holding a large orange drink, which splashed all over me.

"Oh my god," I said, getting my balance back and looking down at myself. My dress was now splotched with bright orange stains. It was on my hair, on my hands—sticky and sweet smelling.

"Oh no!" Bryony said, as she caught up with me. She looked at my dress, her expression going grave. "I have a Tide pen?" Her hand strayed toward her purse for a moment but then dropped. We both could clearly see this was far beyond the help of a Tide pen.

"I'm so, so sorry," I heard a crisp British accent say. I looked up at the guy who'd crashed into me and blinked. He was a few inches taller than me and *very* cute. He was South Asian, with dark curls, one of which had tumbled over his forehead like he was a character in a Regency romance novel. He looked my age, and was wearing jeans, sneakers, and a green T-shirt that read EXCALIBUR!

"What was that?" I asked, looking at the orange-splotched mess I had become.

"Irn-Bru," the guy said with a grimace.

"Irn what?" Bryony asked.

"Irn-Bru," he said again, louder, like increasing the volume would make things clearer. He glanced at Bryony. "I didn't get you, did I?"

"No, I'm okay. Just Cass."

"That's you? Cass?" Despite everything, I couldn't help but appreciate the way he said my name. Why were British accents always so *good*? "I'm terribly sorry, really. Irn-Bru is a Scottish soda? I was bringing it for Niall, you know, like a peace offering, but . . ." He stopped and shook his head. "Never mind. I really am sorry. Is there anything I can do?"

I was just staring at him, and I realized this a second later and looked away. He somehow seemed familiar, but I was pretty sure that I would have remembered meeting a guy this cute. Because he *really* was. My heart was pounding hard, and I realized all at once I hadn't had an instant crush like this in a while. Not since Bruce. "Oh, I mean, it's groovy. Don't worry about it."

There was a sound like a cough, and I looked over to see Bryony widening her eyes at me. I could tell from one glance that she had totally clocked that I was crushing on this guy and that she was not about to let me forget that I'd just said the phrase *it's groovy*.

"Well," he said. He raked a hand through his curls in a way that honestly should have been illegal. "Truly, my deepest apologies."

Had anyone ever said that outside an Austenian drawing room? It was like I could practically feel myself going into a swoon. "No worries," Bryony said, when it was clear I had lost the ability to reply.

"I have to go, but—sorry. Again." The guy gave me a smile, and then turned and walked away, past some shops and a bathroom—in the direction of where I was pretty sure Grizzly Peak was.

I watched him go, then turned to Bryony. "*Oh* my god."

"I'm so sorry about your dress. That sucks."

"Oh right." Between the curls and the accent and the Mr. Darcy fantasy that had been forming in my head, I'd forgotten about it. "It's not that big a deal. Did that guy look familiar to you?"

"No," Bryony said with a shrug. "But could you have *had* more of a crush on him? My god, Cass."

"Who knew I had a weakness for British accents?"

She sighed. "We all do. It's American kryptonite."

"So, what do you think? Swings?"

"Sounds groovy!"

I laughed, and we headed in that direction, but it seemed like everyone else had *also* decided at that moment that the swings were a great idea—the line was longer than I'd ever seen it. Neither of us wanted to wait, so we walked farther down the boardwalk section of Pixar Pier.

"Ferris wheel?" I asked.

"Great," Bryony said, picking up her pace. "Let's hurry before that gets mobbed, too."

As we got closer, I could see this wasn't actually called a Ferris wheel—it was the Pixar Pal-A-Round, which explained why all the cars had Pixar characters painted on the sides of them. There were two lines leading to the ride—one to the right, one to the left. And whereas the left-side line was pretty full, the right was almost empty. "This way!" I called to Bryony as I ran toward it. She laughed and we ran together, around the corner to where the cars were stopping and cast members opened the doors of the cars to let people out and get new riders on. As we got into line, I felt a little smug. What was everyone else *doing*? There were only four people ahead of us, whereas the other line stretched almost back to the entrance.

A red car came to a stop—I could see it had Remy, from *Ratatouille*, on it—and four people got off, all of them looking distinctly queasy. I shook my head. It may have had a different name, but it was essentially a Ferris wheel—even *I* could handle a Ferris wheel.

The four people in front of us got into their car, and the wheel spun on. A breeze lifted my hair and I felt myself shiver slightly. It wasn't cold enough to need my jean jacket—not yet—but I was still glad I packed it. I had a feeling I'd definitely need it in an hour or so. "So glad we picked this line," I said to Bryony as I pulled my bag higher on my shoulder.

"Yeah," she said slowly as she looked around, her brow furrowing. "I actually think . . ."

"How many?" the cast member assigning people to cars asked us as another came to a stop—this one had Anger, from *Inside Out* on it—and discharged another foursome. They spilled out, high-fiving and talking about how awesome it had been.

"Two!" Bryony and I said at the same time. The cast member gestured us toward the waiting car, and I got in first, Bryony sliding in next to me.

"Two? Do I have a party of two?" the cast member called, looking around.

"Us!" I heard someone yell, and saw two girls hurry to join our car.

I bent forward to tuck my bag between my feet, and when I straightened up, I had a clear view of the girls who were sitting across from us—and blinked in surprise when I realized I knew them.

They were Greta Franklin and Nora Silver, from when we'd lived in Arizona, two years and I don't know how many schools ago. I hadn't seen them since we'd left, but they looked the same. Greta was Black, tall, with oversize glasses; Nora was white, petite, and more intense. When I'd known them, they'd been best friends, and since they were here together it seemed like that hadn't changed.

I stared at them, trying to process this. It was one thing to see people from my school in Los Angeles—but from Arizona? It just *was* funny we'd ended up in the same car, and I was just about say something like *Of all the Ferris wheels in all the world*, when Greta leaned forward.

"Cass?" she asked, her voice tentative.

I smiled at her. "Hi—" I started, when Bryony interrupted.

"Wait, you guys know each other?" She raised an eyebrow at me. "Do you know *everyone* at Grad Nite, Cass?"

"We do know her," Nora said, her voice frosty. *"Unfortunately."*

I blinked at that, startled, and glanced between Greta and Nora. All at once, I noticed that neither of them looked particularly happy to see me. "Wait, what?"

At that moment, the cast member stuck her head in. "Everyone all set?" she asked, but without waiting for an answer, said, "Enjoy!" Then she shut the door, locked it, and the car—with all of us stuck inside—rose up into the air.

1

looked across the car at Nora as we rose up and then stopped abruptly as the car below us let people off and picked up new riders. "Wait, what do you mean *unfortunately*?" I crossed my arms and started to lean back, but at that moment, the car swung down and forward, rocking sharply back and forth.

"Uh-oh," Bryony said, her eyes wide as she looked around.

"Is our car broken?" I braced myself against the side, my heart pounding hard. "Is there something wrong with the ride?"

"Um, *no*," Greta said, rolling her eyes. "This is one of the swinging cars."

I stared at her. My stomach plunged—and then plunged again when our car rolled sharply back as we started to rise again. "No," I said faintly, even though all the evidence—like the fact that we were sliding all around this track and swinging freely in space—was contradicting me.

"There were signs when we came in," Nora pointed out.

"You know, I did have that thought when we got on," Bryony said. "All of a sudden, I wondered why the other line was so much longer. I think it's because that was the one for the non-swinging cars."

"Oh god," I said, as the car plunged forward again, then swung wildly in space. I closed my eyes, hoping that would make it better, but then opened them immediately when I realized that made it worse.

"Cass doesn't like roller coasters," Bryony explained in a low voice. Then she shook her head. "Oh sorry—I'm Bryony."

"Greta."

"I'm Nora."

"So nice to meet you!"

"You too," Greta said. "I love your shirt."

"So, you know Cass?" Bryony asked, looking from Greta and Nora and back to me. She widened her eyes like she was saying *What the heck.* I started to shake my head at her—letting her know I thought this was crazy, too—but that just made things feel extra spinny, so I stopped.

Nora folded her arms. "We *thought* we knew Cass."

"But clearly we were mistaken," Greta added, shaking her head.

"Uh," I said, looking from one to the other, trying to figure out what this weird vibe was. I turned to Bryony, who also looked baffled by what was happening. "Of course you know me," I said. "We were in school together when I lived in Arizona," I explained.

I'd gotten to be friends with Greta and Nora when I'd joined the quiz bowl team, something I'd never heard of before we arrived in Prescott but which was, at least at Sunrise Academy, a *very* big deal. My dads had teased me that I'd been preparing to join a team like this my whole life—that my love of facts was finally coming in handy. And I don't know if that was the reason, but our team was *good*. We made it through Regionals, won State, and got to represent Arizona in the Nationals, but ended up coming in second to the winners from North Dakota. Greta had assured me that I shouldn't feel bad about it—North Dakota always won. Apparently, when you couldn't go outside for six months of the year, there was nothing to do except memorize facts.

We'd left Arizona early that summer, heading to La Jolla, where my dads were working on a seaside renovation. Every now and then I'd get a question right when Angelo and Oscar were watching *Jeopardy!* and I'd smile, knowing it was because of my time on the quiz team. I'd really liked Greta and Nora and I'd had nothing but good memories of my time in Arizona. So I didn't understand why they were both acting like this now. "It's really surprising to see you here," I said to them, then drew in a sharp breath as the car started rising again.

We were almost at the summit, which I really didn't like, because that meant I could see just how high up we were as the car rolled back and forth over the track, swinging a lot harder than really seemed to be necessary. I could see most of the park now, lit up and glowing against the darkness—and just in front of us, I could see the Silly Symphony Swings—the ride I *should* have been on.

"So, you thought you'd never see us again, huh?" Nora asked, narrowing her eyes at me. "That's what you were counting on?" She paused and sniffed. "Does anyone else smell orange soda?"

I felt my cheeks burn. "What do you mean, what I was counting on?" The ride started to move again, going faster now, but at least we were starting to go downward, which meant it was almost over. "And why are you mad at me? I haven't seen either of you in two years." I shook my head before I remembered that I shouldn't do that.

"Exactly." Greta pointed at me like I'd just proven something. "Because you were just *gone* when school started junior year."

"Yeah, because I *moved*." What was she so mad about? I'd stayed until the end of the year, after all. We'd gone to Nationals and had brought home a trophy. I'd done what I always tried to do—depart at the top, with everyone happy. "I told you, my dads' jobs mean—"

"But you never told us you were leaving," Nora said, and I was surprised to hear a ribbon of hurt running underneath her words, breaking through the anger and annoyance.

"You didn't tell them?" Bryony asked, sounding shocked.

"Well," I started, just as the car stopped again. I peered out of the car, trying to see where we were. If six on a clock was the ground—which I desperately wanted to return to—we were at three. We were so close—why weren't we *done*? My stomach dropped and flipped again as the car, once more, slid back and forth. I took a deep breath, then made myself let it out slowly. Why would anyone ride this? Did people actually *like* feeling this way? Or were they just pretending?

"She didn't tell us," Greta confirmed, folding her arms over her chest.

"Look, I don't know what you want me to say," I said, making myself sit up straighter. I was learning in real time that it's hard to be in an argument when you're also worried you might throw up in front of everyone in an enclosed space. "It wasn't my decision to move."

"But it was your decision not to tell us," Greta said. "School started and you just weren't there. Suddenly, all your social media had vanished and you weren't responding to texts. . . ."

"Not to mention," Nora chimed in, "you totally screwed us with AQB."

"With *what*, now?" Bryony asked.

"Academic quiz bowl," Greta, Nora, and I all said at the same time.

"Quiz bowl?" Bryony echoed. "Like—bowling?"

"No," Greta said, sounding horrified. "It's an academic knowledge competition, and—"

"And . . . you did this?" Bryony turned to me, sounding more confused than ever. "Is *this* why you know so many random facts?"

"No, that predated this. I told you about it," I said, even as I tried to think back. I must have mentioned it at some point. I was pretty sure.

"No, I definitely would have remembered you telling me you did something called *quiz bowl*." A second later, she glanced over at Greta and Nora. "Uh, no offense."

"We were really good," Greta explained to Bryony, like the reason she wasn't impressed by the idea of quiz bowl was because she didn't know our stats. "We went all the way to Nationals when Cass was on our team. We came in second!"

"Oh." Bryony looked over at me, and it was like she was trying to figure out who I was. "Um. Congratulations?"

"And we would have won the next year," Nora said, shaking her head. "But then Cass screwed it all up for us."

I frowned at that—it was one thing to have people mad at you for what you'd done. But to be blamed for something you weren't even *present* for seemed unfair. I took a breath to point this out, when we started moving again. We were approaching the ground, and I couldn't be happier about it. But instead of stopping in front of the cast members and getting off, the car just kept on going. "Wait, stop," I called, as we rose up into the air, the car swaying more violently than ever. "Why are we going around again?"

Bryony shot me a sympathetic look. "You go around twice."

"We have to do this *again*?"

"Uh. Yeah. But just one more time!" Bryony said with the tone of someone clearly trying to find the bright side but not quite pulling it off.

The car rolled sharply forward, then swung back, and then tipped forward once more. I gripped the seat, trying to breathe. I glanced over at Greta and Nora and realized I'd never gotten an answer. "Wait a second, you said I hurt the *next* year's team?" They both nodded. "How did I do that? I wasn't even on it!"

"Exactly!" Nora said. "You *weren't* there. And that was the problem. If we'd known you wouldn't be a part of things, we would have been actively recruiting. Instead, when the year started, we were a team member down and scrambling. We ended up with this completely useless freshman."

"But you guys still did okay, right?"

Greta and Nora exchanged a look, and I felt my stomach sink in a way that had nothing to do with how the car was swaying. "You made it to Nationals again. Right?" They just stared at me, and I started to get a very bad feeling. "Regionals?"

"Knocked out in Regionals," Nora said, her voice flat. "First round. We lost on a question about how many wives Henry the Eighth had."

"Six," I said immediately. "Everyone knows that."

"Apparently Sarah Rudolph didn't," Nora said.

"Oh." We stopped again, and a heavy, awkward silence settled over the car. I looked down, willing this to be over. I wanted to be off this ride and on solid ground, and not having to confront people who were looking at me like I'd done something wrong. After all, it wasn't *my* fault they'd lost. But the fact they hadn't even made it through Regionals . . . Along with nausea, I was feeling the acrid burn of guilt in my stomach. And I didn't like it.

More than anything, I wished I could have a do-over. I'd go back, we'd go on the non-swinging cars, and I wouldn't have to have this conversation. I could return to thinking that everything was fine when I left Arizona, like I'd believed fifteen minutes ago.

"You still haven't said sorry," Nora snapped, breaking the silence.

"Sorry—for moving?"

"Sorry for the way you left! For costing us Nationals—it wrecked my whole transcript."

"But I didn't know you'd lost!"

"Because you never reached out! Because we never *heard* from you again!" Nora's voice broke on the last word, and she sat back hard against the car. It sent it swaying, as we rose up in the air again, heading back around, finally, toward the ground.

"Could you not do that?" I asked faintly as we rocked back and forth.

"What—make the car move?" Greta asked, also leaning back against the seat, and setting the car swaying. Suddenly, there was a gleam in her eye that I didn't like at *all*. "Does this bother you or something?"

"Oh my god," I muttered as I stared out the window, trying to find anything that would serve as a steady horizon. My thoughts were whirling and my stomach was clenched, but I knew it wasn't just the motion sickness. It was everything they'd said, everything that I would have very much preferred not to hear. I was mentally composing a response to Greta and Nora—something about how I couldn't be expected to be psychic, and that people not knowing facts about the Tudor court wasn't my fault—when we finally came to a stop.

The cast member opened the door for us to get out, and Nora and Greta gathered their bags, then paused for a moment, looking at me.

"It was nice to meet *you*, Bryony," Nora said pointedly. "Cass, I'd say keep in touch—but we both know you're not going to do that. So." She shook her head, then climbed out. Greta followed, and they walked off, neither one of them looking back at me.

1

You doing okay?" Bryony asked.

"Better," I said, mostly to the ground. I was sitting on a nearby bench, bent over my knees. When we'd gotten off the ride, Bryony had taken one look at how pale I was and had hustled me over here. Then she'd gone to Angry Dogs to get me a Sprite that she insisted that I drink to settle my stomach.

It had been about ten minutes, and my inner ear was getting back to normal. But my mind was still churning, in a way that I really would have preferred it wasn't.

I took another sip of the soda, then placed the bottle by my feet and straightened up. "So!" I said, making my voice upbeat and positive. "What should we do now?" I tried to think of things that didn't involve getting back on a ride . . . or eating anything. "Um, we could keep trying to find the Mickey ears?"

"Sure," Bryony said, but she sounded distracted. She glanced back at the ride, circling around and around in its loop. "That was weird, though, right? I mean . . . we keep running into people you know."

"It *is* weird," I agreed, glad that we could actually talk about it. "Like, I know there's a lot of schools here, but I was not expecting it."

"And everyone—seems to be mad at you?" She put a comedic spin on this, but I could see that her eyes were troubled.

"I'm not happy about it either," I assured her. I kept my voice light, like I was trying to shake it off, but it wasn't shaking easily. It wasn't that I thought that all the people from my previous schools disappeared the second I left. I understood about object permanence, after all. But I really hadn't let myself think too much about my old friends, the people who'd once meant so much to me—especially Bruce, in Washington.

It was like I'd pushed those memories down into a box and closed the lid firmly after each move, trying not to notice that each time, doing this got harder and harder.

But tonight, actually seeing Greta and Nora—and even Reagan and Zach—was making me feel rattled in a way I was having trouble getting my head around. I just wanted to put it behind me.

"So, you just didn't say goodbye to them?"

"We moved," I said, feeling like this seemed to be getting lost in all these conversations. It wasn't like I was ever choosing to go. I was being yanked along on my dads' whims. I shook my head, trying to stop this train of thought. It had been a long time since I'd even complained about one of our moves—we were a team, after all. "It's not like it was my choice."

Bryony nodded, but I could see that she still looked unsure. "I just . . ."

"I think they were just mad that they didn't do better at Regionals," I said, ready to move past this. "Easy to scapegoat me, you know?"

She looked at me for a moment longer, then grinned. "I can't believe you did something called academic quiz bowl."

I laughed, feeling some tension leave my shoulders. "I'll have you know it was *very* cool in Arizona. We had jackets and everything."

"Well, see, I didn't know about the jackets. Where should we go? Cars Land?"

"Sure!" I didn't care where we went, really—I was just glad Bryony and I could go back to having fun. "Sheridan did say there's a DJ. And maybe at some point I'll be able to go on a ride again and then . . ."

"Radiator Springs Racers?"

"I mean, while we're there, we might as *well*."

We headed over, and as we made the right turn into Cars Land, I smiled when I saw the famous tow truck from *Cars*, Mater, with a mortarboard—Materboard?—and a line of teens queueing to get pictures with him. I turned to point him out to Bryony, when something caught my eye.

It was a large, stylized poster on a stand, seeming to glow under the flashing lights. ETON MESS was printed across the top in capital red letters. Underneath was written, LIVE! ALL THE WAY FROM ENGLAND! SHOWTIME 12:00 A.M. And then under this was a black-and-white picture of four guys in their deconstructed prep-school uniforms, the same picture Bryony and I had seen over by Pixar Pier, only bigger.

"Hey!" I stopped short when I realized I recognized one of the faces on it. The guy who'd spilled orange soda all over me—and had caused me to briefly lose my power of speech—was one of the four guys in the band. FREDDIE, read the name under his picture. And he, at least, seemed to understand this was all a little ridiculous. Where the other guys were smoldering, he was raising an eyebrow that seemed to indicate that he was very much in on the joke. He held a bass guitar and wore a striped tie over a T-shirt. I realized after a moment that it was the same one I'd seen him in earlier tonight, the one reading EXCALIBUR! The changing lights seemed to linger on his silhouette for just a second longer than they should have, before moving on.

One of the other band members had a microphone slung around his neck, and was pursing his lips at the camera. NIALL was written under his picture, which rang a bell for me. Hadn't the guy—Freddie, apparently—said something about a Niall? The other two also had their names written under their images—TRISTRAM and ALFIE.

"What?" Bryony asked, also leaning closer to look at the poster.

I pointed to it. "It's the guy who spilled orange soda on me! I thought he was just here as a senior, but apparently not."

"He's in a *band*?" She shook her head. "Man. And I thought you were far gone before."

"I was not," I protested weakly, even though I knew it was pretty much the truth. I shrugged and shook my head, giving up the pretense. "It was the accent. And the hair."

Bryony nudged me with her shoulder. "It was cute! I feel like I haven't seen you that flustered around a guy before."

I nodded, realizing this was true. "I mean, there was my ex from SLO."

"The lab partner?"

"Yeah." At my last high school in San Luis Obispo, I'd dated my environmental sciences lab partner for two months. But we never seemed to have all that much to talk about, and when we finally decided to end it, I could sense that both of us were relieved. But I hadn't had a crush on anyone at Harbor Cove, so it really did feel like it had been a minute. "I guess I haven't had a real crush since Bruce." A second later, I realized what I'd done. "I mean . . ."

"Wait, you've never mentioned a Bruce."

"I . . . haven't?"

"No, I would have remembered. Because I would have said something like, *Who's named Bruce these days?* But seriously, who's named Bruce these days?"

I smiled, even as I felt my heart squeeze. I'd had a very similar conversation, the very first night I'd met Bruce Preston. "Yeah. It wasn't a big thing," I lied. "We were supposed to go to the prom together, but it . . . didn't work out."

Bryony turned to me, her eyes wide and sympathetic. "He broke up with you before the prom?"

I swallowed hard, trying to push the memory away—of the text I'd sent, the way I'd turned off my phone to avoid the fallout. "Something like that." I nodded toward the Eton Mess poster, more than ready to change the subject. "But maybe we can go see this band later. At midnight?"

"Sure," Bryony said easily. "Sounds good."

We headed toward Cars Land, and I glanced back at the poster for one more moment before hurrying to catch up with Bryony.

An hour later, we'd danced to the DJ, and my stomach had settled to the point where we'd been able to go on Radiator Springs Racers *twice*, in addition to getting ice cream at the Cozy Cone. We'd finally gone on the Silly Symphony Swings after all, and Bryony had insisted on taking my picture in front of the Aunt Cass Café in San Fransokyo Square. And then, because it was getting close to midnight, we made our way over to where the crowd had gathered in front of the stage by Pixar Pier.

"Okay," Bryony said, looking down at her phone. "Emma R. says they're all here, too. And that the other Emmas have been acting kind of weird...."

"Weird how?"

Bryony shrugged. "She doesn't say." She nodded toward the stage. "You think they'll be any good?"

"I mean, probably not," I admitted. From the pictures, it kind of seemed like this band was a One Direction knockoff. But hopefully they'd be fun, at least. There was a countdown clock above the stage, letting us know the show would start in ten minutes.

There was nobody on stage yet, but it looked like the stagehands had finished their work—there were two mic stands, a drum kit in the back, and speakers placed all around.

The crowd started to grow, with more people arriving from what seemed like all corners of the park, and you could practically feel the anticipation in the air. I glanced around, looking for the mysterious celebrity that was allegedly here. But the only slightly fancy person I saw I didn't recognize. She was a woman who looked to be in her late twenties, dressed in an all-black outfit and heels, which made me think she wasn't a teacher. She also sported a designer cross-body bag that I wasn't sure would be in the budget of any faculty chaperones. I turned to Bryony to mention this just as Emma R. crossed toward us, waving.

"Hey, guys!" she called, maneuvering her way through the crowd. She smiled, but it looked a little strained. "Have you been having fun?"

"Yeah," I said, glancing behind her to Emma J. and Emma Z., who were standing next to each other with their arms folded. You could practically feel the tension zinging off them, the way the air feels just before a thunderstorm. "Is everything okay?" I asked, lowering my voice. I remembered they'd been a little bit strange when we'd first gotten to the park, too—and it seemed like things had gotten worse.

Emma R. glanced back at her friends, her expression clouding. "I'm not sure."

"Well, the band should be fun, anyway," Bryony said, clearly trying to change the subject. She grinned at me. "Cass has a crush on one of the musicians."

Emma R. clapped her hands together. "You do?"

I could feel my cheeks get hot. I'd barely interacted with Freddie, so why was I so excited to see him onstage soon? I shook my head, trying to clear it. "I mean, I just think he's cute. He spilled orange soda on me."

Emma R. gasped. "A meet-cute!"

Bryony nodded wisely, but I shook my head. "I really don't think that qualifies."

"It totally does."

"But want to know the etymology of the term?" I asked, pleased as always to have a fact to fit the situation. "*Meet-cute* comes from the thirties, the director Ernst Lubitsch coined it, and—"

"—didn't even *want* to!" I heard Emma J. hiss before Emma Z. pulled her away a few steps.

I turned back to Emma R., who just shrugged unhappily. "Don't ask me."

A group jostled past me, and I stepped aside for them, then stopped short when I realized I recognized the logo on the back of one of their sweatshirts.

It was a silhouette of a horse, done in green, with green letters underneath spelling out *Evergreen High—Home of the Mustangs.*

I could feel cold sweat starting to bead on the back of my neck. Even as I was staring at the sweatshirt in front of me, I tried to tell myself it wasn't possible. That it was just a coincidence. That a *lot* of schools were probably called Evergreen High, and there were only a limited number of potential mascots, that was all. And who didn't like a mustang? It didn't necessarily mean it was *that* Evergreen High. . . .

"Cass?"

I looked up and felt my heart sink like a stone.

Bruce Preston was standing in front of me.

1

'd met Bruce when we'd moved to Evergreen, a suburb of Seattle. We stayed in the back house—the ADU—while Oscar and Angelo did a gut renovation of the main house. Bruce lived next door with his family; we'd met the very first night we arrived. We'd ordered a pizza, and I'd come out to see Bruce arguing with the delivery girl. He was convinced it was a prank, since he hadn't realized anyone was living in the house. He hadn't been expecting me—and I hadn't been expecting him.

We became fast friends—our bedroom windows faced each other, like something out of a Taylor Swift music video. I quickly developed a crush on him, and while I sometimes got that vibe from him, too, nothing had ever happened between us. We'd agreed to go to the prom together but just as friends. Which made sense, since by that point, I knew that we were moving on again.

But when prom night rolled around, I hadn't felt well enough to go. I'd texted him and then had turned my phone off. We'd left the next day, but the feeling that I hadn't handled things well had followed me to San Luis Obispo. And it hadn't ended there. A week later, a letter had shown up in our mailbox, forwarded by the house's owners. I'd only read it through once—Bruce was upset, asking me what had happened, what he'd done. I had immediately stuffed it back in the envelope. And though I'd thought about it, I hadn't been able to throw it away. But I'd never responded—and I had never seen Bruce again.

Until this moment.

Right here, at Grad Nite.

"Hi," I said, my voice catching in my throat. "I . . . Wow. I didn't realize you'd be here."

Bruce just looked at me for a moment. He looked pretty much the same—tall, with light brown hair and dark green eyes. His hair was a little longer now, and it curled up slightly at the nape of his neck. There was something else that was different about him, but it took me a moment longer to figure out what it was—it was that he wasn't smiling. In fact, he did *not* look happy to see me.

"That makes two of us," he said.

Bryony cleared her throat loudly, and I looked over to see her staring at Bruce. She'd started fussing with her bangs, which she only did when she was around a guy she thought was cute.

"Um, what are you doing here?" I asked, my heart beating hard. Between the way he was looking at me and the tone of his voice, it suddenly felt like

I'd been caught, like I was in trouble. Which, I told myself very firmly, was ridiculous. If he was still upset I'd gotten sick on prom night a year ago, that was a *him* issue.

"Grad Nite," he said, as though it was obvious, slight edge to his voice I'd never heard before.

"Yeah, I know," I said, shaking my head, trying to get my thoughts together. "I just— It seems like a long way to come. From Washington." I was speaking these words and trying to stay calm, even as everything in me wanted to scream *What is happening?!* Between Bruce, Greta and Nora, and Reagan, it was like I'd been dropped into some kind of alternate universe where my past was going to keep confronting me. Like this was my version of *A Christmas Carol*, but in June.

Bruce shrugged. "We won this national academic award, so they let us vote on what we wanted to do to celebrate. And this won out."

"Oh, gotcha. That's—that's cool." I looked up at him, and then immediately had to look away again. Seeing him now was having to actually face how things had ended with us—like the letter he'd sent I hadn't responded to—and I didn't much like it.

"Hi, I'm Bryony," Bryony said, stepping forward and widening her eyes at me. She was giving me very clear introduce-me-to-this-guy signs. And while normally I wouldn't have hesitated, the fact was, I wanted this interaction to end as soon as possible.

"Hi," he said. And I noticed he blinked as he looked down at her, like he was trying to get his bearings. "I'm Bruce."

"Bruce!" Bryony looked at me, then back at him, her eyes narrowing. "You're the one who dumped Cass on prom night?"

Bruce just stared at me for a moment, his face falling. "Is that what you've told people, Cass? *Really?*"

My heart was starting to beat hard. I'd never had a panic attack before, but I was pretty sure this was what one felt like. "It's . . ." I started. I looked at the stage, thinking that any time now would be a *great* moment for the band to start playing.

"Is that not . . . what happened?" Bryony asked, her brow furrowing in confusion.

"Hi, I'm Emma," Emma R. jumped in, not reading the room at all.

Bruce just gave a short laugh, the kind without any humor in it. "No, it's *not* what happened. The opposite, in fact. The last time I heard from Cass was when she stood *me* up on prom night."

Bryony stared at me. "You what?"

"I didn't stand you up," I said, even though I knew I kind of did. "I texted—"

"And then the next day, she was just gone, no goodbye, nothing."

Bryony turned to me, frowning, like she was putting something together. "You did that?" she asked slowly. "Cass?"

"Wait." One of the girls in Bruce's group looked up from her phone. She raised an eyebrow at me. "*You're* Cass?"

"Uh," I said, frowning. I didn't recognize her from my time at Evergreen. "Yes. Do we know each other?"

She shook her head and widened her eyes at Bruce. "I've just heard stories."

What was *with* everyone tonight? Had there been some sort of announcement about me? "Uh, okay."

"Why did you do that?" Bryony asked. She was looking at me like she had no idea who I was.

I swallowed hard, looking between Bryony and Bruce. It felt like I was on trial for some terrible crime, when I actually hadn't done anything wrong. Was I not allowed to get sick, or something? "It was . . ." I started, then took a shaky breath. "There were extenuating circumstances—"

"Did you even say goodbye?" Bryony asked. Hurt was lacing her words.

I felt my heart pound, well aware that my former prom date and his friends—and the Emmas, I could see now—were all listening to this conversation and not even trying to hide it. "Look," I started. "It's— I move a lot, okay? And it was just the best way."

"I would disagree with that," Bruce said, folding his arms across his chest. "You disappear an hour before we were supposed to go to the prom . . ."

"As friends," I said weakly.

"And then you're just gone. And I never heard from you again? You never responded to my letter. It was like I didn't matter. Like what we had didn't matter."

I blinked hard, trying to get my bearings, but it was a challenge. It felt like the ground had been yanked out from underneath my feet, and I couldn't find stability anywhere. And this—seeing Bruce, having him look at me this way—was almost more than I could take. Especially after Greta and Nora and Reagan. "I . . ."

"You know, I spent a really long time trying to figure out what I'd done wrong," Bruce went on. "If I'd hurt you in some way. But I couldn't think of anything, which meant I couldn't understand why you would just ghost like that."

I opened my mouth to reply—but before I could, Bruce turned and walked away.

I took a shaky breath, trying to pull myself together. Between all the people I'd run into tonight, that had been the worst. I glanced at my friends—Bryony and the Emmas were all staring at me like they'd just witnessed a car crash. I swallowed hard, and forced out a laugh. "So, that was weird, huh?"

"It's not the word I'd use," Bryony said. She shook her head, and when she spoke it was like she was putting something together. "It seems like you do this a lot, Cass? Right? You just . . . disappear."

Emma R. looked from me to Bryony and then, maybe finally picking up on the vibes, turned away and pretended to be absorbed in her phone.

I knew I was on unsteady ground—a foreign land I wasn't entirely sure how I ended up in but was very certain I didn't much like. "It's simpler," I finally said. "Otherwise friendships just fall apart slowly and you lose touch and become strangers. . . ." My voice started to wobble.

A group of happy, loud seniors, all wearing different college sweatshirts—probably indicating where they were going next year—ran past us, yelling and laughing. When they'd passed out of sight, I took a breath and made myself finish. "It's just better this way, okay?"

"Better for who?" Bryony asked, then paused. "Whom?"

"Probably? But it sounds pretentious."

She laughed, then caught herself. "No," she said, her voice firm. "Maybe it's better for *you*. But based on the people we ran into tonight, they were pretty upset. They didn't just get over it."

I shook my head, but even as I did, I was flashing back to Reagan's expression, and the truth that I hadn't wanted to process—that they weren't really mad about the churros. The betrayal on Greta and Nora's faces—their shock and hurt when they saw me. It was all piercing through the protective layers I'd had built up around me for so long, letting in light I'd fought to keep out. "But . . ."

"Before, you said you couldn't go to the concert," Bryony said slowly. "And you haven't committed to any of our summer travel plans. . . ." It was like I could practically hear the wheels turning in her head, and I started to get a very bad feeling. "Are you leaving, Cass? Are you going to ditch me the way you've ditched everyone else?"

I opened my mouth to reply, my heart beating hard. All I had wanted was for us to have one fun last night together! Why was this happening? "I . . . No," I said, but even I could hear it sounded unconvincing.

"Did you even apply to the Mermaid Café?" Bryony asked, crossing her arms over her chest. "Or did you lie about that?"

"It's . . . I . . ."

"Show me," Bryony said, and I could hear the hurt in her voice as clear as anything. "If you really applied. Show me the email. Show me you haven't been lying to me. For *months*."

Hot tears stung my eyes. I had no idea how to get out of this. I had no idea that it would feel this bad, having to stand here and see the look of betrayal on Bryony's face. But there was nothing else to do—except tell the truth.

"We're moving to Oregon," I made myself say. "Tomorrow."

"Tomorrow?" She stared at me, the color draining from her face as she processed this. "Really?"

I swallowed hard and nodded, and I felt in the silence that followed the depth of this hurt I was causing.

Bryony was looking at me like she had no idea who I was. "But you knew better than anyone how hard it was for me when everyone ditched me after my breakup. And you were still going to leave? Without even saying goodbye?" Her voice broke on the last word.

Even though we were outside, it suddenly felt like there wasn't quite enough air, like the walls were closing in on me. I started backing away, and

Bryony's jaw dropped open. "You're really going to walk away?" she asked, incredulously. "Seriously?"

I knew I shouldn't, but I didn't know what else to do. I turned and hurried away from the stage, like if I kept moving, I could outrun this awful moment.

I didn't know where I was going, but I knew I couldn't be there any longer. I broke into a run. Tears blurred my vision as everything that had happened tonight felt like it was hitting me at once. All I knew was that I had to go, get out, find somewhere that I wouldn't be confronted, at every turn, with all these people from my past. I didn't understand why they were all cropping up here, on what should have been an amazing night, at what was literally the happiest place on earth.

And even though I knew it wasn't anywhere near the top of things that were going wrong right now, the thought that I wouldn't ever get to see Freddie again was hitting me hard, disappointment mingling with all the rest of my jumbled feelings.

I didn't have anything close to resembling a plan. I just knew Bryony was furious at me, and any hope I'd had for having one last amazing adventure with her at Grad Nite was ruined. And so why would I want to stay, surrounded by people who were mad at me, knowing that my presence was just making their nights worse? I was going to leave everyone from Harbor Cove High behind tomorrow anyway; I'd just get started on it a little early. There was no point in sticking around. I was *out* of there.

I slowed my steps, brushed my hand across my eyes, and looked around. I'd made it to Carthay Circle. I tried to get my thoughts together, make a plan. I needed to find this faculty lounge and tell Ms. Mulaney I was sick or something. I didn't care that it meant I wouldn't be able to come back to Grad Nite. As far as I was concerned, that was a pro, not a con. I'd just get an Uber home. And tomorrow I'd head to Oregon, and I'd try to forget that any of this had ever happened.

I saw a cast member standing across the road from me and started to make my way to them—surely they'd tell me where the faculty lounge was.

But before I could make it over to them, there was suddenly a group of cast members running fast toward me, surrounding someone. I took a step back, out of the way, and saw that people were following the cast members, phones out, recording and taking pictures.

This must have been the celebrity—it seems one had been here after all. I looked around, trying to see who it was, but they were already gone.

"Apparently someone saw her and sold the pictures to DitesMoi," the girl passing me was saying to her friend. "And then everyone knew she was here, and she got swarmed."

I was about to ask who they were talking about, but they were already gone, and I didn't want to run after strangers and demand gossip. But I felt bad for this celebrity, whoever they were. They'd probably just wanted a night to act like a regular high school senior—but it seemed like they hadn't gotten it.

I was about to head over to the cast member when I saw that my sneaker was untied. There was a circle of benches over by the ATM, restrooms and water stations to the side of Carthay Circle. I headed over there and sat down on the closest bench. A girl I didn't recognize was talking on the phone, AirPods in. I leaned over my sneaker as she burst into laughter.

"No, I can't believe you missed it. Unbelievable. Yeah . . . Eton Mess? I think? I've never seen anything like that ever. *Totally* unforgettable. They're already blowing up online. You should have been there. . . ." She got up and walked away, and I glanced back toward Pixar Pier, where the stage was.

Even though I hadn't seen it, I was happy that Freddie's performance had gone well. I was just glad that *someone* was having a good night.

Shoe tied, I tried to focus back on my mission—looking around for Ms. Mulaney or, frankly, anyone else I recognized to tell them I was going. But all at once, I realized that I was *done*. I'd text someone from school and ask them to tell Ms. Mulaney that I'd left. It wasn't like I could get in trouble anymore. I knew in my bones that I couldn't stand to be there any longer, steeped in humiliation, covered in soda, and surrounded by living proof of all the ways that I'd messed up.

So, I turned and headed back toward the Avengers Campus, the way we'd come in. Ms. Mulaney had said that we'd leave through the same door we entered, and right now, that was enough for me. I'd escape and figure out what came next once I was safely out of the park.

With renewed purpose, I started walking faster, keeping my eyes fixed on where I was heading. And with every step that took me closer to the exit, I felt more and more sure that I was doing the right thing. I had no practice sticking around when things got hard, if I was being honest. I could leave all of this—all these mistakes and miscalculations—behind. And then I'd have a chill summer in Oregon and start college in the fall with a totally clean slate, no attachments making things harder.

Even as I tried to convince myself, I knew deep down that it wasn't ideal to be leaving in the middle of a fight with Bryony. But it wasn't like I was going to be able to do anything about it now—I couldn't change any of the things that she was mad at me about. I'd just have to put it out of my mind, that was all. Sometimes things just didn't go the way you wanted, and there was nothing you could do about it.

I pulled out my phone and saw it was 12:15 a.m. It had only taken three hours for my whole world to come crashing down.

I rounded a bend and saw it there in front of me—the wooden door we'd all come in through. It was still open, with cast members waiting by the threshold. But the flood of people we'd come in with had slowed to a trickle. It seemed likely that everyone who was going to be at Grad Nite was already here. I picked up my pace, keeping my eyes on the door. I was almost there. . . .

"Cass?"

I turned to see Amy sitting hunched on a nearby bench. "Hey," I said, waving without stopping, not wanting anything to slow my momentum. I was *so* close, after all. But then a second later, I took another look at her. Amy's face was red and puffy, and she looked absolutely miserable. But strangest of all—she was *alone*. Amy was *always* with Carlos. Seeing her by herself was like suddenly seeing someone without thumbs, or eyebrows, or something. I headed over toward her. "Amy, you okay?"

"No." Her voice was thick as she rubbed a hand across her face. "Carlos and I broke up."

I felt my jaw fall open. I'd only been at Harbor Cove High for six months, but it was long enough that I'd understood AmyandCarlos to be, well, AmyandCarlos—a solid, unshakable unit. Hearing this was truly earth shattering. "You did? I'm so sorry— What happened?"

"We got into this fight," she said, shaking her head. "Like, it all started when Bryony fell and he didn't even try and help her up. And then all these other things started coming out, and then we were yelling at each other. . . ." Her voice hitched, and she bit her lip and looked away.

I felt my stomach sink. "But it was just a silly fight, right? I'm sure you guys will be okay. I mean . . ." I searched for the words to express what I was feeling. Because if Amy and Carlos weren't AmyandCarlos, I no longer knew what I could believe in. Was the earth actually flat? Was the planet spinning backward? "You guys—you're AmyandCarlos."

Amy's face crumpled as I said it. "We're *not* anymore, though." She shook her head, and then her eyes widened as she seemed to really take me in for the first time. "Did you spill something on your dress?" She looked around. "And where's Bryony?"

"It's a long story," I said, pulling out my phone just to have a prop, something I could look at and not have to see Amy's expression. The time on my screen read 12:20 a.m. I dropped it back into my bag and started to edge away. The last thing I wanted to do was go into what had happened with Bryony, and I headed toward the big wooden door that was beckoning me. "I'm actually not feeling so great, so I'm going to go. Will you tell Ms. Mulaney for me?"

"What?" I heard Amy ask. But I was already walking faster, heading toward the exit, focused on my goal, which was getting ever closer. But as I crossed the last few feet to the door, it hit me that I was giving up my one chance to go to Grad Nite. And I was leaving behind all the people I'd met at Harbor Cove—probably forever.

For just a second, my feet slowed.

And in that moment, I let myself wish—something I hadn't done since I was a kid and only then in the presence of birthday candles or the occasional shooting star. I wished that I could go back and do it again. I'd fix this—I'd be able to make things right. If I could just have another shot . . .

The streetlight that was nearest to me flickered for a moment, the light dimming and sputtering before returning to a uniform brightness. I gave it a look, but it seemed to be working again—probably just a power surge of some kind, the Cars Land DJ using too many amps or something.

I shook my head and started walking toward the door again. I could wish all I wanted, but there was no fixing things. I was going to leave and start a new life in Oregon. It was done, and that's all there was to it.

And with that thought, I took a deep breath and walked over the threshold, and through the door.

Part Two

In switching to two-player mode, it's necessary
to start from the beginning.

Your Treasure Tokens™ will not transfer. But never fear!
Your knowledge on how to play the game surely will.

—*Excalibur!* video game manual, page 19

2

Who's ready to have the best night ever?" Sheridan yelled.

I blinked, trying to understand what was happening. I was standing just inside the entrance to California Adventure, right by the door I had just walked *through*. But I was back, somehow. And Sheridan was, too—and yelling the same thing he said as when we first arrived?

I glanced to my right—and saw Bryony standing next to me.

"Oh my god!" I gasped, as shocked to see her as I would have been to see a ghost. How had she gotten here so fast? I would have seen her, surely? And—why didn't I remember coming back into the park?

"Me! I am!" Manny yelled, just like he had earlier in the night. He stopped to take a selfie right in the middle of the entrance—also just like before, causing the same bottleneck.

I saw that same group that had been running around him and instinctively took a step to the side, grabbing Bryony's arm and yanking her out of the way just in time, so she didn't get knocked over like before.

"Wow, that was close," Bryony said, shaking her head. Then she leaned forward to look at me, her brow furrowing. "Cass, are you okay?"

"Bryony," I said, my voice catching in my throat. Did the fact that she'd found me here mean that we could move past everything somehow? "I'm so sorry about our fight, and I know I shouldn't have left things like that—"

"Fight?" Bryony's eyebrows flew up, disappearing behind her bangs. "What are you talking about?"

"You know . . ." My voice faltered as I searched her expression, trying to figure out what was currently happening. Was Bryony trying to say she just wanted to forget about our argument, all the things we'd said, and pretend it had never happened? As far as I was concerned, that would be *amazing*.

Bryony shook her head. "We didn't have a fight. I'm pretty sure I would have remembered."

"But . . . we did," I said, even though I was tempted to just go along with what she was saying. I took a deep breath—which was when I noticed my dress.

It was perfect.

Fresh and unwrinkled, and totally free from orange soda stains. "What?" I gasped. I pulled the fabric away to get a closer look. "What the *heck*?"

"Cass," Bryony said, her eyes wide as she looked at me. "I'm getting a little worried."

"Me too," I admitted. I saw a bench nearby—the same one that Bryony had sat on after getting knocked over. The same one Amy had been sitting on when she told me she and Carlos had broken up . . . My thoughts were swimming. Feeling like my legs might not be up to the job of keeping me standing for much longer, I made my way over to the bench and sank down on it.

"You look really pale," Bryony said, frowning. "Are you sick?"

"I . . ." I took a shaky breath, trying to get my spiraling thoughts under control. "Maybe? I'm not sure. . . ."

"I'm going to get you some water, okay?" Bryony asked, already backing away. "Don't move!"

I nodded, and she hustled off, leaving me alone. I looked around, trying to understand what I was seeing. Crowds of people were pouring through the door, talking and yelling and laughing with their friends. It didn't look at all like this when I'd left, when the area was practically deserted.

Instead, it was exactly the way things had looked when we'd first arrived. *Exactly.*

It was almost like . . .

"No," I said out loud, shaking my head at the absurdity of it, trying to banish the very thought. "It's not *possible.*" I knew that sitting alone, talking to myself on a bench wasn't the best look, but it felt like I had to work this out. And if I just kept in my head, I'd keep going in circles. I pulled out my phone, reasoning that maybe I could get my thoughts down in my Notes app, or something. The lock screen lit up, showing the picture of me and my dads at a roadside In-N-Out. But I couldn't even take in the photo right now, because my eyes were fixed on the time.

9:29 p.m.

I locked the screen for a moment, thinking maybe it just needed to reboot or something. Because I'd just looked at the time before I'd headed out, and it was 12:20 a.m. Which meant that now, it should be closer to

12:30 a.m. I waited another moment, then tapped the screen again—9:30 p.m., the numbers clear as anything.

Had I . . . traveled back in time? But only by two and a half hours? No—of course I hadn't. My phone was malfunctioning, that was all. Maybe when the orange soda hit me? My phone must have gotten wet and short-circuited.

I looked back down at my dress, which had clearly never encountered an orange soda in its life. But there was some explanation. There just *had* to be.

"Hey, Cass!"

I looked over to see Amy and Carlos, arms around each other, walking toward me. I felt my heart lift a little at the sight. They were AmyandCarlos again! This was proof that at least part of the world was still making sense. "Hi," I said, smiling at them, and hearing the relief in my voice. "You guys made up! I'm so happy to see it."

They shot a glance at each other, then looked back at me. "Made up?" Amy echoed. "Why would we need to make up?"

"Because . . . you broke up. We had a whole conversation about it. Right here."

"Is that a joke?" Carlos asked. "It's not funny, Cass."

"Not at all," Amy said, looking at me with wide, hurt eyes. "Why would you say that? Like why even bring that idea into the universe?"

"Seriously. Knock wood!" Carlos said, knocking on his own head. I could have sworn I saw a flicker of irritation cross Amy's face, but then it was gone a second later like it had never been there.

"Sorry," I said, rubbing my hand across my eyes, trying to understand this. What happened after I left through the door might have been fuzzy, but I could recall my conversation with Amy perfectly—probably because it had *just happened*. She had been crying on the bench, she'd told me about the breakup . . . I looked up at them, arms around each other, so clearly a unit, and felt my confidence weaken a little. "Um, what time do you guys have?"

Amy pulled out her phone. "Nine thirty-four."

Carlos glanced at his watch and shook his head. "Nine thirty-five. I set it by the Naval Observatory Master Clock, so it's more accurate."

"More accurate than a *satellite*?" Amy asked, a tiny ribbon of irritation threading through her voice.

"Well, *yes*, actually—"

"Thanks so much," I said quickly, wanting to head this off at the pass. "I just thought my phone was off. But I must have been mistaken." They were still looking at me a little skeptically, and I plastered a big smile on my face that I hoped seemed somewhat natural. "But you guys have a great time! I'll catch you later!"

They headed off, though I could hear them still bickering about time accuracy. I slumped back on the bench again and raked my hand through my hair, trying to bring my thoughts into some kind of order.

I closed my eyes for a long moment, hoping that when I opened them again, I would find myself back in a world that made sense. I'd be walking out the door, on my way to get an Uber, go home, and finish packing for Oregon. This was just . . . an anomaly. It was a very specific kind of déjà vu, that was all.

I opened my eyes and looked around. Everything was just the same as it had been a moment ago. The crowds of laughing seniors, the cast members checking wristbands, the clock on my phone reading 9:37 p.m.

I looked at the groups of happy people running off to start their nights, and felt frustration start to build in my chest. Because this had *happened* already. I'd lived through it once before! That was what I just couldn't get my head around. Why was it happening again? Things like this just didn't occur outside of movies and books. It wasn't . . .

The words *time loop* floated across my mind for just a second, before I immediately dismissed them. There was no such thing as a time loop. Which meant there had to be a rational explanation. There *had* to be. I put my head in my hands, trying to block out any distractions, needing to concentrate. What *exactly* had happened as I'd left? Maybe the answer was somewhere in there. I tried to mentally retrace my steps.

I'd been having the worst night ever. Freddie the cute musician had dumped orange soda on me. I'd run into Reagan, Greta and Nora, and worst of all, Bruce. Bryony had discovered I'd been lying about the Mermaid Café, and that I was leaving, and we had a friendship-cratering fight. Amy told me she and Carlos had broken up, and I'd headed for the exit, wishing—

My head flew up, and I drew in a shocked breath.

I'd made a *wish*. I'd wished that I could have a chance to do things over and make things right. I'd wished that I could *do this again.*

My jaw dropped open, and I immediately closed it. I was remembering now, just after I'd done this, how the streetlight had flickered. At the time, I hadn't thought much of it—just assumed it was the Cars Land DJ. But . . .

Could it be?

It wasn't rational—I knew that. But I *was* at Disneyland. If something like this was going to happen, if a wish was going to come true, it was going to be here, wasn't it? All at once, I regretted not wishing for millions of dollars, or Timothée Chalamet's phone number, or a puppy.

Accepting this went against all my instincts and everything I'd been led to understand about how things worked. But I honestly wasn't sure there could be any other explanation. So maybe the best thing to do was to accept that this seemed to be happening, and just . . . go with it?

"Hi!" I looked up to see Bryony hurrying toward me, carrying a sweating bottle of Dasani in one hand. Ms. Mulaney was hustling alongside her, her expression concerned.

"Are you okay?" Ms. Mulaney asked, pushing her long dark hair behind her ears. She leaned closer to look at me. "Bryony said you were sick."

I took the bottle from Bryony, then took a long drink. "I'm okay," I said slowly. I looked between the two of them, my wheels turning, assessing the situation. "So—we just got here, right?"

Bryony and Ms. Mulaney exchanged a quick, worried glance. "Do you maybe need something to eat, Cass?" Bryony asked. "Would that help?"

I shook my head. "No, I'm okay. But we did just get here, didn't we? We've only been in the park for a few minutes?"

"Yeah," Bryony said like it was the most obvious thing in the world. "Like, fifteen minutes, maybe? Tops?"

I nodded, a bit relieved that this wasn't some giant prank that was being pulled on me. However this was happening . . . it was *happening*.

"Okay, cool," I said, realizing they were both still looking at me, worried. "Just checking. The clock on my phone is acting kind of weird. That's all." I smiled at them—a real smile. "I promise I'm all good. We should go check things out, right?" I asked Bryony.

Bryony frowned, her head tilted slightly to the side, like she was trying to figure me out. "Are you *sure*?" she finally asked. "You looked really pale, Cass. Like, even more than usual."

"Hey!" I said, laughing. It was a joke between us—how Bryony would tan whenever there was sun, and I would inevitably burn, no matter how much SPF 75 I put on. But I didn't even mind the teasing. Just to get to laugh with Bryony again—when only a little while ago it had seemed impossible—felt like the most amazing, unexpected gift.

"Well," Ms. Mulaney said, looking between the two of us, "if you're sure you're okay, you two should go have fun. But if you start feeling sick again, come find me in the chaperones' lounge."

"Is that where you went?" I asked Bryony.

She shook her head. "I caught up with Ms. Mulaney before she'd gotten there."

"It's by the Trattoria," Ms. Mulaney said. "You'll be able to spot it because it's full of teachers trying desperately to stay awake. As you head toward Pixar Pier—" She gestured and the tote bag on her shoulder slipped off and fell to the ground, its contents spilling out. "Agh," she muttered.

"I'll help," I said, bending down. I gathered up stray pens, a lip gloss that was rolling away, and a big pile of paper bound with a rubber band. *Hurricane Madison* was typed on the first page, with Ms. Mulaney's name underneath it. But before I could see anything else, Ms. Mulaney scooped it up. "Here," I said, holding out the pens and makeup. She put the papers back in her bag, and I couldn't help asking, "Was that— Are you writing a novel?"

"Wait, really?" Bryony asked, her voice going high and excited.

"Well," Ms. Mulaney said, her cheeks turning pink. "It is. What I hope will be a novel, at any rate. I've been working on it for so long. I'm actually waiting to hear from an agent about it. They promised they'd let me know if they were interested by the end of the week, which is . . . now, basically."

"Of course they'll want it," Bryony said.

"Absolutely," I agreed.

Ms. Mulaney gave us a smile. "Thanks, girls. Well, go have fun. But take it easy, Cass, all right? Don't push yourself."

"I promise."

"Okay, then." She gave me a nod, then shouldered her bag and headed off, melting into the crowd of seniors and chaperones until, a moment later, I couldn't pick her out anymore.

"You're *sure* you're okay?" Bryony asked.

I nodded emphatically. "I'm fine." And then a wave of joy overtook me. "You know, I'm better than fine. I'm great! Because we're best friends!"

Bryony laughed. "Well, that's certainly true. So, what should we do first?"

"Bry!" I looked over to see—like before—the Emmas coming toward us. I made a mental note of it—that everything, truly everything, seemed to be happening the same way it had happened before. Somehow, *I* knew what was going to happen and could make different choices. But everyone else seemed locked into doing the same things they'd done the first time around.

"Look!" Emma R. said as she reached into her plastic Disney bag and—just like I knew she would—pulled out the Mickey ears with the mortarboard. "Isn't this so—"

"Cute, yes," I finished for her. "But where did you get it? We looked everywhere."

"Uh," Emma R. said, looking taken aback. "You did?"

"When was this?" Bryony asked.

"I mean," I said, trying to cover, feeling my heart beat harder, "I looked . . . online. Beforehand."

"I might need that one," Bryony said.

"Why don't you show us where it is?" I asked. "You guys are going back that way, because you're thinking about doing the Incredicoaster, right? Or Soarin'?"

The Emmas all exchanged a surprised look. "We are," Emma J. said. "But . . ."

"Great!" I said. "Let's all go!" In addition to wanting to track down these Mickey ears, I also didn't want to hang around this area longer than I had to. This was where we would eventually run into Reagan and Zach, after all. But then a second later, I realized that this, my do-over, meant that I wouldn't have to see Reagan or Zach tonight. Or Greta and Nora, either—and *certainly* not Bruce. I could press a reset button on all of it.

I realized, with a wave of relief, that this would be better for all of us. They'd be happier not to see me, I'd be happier not to have an awkward interaction, and Bryony wouldn't start to ask the questions that would lead to our fight. This redo meant it was a chance for *everyone* to have a better version of tonight, not just me.

I felt a spring in my step as the five of us started walking together. Everything around me seemed better, and brighter, and shinier. I felt fond of everyone as I looked around at them, even all the Emmas. And I noticed that all the people surrounding us had that beginning-of-the-night energy—running past with their friends, laughing and excited about what tonight would bring. Everyone's slates had been wiped clean, set back to the beginning again—even if I was the only one who seemed to realize it.

"So," I said with a smile as I turned to Bryony. I was still beyond grateful that we could do this, that we didn't have to sort through the wreckage and aftermath of the fight. "After we get the ears, want to go on Soarin'?"

Bryony raised an eyebrow at me. "Sure you can handle it?" Soarin' wasn't really a roller coaster, but there were some dips in it, to the point where the initial time we'd gone on it, I'd shrieked the first time we dropped down. Bryony had never let me forget it—especially since the very small child strapped in next to us had been completely fine.

"Yes," I said a little defensively. "I mean, I got through the swinging cars on the Ferris wheel, remember?"

"You *did*? When was this?"

"Oh," I said, trying to think fast. "It's . . . um . . ."

"Chip!" Emma Z. yelped, pointing. And sure enough, I saw that once again, the chipmunk was walking toward us in his graduation robes. He waved at all of us as the cast member hurried him along, and everyone around us pointed or tried to get pictures before he passed out of view.

"It's Dale," I said. "You can tell because of his nose."

"I think it's Chip," Emma Z. insisted, her voice firm. I took a breath to argue with her, and then remembered about how she'd lost her scholarship. I decided not to push it—maybe she needed this win, even if she was incorrect.

"The *characters* are in graduation outfits?" Bryony asked, looking delighted. "I had no idea! This is the best thing ever!"

"I know!" I said. "So, we'll get your ears, we'll do Soarin' . . . maybe Radiator Springs . . ." I decided not to suggest the Ferris wheel—just in case we saw Greta and Nora there. Though I was pretty sure that wasn't going to happen. Enough things had already been different tonight. This was the butterfly effect, right? The tiniest changes rippling out and altering everything. But I wasn't *entirely* sure. I suddenly wished that, over the years and all my various schools, I'd paid more attention in physics.

Bryony and I followed behind the Emmas, who were walking three across, despite the fact this meant other people—including Thor—needed to dodge around them.

"Oh!" I said, turning to Bryony, remembering the intel I'd gotten at the end of the night. "It turns out Sheridan is right. There is a celebrity here tonight."

"There is? Who is it?"

"I'm not sure," I said, looking around. "But it's definitely a *she*."

"Well, that narrows things down," Bryony said, deadpan, and I laughed. "Wait—how did you know that?"

I was saved from having to reply when a guy walked past us, and I realized with a start that I recognized him. "Oh my god!" It was Freddie, from Eton Mess—without a soda in his hand this time.

"What?" Bryony asked, looking at me curiously. "Do you know him?"

"It's Freddie! He spilled a drink on me!"

"When did he spill a drink on you?" Bryony asked, looking baffled. The Emmas stopped walking as well, and all three of them looked at me, waiting for an answer—and I realized a second too late what I'd done.

"Oh, nothing," I said quickly. "Never mind. I—don't know him. I thought it was someone else. From before. Anyway. Let's see if we can find the Mickey ears!" I started walking fast, silently admonishing myself. I wasn't used to having to think this carefully before speaking, forgetting that I had knowledge that other people didn't. I'd just have to be more careful, that was all.

As I passed Freddie, my feet slowed slightly. And before I even knew I'd made a decision, I was changing direction and running toward him. "I'll catch up with you!" I called to my friends as I hurried after Freddie.

"Wait, what?" I heard Bryony call.

"Hi," I said, as I got closer to him. "Um. Freddie?"

He stopped short and turned to look at me. "Hi," he replied, a question in his perfectly accented voice. He took a step toward the side of the path, outside the crush of people. "Have we met?"

I blinked, trying to process this. It was very strange to have him looking at me like he'd never seen me before. There was no jolt of recognition, no sense he remembered me at all. Which of course he didn't—but it was jarring to realize that *I* knew him, but as far as he was concerned, I was just another stranger.

"Um, not really." I wasn't sure how to tell him that we'd already met, but it hadn't happened yet without sounding deluded. "I just . . . wanted to say hi? And good luck with your show later." I thought about the girl on the phone, describing the show to her friend—that it was unbelievable and unforgettable. "I know it's going to go great."

His face relaxed into a smile, and I felt myself smiling back at him—automatically, like it was a reflex, something you couldn't stop even if you wanted to. "Really? That's awfully nice of you to say. Thank you."

"Sure," I said. I hoped there would be more—I wanted there to be more—but after a moment, he just gave me a nod, and another smile, and then walked away. I didn't know how to continue this interaction without coming off like a stalker, so I turned in the other direction, and hurried to catch up with my friends.

The Emmas and Bryony were standing around a kiosk—I assumed the one where Emma had bought her ears—but as I got closer, Bryony shook her head. "They're all out."

"What?"

"Sorry about that," the cast member working at the kiosk said. His name tag read JOHNNY, PROVO, UTAH.

"But didn't you *just* have some?" I asked, looking at Emma R. She pulled hers out of her bag and held them up as proof.

"I did. Unfortunately, someone just bought the last pair."

"Are there any other places that have them?" I could feel myself start to get frustrated. Last time around, Bryony and I had looked at a fair number of kiosks. Was it possible that Emma R. bought the last one in the whole park?

Johnny shrugged. "There should be more somewhere. I'm sure you'll find them. As with anything worth searching for, the quest is part of the journey."

"Okay, thanks," Emma R. said, giving him a nod. She turned and walked away from the kiosk with the other Emmas, and Bryony and I started walking behind them.

"That's such a bummer," Bryony said with a sigh. "Maybe we could check the kiosk over there—"

"They don't have any," I said, cutting her off.

"They don't? How do you know?"

"I . . . just do." I turned to the Emmas. Emma J. and Emma Z. were huddled together, looking at something on their Emma Z.'s phone, talking in low voices. "Emma," I said.

"Yes?" all three Emmas replied.

"Oh sorry—Emma R.," I said, and the other two turned back to the phone.

"Because it's going to be worth it," I heard Emma Z. say under her breath.

"What?" Emma R. asked, bringing me back to the task at hand.

"How long after coming into the park did you get to this kiosk? Like, did you come here right away?"

"I mean, maybe five minutes?" Emma R. said with a one-shouldered shrug. "We got here, and I saw these right away, and knew I wanted them, so it wasn't like I spent a ton of time looking at other stuff, you know?"

"Cool," I said with a nod. "Got it." And then I turned and headed for the doors, walking fast.

"Cass?" I heard Bryony yell after me. "Where are you going?"

"I'll be right back!" I yelled behind me. If this was a time loop, when I came back, I'd have enough time to get Bryony her ears. And if it wasn't—if this was just the world's weirdest version of déjà vu—then that question would be answered, too.

I walked faster, and as I got closer to the Avengers Campus, I saw Amy sitting on a bench, and Ms. Mulaney sitting next to her. I slowed when I saw that Amy was sobbing, crying into her hands. "What's wrong?" I asked, as I walked over to them—even though I had a sinking feeling that I knew.

"Amy and Carlos broke up," Ms. Mulaney said, mouthing the last two words to me, like even saying them out loud might be too much for Amy right now.

"Again?"

Amy looked up, tearstained and confused. "What do you mean, *again*?"

"Nothing," I said quickly. "I just mean, why?"

Amy took a shaky breath. "It started small and stupid, you know? We were arguing about who had the more accurate time—just so silly, you know? But then that turned into a bigger fight, and before I knew it, things were over."

I swallowed hard. Once again, I'd inadvertently been the cause of their breakup. How had this happened *twice*? If I got another shot, I resolved to just not talk to them the whole night. That way, if anything happened, there was no way it could be my fault. "Oh no," I said, trying to sound surprised. "I'm shocked to hear it! For the very first time. I'm so sorry, Amy." She gave me a quavery smile, then it turned into a frown and she started sobbing again.

I looked at Ms. Mulaney—should I even bother telling her that I was leaving? On closer inspection, it didn't look like Ms. Mulaney was doing great either—her eyes were red-rimmed and puffy. Was she just really feeling Amy's pain? Or was something else going on? Whatever it was, I figured the last thing she needed at the moment was more student stress. So I just gave her what I hoped was a sympathetic nod, which she returned with a wan smile.

Then I started toward the exit, my eyes fixed on the big wooden door. Before I reached it, though, I took out my phone and opened my notes app. *TEST*, I wrote, all in caps. I made sure it saved, then I locked my phone and dropped it into my bag.

Picking up my pace, I reached the exit—and stepped through.

3

W ho's ready to have the best night ever?" Sheridan yelled.

I blinked, looking around. Just like last time, I hadn't been able to get past the door. I pulled out my phone to check the time, but it was as I'd suspected—it was 9:19 p.m., even though seconds ago it had been much later. Once again, I'd gone back to the beginning of the night.

"Me!" Manny yelled. He stopped to take a selfie right in the middle of the entrance, and almost too late, I remembered what came next. I yanked Bryony out of the way of the girl who otherwise was going to crash into her, just in time.

"Wow, that was close," Bryony said, looking at the girl and her friends, who were running off and laughing, with no idea of what almost happened.

Though I remembered a second later that this was also pretty much the way they'd reacted when they'd knocked Bryony over. "Thanks."

"Of course," I said. I opened my Notes app, my breath half-held in my throat as I looked at them. But sure enough, the *TEST* note was gone. So if this was a time loop situation—which it certainly seemed to be—it seemed everything reset for me each time, full stop. I could remember what had happened, but I couldn't take anything with me, not even an electronic note.

I glanced toward the door, the barrier that I was suddenly unable to pass through, and figured it couldn't hurt to make sure, just in case this was a three-time-only wish kind of situation. "Be back in a second," I said to Bryony. I started to head back toward the door just as Amy and Carlos walked over.

"Wait, where are you going?" Bryony called.

"Where is Cass going?" I heard Carlos ask.

"That's what Bryony *literally* just said," Amy snapped.

I tried to block all of this out. I pushed my way through the crowd, feeling like a salmon swimming upstream as I tried to reach the door.

"Did you forget something in the tent?" the cast member by the door, the one checking wristbands asked.

"Uh, sure," I said. "I'll just . . ." I pointed toward something just beyond her and dodged around an incoming group to step forward, through the doorway.

4

"Who's ready to have the best night ever?" Sheridan yelled.

"Okay," I said, nodding, as I oriented myself. Everything was just like before—my classmates streaming in, everyone happy and excited to begin the night. Bryony next to me, smiling, still firmly my best friend, not looking at me with hurt in her eyes.

I saw Manny take a deep breath to respond like he always did, but this time I preempted him. "Manny is!" I called. He stopped and looked over at me, surprised. I pulled Bryony out of the way before she even knew she was in any danger, and steered us over to the bench that I already felt like I was getting to know well.

"You okay?" Bryony asked me, her brow furrowing.

I nodded. "Just needed a second." I sat down, took a deep breath, and then let it out slowly, the way Oscar's meditation app was always telling him to do. I wasn't sure if it helped, but it gave me a moment to just sit and try and assess the situation.

Because it seemed like I could keep walking through the door, but I was fairly certain I'd keep getting the same result. There was truly no other explanation that I could seem to get my head around. The facts, unbelievable as they were, were also undeniable.

I was in a time loop.

On Grad Nite.

My only experience with time loops had been movies and books, so I wasn't sure how it normally worked, but I was relieved that unlike the ones in *Groundhog Day* or *Palm Springs*, I didn't have to either go to sleep or die in order to reset things. And though I had no way of telling for sure, it didn't seem like I had a limited number of these.

But then, I was still waiting for the wise guide to show up and explain all of this to me. It didn't seem very fair that I was in a time loop with absolutely *no* instructions. Where was my handbook? Or at least someone giving me the dos and don'ts? Nobody seemed to be putting themselves forward, so I figured I'd just have to sort this out on my own. I honestly didn't see any other solution here.

But *why* was I in a time loop? That's what I couldn't get my head around . . . why this was happening. I'd seen enough of these movies to know there was always a *reason* someone found themselves in a time loop—something they had to learn or fix.

I'd first wished to do this over because of how disastrously the night had gone—running into everyone from my past, and this eventually leading to the fight with Bryony. But now, none of that needed to happen. There *was* no fight with Bryony, no running into Reagan and Zach, or

Greta and Nora, or Bruce. I knew they were all here, somewhere else in the park, but I could avoid them—or start things over if I saw them.

So that meant the reason for this loop had to be something else . . . and in a flash of inspiration, I suddenly had an idea.

Emma had even pointed it out to me, I just hadn't clocked it at the time—*the meet-cute.* Freddie the British musician. All at once, it seemed so obvious. I never just ran into cute guys—literally or otherwise. His soda had spilled on me, we'd had a conversation . . . I remembered the way I'd felt drawn to talk to him in my second loop. It was like we had a connection that went past just soda-spilling. It had to be that, right? That maybe something was supposed to happen with us? I decided to find out.

"Hey!" I looked over and saw, right on time, the Emmas coming toward us, Emma R. with her blue plastic Disneyland bag, the other two Emmas looking preoccupied as usual.

"Hey, guys," Bryony said.

"So, what's your plan?" I asked, hoping to skip the graduation ears conversation since it seemed clear that, no matter how many times I tried, we really weren't going to get them.

"We were just debating what to do," Emma J. said, glancing at her phone. "Either the Incredicoaster or heading to Soarin'. There's, like, no line right now."

"You should do the Incredicoaster!" I said immediately.

Bryony blinked at me in surprise. "Cass, you don't like roller coasters."

"No, I know," I said, nodding. "And so that's why you should go on it with the Emmas. Along with all the other ones I can't do. Like maybe the Guardians ride, too, and the Ferris wheel with the swinging cars . . ." I flashed back to our disastrous ride and wasn't able to stop myself from shuddering.

"But you wouldn't be able to go with us."

"I know," I said, trying to sound sad, and not like this was all part of a plan. "But then we can meet up afterward and you'll tell me about how I could have handled them, and I won't believe you."

Bryony frowned. "But we're supposed to hang out together."

"And we will! It's just that this way you'll get the full Grad Nite experience." My heart clenched a little as I flashed back to Bryony, on the verge of tears, confronting me about lying to her. That version of her night had been totally wrecked. And even though she didn't remember it, I did. I needed to erase that entirely, make sure she had the best time. "We can do my wimpy rides once you've done all the daredevil ones."

"Are you *sure*?" Bryony asked, her brow furrowed.

"Chip!" Emma Z. yelped, pointing to the costumed chipmunk in his graduation robe.

"*Dale*," I muttered, even though I knew from experience I wasn't going to win this argument.

"It's Chip," Emma Z. insisted, like I knew she would.

"I had no idea that the *characters* would be in graduation outfits!" Bryony said. "This is—"

"The best thing ever!" I finished for her. "It really is. So, you guys go ride your rides and I'll meet up with you when you're done!"

"Awesome," Emma R. said with a nod. "We'll text you, okay, Cass?"

I nodded. "Perfect."

Bryony looked at me, her expression concerned, and a thought snaked its way into my brain before I could stop it: that Bryony was worried about leaving me alone for a few *hours*. And she had no idea that I was going to leave her, probably forever, tomorrow morning. I shook my head, trying to clear this thought away, but it lingered, like how a bad perfume smell sticks around in an elevator.

"I swear I'm fine," I said, swallowing the lump in my throat and making myself smile at her. "We'll hang out the rest of the night."

"Okay," Bryony said. "I'll text you when we're done riding the real rides."

"Hey," I said, even though I was laughing. "Silly Symphony Swings *is* a real ride, I'll have you know. It's just not as *flashy* as some of the other ones."

"Sure," Bryony said with a grin. "Whatever you have to tell yourself."

"Let's go!" Emma J. said, and I watched as the three of them took off, heading toward Pixar Pier. Bryony turned around once to give me a wave, and then they passed out of view, leaving me standing alone.

"Cass?" I turned to see Ms. Mulaney heading toward me. "You okay all by yourself?" She looked around. "Where's Bryony?"

"She went to ride the roller coasters," I explained. "I'm a roller coaster wimp."

She smiled at me. "I'm the same way. I've never understood what's fun about getting motion sickness."

"Exactly!"

"Well, if you do need anything, I'll be in the chaperone lounge. It's that direction. . . ." She pointed, and just like before, the tote bag over her shoulder slipped off and fell to the ground, its contents spilling out. "Agh," she muttered.

I reached down to help her like before, picking up spilled pens and the thick manuscript. "Here," I said, handing it back to her.

"Thanks," Ms. Mulaney said, tucking everything back in her bag.

"That was your novel, right?" My teacher blinked at me in surprise, and I remembered a beat too late that I wasn't supposed to have known that.

"Well," Ms. Mulaney said, her cheeks going pink. "It is. What I hope will be a novel, at any rate. I've been working on it for so long. I'm actually waiting to hear from an agent about it. They promised they'd let me know if they were interested by the end of the week, which is . . . now, basically."

"Of course they'll be interested!" But then a second later, I thought about when I'd seen Ms. Mulaney later in the night, and her eyes had been red-rimmed and puffy, like she'd been crying. It really was kind of head-spinning, that I had a preview of what was going to happen to people, and they were just living their lives, for what they thought was the first time. But maybe Ms. Mulaney was crying for a completely separate reason! I had no idea.

"I mean, I hope so. But I'm not sure. . . ." She stopped suddenly and reached into her tote bag for her ringing phone. "That's the agent," she said, and her voice had gotten high and nervous. It was strange to see my teacher—who'd always seemed so in control of everything—this flustered. "I need to take this."

"Of course," I said, already backing away. I gave Ms. Mulaney a smile. "Good luck!"

She nodded at me, and tucked her hair behind her ears. Then she took a deep breath and answered the call. "Hello? This is Courtney Mulaney."

Feeling like I should give her some privacy, I walked a few steps ahead, then stopped, when I realized I wasn't sure where to go. If this whole thing had something to do with Freddie, I needed to run into him again, right? I looked around, thinking once again that it would be a great time for a wise guide to show up and give me some instructions.

But when nobody appeared, I just tried to trace things back and remember where I'd crashed into Freddie, the first time. Things were getting a little fuzzy—all the loops were starting to blur together.

All at once, I remembered seeing the profile of the bear carved into the mountain, lit up dramatically by the lights.

Feeling like I finally had a plan, I changed direction and headed toward Grizzly Peak.

4

was almost to Grizzly Peak—I'd just reached Carthay Circle when my
phone beeped with a text.

> BRYONY:
> Sure you don't want to change your mind? You
> might not get another chance!

Under that, she'd sent me a picture of her and the Emmas waiting for
the Guardians ride. She and Emma R. were smiling, but Emmas J. and Z.
were locked deep in conversation, their heads bent together, neither one
looking happy. I started walking again, texting as I went, which meant
I wasn't paying attention at all to where I was going—which was how I

ended up colliding, hard, with someone who had stopped in the middle of the path.

"Ow!" I yelped, stumbling backward a few steps.

The guy I'd crashed into nearly fell over, wobbling before righting himself, but sending his phone, which he'd also been absorbed in, clattering to the ground. He turned around and my eyes widened when I realized it was Freddie. I'd literally stumbled into him! It was all making sense—this *had* to be why I was here. Otherwise, would we keep literally bumping into each other like this?

"Oh no—so terribly sorry," Freddie said. "Are you okay?"

"Hi! I mean— I'm fine. Hey, Freddie." As before, he was wearing his green *Excalibur!* T-shirt, and he was just as cute as ever, but maybe even more so, because this was the closest to him I had yet been, and I wasn't distracted by orange soda spilling all over my dress, or by the fact my friends were waiting for me. Now that we were standing close, I could see he was a good four or five inches taller than me, and his dark eyes were fringed with long lashes. His curls cascaded over his forehead in a way that really seemed unfair—what was next, a dimple? But then he smiled at me, and, sure enough, a single deep dimple appeared in his left cheek.

"Er, yes." His smile was perfectly polite, but very confused. "You're spot on. Sorry—have we met? I apologize if I don't ..."

"A few times," I said, nodding. "But it was earlier. Don't worry about it—you wouldn't remember. It hasn't happened yet."

"I ... Sorry?" He glanced back down at his phone, his eyes scanning the screen. Then he stared into space for a second, seemingly lost in thought before he focused back on me. "Apologies. That was just ... Never mind. I'm so sorry. I shouldn't have just stopped like that."

"Is everything all right?" I asked, nodding down at the phone. "Does it have anything to do with why . . ." I paused, trying to call up the details from our first encounter. "You bought Irn-something for . . . Niall?"

Freddie stared at me, his eyes wide. "Irn-Bru," he finally said, his voice coming out strangled. "I was just thinking I should get some for him. But how did you know that? How could you have *possibly* known that?"

We were standing to the side of the path, but not all the way over, and as a rowdy group of seniors came running around the curve, Freddie stepped to the side, touching my elbow lightly to guide me out of harm's way. I couldn't help but notice the *zing* that shot up my arm when he touched my bare skin.

"Because," I said, trying to think about the best way to go about this. I knew any explanation would just sound like I was losing my mind. But if my being in this loop had something to do with him, *shouldn't* he know about it? "You bump into me later and spill orange soda all over my dress. And you tell me you got it for him as a peace offering."

"But that . . . hasn't happened," Freddie said. He was speaking slowly, his eyes searching my face like he was trying to figure out how I was pulling off this trick.

"I know. But it will. Or maybe it won't, now that we're having this conversation."

Freddie just stared at me for a moment, then seemed to make a decision. "Right," he said, nodding. "Are you hungry? Do you want to get some food? Because I have heaps more questions, but I'm not sure I can ask them on an empty stomach."

As if on cue, my stomach grumbled audibly enough for us both to hear it. "I *am* hungry," I admitted.

"Fantastic. I know a great place." He smiled at me then, the dimple deepening. "I'm Freddie, by the way. Freddie Sharma. But clearly, you know that." He held out his hand to me.

"Cass Issac," I said, shaking it. "And this is actually the first time we've officially met."

"Well." He held on to my hand for a beat longer before dropping it. And even though he was smiling, it was like I could practically see that his thoughts were spinning a hundred miles an hour. "Then it's nice to meet you, Cass. Officially. Ready to go?"

I nodded and gave him a smile. "Lead on."

4

The place Freddie was talking about turned out to be the Hollywood Lounge, in the Hollywood Land section of the park. It looked like an old fifties-style hamburger stand—no indoor seating, just a walk-up window and then tables and chairs outside. There was a checkerboard tile pattern, and ICE COLD REFRESHMENT was spelled out along the top of the roof in neon letters that glowed brightly against the darkness. Freddie went to the food trucks that were parked nearby, but I stayed put and contemplated the menu.

I decided on a burger, fries, and a Coke, feeling like I could use a little jolt of caffeine. Freddie got his food—a burrito and a sparkling water—around the same time I did, and we sat down at one of the white metal outdoor tables in front of the restaurant. We had our choice of seats, since the tables were mostly empty. The only other person there was a guy who I assumed was a chaperone, yawning over a plate of onion rings. But it made sense it was so deserted—everyone else at the park was trying to get everything they could out of tonight. They were having a blast on all the rides and dancing at the DJ stations and probably didn't want to waste any time sitting down to eat a meal.

It wasn't until Freddie and I were sitting across from each other, bathed in the glow of the neon, that I started to feel a little bit nervous. I knew that this wasn't a date—I had only, just moments ago, even been officially introduced to this guy. But there was something about this—the night, the neon, sitting across from him in a nearly deserted sea of tables—that made it *feel* date-ish.

Not that I'd had a ton of experience on dates, or with guys in general. There was my SLO lab partner—and Bruce, of course. But both of those guys had felt like they were from a world I understood. Freddie was a British guy in a *band*, and I was suddenly feeling out of my depth.

"You made a good call with the chips. I mean . . . *fries*," Freddie said, putting on an American accent for the word and making me laugh. "They're the best in the park."

"Oh yeah?" I picked up one and bit into it as my stomach rumbled again. Freddie was right—they were crisp and just the right amount of salty. "Really good," I agreed as I reached for my burger.

"The burrito is good, too," he said, lifting it up. "And I sometimes get the burger, but it's just too complicated."

I paused, midbite. "Complicated?"

"I have kind of a weird allergy," he explained. "I can't have any raw fruit or vegetables."

"Really?"

"Yep. If they're cooked it's fine, but I can't do raw. No berries or anything. And so when I get a burger it has to be totally plain—no lettuce, onion, tomato, nothing. And so sometimes it's just easier to get something else."

"I don't think that sounds like a real allergy. I think that's something you made up when you were a kid and didn't want to eat your vegetables."

He laughed, and I felt myself start to relax. "You're not the first one to suspect that, believe me. In primary school, my friends were always trying to sneak things into my food to see if I was lying."

"So you can't have salad? Carrot sticks? *Smoothies?*" He shook his head, giving a little shrug. "What happens if you do have them?"

"Hives," he said matter-of-factly. "My whole face starts to swell up. It's not attractive."

"I find that hard to imagine." A second later, I realized what I'd just said, and took a quick sip of my Coke to try and cover.

Freddie took a big bite of his burrito and nodded appreciatively. "Now, this is amazing. We don't have anything like this back home."

"And where's back home?"

"London," he said, then shook his head. "Well, kind of. I grew up in Croydon. I was only in the city proper for about five months before getting this gig and coming here." He paused and looked at me. "Have we had this conversation before?"

I shook my head. "Nope. This is by far the most we've ever talked."

He set down his burrito and made a go-on gesture. "So, walk me through it. How does it work?"

I regarded him for a moment, just trying to get a sense of what he was thinking. "Are you saying you believe me?"

"I don't know if I'd go that far," he demurred. "Call me intrigued."

"Hi, Intrigued," I said, giving him a wave. "I'm Cass."

He grinned at that, his dimple making an appearance. "I set myself up for that one, huh?" He looked at me expectantly, waiting for me to continue.

I took a breath. I'd wanted to tell someone else about this—I really had—but now that I had to try and explain this to someone, I wasn't sure how it was going to come across. Would I just sound absolutely bonkers? I had no idea—but there didn't seem to be anything to do except jump in. "Okay. So I just graduated a few days ago."

"Hence the trip to Grad Nite," he said, his voice overly serious.

"Well, exactly. I'm here with my school, Harbor Cove. It's about twenty minutes from here. More in traffic. Have you been?"

Freddie shook his head. "Unless there's a bus that goes directly there, let's just assume I haven't been, because it's not like I'm driving. Are you aware people in this country drive on the wrong side of the road?"

"I think *you* drive on the wrong side of the road. We literally drive on the right."

"And you don't even have proper trains!"

"We have trains!" I protested, feeling that America was being unfairly maligned. "There's the surf liner that goes along the coast. And I know we have one that goes to LA."

"I'm quite familiar with that train," he assured me. "But sorry to interrupt. You were here with your class . . ."

"Right. And it was normal at first. Really fun . . ." My voice trailed off, and I paused, not sure how much I wanted to go into. "Well, it got a little weird. I ran into some people that I hadn't seen in a while, and they weren't exactly thrilled to see me. And then . . . I got into a fight with my best friend, Bryony. So I just decided I was done, that I was going home. And as I was leaving . . ." I stopped and took a drink of my Coke, and Freddie leaned forward, like I was getting to the good part of a mystery. Which I supposed, on some level, this was.

"Yes?"

"As I was leaving, I made—a wish. I wished that there was a way I could do this over. And then the streetlights flickered, but I honestly didn't think anything of it at the time." Freddie nodded, listening, his eyes not leaving mine. "I walked out the doors. But then, a second later . . ." I took a deep breath and made myself say it. "I was just—back. But it was the beginning of the night, and I was just arriving. And everything had reset."

"Everything?" he asked, his eyes wide.

"Yes. Like the film rewound and we just started over again. You know, like *Groundhog Day*—"

"*Pettigrew's Loop,*" he said at the same time.

I stopped and blinked at him. "What's that?"

"What's— You've never seen *Pettigrew's Loop*?" he asked, sounding incredulous.

I shook my head. "I assume it's about someone stuck in a time loop?"

Freddie nodded. "Yes. But since Bernard Pettigrew is a mailman and, well, English, he's very attached to his routine and doesn't realize it for a while. Not until he notices the dates on the mail are unchanging."

"But you have heard of *Groundhog Day*, right?" I'd never heard of his movie, but it seemed like the same concept.

"Of course. It's a classic."

"That's what I kept thinking of—that somehow I'm in a *Groundhog Day* situation. And I'm not sure why." I wasn't about to tell him that *he* might be one of the reasons this was happening.

I looked up at him, fully prepared to see him either laughing or scoffing at me—or worse, eyeing me nervously, like I was someone in the throes of a mental breakdown. But Freddie just looked thoughtful, like he was processing everything I was saying.

"I know this probably sounds impossible. And I know you don't know me. But I swear I'm telling the truth." I took a deep breath and made myself ask it. "Do you . . . believe me?"

Freddie looked off to the side and took a moment before he answered. "I mean, I've always *wanted* to believe in something like this," he said slowly. "I always hoped it would happen to me. Ever since . . ." He looked down at the T-shirt he was wearing and pointed to it.

"Excalibur?" I asked.

"Excalibur," he agreed. He cast a quick glance at my fries, and I pushed them across the table to him.

"Be my guest."

"You're sure?"

"As long as you're not going to have an allergic reaction because of the tomatoes in the ketchup. I don't want that kind of responsibility."

He took a fry and gave me a smile. "They're cooked, so I'll be okay. But thanks for looking out."

I nodded toward his shirt. "So, you're just really into the Arthur myth?"

"No, it's a video game."

"Excalibur," I said slowly. This was ringing a bell for some reason. "I think I've heard of it. Didn't it win some kind of video game award?"

Freddie nodded, looking surprised. "Best new game the year it came out. So you've played it?"

"No, I just know a lot of random facts."

He smiled at that. "Well, it's really great. My brother, Jack, and I were obsessed with it growing up. It starts off pretty grounded—you're in the real world, just walking around. But that's your first task—to find your way into the magic world that's running parallel to the normal world. And when you find the way in, it's a whole other kingdom. The colors are brighter, the music is better—and it's magical, literally. It's this spin on the medieval fantasy world that's just so fun. And within the game, you're going on quests and trying to chase down prophecies and collecting Treasure Tokens. It's the best."

"It sounds fun."

"It is," Freddie said, but his voice was growing more serious. "But it wasn't just about the game. What Jack and I always talked about was if it could be *real*. If this was actually the situation we were in—living our lives like the people in the beginning of the video game. That's what always consumed me the most. Like what if there was this whole other world, so close, and you could never get to it. Or you didn't even *realize* it was there."

I nodded, processing this, as Freddie finished the last of his burrito.

"So finding out that this is happening to you—it's like realizing that maybe a tiny bit of that magic *is* possible. In fact, I really should tell Jack. . . ." He pulled out his phone.

"Uh." I glanced down at my watch, trying to do the math. "Isn't it kind of late in the UK? Or . . . early?"

"Ah," Freddie said with a nod, doing the same calculation that I just had. "You make a good point. But I can't wait to tell him. He loved it, too, but not as much as me. I even had an *Excalibur* poster above my bed."

I smiled at that. "When did you finally take it down?"

He just stared at me, his brow furrowing. "Sorry—take it *down*? I don't understand. . . ."

For just a second, I thought he was serious, until he gave me a smile—one that lit his whole face up. "I'm just taking the piss," he said, and then a second later, shook his head. "Britishism. I'm just teasing you. I took it down in sixth form. Geraldine Bewley was coming over to work on a project, and I needed her to see just how cool I was."

"And how'd that work out?"

"It didn't," he said with a laugh. "But not because of the poster."

"Maybe you should have left it up? Maybe she was a secret fan, too."

Freddie smiled at that, then leaned forward. "So, help me understand. The loop starts when you go through the doors?"

I nodded. "The ones by the Avengers Campus. As soon as I step over the threshold, I'm back to the moment I first came to the park."

"Fascinating. So you can reset it whenever you want?"

"It seems like it. I thought at first that there might only be a few of these. But I've done it . . . four times now? I think? So there might not be any limit."

"You don't know how many times it's been?"

I shook my head. "Even if I wrote something down, nothing comes with me. Like, when you spilled orange soda all over my dress . . ."

"Not me," Freddie protested, looking alarmed. "I mean, not this me. But sorry on behalf of that me."

"The next time I went through, my dress was perfectly clean, like nothing had happened to it. Every time I walk through the door, it's like the first time. I remember everything that's happened, but I can't take anything with me."

"Huh." He reached into his messenger bag and pulled out a small black notebook, the same kind Oscar used on client meetings—a Moleskine. He took out the pen that had been in the notebook and clicked the top. "Do you mind if I write this down? It just helps me think."

"Go ahead," I said as I took a the last bite of my burger.

Freddie nodded at it. "Good, right?"

"Yeah," I said, shaking my head. "I was really hungry."

"Well, that's an interesting point," he said, scribbling something in his notebook, then looking up at me. "What about physically?"

I could feel my cheeks get hot and took an extra-long drink of my soda, hoping to cool them down. "I— What do you mean?"

"Well, like, in *Groundhog Day*, things start over when he goes to sleep, right?"

"Or dies," I pointed out.

"And in *Pettigrew's Loop*, it resets whenever he takes a nap. But you've been doing this for a few hours now, right? Are you tired? Do your feet hurt? That kind of thing."

I considered the question. I probably *should* have been more tired, now that I was thinking about it. If time was going in a straight line, many hours would have passed by now—it would have been close to four or five a.m. But I wasn't tired in any extreme way. My feet didn't hurt, and I wasn't exhausted. I did seem to get hungry at the same time every loop—when Bryony and I had gotten snacks from the Cozy Cone, and when my stomach had rumbled this time with Freddie.

"No," I said. "I think maybe I physically reset, too? Which I guess makes sense—as much as anything makes sense right now."

"That's very cool," he said, underlining something in his notebook and raising an eyebrow at me. "It's like you're a superhero or something."

I laughed. "I don't know about that. But it is nice to talk to someone about this. It's been kind of a weird thing to just have in my head as I've been walking around."

"I mean, I do kind of know what it's like."

My head snapped up as I stared at him, surprised. Was this a *double* time-loop situation, like in *Palm Springs* or *Russian Doll*? "What do you mean?" I asked slowly. Maybe *he* was the wise guide who could walk me through this experience! It was high time I got one, after all. "Are you . . ."

"No, no," Freddie said quickly. "I can assure you I'm not in a time-loop situation." He paused. "You ever say a sentence you're *positive* you've never said before?"

"Oh," I said, nodding. I took a sip of my Coke, trying to cover the disappointment I was sure was plain on my face. While it was a relief to finally talk to someone about this, the idea that I could have had someone on this journey with me had been really nice. It was like until this moment, I hadn't realized how lonely it had been.

"I just meant that my life right now is kind of similar," he said with a shrug. "My days here are all the same. We come over from our hotel, we have a few hours free to wander around. Then we go to sound check, rehearse if we need to, then play the same songs in the same order. And the next night, we do it again."

"You mean," I said, thinking of the posters, "with the band?"

"Oh right," he said, shaking his head. "Sorry. I'm in this band, Eton Mess? We perform for the Grad Nites here. Maybe you knew that?"

"I've seen the posters," I assured him. "Why's it called Eton Mess?"

Freddie gave me a rueful smile. "I couldn't tell you. It's not my band. It was put together by some music executives. I was taking a year off before uni, trying to get people to listen to my songs—"

"You write songs?" I asked, impressed.

"Yeah. I've been playing since I was a kid. When I was little, I realized that I could hear something and reproduce it. It's like perfect pitch, but for instruments."

"Wow," I said, shaking my head. "That's really impressive. How many instruments do you play?"

Freddie laughed. "How many do I play *well*? Two. I play bass in the band. I also play piano, but we don't have keys in Eton Mess. I've been thinking for a while we should but . . ."

"I always wanted to learn piano," I said, then immediately felt myself blush. I was sitting across from an actual professional musician, and I knew I'd just sounded like a total amateur. "I've taken a few lessons, but . . . maybe someday, right?"

Freddie nodded, his expression earnest. "You should stick with it. I love guitar, but there's something so rich in the sound you can get from a piano. And I always prefer singing with it. . . ."

"You sing, too?" I was trying hard to keep it together, but between the hair, the dimple, the accent and now the *singing*, it was getting quite challenging.

"I do. Well, not that much in Eton Mess. I just sing backup occasionally—Niall's the singer." I nodded, remembering the guy in the poster pouting at the camera, microphone slung around his neck. "And all our songs are written by some Swedish songwriting team I've never met. At least that's what they tell us. I'm partially convinced it's some kind of AI that's programmed to churn out pop songs. Honestly, with some of these lyrics, it's the only thing that makes sense."

I laughed, then shook my head, trying to focus. "Wait—you said you were trying to get people to listen to you?"

Freddie nodded. "Yeah. I was in London, doing a ton of odd jobs, just trying to get my music out there, and Niall heard about the audition. There was a group being put together—they wanted a band of Brits to play in the

States. And it was a great opportunity, right? I'd never been to America, I'd get paid to play music. . . ."

"That sounds smart," I said, taking a drink but hitting mostly ice.

"Exactly. So I said yes and came here. I've been trying to use this time in America to make some contacts. When we have time off, I take the train up to LA, trying to get meetings. And this music manager really liked some of my songs—she said she's going to be at the show tonight. I've assured her that what Eton Mess plays aren't the kinds of songs I write, but she still wants to come. She says she needs get a sense of how I play live, what kind of a performer I am."

I nodded and remembered seeing a woman at the show who seemed to be dressed a little better than everyone else there—maybe that was her? "That's really exciting," I said, but Freddie only gave me a wan smile in return. "That's . . . not really exciting?"

"I mean, it's a great opportunity—for *me*."

I suddenly remembered what Freddie had said when he'd crashed into me—that he'd brought the soda for Niall as a peace offering. "It's not so great for Niall?"

A ghost of a smile passed over Freddie's face, and he shook his head. "Yeah. I've known him forever. We were in a band together in school. And he's my mate—I don't want to hurt him. He wants to make it, too, but he's only a singer. He doesn't play his own instruments. And I want to sing my own songs. So, if I move forward, there wouldn't really be a place for him."

"Maybe that's what he gets upset about?" I asked. I thought hard, trying to remember what he'd said. "Why you're bringing him a peace offering," I clarified.

Freddie shook his head. "God, it's mental you know that. So, I guess

I must tell him, right? About the manager coming tonight. And he gets upset—"

"You bring him orange soda to apologize, spill it all over me—"

"Sorry, again."

"But you still have to do it, right? You can't hold yourself back. And this sounds like a real opportunity."

Freddie nodded. "I know—and you're right. But it's not so easy, is it? To just leave people behind like that?"

I looked down at the tabletop, sweeping up some imaginary crumbs just to have something to do with my hands. "I don't know. I think that, you know, sometimes . . ."

"Cass?"

I looked up at the sound of a familiar voice.

Bruce was standing next to the table, staring at me in shock.

4

For just a moment, I blinked at him, wondering why I hadn't anticipated this possibility. It wasn't like any of the people I wanted to
avoid here had disappeared, after all. Of course they would be wandering
around in their own loops. And since I'd changed my routine tonight, it
had inadvertently put me in the path of the person I really would have
preferred to avoid.

"Hi, Bruce," I said, then remembered a moment later that I was supposed to be surprised to see him. "I mean . . . Bruce! My stars! What are
you doing here, so very far from Seattle? I'm shocked, shocked, to see you!"
I glanced across the table and saw Freddie raise an eyebrow at me—maybe
I wasn't quite pulling this off. "Uh, why is your school here? Did you do

really well academically and get rewarded with this trip or something?"

"Well, yeah," Bruce said, sounding a little thrown. "That's exactly wh
happened. I can't believe I'm seeing you again."

"You two know each other?" Freddie asked with a smile, clearly n
picking up on the vibe.

Right away, Bruce's expression darkened. "We *did*," he said short
"But I haven't seen Cass in two years. Ever since she stood me up on pro
night."

"I didn't stand you up," I said weakly, even though I knew by now th
this argument wasn't going to get me anywhere. "I texted—"

"And then the next day, she was just gone, no goodbye, nothing."

Freddie blinked at me in surprise, and I felt my face flush with sham
"We moved," I protested faintly.

"And you didn't even have the courage to tell me to my face," Bru
said, his voice cracking on the last word. "You never responded to m
letter—I don't even know if you got it."

"I did," I replied, and then immediately felt ashamed of myself, sin
I'd basically just admitted I was too much of a coward to write him back

"Ah," Freddie said, looking between the two of us. "Well."

"Yeah," Bruce said, shaking his head. "Well, you ruined my prom nigh
Cass. And now you've managed to ruin my Grad Nite, too, so thanks fo
that."

"I didn't—" I started, then took a breath and tried again. "I was only—

"Word of advice," Bruce said, turning his back on me and looking
Freddie. "Don't get too attached. The second you do, you'll never see he
again."

"Bruce," I said, my voice strangled, but he was already walking awa
his shoulders hunched, his head down. I sat back hard against my seat, m

heart pounding. This was now the second time I'd had this conversation with Bruce. But it wasn't getting any easier. In fact, if anything, it seemed to be getting harder. I rubbed my hand across my face, and then raised my eyes to look at Freddie.

I was fully expecting him to make an excuse to go, or be cold and distant, letting me know exactly what he thought about my behavior.

But instead, he gave me a sad smile, filled with compassion. "Want to get some dessert? I know a fantastic place."

I nodded, starting to leave when I saw Freddie's phone sitting on top of the table. "Uh, Freddie?"

He turned back and picked up the phone. "Cheers. I'm always doing that. My mum says I'd lose my head if it wasn't attached to my neck." He tucked his phone into his back pocket and gave me a smile. "So. Ice cream?"

Ghirardelli's ice-cream parlor, over in San Fransokyo Square, lived up to Freddie's description—or maybe it was just that ice cream always hits the spot after emotionally draining experiences. We walked with our scoops, not to any place in particular, just falling into step together. The people around us were still laughing and running from place to place, but I noticed that the pace was definitely a little slower, like the night was starting to tire everyone out a bit. And while most people still seemed to be having a great time, I saw occasional arguments breaking out among friend groups, couples in spats—the shiny perfection of the start of the night making way for the more complicated reality.

"How's the mint chocolate chip?" Freddie asked, looking over at my cup.

"Really good," I said, nodding. "How's the rocky road?"

"Excellent," he said with a smile. "Though it isn't a patch on the place I used to go back home in Croydon. It was called the Sweet Emporium, and it was amazing. Best rocky road in the world."

"Well, the next time I'm in Croydon, I'll be sure to stop on by."

"Tell them Freddie sent you."

"I will." I glanced over at him, wanting to address the awkwardness that had just happened, so we could move on. "So—that was Bruce."

Freddie glanced over at me. We were walking on the Pacific Wharf and I could see the Ferris wheel in the distance, Mickey in the center, the whole thing all lit up, turning in an endless circle. "I take it that's not the first time you've had that conversation?"

"Nope." Freddie made a sympathetic face. "I didn't know he'd be here tonight. I honestly never thought I'd see him again. I guess I didn't . . . think about how he might be feeling." As I said this, though, I knew it wasn't quite true. Bruce—and the way I'd left Washington—had always bothered me. I'd just been able to push it away until tonight.

"When you said that you ran into people you didn't want to see—was that who you meant?"

"Yeah." I could have left it at that—but I also knew it wouldn't have been honest. And for whatever reason—maybe it was the fact that we'd really just met—I found myself wanting to tell Freddie the truth. The *whole* truth. "But it was also some other people, too. I move a lot." I took a breath and explained about my dads, and their business, and always leaving, always finding the next house, the next project to make perfect. "And so over the years, it just got too hard. Constantly saying goodbye to people, saying you're going to keep in touch but knowing it's not going to work."

We'd reached the Pixar Pier, and I stopped for just a moment to look at the water, the lights from the Ferris wheel reflecting down on it. People on the roller coaster nearby were whooshing around and giving the occasional "AAAGH!" before being whisked away again, going upside down in a loop.

"That does sound really hard. Not that I would know. We've lived in the same house forever. Same neighbors, same street, everyone a little too much in everyone's business. Sometimes, home is your favorite sweatshirt that you've outgrown." He paused and blinked.

"You okay?"

"Yes," he said, holding out his ice cream cup to me. "Would you mind . . ."

I took it from him, and he reached into his messenger bag for his notebook and scribbled down the line. He flipped some pages, and I could see they were mostly filled with his handwriting.

"Sorry," he said, dropping the notebook back in his messenger bag. He slung it across his shoulders and then took his ice cream back. "I thought that might have potential for a song. And I didn't want to forget it."

"Is that where you write down all your song lyrics?"

"Pretty much. But I'm sorry to interrupt you."

"You weren't," I assured him. "I—" I stopped short as I realized where we were. We were in front of the Little Mermaid ride, where the stage was set up. It was busy and bustling, stagehands hauling out equipment and taping down cords. One of them, a girl with bright purple hair, waved at Freddie, and he waved back. All around the stage were blown-up pictures—some of the band, but most just of Niall and his soulful pout. There was an electronic sign at the top of the stage, the message reading ETON MESS TAKES THE STAGE IN and then, underneath it, a countdown clock, showing fifty-nine minutes and nineteen seconds.

"Do you need to go?" I asked Freddie, suddenly worried I'd interrupted his night. Even though he'd told me he had some free time, I was sure listening to a girl talk about her time-loop issues was not how he'd been intending to spend it.

"I have a little more time," he assured me. "I'm good."

We tossed out our ice-cream cups, then started to walk again. But just seeing the countdown clock had been enough to remind me that time was moving forward, and that he didn't have all night to just walk around with me. My phone buzzed, and when I pulled it out of my purse, I saw three texts.

> BRYONY:
> Hey! Having fun? Long line at Guardians, we're going to Incredicoaster!
>
> Incredicoaster down, we're going back to Guardians!
>
> On Guardians line now! Will text when we're done!

I smiled and put my phone back in my bag—glad that Bryony was having fun without me. I noticed a bridge across the water that cut back to the start of Pixar Pier. I tipped my head toward the bridge and Freddie nodded.

We started walking down it together—it was practically empty, save for a group of three seniors, all laden down with plastic Disney bags full of souvenirs. They were standing by the railing, laughing and talking together.

Once we were past them, Freddie turned to me. "So what do you think the reason is?"

"What reason?"

"Why this is happening in the first place. Like, do you think you're supposed to learn something?"

"Like *A Christmas Carol*?"

"I mean, not no?"

I laughed at that, even as my thoughts were racing.

He shrugged. "I'm just basing this off all the time-loop movies where that seems to be the case."

"What does Pettigrew have to learn?"

"Ah." Freddie smiled. "Pettigrew has to learn to break from his normal routine and go out and take chances. And also, adopt a cat. But I'm not sure that's part of it."

"I've been wondering the same thing." I glanced over at him, debating if I should tell him that one of the possibilities for why this was happening might be . . . well, *him*. "What's confusing me is that I wished for this. So shouldn't I be able to end it whenever I want? Without having to go through a whole—thing?"

"Maybe?" Freddie replied, and then he broke into a smile. "Honestly, these are questions I've never had to ask myself until tonight."

I laughed at that, and we walked in silence for a few moments. It was really peaceful on the bridge—the neon lights from the rides and the Ferris wheel were reflecting on the water, and there was a faint breeze stirring the leaves of the trees and lifting up my hair. For the first time, I realized I was getting chilly, and I untied the jean jacket around my waist.

"Cold?" Freddie asked.

"Little bit."

"Can I—" He didn't finish the question, just stepped forward and held out my jacket for me. Freddie helped me put it on, and even though this had never been something I'd needed assistance with before, I couldn't help notice how nice this was. Freddie standing close, settling the jacket over my shoulders, letting his hands linger there for just a moment before stepping back. I was very aware that this was the closest together we'd been, and I could feel my heart start to beat a little harder.

"Thanks," I said, giving him a smile.

"Yeah, the nights get a bit nippy here," Freddie said. "I guess I'm not used to it. We have warm nights back home."

"It's because of the humidity," I said, thrilled that I had a fact at the ready. "It's why the temperature drops in the desert—humidity helps keep the air warm. Since we don't have much in California, we get these cool nights."

He shook his head. "Fascinating."

I shrugged. "I guess I'm just used to it. I've lived almost all my life on the West Coast. And that's not changing next year."

"Next year?"

"Oh, I'm going to UC Berkeley."

"Wow," Freddie said, raising an impressed eyebrow. "That's fantastic."

"Have you been to the Bay Area?"

"Never, but I'm dying to go. Bit of a commute, though, when I have to be here performing every night."

"I'll say. But maybe if it works out with this…music person? Then you might have more of your own schedule, more downtime?"

"Maybe." Freddie's expression was suddenly more serious. He leaned forward and rested his elbows on the railing, then looked over at me. "I'm really glad I ran into you, Cass."

"You mean—literally?"

"That part of it I could have done without. But it's been really fun. And a good distraction from the performance tonight. I mean, it's only all my hopes and dreams on the line—no big deal." He smiled when he said it, clearly trying for breezy, but I could see the fear peeking through.

"Well, I've haven't seen the performance, but I did hear two people saying it was unforgettable. So it sounds like it goes well, right?"

"Really? They said that?" I nodded, and Freddie let out a long breath, his shoulders dropping. "That's brilliant. What a relief." He gave me a smile, his dimple deepening. "But if you happen to see someone who looks like a music manager, maybe you could just have a loud conversation near her about how great I am?" Then he paused, his cheeks flushing. "That is, if you're going to see the show. No pressure."

"Of course I'm going to see it," I said quickly. "I wouldn't miss it."

He smiled. "You're the best." Freddie looked down at me and held my gaze. I could feel my heart pound, and I was suddenly very aware of the space between us—how I could have taken just one step nearer to him, and we'd be close enough to kiss.

I kept my eyes on him as I searched his face, trying to glean what he was feeling. He had to be thinking along the same lines, right? This couldn't be wholly one-sided.

As though he'd heard my thoughts, he reached out to me, slowly, like if I wanted to step away, he was giving me time to, and carefully tucked a lock of hair behind my ear. He took a breath, his eyes not leaving mine. "Cass—" he started.

But before he could say more, his phone beeped. He pulled it out and looked down at it. "I have to get going," he said, real regret in his voice.

"Right." I gave him a smile, even as I could feel my stomach drop. Of course he had things to do—of course this moment was going to end. But it still hit me harder than I was expecting. "Well, it was so great to meet you and—" I stopped as I suddenly realized what this meant. "Oh my god!"

"Oh my god what?" Freddie asked, looking alarmed.

"If this starts over again, you're not going to remember me. Or any of this."

Freddie shook his head. "No. That's not possible."

"But it is, though." I could hear my voice rising in frustration. "That's the way this works."

Freddie blinked at me, and it was like I could see this sinking in. That all we'd talked about—our whole night—would be like it had never happened. "Right," he finally said. "Once you walk through the doors, you'll remember everything . . ."

"But you won't," I finished. "It'll be like we never met."

Freddie put both hands on the railing and leaned forward on it, then pushed himself back, his brow furrowed. "I have an idea," he finally said. "If the loop starts again, come and find me. And say *Excalibur.*"

"*Excalibur*?" I echoed. "What will talking about your video game do?"

"No, it's like a code."

"But it has to be a code you would have known about before this conversation."

"But that's the thing!" he enthused. "It *is*. My brother, Jack, and I came up with it yonks ago. When we were kids, we had a pact that if either of us had a magical experience, we would say *Excalibur* to the other, and they'd know it had happened. That we'd crossed into a place where magical is real."

"And that will be enough?" I asked, feeling relief spread through me. If these loops kept going, I would want to find Freddie again for sure. But the thought of not having to take him through this whole explanation again was also very appealing.

"Absolutely," he assured me.

I nodded, wishing this didn't have to end but knowing that we had run out of time. "So . . . *Excalibur*."

He nodded, giving me a smile. *"Excalibur,"* he agreed.

"Good luck," I said, nodding toward the stage. I could see now that the countdown clock showed there were only twenty minutes until the performance—and he had to get going.

"Thanks," Freddie said, giving me a smile. "It was great to meet you, Cass. Maybe I'll see you after the show?"

I smiled back at him. "I'll be here."

He gave me a nod, then turned and started for the stage. He walked along the side of it, then turned and pushed through the door that, I assumed, would lead him backstage. I watched him go, feeling a few giddy butterflies start to take flight in my stomach.

I had met someone I liked. Like, *really* liked. Was that why these loops had started—so that we could meet? So that this could begin? I felt myself smile as I leaned back against the railing, looking up at the stars and feeling like something was finally on the right track.

4

knew I didn't have a ton of time, but I took advantage of the fact that I had a little bit of a window before Eton Mess would be onstage. I walked to the bathroom across from the door that Freddie had gone through. Now that I was closer, I could see it was wooden and marked with an EMPLOYEE ACCESS ONLY sign.

I used the bathroom, washed my hands, and then dug in my bag for the tinted lip balm I was sure was rolling around in there somewhere. If I'd known I was going to be meeting a cute British musician at Grad Nite, I might have tossed in a lipstick or something, but I had to make do with what I had on hand.

I had just raked a hand through my curls, willing them to behave but knowing it was a losing battle, when I heard the unmistakable sound of someone crying in one of the stalls. I walked back over toward them. The crying was louder now—someone sniffling and sobbing.

"Um . . . is everything all right? Do you need help?"

There was no reply. I tried to think about what could be causing someone to have a breakdown here. Was there also a sink at Disneyland that sprayed you in an unfortunate area? All at once I realized that maybe it was Amy and that she and Carlos had, once again, broken up. "Amy?" I ventured.

The door unlocked and opened up, and I took a step back in surprise—because *Tabitha Keith* was walking out of the stall. Tabitha Keith, nepo baby, burgeoning actress, and cosmetics mogul. So *she* was the celebrity that was here tonight!

But she didn't look at all like the Tabitha Keith I was used to seeing in paparazzi pictures and Instagram ads. Her face was puffy and her eyes were bloodshot—she'd clearly been crying. "Who's Amy?" she asked me.

"Oh," I said, blinking. I shook my head and attempted to pull myself together. "Um, she's my friend. She and her boyfriend break up tonight—I just didn't know if it happened yet."

Tabitha frowned, looking confused, but just said, "Oh. Okay." She took a step closer to the mirror and stared at her reflection. "God. I really look bad, huh?"

"No, no," I said quickly, even though my voice was higher than usual. "Just like you've been crying maybe? But not bad." I flashed suddenly to what would be happening not that long from now—remembering the security scrum escorting who I now knew was Tabitha out of the park. Because pictures of her had been sold to DitesMoi, and she was getting swarmed. Clearly, I was just seeing the prologue to that. But was there anything I could do with this knowledge? If the crying was anything to go by, it seemed like she was already well aware that something bad had happened.

"Sure," Tabitha said, shaking her head. She waved her hand under the dispenser to get some paper towels and blotted her cheeks with them. "Just—you think you can trust your friends, right? And then to find out like this. . . ." She let out a shaky breath.

"Why?" I asked, taking a step closer. "Did something happen?"

Just then, I heard the crackle of feedback from a speaker. "Make your way over to the stage," a voice said. "Eton Mess will be going on in just a few minutes!"

"Oh," I said, looking from the speaker and then back to her. "I actually . . ."

"It's fine," she said, waving this off and giving me a smile that didn't meet her eyes. "I'm okay. Thanks for checking on me, though. It was really nice."

She gave me a nod and turned to her reflection, pulling a makeup bag out of her purse. I was half tempted to ask if she had any of her own line with her—and if she did, if I could try her new blush—but realized that was very not appropriate. And besides, I had to get to the show.

"Take care, okay?" I said as I headed for the door. She gave me a nod, and I gave her one back before I pushed my way out of the bathroom.

There was nobody on stage yet, but it looked like the crew had finished their work—there were two mic stands, a drum kit in the back, and speakers placed all around the stage. The whole thing looked so *professional*, I was grateful that I'd met Freddie before I'd seen him perform. If I'd seen him taking the stage in front of this huge crowd, would I have been able to see him as the nice guy I'd had dinner and ice cream with? Would I have been able to open up in the same way? I had a feeling the answer was no.

I pulled out my phone and texted Bryony that I was waiting by the stage. She texted me back that she'd be right there—along with a thumbs-up and three roller coaster emojis.

I looked around for anyone else I knew and spotted the well-dressed woman in black, the one that I now knew was the manager coming to see Freddie. Smiling as I remembered his request, I edged my way over to her. I also wanted to make sure that I wasn't in the same spot where I'd run into Bruce during the first loop. We'd just had an awkward conversation, and I wasn't sure we really needed another one. I pulled out my phone, about to have a pretend conversation about how good I'd heard the bassist of this band was, when someone tapped me on the shoulder.

I turned around to see Greta and Nora, both looking shocked. "Cass?" Nora asked, her eyes wide behind her glasses. "Cass Issac?"

I silently groaned. "Hey, Greta. Hey, Nora," I said, waving, hoping we wouldn't have to go into the whole thing again. I really wasn't sure I wanted a *second* lecture this loop about how I was a terrible person.

They just blinked at me, and I realized a moment later, that I should be more surprised to see them. "I mean—hi! What a shock. That we're all here at Grad Nite!"

"I just think it's shocking that you're here at all," Nora said. "We thought you fell off the face of the earth."

"Seriously," Greta agreed. "You just vanished, Cass. We were worried."

"You were?" I asked. This hit me somewhere deep in my chest, and I blinked, trying to shake it off. "Well—I was fine. I just moved."

"But you didn't tell us. You just disappeared. Like Amelia Earhart in—"

"1937," we all finished at the same time. I smiled. For just a second, it felt like we were back on the quiz bowl stage together.

"It wasn't cool," Greta said, shaking her head. "It was really hurtful."

I opened my mouth, trying to think what to say to this. "I . . ."

"There you are!" Bryony hurried up to me and gave me a quick hug. "Sorry that took so long, we kept switching roller coasters, thinking we could beat the line. We should have done the Incredicoaster first, then Guardians. We definitely went in the wrong order." I glanced behind her and saw the Emmas. Emma R. was holding a cookie shaped like Jack-Jack and looking worriedly at the other Emmas, who were sniping at each other. "Oh sorry," Bryony said, noticing Greta and Nora. "I didn't mean to interrupt."

"You weren't," I said, more than ready to end this interaction. "I was just leaving."

"You're good at that," Nora said, the hurt clear in her tone.

I didn't know what to say to that, so I just turned around and walked toward the Emmas, feeling my heart pound in my chest.

"What was that about?" Bryony asked me, keeping her voice low.

"I went to school with them in Arizona," I said, speaking quickly, trying to move on from this. "They were mad that I moved."

"But it wasn't your fault," Bryony said, looking outraged on my behalf.

"I know, right?" I was well aware that I was skipping over lots of pertinent facts here but was choosing to ignore that for the moment. We'd reached the Emmas, and I turned to Emma R. "Hey, how were the roller coasters?"

"Really fun," she said, giving me a smile that immediately faded as she looked at the other two Emmas. "Cookie?"

I broke off a piece, then handed it back. "What's going on with Emma and Emma?" I asked, lowering my voice.

"We don't know," Bryony said, matching my volume. "But they've been like this all night."

"What did you get up to, Cass?" Emma R. asked me.

"I spent most of my time with Freddie!" I said excitedly. Emma and Bryony just stared at me blankly. "Oh, right, you don't know who that is. Well, he's super cute, he's a musician, he's British. . . ."

"That's amazing," Bryony said, giving me a grin. "Cass has a crush!"

"Bryony does, too," Emma R. said, giving her a shove. "She saw this brown-haired guy and immediately turned into the heart-eyes emoji."

I grinned at her. Bryony hadn't really had a crush on anyone—well, except Tom Holland—since her breakup in December. "That's great! What's his name?"

"I didn't get it." She sighed. "I guess it wasn't meant to be? I wasted my only shot."

"Well," I said, trying to think about how to put this, "maybe not? Maybe you'll have more chances than you think?"

The countdown clock ended, but Eton Mess didn't take the stage. After a few moments, I could see the crowd starting to get restless, a few people peeling off and heading to rides. I could understand it—we were getting close to the end of Grad Nite, and unlike me, they probably thought it would be their only chance to do this.

Bryony took a breath to reply, but before she could speak, the lights onstage started swirling around, and the announcer was back.

"Disney Grad Nite seniors and chaperones! Please welcome—all the way from jolly olde England—Eton Mess!"

Everyone cheered and the band came out onstage. I noticed that Niall and Freddie were laughing together, both of them holding bottles of water as they took their places, and I let out a sigh of relief. It seemed like maybe Freddie hadn't told him about the music manager coming. I figured if he had, they wouldn't look so happy and relaxed, and Niall wouldn't look so pleased with himself—though judging by the poster, maybe this was just his default expression.

The band was wearing the outfits I recognized from the poster—all variations on a prep school uniform, with some of them pulling it off better than others. The drummer, who had long dark hair, mostly looked uncomfortable, flipping his tie over his shoulder as he sat behind his drum kit. And the other guitarist, a shorter redhead with a kind, freckled face, didn't look very happy, pulling at his collar and swallowing hard, his face pale. In contrast, Niall looked good, smiling and winking at the audience, but he had nothing on Freddie. Freddie looked so handsome in his shrunken blazer and striped tie that I had to remind myself that there were bigger things happening right now than my rapidly growing crush—even if it was suddenly hard to remember what those were.

"Hey there, seniors! Congratulations on graduating!" Niall yelled from the stage, and the crowd around me cheered happily. "Are you having fun at Grad Nite?" Everyone cheered louder. Freddie took a drink of water from his bottle and smiled at the crowd. "Chuffed to hear it," Niall said, in an accent I would have described as *posh Brit*, one that seemed to be getting thicker with every word he spoke. "We're Eton Mess, and we're—"

But before he could finish his sentence, the redheaded guitar player groaned, clutched his stomach, and then looked around, panic in his eyes. He tried to run from the stage but couldn't quite make it—and a moment later, he leaned over and threw up.

A collective *Ewwwww!* went up from the crowd, and I stared in horror, feeling my stomach plunge. I whipped around to see the music manager—her hand was clapped over her mouth and her eyes were wide with horror.

"Uh, sorry," Niall said, staring as the redhead staggered offstage, and a series of crashes followed as he must have bumped into equipment. "We're just having a little— Freddie?" he asked, desperation in his voice.

I looked to Freddie but realized with dawning alarm that Freddie didn't look great either. He was scratching at his neck, and his face was slowly getting red and puffy. . . .

"Vegetables!" I whispered.

"What?" Bryony asked, looking from me to the stage. "What is happening here? Is this part of it?"

"Sorry about all this," Niall said, stepping up to the mic as Freddie ran off the stage as well, his face now bright red, his eyes so puffy I wondered if he could even see. "Maybe something a capella from me as my mates get themselves sorted?"

I stared at the stage, still not able to get my head around how everything had gone so wrong, so quickly. I was now rethinking the conversation I'd overheard in a totally new way. The girl had said the performance was unbelievable, unforgettable, and it was blowing up online. I had just assumed she'd meant all of this in the good way. But now, I realized it was the exact opposite—because what had just happened was a complete train wreck.

Everyone around me was holding up their phones, filming, and the music manager was walking away, shaking her head—clearly writing Freddie off and leaving his crushed dreams in her wake.

All at once, it seemed perfectly clear. *This* was the reason I was in the time loop—and the reason that I kept running into Freddie. It was so that I could *fix* this. I could save his performance, and his shot at making it big. Because what had just happened onstage . . . it was worse than just not getting a shot with a manager. Judging by how everyone was recording and posting and commenting, this would be something that would follow him forever, wrecking any other prospects.

I turned away from the stage and started hurrying toward the exit.

"Cass?" I heard Bryony call after me. "Where are you going?"

"To fix it!" I yelled behind me. I knew what I had to do—I had to stop Freddie from eating whatever vegetable he'd just consumed and save his chance of becoming a star. I could make this better. I was sure of it.

I was almost running as I made my way back toward the wooden door. The wind had picked up, and it was blowing paper out of a trash can. One page practically hit me across the face so I crumped it up and grabbed a piece off the ground as well, bringing them back to the bin. I was about to throw them away, when I noticed the footer on the paper, next to the page number. It read *Courtney Mulaney/Hurricane Madison.*

I just stared at it for a moment before looking down into the trash can—where the rest of Ms. Mulaney's manuscript had been thrown away. The last time I'd seen her, she'd been getting on the call with the agent. But now, looking at her novel in the trash—it seemed like it hadn't gone well.

I threw away the papers and then picked up my pace, eyes on the door. The sooner I started this over again, the sooner I could start fixing things.

I saw Amy huddled on the bench, her face in her hands, and my heart sank as I realized that, once again, she and Carlos had ended the night broken up once more. "I'll fix that, too," I muttered to myself, practically running now, getting closer to the door. . . .

5

tapped Freddie, who was staring at his phone, on the shoulder. He looked up at me, eyebrows raised. "Yes?"

"Excalibur," I said confidently. I'd done everything the same as last time: encouraged Bryony to go on the real roller coasters and made sure to tell her to start with the Guardians ride. Then I'd had a quick chat with Ms. Mulaney, and headed over here as soon as she got her agent call. So I'd known just where Freddie would be—staring at his phone, reading the email from the music manager, the one that told him she was coming tonight.

Freddie just blinked at me. "Pardon?"

"Excalibur," I repeated, more slowly this time.

"Yeah," Freddie said. He nodded down to his green shirt, with *Excalibur!* written across it. "I take it you're a fan of the game, too?"

"No." I shook my head, wishing that Freddie had decided to put on a different shirt, so me knowing about this wouldn't just seem like a coincidence. "*Excalibur.* You told me to say it?"

"I— What?" He glanced around, like he was hoping someone could explain to him what was happening. "I don't think we've met before, have we?"

"Like, three times!" I had to turn away for a second. It was too hard to see Freddie looking at me like I was a stranger, like our whole night had just never happened. Because it *hadn't*, for him. Which I knew intellectually, but it didn't make this hurt any less. But just a little while ago, Freddie—this same person—was looking into my eyes and tucking my hair behind my ear and telling me with confidence that all I needed to say was *Excalibur* for him to understand, to remember, to allow us to skip all of this.

"When was this?" Freddie asked, his brow furrowing.

"Never mind," I said, trying my best to remember details he'd told me. "So—you're Freddie. You have a brother, Jack. You write your song lyrics in your little black notebook. And you told me to say *Excalibur* to you—that you'd understand."

Freddie took a step back, his eyes wide. "Are you a fan of the band, or something? Did you look me up, find out that information about me?"

"No," I said, shaking my head, hearing my voice rise. "You told it all to me!"

"But we've never met before. So . . ." Freddie shook his head and took another step away from me.

I let out a short breath, trying to temper my frustration. I was realizing too late that I hadn't thought this through. Freddie had been so confident that I'd just assumed it would work immediately. And I certainly hadn't wanted to come off like a stalker, which was what I was pretty sure was happening now. But not only did I want him to understand, I *needed* him to, and fast. I had to warn him not to eat something that had vegetables in it and see what could be done about the guitarist with the tummy troubles. Otherwise, he was going to throw away his chance of impressing the music manager.

I shook my head. "I guess I just thought this would be easier."

Freddie looked genuinely worried now. "*What* would be easier?"

"Nothing." I realized all at once that I just had to start this over. I'd messed things up too much to salvage this loop. "I'll just try again."

"You will?" Freddie sounded worried. "And, uh—try *what* again?"

"Be right back!" I called as I changed direction and headed back toward the exit.

As I walked toward the wooden doors, I couldn't help but be irritated with myself for believing it would be easy. But I knew better now—and I'd prepare. I'd stop and get my thoughts together first. And then nothing would get in my way—

My feet slowed when I saw Ms. Mulaney in front of me. She was pacing as she talked on the phone, running a hand through her hair. Her eyes were red, and it hurt my heart to see that she looked absolutely crestfallen. "But could you reconsider with some revisions? I could just submit it again?"

I flashed back to the manuscript that I knew, not that long from now, would be in the trash can—that this call was never going to go her way. I walked around her, keeping my head bowed so she wouldn't see me. Once I was past her, I picked up my pace. I just had to get to the door—

"Cass?"

I winced. I had never disliked the sound of my own name before tonight, but I now realized I was coming to dread it. Every time I heard it, it was like getting a warning a bomb was about to go off. Not sure who I was going to see—but not thrilled about any of the possibilities—I turned around. Reagan, Zach, and McKenna were standing in front of me.

"Hey, guys," I said, trying my best to muster a smile but not sure I succeeded. "Enjoying Grad Nite?"

"Uh," Reagan said, looking freaked out. "We *were*."

"I can't believe you're here," Zach said, sounding rattled.

"What's the big deal?" McKenna asked. "Hi, I'm McKenna."

"Cass," I said, giving her a nod.

"How are you acting like this is just normal?" Reagan asked, folding their arms across their chest. "Like you didn't just vanish into the ether when you left our lives."

"Wait, what?" McKenna asked, looking intrigued now.

"We'll catch up later, okay?" I started to walk again.

"Seriously?" Reagan asked, and I could hear the surprise—and the hurt—in their voice. "That's all you're going to say?"

"For the moment," I said over my shoulder. "To be continued!"

Behind me, I heard Reagan scoff, since they didn't realize just how true this was.

I picked up my pace, keeping my focus on the doors that would let me start this over. I just hadn't prepared enough, that was all. But I wouldn't make that mistake again.

6

ass?" Ms. Mulaney asked, her expression concerned. "You okay
all by yourself? Where's Bryony?"

"She went to ride the real roller coasters." I glanced at my watch. "She's
probably getting in line for Guardians right now, though she's going to
move to the Incredicoaster when that line is too long."

Mrs. Mulaney blinked at me. "Oh. Well, that's good. If you need anything, I'll be in the chaperone lounge. It's that direction. . . ." As before, she
pointed toward Pixar Pier, sending her tote bag crashing to the ground and
spilling out its contents.

"I'll help," I said eagerly, a little louder than I meant to. I saw Amy
glance over at me from where she was standing with Carlos. I grabbed
for a loose manuscript page and a pen that had rolled a few feet away. I

folded the paper quickly, stuck it in my bag, and tucked the pen in my dress pocket.

I looked up to see Amy standing nearby, staring at me. "What's going on?" she asked, looking baffled. "And why did you just take Ms. Mulaney's paper?"

"Why is this your business?" Carlos asked her.

Amy shot him an irritated look. "I'm just asking questions, Carlos. Am I not allowed to do that?" Then she turned back to me, her expression expectant.

"I didn't take her paper," I said, even though I knew that, as far as defenses go, this one left something to be desired.

"What paper?" Ms. Mulaney asked.

"The one in Cass's bag," Amy said, pointing at it.

I looked down at it and saw the triangle of the top sticking out of my bag, as clear as anything. "Right," I said, pushing myself up to standing. "If you'll excuse me . . ."

7

If you need anything, I'll be in the chaperone lounge. It's that direction. . . . " Just like I'd been planning, Ms. Mulaney pointed, and her tote bag fell to the ground, its contents spilling out.

"I'll help you," I said, making sure to keep my voice quiet this time.

I bent down to the ground, pretending to help, but keeping my eyes on Amy, doing my best to avoid attracting her attention. When I was sure she wasn't looking at me, I grabbed a stray piece of paper, folded it quickly, and pocketed it along with a pen. Then I straightened up and handed Ms. Mulaney the items I'd picked up.

"Thank you," she said, pulling her bag over her shoulder. She looked at me and raised an eyebrow. "You all right?"

"Uh-huh," I said. I stayed in place, knowing that any minute her phone would ring, and it would be the agent on the other line. Without meaning to, I flashed to the memory of her on the phone not too long from now, her voice cracked and desperate. "Just—maybe . . ."

Before I could say anything else, her phone rang. She fished it out of her bag, and I saw her eyes widen. "I have to take this."

"Good luck," I said, and walked away before I would have to see her expression change. But I couldn't do anything about Ms. Mulaney's crushed dreams—I had to try to save Freddie's.

I found a bench, tucked under a tree, and sat down to try to gather my thoughts. I had to figure this out. I needed to get him to believe me, to get us back to where we'd been three loops ago—and hopefully also stop the Eton Mess disaster from happening and ruining his chances of a future music career.

I pulled out my pilfered paper and pen and stared down at the blank page for just a moment, trying to recall everything that Freddie had said. I knew that I wouldn't be able to keep this piece of paper for more than one loop. If this all started again, it would be back in Ms. Mulaney's bag like I'd never written on it. But I was hoping that maybe the act of writing it would help cement it in my brain. *Freddie*, I wrote across the top of the paper, and underlined this twice. Then I took a breath and started to write.

  - Brother named Jack
  - From Croydon
  - Loves Excalibur/poster above bed/Geraldine Bewley school project
  - Weird vegetable allergy

-*Rocky road ice cream/Sweet Emporium*
-*Manager coming tonight*
-*Mates with Niall from school days*
-*Lyrics in notebook*

I tapped the pen on the paper and then tried to remember the lyric that he'd written in his notebook, the inspiration he'd had while we'd been talking. It was his line, after all. It didn't seem right for him to lose it just because we weren't going to be having that exact conversation any longer. I closed my eyes, trying to recall it, then scribbled what I was pretty sure was right: *Sometimes home is your favorite sweatshirt you've outgrown.* I looked down at the list for a moment longer, trying to memorize as much as possible so that I wouldn't freeze up and lose my train of thought. Then I folded the paper up again, dropped it in my bag, and hurried off to find Freddie.

It didn't take long—he was, as before, standing in the middle of the crowd and staring into space, like he was trying to process the news he'd just gotten. I let myself look at him for just a moment before I hurried over to him and tapped him on the shoulder.

"Hi," I said, when he turned around.

"Hi," he said, giving me a polite, if slightly confused smile.

I held out my hand. "I'm Cass Issac."

"Freddie Sharma," he said, shaking it, even though he still looked a little baffled.

"Can I talk to you a second, Freddie?"

"Uh," Freddie said. He ran his hand through his hair, causing that one lock of curly hair to fall forward on his forehead like a Mr. Darcy dream. "I suppose so, sure. Is there something I can help you with?"

"Kind of." I tipped my head to the side of the path, and we got out of the way of the seniors running around and yelling, off to the rides or the DJ or the games. "But there's also something I need to help you with."

"Me?"

"Yes." I took a deep breath, knowing there was no way to do this but to begin, and just hope it would work this time. *"Excalibur."*

He raised an eyebrow. "What's that now?"

"Excalibur. You and your brother, Jack, used to play the video game. But more than that, you used to talk about the possibility that there was a magical world just alongside ours. And you had that as a code in case one of you found it. The other one would come back and say it, and you would know."

Freddie just stared at me. "You— What are you saying, that . . ."

"We've met before. We've had a whole night where we talked about everything. I know about the *Excalibur* poster above your bed, and Geraldine Bewley and the school project. About the Sweet Emporium and their rocky road ice cream. About the lyrics you write in your Moleskine notebook. About your weird vegetable allergy—"

"It's not weird—"

"And about how you told me to tell you *Excalibur*—that you would believe me when I told you. That you might even . . . remember." I swallowed hard and looked up at him.

Freddie's eyes were wide, but he didn't seem worried that I was an unhinged stalker, like he had before. It was more like his thoughts were churning so fast he could barely keep up.

"So, it's real?" Freddie finally asked as he looked down at me, his voice just above a whisper. "Magic—it exists?"

"It certainly seems to," I said, feeling relief course through me. Freddie wasn't walking away, or calling security, or looking at me like I'd lost my mind.

"Cass," he said, smiling at me, and it was like he was practically vibrating with excitement. "Tell me *everything*."

7

knew we would both be getting hungry soon. But going back to the Hollywood Lounge would mean running into Bruce. So I steered us over toward Grizzly Peak, where I hadn't yet spent a ton of time—and I just hoped I'd be able to avoid running into Reagan or Zach, or Greta and Nora. I glanced at my phone, seeing the same texts I always got from Bryony—telling me that they were waiting on line for the Incredicoaster.

As we walked toward Smokejumpers Grill, I explained as much as I knew to Freddie—occasionally repeating his own theories back to him, which seemed to delight him to no end. He was rolling with the stuck-in-a-time-loop thing a lot better than I had, that's for sure.

"And you said it restarts at the door?" He shook his head. "Brilliant. It's just like *Pettigrew's*—"

"Loop," I finished. "I know."

"You've seen it?"

"No, but you told me all about it."

"This is mental," he said, sounding awed. "It's the kind of thing I always used to dream about, and now it's happening! And I mean, it's happening to you. But I'm here as well, aren't I?"

"You are," I assured him with a smile.

"So why do you think it started? What's the purpose of it?"

"When I was leaving Grad Nite the first time, when I walked through the doors, I made a wish—to get the chance to do things over."

"Why did you want to do things over? Because you were having such a great time?"

I laughed shortly, then shook my head. "Very much not. No, it's . . ." I hesitated, then took a breath and told him the stripped-down version of what had happened, that first time—running into everyone from my past I never thought I'd see again. Getting into a fight with Bryony. Having to leave tomorrow to go to Oregon.

By the time I'd finished, we'd reached the restaurant. Right on cue, I felt my stomach growl, which was one more piece of evidence that everything reset when I went through the doors. Having just had a burger and ice cream not that long ago, I shouldn't really be starving again—but I was. We both ordered—chicken fingers for Freddie and a chicken sandwich for me, sodas for both of us—and took our food to the chairs outside.

"So, if this is happening because you made a wish, how do you make it stop? Just un-wish it?" Freddie asked, once we were sitting across from each other.

"I'm not sure I want to stop it just yet," I said, taking a bite of my chicken sandwich and nodding approvingly. It was even better than the burger had been. "I think it might be happening so I can help you."

"Me?" His eyebrows flew up, and when he smiled, the dimple appeared, just as cute as it had been before. "What do I need help with?"

"Well." I wasn't sure how to put this delicately, so I set my sandwich down and decided to just jump in. "The show tonight—the one the music manager is coming to—"

"You know about that?" he asked, then shook his head the second the words had left his mouth. "I mean, of course you know about that. Never mind. Carry on."

"The show doesn't go all that well. The redheaded guitar player . . ."

"Alfie?"

"Gets sick all over the stage. And then you must have eaten some vegetables accidentally, because you start breaking out in hives, your face gets puffy, and the show ends without anyone playing any music."

"And the manager?" Freddie's voice was hoarse, and he looked like he was afraid to hear the answer.

"She leaves." I winced, remembering her appalled expression as she stormed away.

"Oh my god." Freddie sat back in his seat, looking shell-shocked. "So, my big break doesn't actually happen tonight."

"But maybe that's why this is all happening. I'm going through the loops so I can make sure that the show goes well and we can avoid these problems!"

Freddie frowned. "I'm not sure time-loop magic is really going to be used to get me a record contract."

"Why not?" I asked. "Maybe this is a *Bill & Ted* thing, and you go on to record some really important song and we have to make sure that happens."

"But then *I'd* be in the time loop," he pointed out. "It would be happening to me, and I wouldn't just be a . . . I don't know. What am I here? A supporting character?"

"Or love interest." The second I said it, I felt my face get hot.

"Oh *really*?" Freddie raised an eyebrow at me. He was blushing slightly, but also gave me a grin. "So do we . . ."

"No!" I said quickly, staring down at my chicken sandwich. "We kind of have, like, a moment? We're over by the pier looking at the lights on the water. But we don't even kiss or anything." I heard the palpable disappointment in my voice even as I was saying the words, and when Freddie laughed, I did, too.

"Well, it's still good to know."

"Uh-huh," I said, looking away and willing my blush to subside. "So, we need to focus. We have to make sure the performance goes well tonight."

Freddie nodded, his expression growing more serious. "Yeah. Otherwise, it sounds like it's going to be an absolute disaster."

I didn't want to agree with him too emphatically, but that was the only way to describe what had happened. "Well, not anymore. We'll fix it, right?"

"Right," Freddie said. "So let's figure out what happened—I must eat some raw fruit or veg at some point, right?"

"Yeah. I'm no expert, but you told me your allergy symptoms, and that's what it looked like."

He raised his chicken tender to his mouth to take another bite, then paused and looked at it carefully. "This is okay," he said with a nod, then took a bite.

"How fast after you eat something do you get symptoms?" I asked, taking a bite of my own dinner and giving silent thanks that I didn't have any food allergies to always be on guard for.

"Pretty fast. Like, within a few seconds, I start to have a reaction. So I guess I must have accidentally had something right before I went out onstage? And I just didn't realize it."

"So you'll be careful on your end," I said, glad that this was manageable. "But we have to let your bandmate know and see what's going on with him."

"I can't believe *two* of us get sick," Freddie said, shaking his head. "And that we both get sick from different things? It's not like we catch the same bug. It's kind of a big coincidence."

"I know," I said slowly. It actually *was*. But these things happened, right? I'd seen it with my own eyes. I took the last bite of my chicken and pushed my tray away.

"Ready?" he asked. I nodded, but before I could get my tray, Freddie was picking it up for me. "I've got this," he said, giving me a quick smile.

He walked away, stacking the trays near a trash bin. I picked up my bag and had just started to walk away when I noticed he'd left his phone lying on top of the table, just like he had before. "Freddie?"

He turned and saw me holding up his phone, and his eyes went wide. "Oh bollocks. Thank you. My mum always said I'd lose my head if it wasn't attached to my neck."

I smiled at him. "I know." I handed him his phone, and he tucked it into his back pocket.

"Now," he said, starting to walk toward Pixar Pier. "Let's find Alfie."

I'd never been backstage at any kind of music venue, and I could feel my eyes were wide as Freddie led me up around to the back of the stage that had been set up in front of the Little Mermaid ride. He pushed through the wooden door confidently, not seeming to think it was an issue that it was clearly marked EMPLOYEE ACCESS ONLY. We walked down an outside path, until he pulled open a door that was unmarked and held it open for me. Inside, we walked down a narrow hallway, with three people sitting on cases stenciled with ETON MESS, playing cards. I recognized the purple-haired girl who'd been helping to set up the equipment and was now frowning at her hand as she looked around the circle. ETON MESS CREW was emblazoned in white onto the back of her black T-shirt. The other two guys also looked like they might be in the crew—they were both wearing black as well and had walkie-talkies clipped to their belts.

"Call," one of the guys said, raising an eyebrow.

The girl narrowed her eyes. "I feel like you're bluffing," she said. She looked up and smiled at Freddie. "Hi, Freddie. Is Van bluffing?"

"Hey, Violet. I can't tell you that," Freddie said with a smile. "Hold on. Let me get a picture." He took a picture of the poker game with his phone—everyone shielded their cards—then set it down on the case closest to him. "Is everyone else in the greenroom?"

"Not His Majesty," Violet said with a roll of her eyes. I took a breath to ask a question, just as one of the other guys cleared his throat. "Right. Okay," she said, focusing on her cards again.

Freddie headed down the hallway, and I heard Violet groan—apparently the hand hadn't gone her way. "His Majesty?" I echoed as I followed behind Freddie.

"Oh yeah," he said, giving me a slightly embarrassed smile. "That's what some of our tech crew call Niall. Not to his face," he added quickly.

"Why?" Judging from his picture and his demeanor onstage, I was pretty sure I had an idea. But considering this whole band was made up of Brits, I didn't know if it was because he was actually, like, twentieth in line for the throne or something.

"Well," Freddie said, taking a deep breath, "he can sometimes be a little ... self-important? He doesn't mean to be—but he *is* the lead singer. Niall's always wanted to be the star."

"It doesn't bother you?"

"I mean, I've known him forever. I think I maybe I understand him better than other people? He means well," he assured me as he opened up a door marked GREENROOM in the Disney font.

We walked inside, and I looked around, taking it all in. It was a small room, with a couch, several chairs, and a food station on a table in the corner—a fruit platter, a veggie tray, rows of bottles of water lined up neatly. Along the side of the wall were rolling clothes racks with the outfits I recognized from the performance.

"Hey, Fred! Where've you been?" the redhead—the one I'd last seen stumbling from the stage in misery—was walking over to us with a happy smile, a paper plate in his hand.

I stared at him, trying to hide my surprise. It was unsettling, to know what would happen to him later, whereas he had no idea. For the first time, I felt a kinship with the ancient forebearer of my name—Cassandra, who could tell the future. In her case, though, nobody ever believed her, which I was hoping wouldn't be the same with me.

"Sorry I'm late," Freddie said as he set his messenger bag down and glanced up at the wall clock.

"Hi!" the redhead said cheerfully to me. "I'm Alfie."

"Cass," I said, tilting my head to the side as I tried to place what I'd just heard. All I knew for sure was that he did *not* have a British accent. "Are you . . . Australian?"

"Naur," Alfie said, then he grinned. "Guilty. They couldn't find enough Brits who could get work permits fast enough, so they turned to the better country." At this, Freddie snorted, and Alfie shrugged. "At least I'm from the Commonwealth, though. Not like 'Tristram.'" He put air quotes around this, and I frowned, just as the dark-haired drummer emerged from a door at the back of the room.

"Speak of the devil," Freddie said, giving him a nod.

He looked at me, then pointed at himself, his eyebrows raised. "It's okay," Freddie said. "Cat's out of the bag."

"Oh cool," the drummer said, in an unmistakable American accent. He nodded at me. "Hey, I'm Doug."

"Cass," I said, trying to figure out what exactly was happening.

"He's Tristram in all our official bios," Freddie explained, picking up on my confusion. "The execs who put this group together think it's better if we're all Brits."

"So I just don't talk much," Tristram/Doug said with a shrug. "I'm actually from Chicago, but if someone asks, I'm supposed to say . . ." He paused, furrowing his brow. "Hertfordshire?" he asked, pronouncing every consonant separately.

"Close enough," Alfie said, scooping up a forkful of food from his plate.

"What are you eating?" I asked, my voice sharp, refocusing on our mission.

Alfie glanced up, surprised. "Uh—a stir-fry. I got it from a strip mall down the street."

"What kind of stir-fry?"

Alfie blinked at me, his expression hurt. "What? I'll have you know that I've been really good about my carbs."

"We don't care about that, mate," Freddie assured him.

"Well, Niall does," Alfie said with a sigh. I took a step closer, trying to see what was in his dinner, and he tipped the plate slightly toward me. "It's prawns. All right?"

"Prawns?" I echoed.

"He means shrimp," Tristram/Doug explained from the couch, and I nodded, feeling like I'd discovered the reason Alfie had gotten sick. Any time either of my dads got food poisoning, shrimp always seemed to be the main culprit. And if Alfie had brought this with him, who knew how long it had been unrefrigerated.

"They have all kinds of crazy words for food," Tristram/Doug continued. "It took me forever to understand what they meant. Courgettes, aubergine, rocket . . ."

"Rocket's normal."

"No. To them, it means 'lettuce.'"

"Wait, *what*?"

"I think we might be getting off topic," Freddie said. He took the plate from Alfie and tossed it in the garbage.

"Oi!" Alfie yelped. "That's not on. That was my dinner, wasn't it?"

"It's for your own good," Freddie assured him, clapping him on the back. "Trust me."

"All right," Alfie said, looking a little weirded out as he wandered over to the craft services table. "Suit yourself."

Freddie turned to me, eyebrows raised. "What do you think? Did we do it?"

I looked over at Alfie, who was now sitting on the couch next to

Tristram/Doug and opening up a mini bag of Ruffles. He certainly didn't have the look of someone who was going to be violently ill soon, and I let myself breathe a sigh of relief. I smiled up at Freddie. "I think maybe we did."

"Well, thank you," Freddie said. "You really saved the day."

"Hopefully," I said, not wanting to get too far ahead of this—after all, the day wasn't over yet. But before I could say this, the door flew open and Niall sauntered in.

I recognized him right away. His blond hair was a little long and pushed back, and he was wearing sunglasses, despite the fact we were indoors. And it was night. But he also had something else—a kind of swagger, an anticipation of attention, like he was already performing and expecting an audience to appreciate him. It was wholly missing from Freddie's way of moving through the world, and I found that I really didn't love it.

"We ready, gents?" Niall asked, but in a Scottish accent—very different from the one he used onstage. He flopped into one of the chairs and pushed his sunglasses on top of his head. He looked around the room, and his eyes widened when he saw me. "Are you . . ." he asked, sitting up straighter, suddenly looking nervous as he glanced from me to Freddie.

"That's Cass," Freddie said, and I lifted a hand in a wave. "She's here for Grad Nite."

Niall nodded, and it seemed like this information put him at ease. He relaxed back into his chair again and pulled a phone out of his tracksuit pants. "Fredward," he said, holding it out, "you forgot your phone *again*. I found it in the hallway."

"Oh bollocks." Freddie sighed as he took it from him. "I really do have to keep better track of it." Every other member of the band nodded at once, clearly in agreement. "Cheers."

"Sure," Niall said with a smile. It seemed a little forced to me, but maybe that's just what his smiles were like? I didn't have a big enough sample size to tell. Then he looked over at me and raised an eyebrow. "We do have to get to rehearsing."

"Of course," I said, nodding. This was a professional band, after all, here to do a job, and I didn't want to get in the way of that. Especially since the performance going well was crucial to Freddie impressing this manager. "Good luck," I said, glancing around at all the band members. "Break a leg!"

Alfie waved at me cheerfully. "Nice to meet you, Cass," Tristram/Doug said, giving me a smile. But Niall didn't look up, just scrolled through his phone, clearly otherwise occupied.

"I'll walk you out," Freddie said, holding the door open for me. I thought I saw Niall roll his eyes at that, but I was already walking through the door and couldn't be sure. Freddie glanced down at his phone, then looked up at me with a smile. "The manager confirmed," he said. "She's going to be there."

"I mean, I could have told you that."

"Oh right," he said, shaking his head. "I keep forgetting you know the future."

I laughed at that. "Just for this one specific instance. But I think we should be okay now. We stopped Alfie from eating the shrimp, you're not going to eat anything ..."

"I'm really not," Freddie said fervently. "I wonder what it was last time?" He pondered this for a second, then shook his head. "Who knows."

"I'll let you rehearse." Niall had seemed annoyed enough about losing time, I didn't want to make it even worse. "It's an important performance, after all."

Freddie nodded. "It's strange, isn't it? To know that your moment of destiny is just around the corner." He blinked, and his expression was one I recognized. Sure enough, a moment later, he was patting his pockets, like he was looking for his notebook. "That could be a good lyric."

"Here," I said, pulling the pen out of my bag, along with the piece of paper.

"Freddie," he read off it, then looked at me, eyebrows raised.

"I just wanted to make sure I remembered," I explained, feeling my cheeks get hot. "When I was trying to tell you that we'd met before."

"I don't think anyone's ever given me a list like this before," he said, looking back down at it, a smile playing around the corners of his mouth. "It's really . . ."

"Weird?" I finished with a half-laugh.

"Amazing," he said at the same time, and I looked up at him in surprise. "I mean," he said, and I could see that he was also blushing slightly. "It means someone likes you, right? If they're paying attention?"

I looked at him, feeling my heart beat faster. He took a half step toward me, and I took one toward him, closing the space between us. He reached out and tucked the lock of hair behind my ear. He didn't pull his hand away right away, but let it rest there, right by my cheek, turning my hair around his fingers. "Cass," he started, then took a breath.

"Oi!" Niall stuck his head out the door, making both of us jump, and I took a step back. "Sorry to interrupt," he said, even though his tone said the exact opposite, "but we do have a show to do, superstar."

"Right," Freddie said, nodding. "There in just a moment." Niall disappeared back into the greenroom, the door slamming behind him harder than seemed strictly necessary. "I really should go."

"It sounds like it," I agreed.

"But maybe I'll see you afterward?"

I nodded, smiling at him. "I hope so. Good luck—you'll do great." I gave him a nod, then started walking out the way we'd come in.

"Cass?" Freddie called, and I turned around. I couldn't help but notice how much I liked the way he said my name. It might have been the accent, but I didn't think it was *just* that.

"Yes?"

"What's this?" he asked, pointing toward the bottom of the page. "This thing about home being a sweatshirt you've outgrown?"

"It's a song lyric."

"I love it," Freddie said, looking down at the paper. "Who wrote it?"

"Well—you did." He glanced up at me in surprise and I smiled at him. "See you later." Then I turned around and headed back down the hallway, the words feeling a little bit like a promise. And as I rounded the corner, I hoped they would be true—that now the performance was saved, and maybe when I walked through the doors, it would be into a future that unspooled in a straight line, instead of circling around in an endless loop.

As before, the crowd was starting to gather in front of the stage. The music manager was in the back, at her same spot. I could see the count-down clock and realized why Niall had been so insistent on getting me out of there—the band was set to go on in fifteen minutes. What if this was going to be the last loop? What if I'd fixed things?

I looked around until I saw Bryony in the crowd, standing with the Emmas, and felt a wave of guilt hit me. I'd needed to get things on track with the band, but doing that had meant I wasn't getting to spend time with my best friend—and on the last night we'd get to hang out. But surely it was for the greater good. Right?

I walked through the crowd, keeping my eyes fixed on her, trying not to lose her in the shifting group of people—and also keeping my eyes peeled for Bruce, who I would really prefer not to run into right now.

I saw Bryony's eyes widen as she saw me, and I waved at her, closing the distance between us. "Hi!" I called as I got close enough for her to hear me.

"Where have you been? I texted you," Bryony said.

"Oh, sorry," I said, pulling out my phone. "I was kind of distracted. How were the roller coasters?"

"It was all your idea! I didn't even want to do it!" Emma J. was yelling at Emma Z. Emma R. walked up to us, her expression worried as she glanced back at her friends.

"They're still at it," she said to Bryony, shaking her head. Then she smiled as she saw me. "Hey, Cass! How's it going?"

"Good." I glanced back at the other two Emmas, who were huddled together, having a whisper-fight, both of them looking beyond stressed out. "What's going on with them?"

"We have no idea," Bryony said, exchanging a look with Emma R.

"But it's been happening all night," Emma R. said, frowning. "And I keep asking, but they keep telling me it's nothing. But it's *something*. They started being weird when we saw Mater in his graduation cap. And—"

Before she could continue, the announcer's voice crackled over the loudspeakers. "Disney Grad Nite seniors and chaperones! Please welcome—all the way from jolly olde England—Eton Mess!"

Everyone cheered, and the band strode out, wearing their prep-school outfits. I saw Niall and Freddie laughing together as they walked. Like before, they were both holding their bottles of water, and Niall slapped Freddie on the back as they took their places on stage.

Freddie caught my eye and waved as he picked up his guitar and lifted it over his head. I smiled back at him, and it felt like everyone in the crowd turned to look at me—including Bryony and the Emmas.

"Did the cute bass player just wave at you?" Emma R. asked. She gave me an impressed thumbs-up. "Nicely done."

I felt my cheeks get hot. "I mean—kind of?"

"How do you know the bass player?" Bryony asked.

"Well—"

"Oh my god, Cass, tell me everything!"

I laughed, but as I did, I felt a little guilty twist in my stomach. I *wanted* to tell her about Freddie, about the boy I'd met, about how cute and nice he was. Because I always talked to Bryony about the things that mattered. Things didn't seem real until I got to discuss them with her.

But assuming I'd fixed the issue with the band, the time loop was about to end. And then I'd just . . . never see her again? The plan that had seemed so clear earlier tonight was starting to get murky. I shook my head, trying to clear it. "I just—"

"Hey there, seniors! Congratulations on graduating!" Niall yelled. Everyone around me erupted in cheers. "Are you having fun at Grad Nite?" Freddie took a drink of his water, then set the bottle down at his feet. He met my eye again, and I made myself smile at him, even though my thoughts were spinning.

"Chuffed to hear it," Niall said. He was back to using his posh British accent, all traces of his Scottish brogue gone. "We're Eton Mess, and we're—"

Just as he said this, Alfie groaned and clutched his stomach. Freddie stared at him in alarm, then looked at me. "No," I whispered, shaking my head, not quite able to believe what I was seeing. How had we not fixed it? But then—just like before—Alfie tried to run backstage. He didn't quite make it though, throwing up on the stage as Tristram/Doug scrambled out of the way.

The crowd all around me yelled *Ewwwww!* and everyone started to pull out their phones—eager to record and document this car crash.

"How is this happening?" I asked, raking my hands through my hair.

"Seriously," Emma R. said, looking nauseated. Even the other Emmas had stopped fighting long enough to stare, open-mouthed at the spectacle.

"This isn't supposed to happen again!" I said, shaking my head.

"What does that mean?" Bryony asked, frowning at me.

"It's just—I thought we fixed it."

"Fixed what? Who's *we*?"

"Uh, sorry," Niall said from the stage, looking discomfited. "We're just having a little— Freddie?"

I turned to Freddie, hoping that maybe, this time, he would be able to do something about it. I glanced behind me and saw that the music manager looked repulsed, but she hadn't left yet. And maybe she wouldn't hold Freddie responsible for the fact that Alfie loved prawns. Maybe Freddie could still fix things, get things back on track. I turned back to the stage and felt my stomach plunge as I realized this was absolutely not going to happen.

Just like before, Freddie was scratching at his neck, his face getting red and puffy, his eyes filled with dread. "How?!" I practically yelled. I turned to see, right on cue, the music manager storming off just as Freddie fled the stage and Niall stepped up to the mic.

"Sorry about all this," he said smoothly, with a wink to the crowd. "Maybe something a capella from me as my mates get themselves sorted?"

"I have to go," I said, already heading toward the exit.

"You're leaving?" Bryony asked, sounding confused. "You just got here!"

"I'll be back," I promised, breaking into a run. "Just give me a second!"

8

I found Freddie just where I knew he'd be. In his inconvenient spot, standing in the middle of the path. This meant everyone had to walk around him, but Freddie—lost in the good news that he'd just gotten—was oblivious to all of it. I could see his face was back to being regular-size, not red and puffy.

I'd hurried through what was now becoming a routine with Bryony and Ms. Mulaney—encouraging Bryony and the Emmas to go on the roller coasters, splitting off from Ms. Mulaney when she got her ill-fated agent call. The only slight detour I'd taken was to write out the Freddie list once again—this time, adding the new things that I'd learned.

Freddie
- *Brother named Jack*
- *From Croydon*
- *Loves Excalibur!/poster above bed/Geraldine Bewley school project*
- *Weird fruit and vegetable allergy*
- *Rocky road ice cream/Sweet Emporium*
- *Surf liner up to LA for meetings*
- *Manager coming tonight*
- *Mates with Niall from school days*
- *Lyrics in black notebook*
- *Tristram's real name is Doug: he's from Chicago. Alfie is Aussie. Lettuce is rocket??*
- *Always losing phone*
- *Mum told him he'd lose his head if not attached to his neck*

Sometimes the only home you've ever known/is the favorite sweatshirt you've outgrown.

Knowing your moment of destiny is just around the corner.

But I wrote this list as fast as I could and then hurried to find him, because we didn't have a surfeit of time. Clearly, it hadn't been enough to throw out Alfie's dinner—he must have eaten some of the cursed stir-fry before we got to the greenroom, which meant we needed to stop it as soon as possible.

I walked right up to Freddie—he was still staring at his phone, reading the email about the manager coming. And I hated that I had to burst his bubble so soon after getting good news, but the faster we got through this part, the sooner we could start fixing things.

"Hi," I said, coming to stand right in front of him. "I'm Cass Issac. *Excalibur.*"

Freddie just blinked at me, then looked down at what he was wearing. "Like, my shirt?"

"Not exactly." I gave him a smile, took a deep breath, and launched into my explanation.

It didn't take as long this time, or maybe I was just getting better at going through the situation. But by the time I got to the part about what was going to happen with the performance unless we intervened, Freddie started nodding.

"Okay," he said. He looked down at the Freddie list I'd handed him during my explanation and then back at me, his eyes wider than usual. "I'm just trying to get my head around this."

"I know," I said, "and it's okay if it takes you longer. But right now—right this moment—you have to call Alfie and tell him not to eat the shrimp. Er, prawns."

"Right," Freddie said. He pulled out his phone and pressed a button to make a call. "But this is amazing! I always wanted to believe something like this was possible."

I smiled at him. "I know."

He laughed. "Right, of course. It's ringing," he said, then frowned. "Voicemail . . . Alfie, mate! I need you to stop eating your prawn . . ." He glanced at me.

"Stir-fry," I supplied.

"Stir-fry," Freddie continued.

"Tell him it's not a carb thing," I whispered.

"It's, uh, not a carb thing," Freddie said, looking a little taken aback. "It's just for health and safety. So just bin it and get something else to eat, okay? And maybe avoid seafood altogether? Cheers." He hung up and looked at me. "Think we did it?"

"I don't know." I honestly wasn't sure I could take seeing Alfie throw up again, and I wanted to do everything I could to try and prevent it, for my own sake as much as Freddie's. "Maybe we should go check?"

Freddie nodded. "That's a good idea. I am going to need to eat something, though."

As though on cue, my stomach grumbled. "Me too. But maybe, let's get it to go?"

We ended up getting hot dogs at Angry Dogs. Freddie got the full Angry Dog, whereas I decided I might not be up for that level of spice at the moment and chose the Slightly Annoyed Dog. We ate them as we walked toward the stage where Eton Mess would be performing, trying to work out what, exactly, happened to give Freddie his allergic reaction.

"It happens onstage?" he asked, taking a bite of his Angry Dog.

I nodded. "You start out fine, and then, like a minute later, you're having this reaction. And you *knew* about it last time—you promised me you weren't going to eat anything, just to be on the safe side." He took another bite of his hot dog, and I nodded at it. "How is that?"

"Really good," he enthused. "You should have gone for spicy."

"I think I'm okay," I assured him.

"Now, while these are good, the hot dogs at Award Wieners are slightly superior."

I laughed. "At *where?*"

"The name might be silly, but the hot dogs are not," Freddie assured me. "Honestly, I think at this point, I've tried all the food at the park, so you should really trust my opinion."

"I mean, I'm getting there," I said, realizing with some surprise that this was the third dinner we'd had together. "A few more loops and I'll catch up to you. But maybe be *extra* careful this time, okay? I just don't understand where this allergic reaction is coming from—"

I stopped short when I realized that Reagan, Zach, and McKenna were walking toward us. They hadn't seen me yet, but unless I wanted to have a very awkward conversation with all of them—mostly revolving around why I was a terrible person who hadn't brought churros—I had to get out of sight, and fast.

"You okay?" Freddie asked, his brow furrowed.

"Yeah, we just need to hide."

"Hide?"

I looked around in a panic, knowing I was about to be spotted unless I moved quickly. But where could we even go?

"Here," Freddie said, jumping into action. He grabbed my free hand with his, and the moment we touched, I felt that *zing* travel all the way through me. He pulled me behind the nearby cookie stand so that we were out of sight. "Okay?" he asked.

"Maybe." I glanced around to try and see Reagan, but attempted to do it surreptitiously. Seeing where I was looking, and still holding my hand, Freddie steered me so that he was facing the direction the trio was coming, with my back to them. Then he dropped my hand and leaned his arm against one of the posts holding up the cookie stand.

I looked up at him. And I hadn't realized, until this moment, just how close together we were. I could have risen up on my toes and been near enough to kiss him. I wasn't going to—we were both still holding hot dogs, and we had to stop Alfie from eating the shrimp. But it was more than that. It was the fact that this wasn't the Freddie who'd stood close to me in the moonlight and tucked my hair behind my ear. It wasn't the Freddie who'd turned my hair around his fingers in the hallway, asking if he could see me after the show. This Freddie had just met me, and while I hadn't just met him, I still wanted to be respectful of that. Even though, standing this close and breathing him in, seeing his strong arm resting on the post above me, I could feel my resolve start to weaken.

He looked down at me and raised an eyebrow. "Think we're okay?"

I nodded, trying to get a hold of myself. We were on a mission here, and I couldn't lose sight of that just because Freddie had an accent and a dimple and a lock of hair I was dying to run my fingers through. . . .

"Right," I said, forcing myself to look away from him. I took a step back and glanced over where I'd seen my former friends. I could see their backs now, walking away with no idea of how close I'd been. "Okay, let's go."

"Sure," Freddie said, falling into step with me as we headed toward the stage area. "But you really are going to have to explain what that was."

"Of course," I said, shaking my head. "Sorry. I did explain it to you already. But not *this* you. It's— Well. Those were people I used to be friends with, back in Los Angeles. And I found out tonight . . . that they're pretty mad at me." I tried to push it away, but the look that Reagan had given me when they'd first recognized me—the shocked betrayal—was seared in my brain.

"Why are they mad at you?" Freddie asked, taking a bite of his hot dog.

I took a bite of my own, then told him the story—my dads moving all the time, the way I always had to leave schools just as I was starting to make friends. How I was never able to really relax or settle in.

"So," I said, when I'd finished giving him the abridged version and we'd both tossed the remnants of our dinners away, "because of all that, I've found that it's easiest to just try and make a clean break with people. And I thought it was fine! But then I ran into them, and, well . . ."

"So that's why you're avoiding them."

"Yeah. Well, not just them." Freddie raised an eyebrow at me, and I took a breath and explained about Nora and Greta, and even though I didn't really want to—Bruce. "And since I'm stuck in this loop, it's like I'm always looking over my shoulder. The last thing I want is to run into them so they can tell me how mad they are at me." My mouth twisted as I said it. These words, which I'd been trying to toss off, instead landed heavily.

Freddie shook his head. "Our worst mistakes are a hall of mirrors—reflecting back to us all we shouldn't have said." He blinked, like he'd just surprised himself, and his expression was one I was now getting quite familiar with. "That might actually be a good—"

"Lyric?" I finished for him, with a smile, already pulling the Freddie list and Ms. Mulaney's pen out of my bag.

"Uh, yeah," he said, looking a little abashed as he scribbled it down. Then he pointed to the two other lines he'd come up with. "Who wrote these?"

"You did," I said, and smiled when I saw his surprised expression. He tore off the bottom part of the list, then handed it back to me.

"Sorry about that," Freddie said, still staring at the song lyrics on the page—including the ones he'd written but had no memory of. He shook his head, then looked up at me. "Lyrics aside, always having to move around that much—that must have been really hard, Cass."

"Thanks. But it's the way my dads' business works. It's just the way it's always been."

He looked at me for just a moment before speaking. "It sounds like you're mad at them."

I just blinked at him. "Mad at who? My dads?" Freddie nodded, and I just shook my head automatically. I was honestly a little surprised by the turn this was taking—it hadn't come up in any of our conversations so far. "I'm not mad at them." The second I said it, though, I wondered if it was true.

"It's okay if you are," he said, giving me steady look as we approached the door that I now knew would take us backstage. "It can't have been easy, growing up like that."

"Well, no. But . . ." I stopped as Freddie pulled the door open for me. I stepped into the corridor, my thoughts spinning. *Was* I actually mad at them? Had I been for a while now—and just hadn't let myself see it?

"Hey, Violet," Freddie said, as he approached the three stagehands playing their poker game. We were here earlier than before, and I noticed that the pot in the center had a lot less money in it. "Who's winning?"

"Me, so far. I just can't tell if Van is bluffing," she said, raising her eyebrow at the guy across from her.

"He is," I said immediately, remembering how the last hand had gone.

"What?" the guy, Van, asked, frowning at me. He looked disconcerted. "Who even are you?"

"No one," I said quickly, even as I widened my eyes at Violet, trying to communicate that I knew what I was talking about. "Never mind."

"Let me get a picture," Freddie said, taking out his phone like before. He snapped it, then smiled at them. "Nice."

"We should go," I said, nodding toward the greenroom. I was all too aware that shrimp-eating could be happening right now, and we were wasting precious time.

"Right," Freddie said, his expression growing more serious. "Of course. See you guys." We hurried down the hall, and I remembered a second too late that he'd left his phone again—but I figured we'd deal with that after we'd talked to Alfie.

Freddie pushed open the door to the greenroom. Tristram/Doug was sitting on the couch, twirling his drumstick, and Alfie was holding a plate, the fork in his hand traveling up to his mouth. . . .

"Prawns!" Freddie yelled. Alfie jumped, and his plate fell to the floor.

"What?" he asked, looking spooked as he glanced around in a panic. "What's going on?"

"Did you eat any of it yet?" I asked, hurrying up to him. He just frowned, looking from me to Freddie like he was trying to figure out what exactly was happening. "The shrimp," I said, my voice rising. "I mean, prawns. Did you eat any?"

"I had some at the strip mall. I brought the rest with me. Uh—who are you, again?"

"That's Cass," Freddie said, picking up the shrimp stir-fry plate from the floor and tossing it in the garbage. "She's very worried about people getting food poisoning."

I shot a look at Freddie that he returned with a grin. "Do you feel okay?"

"Well, I'm a little shaken up," Alfie said. "I was just enjoying my dinner when you lot burst in here."

"Sounds like they were trying to help," Tristram/Doug pointed out, in his American accent. Then he paused, his eyes widening. "I mean," he said, in what was very likely the worst English accent I'd ever heard. "They were just 'elpin', wot?"

"It's okay, Doug," I assured him. "I know the truth."

"Oh thank god," he said in his regular voice, relaxing back against the couch cushions.

"You know about Doug?" Freddie asked me in a low voice.

"We've met before," I assured him. I glanced over at Alfie, who was making his way over to the snack table, still looking disconcerted. "What do you think? Are we okay?"

"Well," Freddie said, knitting his brows in concentration. "Hopefully? Maybe the ones he ate at the restaurant were fine, and it's only the unrefrigerated prawns—the ones he ate here—that were the problem?"

I nodded—that made sense. And plus, in the other loops, the sickness came over Alfie pretty soon after he'd eaten the shrimp. And since he seemed okay now, hopefully we were out of the woods. "Let's hope so," I said, giving him a smile.

"So, um," Freddie said, sticking his hands in his pockets. "Did you want to hang out, or . . ."

I did—but even more than that, I wanted to try to find Bryony. If we'd finally fixed this, it meant time with my best friend was slipping away, and I wanted to get as much of it as possible. "I should let you rehearse," I said. "Big night tonight, right?"

"Well, I'll try not to let you down. Are you getting totally sick of our music? How many times have you seen it?"

"You've been to more than one Grad Nite?" Alfie asked, wandering back over with a plate of crudité and chips. "I didn't think that was allowed."

"Oh no, I haven't seen performances. Just clips. Online," I said quickly, trying to cover. He nodded, apparently satisfied with this, and flopped down next to Tristram/Doug on the couch. "I actually haven't ever seen you guys play," I said to Freddie in a lower voice when I was sure Alfie was out of earshot. "Every time I've tried, you've never been able to actually perform."

"Right," Freddie said, raking a hand through his hair. "Well, let's hope we've changed that tonight."

I nodded. "But you have to be really careful, okay? Don't eat *anything*. Every single time, you've had an allergic reaction."

"I won't," he promised me, making the cross-your-heart gesture for good measure. "But maybe after—hoping it all goes well—we can hang out?"

I smiled. This wasn't the first time Freddie had asked me this, but hearing it still made me just as happy. "I'd like that."

He opened the door to walk me out, and we headed down the hallway. My feet slowed when I saw that Niall was standing next to the stagehands playing poker. He was frowning as he looked down at something. He turned slightly, and I realized what he was looking at was Freddie's phone.

"Niall?" Freddie called.

Niall startled, and for just a moment there was a caught-out expression on his face before it was replaced by the big, confident smile I'd seen onstage. "Hey, mate," he drawled, holding up Freddie's phone. "Looks like you forgot this again."

"Agh," Freddie said, shaking his head. "I really have to be better about it. My mum always said—"

"Why were you looking at his phone?" I interrupted, trying to figure out what I'd just seen.

"What do you mean?" Niall asked, his smile widening, getting even more charming. But his eyes, I couldn't help but notice, didn't match this expression—they were cold and calculating. "And who are you, again? I don't believe I've had the pleasure."

"This is Cass," Freddie said quickly, stepping in between us and taking his phone from Niall. "She's here for Grad Nite."

"Did you two just meet?" Niall asked, looking between us like he was trying to work something out.

"Kind of. Feels like I've known him longer, though." Freddie laughed at that, and I smiled at him. "I should let you rehearse. Good luck."

"Thanks," Niall said, giving me another grin that didn't meet his eyes and clapping Freddie on the back. "Come on, superstar. Let's get ready."

"I'll see you after?" Freddie called, as Niall steered him away.

"Absolutely," I called after him, crossing my fingers that this would turn out to be true. They disappeared into the greenroom, and I just stood in the hallway, trying to work out what was bothering me about Niall. But after nothing came to mind, I tried to shake it off.

I headed around the corner, where Violet was opening the equipment cases and starting to unpack them. I gave her a nod as I headed to the exit, but she straightened up and smiled at me. "Hey!" she said cheerfully. "Thanks for the tip about Van. He *was* totally bluffing. How did you know?"

"Oh," I said, with a shrug, "I guess I'm just good at reading people? Have a good night."

"You too," she called after me, going back to work.

I took a deep breath, then pushed my way out the doors, heading off to find my best friend.

8

On my way to the stage, I stopped by a different bathroom than the one I knew that Tabitha Keith would soon be weeping in. There wasn't anything I could do about that now—in this moment, I just wanted to find my best friend and spend as much time with her as possible.

I looked around the crowd that was starting to gather in front of the stage but didn't see her and the Emmas anywhere. I was here earlier than I normally was—there were ten minutes on the countdown clock—so I wasn't sure exactly when she'd be arriving. I looked down at my watch, to try and note the time, before I gave it up. I was already keeping so much in my head—where people were at any given moment, facts about Freddie, random poker players' cards—I wasn't sure I could add more to it without osing something. I pulled out my phone, figuring that maybe it would be better to text Bryony so that she wouldn't be shocked to see me.

But just for a moment, I stared down at the picture on my lock screen—Oscar and Angelo and me. Freddie's words were rattling around in my head, and I was trying my best to dismiss them. I wasn't mad at them. Maybe I was mad at the *situation*, but not at them. It wasn't like they could have done anything different . . . right? I'd been working so hard to be part of our little unit, a team player, that these were questions I'd never asked.

I realized with a shock that I'd never once told them how I felt about it all. And suddenly, standing in the middle of a Grad Nite crowd, looking down at a picture of our smiling faces, I wished that I had.

"Cass?" It was a guy's voice, and I felt my heart lift as I looked up, expecting to see Freddie standing in front of me. But a second later, I registered that the voice had been American, not British. Which made sense, because Bruce was standing in front of me, arms folded across his chest.

I inwardly sighed as I realized that I hadn't accounted for him here, which I absolutely should have. I'd run into him twice before, after all. But constantly avoiding people, and having to keep ever-changing maps in my head, was truly starting to get exhausting.

"Hey, Bruce," I said with a wave, as he stared in surprise at me. A second later, I remembered that I wasn't supposed to be expecting to see him here. "I mean," I said, scrambling. "Hey! Bruce? I'm so very surprised to see you here. Why are you so far from home here, in California?"

"We won an academic award," Bruce said. His eyes were still wide as he looked at me, like he'd just seen a ghost—which was probably what this felt like for him. I'd seen him enough tonight that the shock was wearing off. He was even starting to look familiar—his light brown hair, black backpack, *Cereal* T-shirt . . .

"Wait," I said, taking a step closer. His Evergreen High sweatshirt was off, and now I could see that he was wearing a T-shirt touting Bryony's favorite podcast. His read SNAP CRACKLE POP CULTURE under the *Cereal* logo. "You listen to *Cereal*?"

"Uh, yes," he said, looking a little discomfited. "Do you?"

"No," I said immediately. "But I've heard a lot about it, believe me. In fact . . ." I turned away, scanning the crowd, which was getting steadily bigger. I could see the music manager taking her spot, I could see people jockeying for better positions. I could even see . . . "Bryony!" I yelled the second I spotted her, rising up on my toes and waving.

"Cass?" she called, then started to make her way over to me, Emma R. following behind her. The other two Emmas, as expected, were bickering together in low tones, both looking miserable. "When did you get here? Why didn't you text me?"

"I was about to," I said, holding up my phone like it was proof. "But I knew you'd be here soon." She took a breath, and I continued on before she could ask a follow-up. "But I wanted you to meet Bruce."

"Hi!" Emma R. said, striding forward to wave at him. "I'm Emma."

"Hello," Bruce said politely, even as he was looking increasingly confused.

"This is Bryony," I said, gesturing to her, and noticing that she was playing with her bangs again, which was all the sign I needed. I knew now I hadn't been imagining the sparks I'd felt between them earlier. "I just thought you should meet, since you're both *Cereal* fans." I saw them both clock the other's shirt.

"Cereal, like for eating?" Emma R. asked, sounding baffled.

"It's a podcast," Bryony and Bruce said at the same time, then smiled at each other.

"Is it a murder podcast?" Emma R. asked. "Because those are the only ones I listen to."

I turned to her. "Wait, really?"

She shrugged like this should have been obvious. "Of course."

"How do you know Cass?" Bryony asked, looking up at Bruce and fussing with her bangs again.

"We knew each other in Seattle," I said, jumping in before Bruce could. "We were neighbors. Friends. And then . . . I wrecked everything." I didn't know I was going to speak the truth before I was saying it, and it just reverberated between us for a moment, like when a tuning fork finds the correct pitch.

"You—what?" Bryony asked.

I looked at Bruce and saw that his expression had softened a little. The hurt fury that had been on his face every other time we'd seen each other tonight was starting to fade.

"Okay, I'm going to need this story," Emma R. said.

I took a breath to answer, just as the lights started to swirl and the announcer's voice crackled over the loudspeaker. "Disney Grad Nite seniors and chaperones! Please welcome—all the way from jolly olde England—Eton Mess!"

I turned to the stage, feeling like my heart was in my throat. "Please," I muttered under my breath. "Please, please."

As before, I could glimpse Niall and Freddie backstage. But this time, I saw Niall hand Freddie his bottle of water right before they stepped out onstage, Niall slapping Freddie on the back.

"Hey there, seniors! Congratulations on graduating!" Niall yelled, the way he always did. But I wasn't looking at him—I was focused on Alfie, who looked a little better than he normally did. "Are you having fun at Grad Nite?" Niall asked as Freddie took a drink of his water.

I glanced behind me and saw the manager, dressed all in black, her eyes fixed on the stage. I turned back to the band, my eyes scanning all the members of Eton Mess—well, except for Tristram/Doug; he never seemed to be part of the problem—looking for indications that things might be going off the rails again, hoping this was the one time they wouldn't.

"Chuffed to hear it," Niall said to the crowd in his posh accent that I now knew was totally fake. I remembered the coldness in his eyes and the startled look he'd had when we'd caught him with Freddie's phone. My eyes drifted to the bottle of water in Freddie's hand—the bottle that Niall had handed him—and I started to get a bad feeling. "We're Eton Mess, and we're—"

As if on cue, Alfie clutched his stomach. "NO!" I said, louder than I'd intended. Many people in the crowd—including Bryony, Bruce, and the Emmas—turned to stare at me.

"You okay?" Bryony asked.

"No," I said, shaking my head. "It's—" But before I could continue, Alfie tried to run backstage. Like before, though, he didn't make it, throwing up onstage yet again. The crowd around me reacted with horror, but I looked away from Alfie, my eyes focused on Freddie's face. I wanted to be wrong about the theory that had started percolating in my head, I wanted him to be fine. . . .

"Uh, sorry," Niall said from the stage, his expression appalled. "We're just having a little—Freddie?"

I realized I wasn't even surprised as I saw the red rash creeping up Freddie's neck, the way his eyes were getting puffy.

"Is this part of the show?" Emma R. asked, frowning. "Like performance art? I don't think I like it."

Freddie ran off the stage, and I turned around, knowing what I was going to see—the music manager leaving.

"Sorry about all this," Niall said smoothly, with a wink to the crowd. "Maybe something a capella from me as my mates get themselves sorted?"

"What was all that?" Bryony asked, sounding horrified.

"It was betrayal," I said, my heart heavy. Bryony, Bruce, and Emma R. just stared at me, baffled, and I started to back away, heading for the exit. "If you'll excuse me . . ."

9

P rawns!" Freddie yelled.

Alfie jumped, and his plate fell to the floor. "What?" he asked, sounding spooked as he glanced around in a panic. "What's going on?"

"We're here to help," I assured him. I'd done the same thing as before—shaken off Bryony, rushed to meet Freddie, given him the rundown of what was happening. We hadn't taken the time to eat, just hurried right into the greenroom, past the stagehands who were just starting to deal their cards for poker. But when Freddie paused to take his picture, I didn't stop him—or remind him to get his phone when he left it the way he always did. I'd realized that it was important that he leave it behind. "That stir-fry is not your friend," I told Alfie as I tossed out the paper plate.

"And the portion you ate at the strip mall is going to give you food poisoning right as your show starts."

"I'm sorry, what?" Alfie turned to Freddie, then looked back at me. "Are you having a laugh?"

"Nope," I said.

"Wait, who are you?" Tristram/Doug asked, then paled. "I mean, erm, who d'ye be, lass?" His accent this time—as far as I could tell—was veering into very bad Irish.

"It's okay, I know you're from Chicago," I assured him, and he visibly relaxed. "And I'm Cass. Just trying to help out the band."

"It's for the best," Freddie assured Alfie.

"So you can't perform tonight," I said, and all three bandmembers' heads whipped over to stare at me.

"Sorry, that's . . . naur," Alfie said, shaking his head. "I'm the guitarist, y'see?"

"Yeah," Freddie said, turning to me. "He's a pretty important part of the band. What do you mean, he can't play?"

"He can't play," I said, then lowered my voice so only Freddie could hear. "We *just* tried this. Even if we get him to stop eating now, he still gets sick. He can't go onstage unless you want him to vomit all over it and wreck *your* shot."

"Well, obviously I don't want that," Freddie said, his eyes going wide. "How are we supposed to play without a guitarist?"

"You play guitar," I pointed out, wondering what the problem was.

He shook his head. "I play *bass*."

"Isn't that the same?" All three band member erupted in identical sounds of disbelief. "Well, they're both guitars," I said defensively.

"We need a guitar player," Tristram/Doug insisted. "Or at least someone on keys. But you can't have a band with just bass and drums."

"I mean—Death from Above 1979 does," Alfie pointed out. "And . . . Megachurch?"

Freddie shook his head. "I don't think you're helping your argument here."

"Can't you do it?" I asked Tristram/Doug.

"I play drums," he said, and held up his sticks, like I might need a visual aid. "We need drums, too."

"And Niall doesn't play *anything*?" Not that I wanted to have to rely on Niall, but this was an emergency.

"Just mind games," Alfie said grimly.

"Wait," Freddie said, looking surprised. "That's not on. He means well, Niall, it's just . . ."

I shook my head. "He really doesn't."

Alfie pointed at me. "See, Cass gets it!" Then he frowned. "Wait—how exactly do you get it?"

I glanced at Freddie—I was suddenly very aware of the other two band members watching us, leaning forward to hear every word. "Can we talk somewhere?" I asked, lowering my voice.

"What did you mean, Cass?" Freddie asked when we'd stepped into the hallway for some privacy. "About Niall?" His brow was furrowed as he looked down at me.

I took a deep breath before answering. It wasn't that I was a *100* percent sure about this—but it was the only explanation that made sense, given everything that I'd seen. "It's your allergic reaction."

Freddie grimaced. "Right. When I get hives because of something I eat."

"Not eat. Something you *drink*. Niall gives you a bottle of water right before you go onstage. And I think he puts something in it—something to make you sick."

"What?" Freddie blinked at me, then gave a stunned half laugh. "No. He couldn't have."

"It's the only thing that makes sense." I glanced down the hallway toward the stagehands, but they all seemed much too immersed in their game to pay any attention to us. "He puts—I don't know, cucumber or fruit or something in it. He knows about your allergy, right?"

"Well, yeah. But . . ."

"And you said the reaction happens pretty soon after you eat or drink something. Right?"

Freddie nodded, a little reluctantly. "Yes."

"The last two times, I told you about your allergic reaction, and you promised not to eat anything. But right before it happens, you take a drink of your water bottle. The water bottle *Niall* gives to you."

"Why would he do that? It makes no sense—"

"It's your phone." Freddie frowned and started patting his pockets, and I pointed to where he'd left it on the instrument case. "You leave it there, and he picks it up and sees the text from the manager confirming she's coming."

"But I still don't think that he'd . . ."

"He got really upset, back when you just tell him," I said. "You try and bring him Irn-Bru to make up for it."

"Well, that's understandable. . . ."

"You told me yourself that he always wants to be the star. What if he didn't like the idea that you were going to get your big break—and not him? And maybe he decided he wasn't going to let that happen?"

"No!" Freddie said, and I could hear the frustration in his voice. "Niall wouldn't do that."

"But he does! And I've seen it. I don't know what else to tell you."

Freddie stared down at the ground, his brows knitted together. I felt my heart squeeze as I looked at him—I could only imagine how I would feel if someone told me Bryony was going to betray me. But then a second later, it hit me—was this how Bryony felt when she found out I hadn't applied to the Mermaid Café and was planning on leaving? Like I'd betrayed *her*?

"I'm sorry," I said quietly. "I've just seen you guys crash and burn four times now. And I know this is important to you. I'm trying to help."

Freddie looked up at me, and I could see the hurt in his eyes. "Right," he said, shaking his head. "I know you are. It's just . . . hard to hear."

"Yeah," I said, crossing my arms, then putting my hands in my pockets. We were in uncharted territory here, and I wasn't sure what came next.

"Well," Freddie finally said, breaking the silence. "I should probably get ready for the show." The lightness, the buoyancy that he always seemed to have was gone, replaced with a weariness I hadn't seen before.

"Oh," I said, taken aback but trying not to show it. A second later, it hit me that of *course* things would be different this time. He wasn't going to smile at me and tuck my hair behind my ear and tell me that he hoped we could hang out after. I'd just told him his best friend was about to betray him. "Right, of course."

"Okay," he said, giving me a sad smile as he turned back to the greenroom.

"Good luck," I called after him, and Freddie gave me a half wave before heading inside, leaving me alone in the hall.

I didn't want to see Bryony, or Bruce, or any of the Emmas. I didn't want to see anyone I knew—I just wanted a place to watch the show. I needed to see if I was right, of course, but mostly, I wanted just *once* to see the band's set go off without a problem. It didn't seem right that this was Freddie's big chance, and not only did it go badly, but I was forced to watch it, over and over again.

I found a spot outside the bulk of the crowd, by the water. I pulled my jean jacket on for warmth, and then looked around, hoping that nobody would notice me. I had a feeling I would be okay—most everyone was turned the opposite way, facing the stage, but even so, I needed to be vigilant.

The speakers crackled and, as always, the announcer's voice sounded. "Disney Grad Nite seniors and chaperones! Please welcome—all the way from jolly olde England—Eton Mess!"

I watched, heart in my throat, as the band members took the stage, all of them looking disconcerted, like there had just been an argument before they'd walked out. This was not the smiling, confident group I was used to seeing take the stage. I glanced over at the music manager—I had a perfect view of her from where I was sitting. She pocketed her phone and focused on the stage, and I crossed my fingers on both hands.

I let out a sigh of relief when I saw that Alfie wasn't with the band. There was a spotlight on his microphone, but no Alfie appeared. Freddie had the bottle of water with him, but he put it down by his feet as he pulled his guitar over his head, and I was relieved to see that it didn't look like he'd opened it.

"Uh, hello, seniors! Congratulations!" Niall called. He kept glancing over at Freddie and at the bottle at his feet, his expression disgruntled. He definitely seemed more scattered this time, less smoothly composed. "Are you having fun tonight?"

The crowd yelled enthusiastically, but I just sat still, my eyes fixed on Freddie, willing this to turn out well.

"We're down a guitar player," Freddie said, speaking into the mic. And even though I knew it wasn't possible, it felt like he looked right at me as he said it, like his eyes had found mine in the crowd. "So I hope we'll still be able to put on a good show for you."

"'Course we will," Niall snapped, losing his posh accent for just a moment. Then he pushed back his hair and smiled at the crowd. "Here we go!"

Tristram/Doug counted out *one, two, three* on his sticks, and then the band started to play.

And it . . . wasn't good.

It was *fine*—certainly better than the versions of this show where people got sick onstage and erupted into hives. But there was obviously something missing. Clearly, I had been wrong, and it really *did* matter when you were down an instrument.

All the songs sounded just a little bit off, and Niall was distracted, messing up words, glancing over at Freddie throughout, clearly wondering why he was still absolutely fine. But it was like without Alfie on guitar, everything was unbalanced, the timing wrong, the music never finding its groove. The crowd was picking up on it—people were looking at their friends and whispering, and there was just a sense in the crowd of *something is wrong* that you could palpably feel. When the whispers turned into murmurs, I saw Freddie looking out to the crowd, his expression worried even as his fingers flew over the neck of his bass. It was the first time I was seeing him play, and even though it clearly wasn't the best showcase for the band, I could tell that *he* was great, playing with a skill I wouldn't have thought was possible in someone around my age.

But even Freddie's bass abilities weren't enough to salvage this slow-motion car wreck. And when Niall messed up three lyrics in a row, he stopped singing, stepped back from his microphone, and shook his head. "This is *bollocks*," he said, then stormed off the stage, petulantly pushing the mic stand as he went. He clearly meant for it to topple over, but instead it just wobbled back and forth a little before righting itself. Freddie stopped playing, and so did Tristram/Doug, who looked around for a moment, then got out from behind his drum kit and walked offstage, leaving Freddie there alone.

Freddie looked out into the crowd, and for a moment, I wondered if he was going to take the stage, the way Niall was so eager to in the rest of the loops when his band became otherwise indisposed. But if I knew anything about Freddie by now, it was that he thought about other people much more than himself. So I wasn't surprised when he just leaned close to his mic and said, "I'm so sorry. Apologies."

Then he set his bass down and turned and walked off the stage as well—leaving it empty, the spotlights still swirling around nothing.

"Um, that was Eton Mess!" The announcer was back, his voice crackling through the loudspeakers, and even though he was a professional, he couldn't quite disguise the confusion in his voice. "You have more than an hour left of Grad Nite—so be sure to visit any attractions that are still on your list! Be safe and have fun!"

As soon as he stopped talking, the music came back on, and the stage lights snapped off. The crowd started to break up and wander off—and

I looked over to see the manager gathering up her things, an annoyed expression on her face. "No," I heard her say into her phone as she strode past. "It was a complete waste of time."

I winced, feeling my heart squeeze. Even though I'd done everything I could to try and fix this, it had still been a disaster—just a different *kind* of disaster than before. I walked slowly up to the stage as the crowd thinned out, everyone off to get their last Grad Nite adventures in—because, for them, this was a night that would never come around again.

I was pretty sure I wasn't allowed, but even so, I pushed myself up onto the stage. I stood there for just a moment, then picked up the water bottle that Freddie hadn't touched. Sure enough, I could see that the little seal on the cap had been broken—and I was sure I knew by whom.

"Hey."

I turned around and saw Freddie standing on the stage behind me, looking surprised to see me there. "Hi. Um, that was . . ."

"Awful," he finished, his voice cracking as he said the word. He walked over and picked up his bass. "The manager . . ."

"I think she left."

"Yeah. That makes sense. Why would she stick around after that?" He looked at me, and I saw the hurt—the anger—in his expression. "You know, we might get fired? All of us sent back home for unprofessional behavior." He shook his head. "Maybe if we'd just gone ahead and played like we'd planned, it would have been okay. But you seemed so convincing . . ."

"Wait." I took a step closer to him. "You don't believe me?"

"I don't know what I believe!" His voice was rising. "It *is* pretty fantastical, Cass, you know that. You know what it sounds like. But maybe if we'd just gone through with it—"

"Alfie would have gotten sick. *Onstage*. Is that what you want?"

"No, but at least then it wouldn't be our faults! We wouldn't be about to get fired!"

"But you don't want to be here anyway!" Somehow, without my noticing, this had switched from a conversation into a fight, both of our voices getting loud enough that some people passing by glanced up at us, like they were trying to figure out if this was part of the show—or some kind of experimental theater. "You told me you're tired of playing the same music every night, singing someone else's songs. . . ."

"Well, maybe that was stupid. Maybe I shouldn't have tried for so much more. Shouldn't have tried to *make it in America*. I mean, how silly is that—to think that it could happen?"

"It's not silly. And I'm sorry. I—" A second later, it was like I'd just heard myself, and shook my head, getting mad all over again. "Wait, why am I *apologizing*? Do you know how much time I've spent trying to help you? Trying to fix this?"

"Yeah." Freddie slung the bass over his shoulder and folded his arms as he looked at me. "Why?"

"What . . . What do you mean, *why*?" It felt like everything I'd been attempting to do—and all the help I'd been trying to give him, everything I'd done to save this performance—was being thrown back in my face. "I guess you'd rather be having hives right now? Sorry for trying to help you."

"But *why* are you so focused on helping me? You've just said you've spent a lot of time trying to fix this. But why aren't you trying to fix things with your friends? Your *real* friends?"

I swallowed hard. "Because—this is what I'm meant to do here. The loops are to fix this."

"But that doesn't make sense. I'm someone you just met tonight. This is *your* journey. You really think this is happening to you so you can save our performance?"

"I mean . . ." I blinked at him. This was the *problem* with not having a wise guide to walk you through things. You didn't have answers to fairly basic questions like this.

Freddie took a step closer to me. "You told me yourself that there are a bunch of people from your past here tonight, people you're avoiding. Don't you think that *maybe* this is happening so that you can make things right with them?"

I shook my head, my heart beating hard, as I tried to gather my thoughts and get them in some kind of order. "That's . . . It's not . . ."

Freddie gave me a long look, his head tipped to one side. "You know what I think? I think it's easier for you to try to fix this performance than deal with the people you've hurt. The ones you keep leaving behind."

I drew in a sharp breath—it felt like I'd just been slapped. "That's not fair."

"But it's right. Isn't it?" He just looked at me for a moment. "I don't think you want this to end. I think you like being in the loops. It's the way you've lived your whole life, right? Always starting over, leaving everything behind and rebooting somewhere else?"

I felt tears spring to my eyes. And even though I was trying to deny these words, the truth of them was making me feel shaken—like the ground was no longer as steady as it had been just moments before. But rather than face this, I just folded my arms over my chest, and when I spoke again, my voice was cold. "Look, I don't think there's any fixing this." I gestured to the instruments, trying not to think about the fact that maybe I also meant *us*.

"Because either Alfie gets sick, or he doesn't play and the songs don't work. And it looks like I was just wasting my time trying to help."

"I don't think I would call it *help*, Cass. This was a disaster."

"This disaster was better than all the other ones I've seen," I said, my voice starting to rise again. "At least you didn't have an allergic reaction this time!" Freddie just shook his head, and I frowned. "You believe me, right? About Niall?"

"About my best friend betraying me? Going behind my back?" Freddie raked his hands through his curls, which felt like something that should absolutely not be allowed when you're trying to stay mad at someone. When he looked at me again, his expression was pleading. "I mean, you don't know for sure, right? It's not like you *saw* anything."

"I saw enough." For just a second, a crack appeared in the wall I'd put in front of my heart, to shield it from everything Freddie had just said to me. I felt it weaken as I looked at how crestfallen his expression was. To lose your big chance *and* your best friend was an awful one-two punch to take, even without adding the girl and her time-loop problems to the mix. "Look, I'm sorry Niall turned out to be a terrible friend. But I'm not lying to you. I wouldn't do that." Freddie just looked away, and I held out the bottle of water. "Here. Drink if you don't believe me. It's not like I want to be right about this."

Freddie just looked at me for a long moment, like he was weighing something. Then he took the bottle from me, unscrewed the cap, and took a long, almost defiant drink.

He lowered it and looked at me, a relieved smile spreading over his face. "See? I'm . . ." But almost immediately after he'd said this, it started. The red rash creeping up the sides of his neck, his eyes getting puffy. "Oh," he said, blinking, his voice heartbreakingly sad. "You were right. I'm sorry, Cass."

"I'm sorry, too." And I was—about Niall, and the performance tonight, and all the ones that had come before. But I also meant the two of us. Because even though Freddie might not remember—I wasn't sure there was any coming back from this.

"I have to go," Freddie said, already backing up, his face getting blotchier and blotchier. And before I could say anything else, he ran offstage.

I stood there, alone on the stage, blinking back the tears that were threatening to spill. As much as I wanted to ignore Freddie's words, they were bouncing around in my head, reverberating, making me think about all the things I usually pushed as far away as possible.

"Hey!" I turned around and saw a security officer looking up at me. "You can't be here," he said.

"It's okay," I said, as I walked to the end of the stage and climbed down. "I was just leaving."

10

Freddie was in his usual spot—staring at his phone, a small, hopeful smile playing around the corners of his mouth. I'd done the same routine as always—roller coaster talk, Bryony, Ms. Mulaney—barely even paying attention to what I was saying, like I was an actor in a play that had run a hundred times. Because I was focused on Freddie. I just wanted to get here, to him, to try and . . . what?

I had nearly reached him, but as I considered this question, I felt my feet slow, then stop. What was I actually going to do here?

There truly didn't seem to be any way to salvage Eton Mess's show tonight. It wasn't like I could procure a guitarist in time, and either Alfie got sick and the show was ruined, or Alfie sat it out and the show was ruined. And as I turned this over in my mind, I thought about what Freddie had

said—that maybe it was actually *better* not to have known what was goin
to happen. If it was truly just food poisoning, maybe the band wouldn
get fired for being unprofessional and walking off the stage. Maybe lettin
them know what was coming, if all that was coming was bad, was actuall
just cruel.

I looked at Freddie now, his eyes wide as he read the email, like he wa
afraid to believe it was real. There was a piece of me that wanted to wal
up to him, start the explanation, begin our night together. I wanted to ea
a meal with him and learn new things to add to the list of Freddie fact
and see if he'd come up with any new song lyrics. I wanted to walk witl
him and see the light from the Ferris wheel play over his face and feel th
butterflies in my stomach as I realized we were close enough to kiss.

But that's all it would be.

It would be just a handful of hours, hours that he wouldn't remembe
once they were over. This was never, I realized like a punch in the gut, goin;
to *go* anywhere. I might feel like I was getting to know him better eacl
time, but I was always just going to be the girl he'd met a few hours befor(
There wasn't any future here. Just a continuous fresh start.

It was like Freddie had pointed out—that this was what I did witl
everyone in my life. I started over—a new town, a blank slate. Leavin;
people behind, only to discover tonight—over all the tonights—that the
hadn't actually gone anywhere.

But as I looked at Freddie, the lock of hair falling over his forehead,
realized I didn't want that anymore. I didn't want any of this.

Freddie looked up from his phone and blinked when he saw m(
Which was understandable—I must have looked odd, standing frozen ii
front of him. While everyone else was swirling around us, off to their nex
adventure, he and I were standing stock-still in the middle of the path. Fo

just a second, and against all logic, I hoped that maybe he might recognize me. That somehow what we'd shared—even the fight we'd just had—would have carried through.

But then he just gave me a small polite smile, the kind you give to strangers. "Hi," he said, a question in his voice, like he was wondering why I was staring at him. "Sorry . . . do we know each other?"

I looked at him, trying not to let him see what I was feeling, trying to cover up the fact that it felt like my heart was breaking. Then I took a breath and made myself reply. "No," I finally said. "We don't."

And then I turned and walked away.

10

I walked away from Freddie, tears stinging my eyes as I realized he'd probably already forgotten that brief interaction we'd just had. Why would he have held on to it? I was just a stranger, after all. And unless I did something about it, that was all I'd ever be. If I couldn't fix this situation, I was going to be stuck here. Possibly forever.

The thought was chilling enough that it stopped me in my tracks. What had started as a fun adventure, and then a problem to solve, was suddenly stretching forward as an interminable purgatory. I'd just *always* be here, at this particular Grad Nite, wearing this same dress? Never able to move things forward with Freddie or escape my past mistakes? The thought was enough to make my stomach clench. That *couldn't* be my future. I wasn't just going to accept it—I was going to do something about it.

I changed direction and started walking, fast, back toward the doors. I'd wished for this to happen, and it had happened. The lights had flickered, and then the next thing I'd known, I was stuck in this time loop. So I'd just un-wish it.

As I picked up my pace, I shook my head, annoyed at myself that I hadn't actually tried this yet. Because maybe things *would* just be that simple. Once again, I lamented the fact that my wise guide had apparently gotten held up in traffic or stuck on a Zoom call or something, because knowing these kinds of rules would have been super helpful.

I slowed down a little as I got nearer to the doors. I took a deep breath and said quietly, "I don't want another chance at any of this. I just want to be back to normal. I want this to end. I'm happy with how everything is." Even as I spoke the words, I knew they weren't entirely true. I wasn't exactly *happy* with how things were going tonight—but I was just through with all of this. It was time to leave, go back to my real life, move on. I couldn't just stay here forever, trapped in this loop and never getting to go forward.

The lights didn't flicker, but I figured that didn't necessarily mean anything. Maybe they only did that at the beginning of a wish, not the conclusion of it.

I crossed my fingers as I got close to the doors, my heart beating hard. But I was feeling secure in my knowledge that I was making the right move. Because I was *done*. It was time to end this.

I took a deep breath and stepped through the doors.

Part Three

There will always come a moment when you'll want to give up the game. This is normal! It's a challenge—and it's the challenges that make success rewarding.

—*Excalibur!* video game manual, page 24

11

W ho's ready to have the best night ever?" Sheridan yelled, running past me.

"No!" I cried in frustration. I looked back toward the doors, like they were the ones who'd betrayed me. I was back—back, once again, at the beginning.

"What's wrong?" Bryony asked, looking at me with wide eyes. "You okay?"

"Me! I am!" Manny yelled, stopping to take his selfie. On autopilot, I pulled Bryony out of the way so she wouldn't get knocked over. Then I ran my hands through my hair, my thoughts in a whirl. I had tried to un-wish this—and it hadn't worked. What was I supposed to do now? How was I meant to stop this? Where were my *instructions*?!

"Cass, what's wrong?" Bryony asked, peering at my face. "You look really pale. Like even more than usual."

I knew this joke was coming, but I smiled anyway, almost against my will. "I just . . . need to think about something."

"Think about what?" Bryony sounded baffled. "Like, what we're doing tonight? You have to make a plan?"

"Uh, kind of." I walked over to the nearby bench and sat down on it, trying to get my thoughts in order.

"What's going on?" I looked over and saw Amy and Carlos heading toward us, Amy leading the way. For the first time, I noticed the strain in Amy's eyes, the way she already seemed on edge, before anything had even happened—before the two of them had any of the fights they were going to have tonight. And I also realized that was probably the reason Amy kept coming over here. She was clearly just looking for some kind of distraction and we were closest.

"No idea," Bryony said, raising an eyebrow at me. "Cass just needs to think about something, apparently."

"Let's think about having *fun*!" Carlos practically yelled, and I saw Amy wince.

"Yeah, you guys go have fun," I said, even though I knew that they wouldn't. "I'm just going to take a second. And then I'm sure we'll see you later."

Amy still hesitated, but Carlos nodded. "Come on, let's do it to it," he said, reaching out his arm for Amy's. She followed, but I noticed her pulling her hand away, fiddling with the strap on her bag instead.

I watched them go, then looked down at the ground for a moment, trying to marshal my thoughts. Un-wishing this hadn't worked. It wasn't going to be that simple.

Even though I'd been trying my best to push them away, Freddie's words were still echoing in my ears—that this wasn't about helping him and the band. That it was about me, and all the people here that I'd left behind without explanation.

So maybe I just needed to apologize to all of them. Surely that would do it? If I had to learn some lesson here, that would cover it, right? I turned this over in my head, trying to find flaws in this logic but couldn't come up with any.

I jumped to my feet, already feeling like I was one step closer to getting my life back on track. I'd say my apologies, walk through the door, and everything would be back to normal. In no time at all, this whole night would feel like one very weird, very long dream.

"You okay?" Bryony looking relieved as I came to stand next to her.

"I'm okay," I said slowly, trying to sort out how best to do this. The easiest way, I decided, was probably just to jump right in. "I just wanted to apologize."

"Apologize? For what?"

"The thing is, I'm actually—moving to Oregon. Tomorrow." I swallowed hard after I said it. Bryony and I had had this conversation before, but that didn't make this any easier. I took a breath and said the rest all in a rush. "I know I should have told you before now. And I'm sorry." I glanced over at the streetlight, hoping that maybe I'd see a little bit of a flicker—like maybe this was enough to get things back on track.

"You're ... moving," Bryony echoed. She blinked at me, like she was trying to make this make sense. "To Oregon? *Tomorrow?*"

I nodded, feeling my heart constrict a little. I had to look away from her face, filled equally with hurt and disbelief. This exact expression was why I hadn't ever wanted to have these types of conversations—why it had always been simpler to just slip away.

"And you're just telling me now?"

"Really, I wasn't planning on telling you at all," I said, and then realized a second too late what I'd done. "I mean . . ."

"You were just going to—what, *leave*?" Bryony's eyes were wide with disbelief. "Just vanish on me?"

"I . . ." I could feel myself start to sweat, even though the night, as ever, was cool. "I thought we could have one last fun night. . . ."

"So was this why you said you couldn't go to the concert? Because you knew you wouldn't be here?" Bryony was speaking slowly, her voice shaking slightly as she put it all together. "But if you're leaving, how can you work at the Mermaid Café with me?" She stared at me for a moment, and then her face crumpled a little. "Cass. Did you even *apply*?"

"Like I said," I said, trying to ignore the fact that my cheeks were getting hot with shame, "I'm sorry. I should have told you sooner."

"You think I'm just mad about the *timing*? I'm mad that you've apparently been lying to me, for *weeks* now. That you were going to . . . going to leave me alone and not even tell me why?" The hurt and disbelief was clear in her voice, and I could see there were tears in her eyes. "You knew how hard it was for me when I got dumped and all my friends ditched me. You knew that and still . . ." She took a shaky breath, and when she spoke again, her voice was breaking, cracking with emotion. "How could you *do* that to me?"

"It's . . ." I shook my head, trying to get myself to focus. "We're both going to college in the fall. So this would have happened anyway . . ." My voice trailed off.

"Of *course* it wouldn't have." Bryony was looking at me like she'd never seen me before. "You can stay in touch, Cass. You don't always have to discard people. You don't always have to be the first to leave, just because you're worried someone's going to leave *you*."

I felt tears sting my eyes, and I took a step away. My heart was beating hard. This wasn't the clean, easy absolution that I'd been hoping for. I wasn't feeling any better. In fact, I was feeling distinctly worse, like I was on the verge of tears myself. All I knew was that I couldn't stay in this fight, with Bryony looking at me like she didn't know who I was. "I have to go—find some people. I'm sorry. . . ."

"Wait." Bryony stared at me in disbelief. "You're just leaving? We're not even going to talk about this?"

"We did talk about it," I said, even though I knew we hadn't, not really. But I wasn't sure I was going to be able to stay there any longer and see the look on her face, letting me know I was making everything worse. "I'll see you later, okay?"

"Cass!" I heard her call after me, but I was already hurrying away, not letting myself look back.

That interaction had *not* gone great, but at least I'd apologized. And I just hoped it would be enough to set things right again. And then once things were back on track, and time was moving forward again, Bryony and I could have a longer conversation about things. We'd fix it. But right now, I had to find the other people I needed to talk to. I was hoping I could find them all fast, end this thing within an hour.

I consulted the map in my head, where I kept track of locations for all these various people—usually, so I could be sure to avoid them. But now, it was very useful for tracking them down. I thought for a moment, then headed off to Cars Land.

The DJ was playing, people were dancing in front of his turntable stand, but I just ignored it all as I made a beeline for the Cozy Cone snack stands. Though as I glanced behind me at my fellow seniors dancing enthusiastically, hands in the air, it occurred to me that for all the time I was spending here at Grad Nite, I hadn't actually partaken in the most fun parts of it. There had been people to avoid and concerts to try to save—and not, apparently, enough time to dance to a DJ or go on Radiator Springs Racers again. And now, on the verge of leaving Grad Nite forever, that was suddenly seeming like a bit of a waste. But there was nothing to be done about it now—I had to concentrate on the task at hand.

I didn't have to wait long before I saw Reagan and Zach, standing in the churro line with McKenna, and I headed straight in their direction. "Hey there," I said as reached them. Reagan's eyes went wide, and so did Zach's, but McKenna just gave me a cheerful wave.

"Cass?" Reagan asked, blinking at me. "Cass Issac?"

"It's me. Look, I just wanted to apologize about the churro thing. I didn't realize they were so important to your party. But since you're already here . . ." I dug in my bag and pulled out my wallet. As I thumbed through my bills, I knew exactly the amount that would be in there—just like everything else, my money reset every time I walked through the door. I held out a twenty. "Here. Now you can buy the churros and we can call it even. Right?"

Reagan just stared at me, and Zach looked from me to Reagan, unsure. But McKenna shrugged and plucked the bill from my hand, giving me a smile. "Okay. Free churros! Thanks a lot."

"That's really all you have to say?" Reagan asked, sounding shocked.

"I mean, I'm sorry," I said again, in case that first one hadn't counted. "So—the churros will make up for everything, right?"

Reagan exchanged a look with Zach, but neither of them said any-thing. And after waiting a few more moments, I figured I'd done what I came to do. "Great," I finally said, and turned to go back where I'd come from. I tried to tell myself that it was fine, that things were even now, the scales balanced, but it really didn't feel that way.

Doubling back to the Ferris wheel, I tried to tell myself that how someone took my apology was not in my purview. All I could do was apol-ogize, and anything else was *their* issue. Right?

As I walked, I realized that I was about to pass the merchandise kiosk—the one staffed by Johnny from Provo, Utah, the one that never seemed to have the Mickey graduation ears I wanted to get for Bryony. I figured by this point in the night, the Emmas would have already been there and Emma R. would have purchased her ears already. But it couldn't hurt to check.

There were two chaperones ahead of me, buying baseball caps. While I waited for them to finish, I walked around the kiosk, trying to see if I could spot the graduation ears—but of course, I didn't see any. When the chaperones walked away with their bags, I headed over to Johnny, who was leaning back in his chair.

"Are you finding everything you wanted?" Johnny asked, and I just blinked at him. He nodded toward the kiosk. "To buy?"

"Oh right," I said. "Um, no, actually. You don't have any of the gradua-tion Mickey ears left do you?"

"Not this time."

"Wait," I said, wondering if I'd heard him right. "What?"

"Not at this time," he said, louder now. "All sold out. Is there anything else I can help you with?"

"No," I said, looking around at all the merch. "Thanks, though."

"I hope you find what you're looking for," Johnny called after me as I turned to go. "Maybe at another kiosk," he added.

I took a breath to say something—I wasn't even sure what, it was just that this interaction seemed a bit *off*—when a group of three friends ran up to the kiosk and started exclaiming over the merch. Deciding to put it behind me, I picked up my pace as I hurried toward the Ferris wheel, where I knew Greta and Nora would be soon.

I heard two familiar voices and turned to see Amy and Carlos walking toward me, bickering. I took a few steps forward and turned my back, hoping that they would be too caught up in their argument to notice me.

"Because we keep having this same discussion over and over again!" Amy said, sounding exasperated.

"We're only having this discussion because you keep bringing it up," Carlos said, sounding equally exasperated.

"Because *you* won't admit you're wrong!" Amy said, shaking her head.

"But I'm *not* wrong, so why would I admit that? Just to end the discussion?"

I didn't understand what exactly was happening with them—they seemed to be having a fight about something different in all these loops. But maybe, just maybe, they'd figure it out and this would be the one that ended with them together and happy at the end, and not Amy sobbing on the bench a few hours from now.

When their voices faded out and I was sure the coast was clear, I headed off in the other direction. I had to find Greta and Nora, apologize to them, and keep this whole thing moving. I didn't have to wait long before I saw them approaching the Ferris wheel—the swinging cars, I could see now. I hurried over to them, stepping into their path before they got on line for the ride and I missed my window.

"Greta! Nora! Hello!" They both gaped at me, eyes wide with surprise. "So funny seeing you here. Such a coincidence! Anyway, I just wanted to say sorry I didn't tell you I was leaving Arizona—I should have let you know so you could have planned the next year's quiz bowl team better. I didn't know it would mess things up. My bad."

Greta let out a short laugh, while Nora just shook her head. "My *bad*?" she echoed.

I looked between the two of them. "Well, it was. But now I've apologized, so . . ."

"So you think everything is fixed?" Greta sounded incredulous. "Also—hi, by the way. We haven't seen you in years and you just start launching into this?"

"Also, how did you even know how your leaving affected the quiz bowl team?" Nora asked, frowning. "It wasn't like it was national news." Then her eyes widened in horror. "Oh my god, *was* it?"

"I just . . ." I willed my brain to think faster as I realized I'd revealed more than I should have. "I figured I might have left you in the lurch and wanted to say sorry. And now I've done that. So . . . we're good?" Just as I said this, a big group rushed toward the entrance, and it was like you could see the line starting to get longer in real time.

"Let's go," Greta said, keeping her eyes on the line. "We don't want to have to wait forever."

They started heading toward the line, not even saying goodbye, and I felt a little flutter of nervousness in my stomach. "So we're good, right?" I repeated as they got in line.

"Whatever you need to tell yourself, Cass," Nora said, glancing over her shoulder at me. Before I could reply, they were walking ahead in line, not looking back. I watched them go, wondering why absolutely none of this was making me feel any better. But maybe it wasn't about me—maybe it was just about making these apologies and saying what I needed to so that I could finally stop this. I could deal with one more slightly uncomfortable conversation, if it meant that the time loop would be over and life could go back to normal.

Luckily, I knew exactly where Bruce was going to be, and I concentrated on that as I headed toward the Hollywood Lounge. I just had to talk to him, and then I was done—home free. I slowed down, however, as I passed the trash can where Ms. Mulaney's book had been tossed out. I realized I didn't know what her timeline was—what happened between getting the call that sounded like didn't go well and seeing that she'd thrown her manuscript into the trash. But right now, there was no manuscript, just empty soda bottles and crumpled popcorn bags. I knew that throwing out her book was mainly a symbolic gesture—since it hadn't been handwritten, I assumed it was backed up on her computer somewhere. But I still remembered how sad it had looked lying there, someone's dreams literally trashed.

Just like Freddie's. The thought flashed through my head before I could stop it.

But I really didn't want to think about Freddie. I just wanted to do this last apology, walk through the doors, and then finally head home. And if that meant that Eton Mess was barreling toward another disastrous performance tonight—well, that was no longer my problem.

I picked up my pace as I walked toward the Hollywood Lounge, keeping my head down, feeling like I was in a totally different reality than all my peers who were surrounding me, laughing and yelling and heading to their next ride, or off to get some snacks. I made a beeline for the table I'd been at with Freddie when Bruce walked up to us.

I'd only been there for a moment when I felt, right on cue, my stomach grumble. In other loops, this was when I'd be having dinner with Freddie, talking and laughing with him and filling in my Freddie list with even more facts. But in this one, I was sitting alone, waiting for my former prom date to come by so I could have an uncomfortable conversation.

Luckily, I didn't have to wait that long. After only a few minutes, I looked up and saw Bruce heading in my direction, his feet slowing as he got closer. I stood up. He stopped in his tracks, blinking like he was trying to figure out what was happening.

I waved, figuring that I might as well get the ball rolling. "Hi, Bruce. How's it going?" I asked, even though he looked like someone who had just been hit with something heavy.

"Cass," he said, but not like a question—more like he was trying to verify that this was actually happening and he wasn't having a dissociative episode.

"Yeah, hi, it's me. I just wanted to say," I said, deciding for once to dispose with my line about being so surprised to see him there, "that I shouldn't have texted right before the prom and bailed on you. That wasn't fair to you. So—sorry." I nodded, waiting for a wave of relief to wash over me, to alleviate the guilty feeling in my stomach that I still got whenever I thought about Bruce and how everything had gone down. But that didn't happen.

"Okay, this is beyond weird." Bruce was still looking at me like I was something out of a bad dream. "I guess we'll just skip over the fact that we're both here at Grad Nite? And you don't even seem surprised to see me?" He stopped and shook his head, then took a deep breath before continuing. "But putting all that aside . . . if you didn't want to go to the prom with me, why did you agree to?"

I swallowed hard. The last thing I wanted was to have a *conversation* about this. I wanted to apologize and get out. "It wasn't that I didn't want to go."

"I mean, why make all those plans if you never had any intention of following through on them?"

"I did," I insisted. "It was just . . ." All at once, I flashed back to the night of the prom. What had actually happened. Not what I'd told Bruce—and frankly, myself—had happened.

I'd been getting ready for the prom in my room. I'd been fixing my hair, and excited butterflies were dancing in my stomach despite the fact Bruce and I had been clear that we were only going as friends.

But then I'd looked through my window—the one that faced his—and I'd seen Bruce standing in front of his mirror. He was adjusting his bow tie, his expression happy and nervous and hopeful. In that moment, I'd seen that he liked me as more than a friend. And this made it clear to me that we'd both been pretending—because I liked him as more than a friend. I had from the first night we'd met, arguing about pizza delivery, when I teased him about the fact that nobody was named Bruce anymore.

This realization—that our just-friends decision was basically a sham—was enough to shake me. I pulled my curtains shut and sat down on my bed. I knew on some level that this should be a *good* thing. We liked each other! And this could be a great night!

But then I came back to reality. We were leaving in two days for San Luis Obispo—and of course, I hadn't told Bruce. But what would be the point of starting something that was only, in a matter of days, going to have to end? It had been impossible enough to try and sustain *friendships* once I moved. Even though I'd never tried, I knew that it would be even harder to carry over a romantic relationship. Not to mention more devastating when it would invariably all fall apart.

And so, sitting on my bed in my prom dress, I'd known what I had to do. I was doing the thing that was actually kinder in the long run—saving us both a lot of trouble and heartache.

I'd texted Bruce I was sick, and turned off my phone so he couldn't write me back. Then I'd put on sweatpants, hung up the dress I knew now I'd never wear, and headed downstairs to tell my dads I wasn't feeling well.

And now, thinking about it, I wondered why they'd just accepted this story. They hadn't asked any follow-up questions, or talked to me about it . . . and shouldn't they have?

But I shook my head, trying to push this away—and feeling almost disloyal for even thinking it. This wasn't about my dads. This was about trying to take responsibility for what happened with Bruce. It was time to say my piece and get my life back on track. "Look, I just wanted to say sorry, okay? That's all."

"That's *all*?" Bruce echoed incredulously.

"Yeah," I said, picking up my bag and starting to walk away. None of the interactions had gone like I'd hoped, but this one was worse than the rest. "Just—sorry, and . . . have a good rest of your night!" Even as I said it, I wondered if this interaction with me was going to make it inevitable that he would *not* have a good rest of his night. But I couldn't do anything about that right now.

I headed back toward the entrance, nearly running as I pushed past people on my way out. With every step, I was sure that I'd done it. This was over—and my regular life was just across that threshold. As I passed the streetlamp, I thought, very carefully and clearly, *I just want to go back to how things were. Back to normal again.* I glanced hopefully at the light, looking for any sort of a flicker—but didn't see one.

As I reached the exit, I told myself that was fine. The lack of a flicker didn't mean anything. If Freddie was right, and this *was* about me, I'd done what I needed to do. Which would mean that this time loop nonsense was over now. I could practically *feel* it.

And with that thought carrying me forward, I took a deep breath and walked through the door.

12

W ho's ready to have the best night ever?" Sheridan yelled.
I blinked at him.

It hadn't worked.

I was back.

I had done the one thing I could think of to do to end this, and it hadn't achieved anything. What did that mean?

What was I supposed to *do*?

Was this just my life now? Never moving on, never moving forward, just endlessly starting over?

"Me! I do!" Manny said, stopping to take his selfie and causing the same bottleneck as always.

"We need to move," I murmured as I navigated Bryony out of the way, my thoughts spinning. I walked over to the bench and sank down on it. Attempting to help Freddie hadn't worked. Un-wishing this hadn't worked. Trying to make amends hadn't worked. So was I just going to be stuck here, at Grad Nite?

Forever?

"That was close," Bryony said, and I mouthed the words along with her, feeling in that a growing sense of dread and unease. Were we going to keep having these same conversations? These same discussions? For *eternity*?

"So, what should we do first?" Bryony asked, as she looked around, her voice bright and energetic. "I definitely want to do Radiator Springs Racers—you do, too, right? And Spider-Man . . ." She looked down at me and her smile faltered. "Cass, are you okay?"

I shook my head—I didn't even feel capable of pretending anymore. Because why say I was okay and then stumble my way through the night, knowing I'd just have to do it all over again, and *none of it would matter*? What was the point?

What was the point of *any* of it?

"I'm not doing so great," I said, my voice coming out faint. It was also how I felt—like the world had just started spinning much too fast. I suddenly remembered a fact about *Groundhog Day*. According to the screenwriter, he'd intended Phil to be stuck in his loop for *decades*.

The thought of that much time, trapped here, crashed down on me like a load of bricks. I couldn't do that. I *couldn't*.

But what if I didn't have any other choice? What were my options?

"I'm going to go get you some water," Bryony said, like I knew she would, already backing away.

"Thank you," I said faintly, as tears sprung to my eyes. "You're such a good friend."

"Just sit tight, okay?" she called, already hurrying away.

I hunched forward, putting my face in my hands, trying not to notice that my heart was racing and my breath was coming shallowly—not great signs, but then, probably reasonable responses to learning that you might be stuck in a loop in perpetuity.

"Cass?" I sat up and saw that Amy and Carlos were walking toward me, Amy frowning. "What's wrong? Are you okay?"

"And where's Bryony?" Carlos asked, looking around.

"She went to go get Ms. Mulaney," I said dully, since I knew that was exactly what would be happening now. Bryony would show up with Ms. Mulaney and a bottle of water. The manuscript would scatter. She'd get a call from her agent with bad news.

The thought of having to live through it again—of nothing ever changing, of this being my life—was enough to make my heart pound again.

"We should get you some help," Amy said, looking more and more worried.

"Help's coming," I assured her. "I mean, as much as one can be helped when there's no future and just an endless purgatory."

"Uh. What?" Carlos asked, widening his eyes at his girlfriend.

"Yeah," Amy said, looking more worried than ever. "What does that mean, Cass?"

"Hi!" Bryony ran toward me, water bottle in hand, Ms. Mulaney next to her.

"Are you okay?" Ms. Mulaney asked. "Bryony said you were sick." She looked at Amy and Carlos and gave them a nod. "Hi, you two. Cass just needs some help, and it might be easier without a crowd, okay?"

"Okay," Carlos said easily, starting to walk away, reaching out for Amy's hand. She pushed it away.

"What do you mean, *okay*?" she asked, shaking her head. "Our friend needs help and you're just going to walk away?"

"Uh, yeah, when a teacher tells me to I am," Carlos said. "What's the big deal?"

"The big deal is that you have to be there for your friends!"

"But not when you're specifically told *not* to be there!"

"Guys," Ms. Mulaney said, her voice firm. "Please just take this elsewhere, okay?"

I gave Amy a nod, and she shot me a faint smile in return. Then she and Carlos walked off—Amy, like always, avoiding holding his hand by playing with her bag strap.

"What's going on?" Ms. Mulaney asked.

"I just . . ." I started, taking the water bottle with shaking hands. "I just don't feel great. Everything is spinning and . . ." I swallowed hard. I didn't know how to explain that we'd had this conversation before, that I'd lived this night before, that the enormity of *infinity* was rising up to swallow me whole, like a whale.

"Let's go to First Aid," Ms. Mulaney said. Her voice was getting teacher-serious, like she wasn't going to brook any arguments, and this wasn't a discussion. "It's that way. . . ." She gestured, her tote bag slipped, the contents spilled out. I watched it all happen but didn't make any move to help. What would be the point? This tote bag was going to forever crash to the ground, whether I picked up the pens or not. It would be a literal exercise in futility, and one I had no interest in undertaking at the moment.

"Let me get that," Bryony said, picking up the rubber-banded pile of papers.

"Thanks," Ms. Mulaney said, tucking everything back in her bag.

This was normally when I asked about the pages that I knew were her novel. But I also knew what happened to the novel by the end of the night. So why bother having the conversation? The agent didn't like Ms. Mulaney's book. Eton Mess's performance ended in disaster. Carlos and Amy would break up. And all of this would just keep happening, over and over again, and there was nothing anyone, especially me, could do about it.

"Bry!" As expected, the Emmas were coming toward us, Emma R. carrying her plastic Disney bag.

"Hey, guys," Bryony said, giving them only a half smile before she turned back to me, her eyes worried.

"Hi, Ms. Mulaney," Emma R. said. "I thought you were going to be in the chaperone area?"

"I was," she said, nodding. "But Cass isn't feeling well. I'm going to take her to First Aid."

"I'll come," Bryony said immediately.

"There's no point." I let out a shaky breath, trying to regroup. "I mean, I think I just need to lie down. See if the dizziness stops. But you—you should hang out with the Emmas. Go on the real roller coasters. Have fun. You deserve that." Tears were leaping to my eyes again, and I blinked hard, trying to keep them at bay.

"I don't want to just ditch you."

"No, you should have a good night," I said, standing up on unsteady legs. "You all should. And I'll join you when I feel better. Promise." I wasn't sure I sounded at all convincing, but Emma J. and Emma Z. nodded, clearly ready to move on with their nights.

"I don't know," Bryony said, her brow furrowed.

"It's for the best," I assured her. "Really. We'll hang out again."

"Let's go to Guardians!" Emma R. said. "And then maybe later you can join us, Cass? When you're feeling better?"

"For sure," I lied, already starting to walk in the direction Ms. Mulaney had pointed.

Ms. Mulaney directed us toward Carthay Circle, and we walked in silence for a moment or two, Ms. Mulaney shooting me concerned looks, while I just concentrated on putting one foot in front of the other. "You're in a lot of pain, huh?"

"Yes," I said, hearing my voice catch. I knew I was a few minutes at best from bursting into tears. "I really am."

She pointed ahead of us, and I could see a door I'd never noticed before. It was tucked away, but printed on the glass door, unmistakable, was FIRST AID. "I can tell," she said, shaking her head. "And on your Grad Nite, too. It doesn't seem fair. You only get to have this once."

"Yeah," I said sarcastically, with a short laugh. "Sure." Ms. Mulaney glanced over at me, surprised, when her phone rang, just like I knew it would. She reached into her tote bag for it, and her eyes widened when she saw her screen. "This—this is a call I really need to take," she said, her voice nervous and hopeful.

"I'll get myself to First Aid." We were just feet away, after all. "And . . . just . . ." I took a breath. I knew I couldn't do anything about what she was about to go through, but I wanted to try and mitigate what I could. Even though it didn't matter, and it never would. "You're the best teacher I ever had. And I think you're great. No matter what what anyone says. Okay?"

Ms. Mulaney smiled at that, looking touched, and I nodded at the ringing phone in her hand. "Good luck," I said, and turned and hurried toward First Aid. I glanced behind me to see her take a deep breath and answer the call.

"Hello? This is Courtney Mulaney."

Ms. Mulaney walked away, and I stood by the entrance, hesitating. This was usually the time of night I would have gone to find Freddie, back when I still had some hope about what the night could bring, when I still thought I might be able to fix anything. But there was nothing else to do—nobody I wanted to see, nothing that was going to change. And so, going to the infirmary did sound like a good idea. It would be a place, at least, where I could sit in a quiet room for a little bit and try and grapple with what was happening.

I must have really looked bad, because the nurse running First Aid—her name tag read HELEN, PISMO BEACH, CALIFORNIA—asked me a series of check-in questions and then pretty quickly showed me to a room lined with narrow blue cots with white sheets, blankets folded on the foot of them. The room was quiet and dark, and seemed so peaceful I felt my shoulders drop a little bit just looking at it. She checked my vitals and took my temperature but seemed assured I didn't have to leave the park and go to the hospital—that I was just dizzy and needed to get my bearings.

"It happens with motion sickness sometimes," she'd said as she pointed out the cot for me to take. "Especially on Grad Nite. You kids do the rides over and over again and sometimes the inner ear just can't take it. But if the vertigo gets worse, let me know, and we can get you to a hospital." She then took my information, and Ms. Mulaney's information, and then headed out, turning off the lights behind her.

I lay down, curled into a little ball, and closed my eyes. I let myself imagine that, somehow, when I opened them, I'd be back at home, and this all would have been a bad dream.

And with that thought in my head, I drifted off to sleep.

★

"Cass?"

I opened my eyes and blinked. I wasn't at home. It wasn't all a dream. I was in First Aid at California Adventure, on Grad Nite. I hadn't actually gone anywhere—I'd just taken a nap. Bryony was standing over me, looking worried. "Are you okay?"

"How are you feeling?" Nurse Helen asked as she bustled in, snapping on the light. I squinted against it.

"Better," I said, pushing myself up to sit. I didn't feel better. In fact, I felt exactly the same—but I didn't want to deal with the nurse calling an ambulance I didn't need.

"It's almost over," Bryony said, her mouth twisting. "You missed it."

"I really didn't," I assured her, rubbing my eyes.

"What?"

"Nothing—sorry. Still fuzzy-headed." I pushed myself up to standing and grabbed my bag. Then I picked up my jean jacket and pulled it on—it was cold in here without the blanket.

"We need to get going," Bryony said, looking down at her phone. "We have to go get the bus."

I blinked at her, taking in what she'd just said. "Because Grad Nite is over," I said slowly. "Because it's ending."

"Uh, right," Bryony said, exchanging a look with Nurse Helen. "You *sure* you're okay?"

"I'm great!" I felt myself smile for what felt like the first time in forever.

"So much better. We should go." I grabbed Bryony's arm and pulled her out of the infirmary, calling my thanks to Nurse Helen behind me as I went. How had I not thought of this? I'd always left *before* Grad Nite ended—enough things had always gone wrong that it just made sense to start things over. But I'd never stayed for the whole night. Maybe this was the missing piece! Maybe this was how I got back on track—I just had to let the whole night play out. Could it be that simple? I felt hope flare in my chest.

"You really missed a lot," Bryony said, matching my pace and falling into step with me as we joined the crowd of seniors and chaperones streaming for the exit. I'd never seen people here this late at night—and there was a distinct difference. They seemed tired and happy, and nobody was walking as fast as they had when the night had kicked off.

"I'm sorry," I said, meaning it. If this was the last time—if now I was finally getting to leave—this would be her Grad Nite, the one she remembered. And we hadn't been able to spend any of it together.

"Don't be sorry," she said immediately. "I'm just bummed we didn't get to spend time together. I'm glad you're feeling better, though."

"So what did I miss?" I asked, giving her a quick glance before looking ahead of me, focusing on the exit. We'd walk through it with everyone else and then maybe—*hopefully*—I'd be able to keep going. I never thought I'd be so excited by the possibility of walking into a parking lot, but it had just turned into the promised land.

"Oh man, so much." She started ticking things off on her fingers. "The Emmas are in some kind of fight, I don't know what's going on. Emma R. doesn't either—but Emma Z. and Emma J. were on their phones practically the whole night and wouldn't tell us why. And! Sheridan was right after all—there was a celebrity here, it was Tabitha Keith! But then a picture showed up on DitesMoi that let everyone know she was here, and she got swarmed and had to be escorted out by security. Everyone was filming her; I felt so bad. . . ."

I nodded, feeling my heart squeeze as I remembered the heartbroken girl sobbing in the bathroom stall next to me. I'd promised to help her—but hadn't. And now if things worked out, I wouldn't ever be able to do anything about it.

"Amy and Carlos broke up! Can you believe it? And Ms. Mulaney seems really upset about something, but I don't know what. And we all went to watch the band play, and it was a disaster. Like, two of them got sick *onstage*. They're already trending. It's really bad, these guys are a joke now. And I, um . . . saw this guy I thought was really cute."

I whipped my head over to look at her and clocked the blush rising in my best friend's cheeks. "You did?" I asked, wondering if she was talking about the person I thought she might be. "What did he look like?"

"Brown hair, tall," she said, a dreamy smile appearing on her face. "But I first noticed him because he was wearing a *Cereal* shirt." I nodded, feeling vindicated that I'd gotten this right—Bryony liked Bruce! I knew it. I hid my smile by pressing my lips together. "Oh, *Cereal* is this podcast I like," she added, deadpan, raising an eyebrow at me.

"I know," I said, a defensive note creeping into my voice.

"I just think you'd like it if you gave it a chance. It's pretty much my favorite thing ever. And then we could talk about it. . . ."

"Wait a second." We were now in a scrum of people all heading for the double doors. They were flung wide open, and people were walking through—and then continuing to walk like this wasn't a rare and precious thing. "You actually want me to listen? I thought we were just joking around about it."

"It's important to me," Bryony said quietly, and I blinked.

"Oh. I'm sorry, I didn't realize."

"This way to your buses!" the cast member nearest to the doors called, making me jump. "We hope you enjoyed your once-in-a-lifetime Disney Grad Nite experience!"

I steeled myself, but didn't stop. I was moving forward with the crowd, surrounded by my fellow seniors. I kept my eyes fixed on the patch of asphalt just past the doors. I was so close—I was almost there. And maybe when I crossed through, this would all be over.

I took a deep breath and walked forward.

13

W   ho's ready to have the best night ever?" Sheridan yelled.

I sighed, then tugged Bryony out of the way before anyone could run into her. The brief flare of hope I'd felt at the idea of an escape hatch had been quickly extinguished. Of course it wasn't going to be so easy as just letting the night unspool.

Which meant I was back where I'd started.

Which was nowhere.

"Are you okay?" Bryony asked. She was looking at me, her expression worried.

"Nope," I said with a weary sigh. "Maybe you should go get Ms. Mulaney. . . ."

I took the same cot as before and curled in a tight ball. What if there really was no escape? What if this was just it, forever? I let my eyes close. I wasn't tired, exactly. But if I was asleep, I could block out the reality of what I was living through. I pulled the blanket over me and let my eyes drift closed.

15

The thing about lying around First Aid in a theme park is that it gets boring after a while.

17

curled on my side, staring straight ahead of me. I'd tried to sleep, but it wasn't coming.

And the blanket was getting really scratchy.

19

I was lying on the cot, shivering in the air conditioning. Feeling like I needed more warmth than the scratchy blanket, I sat up and picked up my canvas bag.

When I reached for my jacket, my wallet caught my eye. I smiled as I looked at it, an idea occurring to me.

If I was really going to be stuck here—and nothing *actually* mattered—I might as well start having a little more fun.

20

W ait, I don't get it," Bryony said as she followed along in my wake. I was running flat out, heading for Johnny's merchandise kiosk, and she was trying to keep pace behind me. "What do you want to buy?"

"Everything!" I called over my shoulder.

When we got to the kiosk, as I'd expected, the Emmas were already there, and Emma R. was taking her blue plastic bag from Johnny. "Any more Mickey graduation ears?" I asked, breathless. Bryony joined me, breathing hard.

"Just sold the last one," Johnny said, nodding his head toward Emma R.

"Mickey graduation ears?" Bryony asked, her face lighting up.

"Look!" Emma R. said cheerfully, pulling them out of her bag. "Also hi, Bryony! Hi, Cass." She glanced over at the other two Emmas, who were huddled over Emma Z.'s phone, just like I'd expected them to be.

"Oh, that's so cute! I might need to get them," Bryony said.

"Not from him," I said, nodding to Johnny.

"Nope. Like I said, I'm out," he said. He raised an eyebrow at me. "How's this night going, Cass?"

I blinked, wondering how he'd known who I was. But a second later, I remembered that Emma had just called me by name—not to mention the fact I was carrying a monogrammed bag.

"It's good," I said, giving Johnny a nod. "So I think we want to buy . . . a lot of stuff."

"We do?" Bryony echoed, frowning. "Since when?"

"Well—I do," I corrected. This was going to be a shopping spree with *no* consequences, and I couldn't wait. I could buy whatever I wanted, and then it would be like it never happened. A second later, I realized that this also meant I wouldn't be able to *keep* any of it. But I didn't want to focus on that right now.

"So I'll get one of everything," I said, with a decisive nod. "And whatever you want, Bryony. And then we can hit some of the other stores, too!"

"Uh . . ." I saw Bryony exchange a glance with Emma R. "I'll get one souvenir, I guess? But you don't need to pay for it."

"Get whatever you want! It's not like money matters!"

"Doesn't it?" Emma R. asked, looking alarmed.

"Not to me," I said blithely, already pulling sweatshirts and baseball caps and water bottles from the kiosk.

"Isn't this going to be a lot to carry around?" Bryony asked, eyes wide as she took in my haul.

I just shook my head and started piling up as many things as I could grab. "It'll be fine."

"No, it's a good point," Emma R. agreed. "What if you want to go on rides? You won't be able to."

"It's fine!" I snapped, hearing my voice get shrill. "This is supposed to be fun. So just go wild."

The total came to an amount I had to blink at. It had a *comma* in it. And even though I knew that this wasn't real—and it would all be reset—my heart was still pounding as I handed over my credit card, the one that was linked to my dads' account and was only supposed to be used in case of emergency.

"You sure about this?" Johnny asked, looking right at me.

"Yes!" I said, maybe a little louder than I needed to. Wasn't he supposed to be encouraging me? What kind of salesman was he?

"Okay," he said with a nod as he tapped my card. As I waited for it to go through, I felt my pulse race. What if it got declined? But a second later, a very long receipt printed out, and I scribbled my name on the line.

Everything I'd bought filled up five bulging bags, and even though Bryony took two, it still wasn't easy to carry. But it was *fun*. Right? Already, the thrill of picking things out was beginning to fade, and I wasn't feeling any spark of joy as I looked down into the bags. I couldn't even remember all the things I'd bought. And it was *night*—why had I gotten sunglasses and a misting fan?

Bryony and the Emmas headed to ride Soarin', but I couldn't with my bags, which was exactly what Emma had pointed out. But I told myself that it was fine, as I walked to a nearby bench and dropped all my bags. I had just started digging through them—I was thinking I might put on one of my new sweatshirts; I'd bought five—when my phone rang.

I pulled it out. Seeing OSCAR CELL on the phone screen, I answered immediately. "Hello?"

"Cass. You're conferenced with both of us."

"Is everything okay?"

"Why are you spending a small fortune at Disneyland?" Angelo asked, his voice angry.

"Don't worry about it," I said, shaking my head. "It doesn't matter."

"Doesn't *matter*?" Oscar echoed, sounding furious. "Of course it matters. That's our money you're spending there."

"You're going to pay us back," Angelo said, and even over the phone, I could picture him shaking his head, practically see his disappointed expression.

I started to agree—anything to make it so they weren't mad at me and end this conversation. But then something stopped me. "Wait," I said. "How am I supposed to pay you back?"

There was silence on the other end. "Well," Oscar said, sounding like he was trying not to smile, "I would suggest getting a job."

"I was *going* to get a job," I said, and I was surprised to hear that my voice was shaking. "I was going to work at the Mermaid Café with Bryony all summer. But then you told me we were leaving. . . ."

"Hold on, now," Angelo said, sounding confused. "You said you were okay with that."

"I know." I ran a hand through my hair, trying to get my thoughts together. "But did I really have a choice?" I blinked at that, surprised. I hadn't even known I'd thought that. Why was I suddenly fighting with my dads about it? All of a sudden, I thought about what Freddie had said— that I was mad at them. And about the flare of anger I'd felt toward them when I'd thought about prom night—how it seemed like they were more interested in making sure I was going along, as usual, than in what was happening in my life.

"Cass," Oscar said, his voice surprised. "We didn't know . . ."

"I have to go," I said quickly. I wasn't sure what conversation I'd wandered into, but I wanted to get out of it as soon as possible. "I-I'm sorry about the money. I'll pay you back."

"Cass!" Angelo said, but I was already hanging up. I knew they wouldn't remember this, but I would. I tried to push this away, tell myself that I was fine. Just like I always was.

A second later, though, I could feel doubt creeping in. Was that true? *Was* I always fine? Or had I kept moving, always looking ahead, so that I wouldn't ever have to think about this?

My phone was ringing again, and I knew without even having to look that it was my dads. Of course they were going to want to talk this out. And if I turned off my phone to ignore the calls, I had a feeling that there would soon be an announcement, summoning me, my name echoing over the whole park.

There was just one thing to do. I left the bags behind on the bench and headed for the exit.

21

I lay on my back, wide awake, staring up at the ceiling. I was back in First Aid, which had become very familiar to me.

I'd tried to sleep through this. I'd tried to go on a shopping spree. But I knew, deep down, that I couldn't spend my whole life this way—avoiding things and hiding and distracting myself. I knew it was time to go.

I pushed myself up to sitting and picked up my bag.

Nurse Helen stuck her head into the room and smiled when she saw me upright. "Feeling better?"

I nodded. "Thanks. I think I just needed a moment."

"I'm glad. You'll want to have fun while you still have time!" She gave me a smile before heading out, and I just sat there for a moment, taking in her words. Thinking about all the things I'd never done because I didn't have the time—and flashing to the keyboard under my bed, the one that came with me on every move, but that I'd never really learned to play.

It hit me that time was suddenly something that I had a *lot* of.

So what did I want to do with it?

Part Four

Above all, don't forget about building your skill level! It takes time and practice and above all, patience. But you'll be rewarded. (Literally! With Treasure Tokens™!)

—*Excalibur!* video game manual, page 37

22

tried to tell myself, as I walked up to the door that led backstage, that it wouldn't be *stealing*. I was borrowing, if anything. And everything was going to reset, so who would be bothered by it?

I'd gone back to the usual routine—telling Bryony to go on the roller coasters, and then splitting off from Ms. Mulaney when she got her phone call—which meant I was free to do some light breaking and entering.

But it wasn't even really *breaking*, I reasoned as I looked around before pushing through the wooden door and walking along the path that led to backstage. It wasn't like anything was locked here. I was pretty sure it was only breaking in if you had to, well, *break in*. Right?

I'd tried to time it as best I could, even though I didn't really know where Freddie was, since I hadn't met him in this loop and we hadn't gotten food or spent any time together. Probably he was off getting Irn-Bru for Niall, to apologize for daring to pursue his own dreams . . . not having any idea that Niall was going to do everything he could to wreck them.

I pulled open the unmarked door, and all the stagehands looked up from their poker game at me.

"Can we help you?" Violet asked.

"Oh," I said, blinking and looking around. "This isn't—the bathroom?" They all just shook their heads. "My bad! I'll just . . ."

23

waited outside the door, feeling my heart beat hard. I knew that there was a window here—after all, I'd lived it. There had been a moment when I'd left the dressing room and walked out to see all the stagehands were gone and I was all alone in the hallway. So I just had to find the right timing and I'd be home free.

"Okay," I muttered to myself. I knew there was only so long that I could stand outside a door I wasn't supposed to be near without attracting attention and questions that I really didn't want. It was time to just go for it.

I pulled open the door, stepped into the hallway, and held my breath as I looked around. It was totally empty, but I wasn't sure how long that was going to be the case. Acting like I had every right to be there, I walked with purpose down the hallway, where I knew the instrument cases were.

As usual, the guitars were lined up, ready and waiting, but I looked past them to the cases of other instruments that seemed to be stored in this backstage area. Obviously I couldn't take a whole piano, but surely I could filch a keyboard. I was just starting to examine them when the door behind me banged open, and I jumped.

Niall was standing there, looking as surprised to see me as I was to see him.

I paused for just a second, trying to recalibrate. Normally, by this time Niall was already back in the dressing room with the other members of Eton Mess, telling me to get lost. But a second later, I realized that since I hadn't intercepted Freddie, he'd gone ahead on the path he went down when he didn't meet me. He'd told Niall about the manager, got him Irn-Bru to soften the blow, and spilled it on my dress. I was realizing a beat too late that I hadn't factored in where Niall was in this scenario. And the answer, apparently, was right front of me, messing up my plans.

"Can I help you?" he asked with a wide, empty smile, his voice going back to lazy posh.

"I was just leaving." I gave him a nod and turned for the door, ready to duck out and hustle back to the entrance, start this whole thing over again. But a second later, it occurred to me he might actually be able to point me in the right direction. "Have you seen a keyboard around here?"

"Uh," he said, looking disconcerted. "There's a spare one in that case, I think." He pointed to one of the instrument cases. "Are you with management?"

I could practically see him weighing me up, like he was trying to figure out if I was someone he needed to impress or not. He was clearly annoyed that I was there, but wasn't sure if he could safely express that annoyance. I saw his gaze travel down to my hand, and his eyes narrowed as he clocked the wristband that confirmed I was just a regular teenager here for Grad Nite, and not someone he had to impress.

"Cool, thanks," I said, reaching for the door just as Niall took a step in front of it, blocking my path.

"You're really not supposed to be back here." His smile, the one that had never met his eyes, was fading by degrees, like someone was hitting a dimmer switch.

"Yeah," I said, crossing my arms over my chest. I wasn't smiling at all now. I was just looking at him, assessing him. He should have counted himself *lucky* to have been Freddie's friend all these years. And then to turn around and try and wreck his chances—and succeed, most of the time—was beyond galling. It was *enraging*. "And you're not really supposed to be giving people allergic reactions, are you?"

His smile dropped immediately, and I thought I saw a flicker of panic in his eyes before it was immediately smoothed out. "I don't— What do you mean?"

"I mean how you're going to mess with Freddie's water. Because you're jealous and small and petty."

He barked out a laugh, like this was just so absurd, but I could see his eyes darting back and forth—could practically hear his brain whirring as he tried to figure out what was happening. "What are you on about?" he drawled, but I couldn't help but notice that his accent had started to slip. "I haven't done anything. And that's— What a thing to say, honestly."

"You're going to," I said, folding my arms across my chest. "You know you've already thought about it. Maybe even started to plan?"

"Okay, I don't have to stay here and hear this," he said with a forced laugh. "I don't have to listen to you accusing me of something I haven't done. Who are you, Tom Cruise?"

"I . . ." I started, then frowned. "What?"

"You know. *Minority Report?*"

I shook my head. "Never seen it."

"Oh it's really good," he enthused. "It's—" A second later, he caught himself. "Why are we talking about this? I don't even know who you are. You shouldn't be here. I'm going to call security—"

"No need," I said, maneuvering past him toward the door. "I'm leaving." For just a second, I tried to think of some snappy closing line, but nothing came, so I just settled for giving him the I'm-watching-you finger point before stepping outside and walking away quickly. And in case Niall actually *was* calling security, I pushed out fast through the main door and then hustled away, ready to give this another shot.

24

knew I had to get in and get out in about three minutes if I wanted to make this work. I checked the time—10:19 p.m. Hopefully I had found the sweet spot between not being seen by Violet and the other stagehands, and being able to miss Niall entirely. Though in all honesty, I really hadn't minded being able to give him a piece of my mind. Even though I knew he wouldn't remember any of it, it had made me feel better just to tell him how awful he was.

I waited one moment more, then took a breath and pulled the door open. As I'd hoped, the hallway was empty. I walked straight up to the case Niall had pointed to, unlocked it, and spotted a keyboard. I grabbed it, closed up the case, and pushed it back to where it belonged. I figured nobody would notice. Since there were no keys in the band, it wasn't like a missing keyboard was going to turn into a huge emergency. I had just started for the door, when I heard Freddie laugh.

I froze and turned around, but the hallway was still empty. Then a moment later, I heard it again—a sound, I now realized, that was so familiar to me I could have picked it out anywhere. It was coming from the green-room, through the door that was pushed open just slightly. Even without being able to see him, I could picture it. Freddie wandering around, chatting to his bandmates, Alfie happily eating the prawns that would betray him, none of them realizing what was coming. I knew that Freddie was nervous about the manager, but he hadn't been able to share this with anyone—because in this version of tonight, we'd never met. Which seemed impossible—but was somehow the truth.

"Hey!" I jumped and turned around to see Niall standing just inside the door, staring at me.

I looked down at the keyboard in my hand, then shook my head and handed it back to him. "Sorry," I said, moving past him toward the door. "Let's try this again."

25

At 10:18 p.m., I pulled open the door, walked directly over to the case, took out the keyboard, closed it up, and left as quickly as I'd come in.

Outside the door, I blinked at the keyboard in my hands, a little amazed that I'd done it. I'd finally pulled off my first heist. But I didn't have time to bask in my victory—I knew Niall was coming along at any moment. I started walking fast, pushing out through the wooden door and stepping into the flow of the crowd again. But I could sense that I wasn't exactly blending in. I was getting some stares, which was frankly understandable—I was walking around Grad Nite with a keyboard. I needed to find somewhere that I wouldn't be in the mix of everyone—and I wouldn't encounter Bryony or anyone I knew. I was supposed to be in the infirmary recovering after all, not wandering around with a Yamaha. I stepped out of the flow of people and shifted the keyboard to my other hand, thinking.

Then I changed direction and walked the other way.

Over my nights here, I'd observed that the quietest part of the park was Grizzly Peak. There weren't as many rides that were open—the Grizzly River Run, the water ride, was closed, which only left Soarin'. There weren't as many people here—no costumed characters or photo opportunities, just the occasional person sitting on a bench, or passing through, using it as a shortcut to the Avengers Campus. But for right now, I didn't mind that things were quiet and it was a little off the beaten path. Especially since I had a feeling I wasn't going to be great at this for a while.

I sat down on a tucked-away bench and turned the keyboard on. I stared down at the keys, then tentatively pressed down on what I remembered from my long-ago lessons was middle C.

Then I googled *video to learn to play piano.*

29

t turns out? Playing the piano is *hard*.

35

Like—*really* hard.

42

t's especially hard when people slow when they pass you, like they're expecting you to be a professional musician, only to realize a second ater that you're far from it. But luckily, there weren't that many people assing by, and I *was* getting better—even if it was taking me longer than d anticipated.

But I did, after all, have time.

I had nothing but time.

55

was improving. I could tell.

It no longer sounded horrible when I tried to play a Taylor Swi
song. And the people that wandered past—I now knew them all, an
exactly when they would show up—now nodded at me occasionally. Som
of them even stopped to listen. This was a *huge* improvement, since not th
long ago, they'd been wincing and speed-walking away.

I played a chord, breathing out as my fingers found their proper pos
tions easily. I could finally do it without having to check the diagrams I
found online, and without having to place each finger down deliberately.
was finally second nature.

I smiled, pulled up the chords, and started to play "Begin Again."

65

I sat behind the piano and ran through my repertoire. I had songs I could play easily now, songs that even people passing by could recognize. I did a Disney medley, a Taylor medley, a Band of Brothers medley, and I'd even learned some classical pieces for good measure.

It wasn't like everything sounded perfect, but everything I played was recognizable as a song. After I reached the end of my last one, I played the final chord and let the sound reverberate around me for a moment before it faded out.

A few of the people walking by gave me a nod, and one of the chaperones I now recognized even gave me a few small claps as she passed. But then there was only silence, and me, sitting alone in front of the keyboard.

I realized I'd come to the end of my project.

And I had no idea what came next.

66

Almost by force of habit, I ended up back in Grizzly Peak. For the first time in a long time, when the loop had started over again, I hadn't snagged my keyboard. I wasn't sure what the point would have been. I'd wanted to learn to play the piano, and I had. But now that I no longer had this goal to focus on, I was starting to get the panicky feeling I'd had earlier, the sense of an endless expanse of time bearing down on me. Like I was staring into an abyss and the abyss was staring back.

Needing a distraction, I looked through my bag, taking the items out one by one even though I was very familiar with everything I'd brought with me. There was my small makeup bag, wallet, mostly charged phone, headphones. And that was it.

There were no surprises, nothing unexpected. When I'd packed up my bag to bring to Grad Nite, I'd had no idea that I might be packing for ... forever? I shook my head, not letting myself think like that. If I went down that road, I'd only start to spiral again. But, I reasoned as I started putting everything back, if I had known this, I might have packed some more books. Or a movie ...

I paused, struck by a thought. I plugged my headphones in, put the earbuds in my ears, and started scrolling through my phone.

67

hated to admit it, but Niall was right. *Minority Report* was a pretty good movie.

68

*P*ettigrew's *Loop* was really good, too.

69

I stared down at my podcast app, eyes widening as I took in the sheer amount of episodes.

But it was important to Bryony—so it was important to me.

Wincing a little, I pressed play on the first episode of *Cereal*.

71

No podcast should have this many episodes.

76

And nobody should be forced to listen to this many mattress commercials.

82

There was just *too much podcast*. Too many episodes—they spanned *years*. I had been listening for hours every night, walking the park in loops or sitting at a table in Grizzly Peak, and I'd barely made a dent.

90

t *was* actually pretty funny, though.

99

mean, it took a while. You had to learn all the inside jokes and get to know the humor of the hosts, Sarah and Zan. I'd started saying their catchphrases out loud along with them, not caring if the people around me thought it was odd that this girl at Grad Nite was suddenly blurting out "It's better with milk!" or "What kind of Cinnamon Toast nonsense is this?" Who cared what anyone else thought? This was all going to reset and they wouldn't remember.

But *I* would—and best of all, I finally understood why Bryony loved it so much.

I scrolled through my podcast app to find the next episode, and pressed play. The opening theme started playing, and I smiled as I turned up the volume.

109

The last mattress commercial faded out, and I pulled the earphones from my ears. I'd done it—I'd listened to all of *Cereal*. I now understood all the references that Bryony had been making since I'd known her. I felt a pang as I thought about all the time that we could have been sharing these jokes and talking about our favorite episodes ... but I couldn't go back and change that. And at least now I knew what I'd been missing out on.

Someone jostled me as they passed, shaking me out of this reverie. I looked around and realized where I was. Almost to Pixar Pier, but not quite. I looked down at my watch, wondering if this had just timed out right.

And sure enough—a second later, I saw him. Freddie, walking fast, and carrying a bright orange bottle of soda.

I moved without thinking, just stepped into Freddie's path. We crashed into each other, the bottle fell to the ground, and the contents exploded, splashing up and hitting my dress.

"Oh no!" Freddie gasped, staring in horror at the orange stain on the hem of my dress. "I'm so sorry—are you okay?"

"I'm fine," I assured him. I looked at Freddie, letting myself take it all in—the lock of hair over his forehead. His dimple. How much I'd missed him.

"But . . ." Freddie looked up at me, his brow furrowing. "Your dress . . ."

"I promise it's okay." I looked down at the orange puddle, the one that all the seniors around us were giving a wide berth to. "What about your soda?"

"No, I think it's a lost cause," Freddie said with a rueful laugh. "It was probably a kind of stupid idea anyway. I was getting it for my friend, as kind of a . . . peace offering, I guess."

"Or maybe," I suggested, "that friend is a mean jerk and he doesn't deserve a peace offering. Or orange soda."

Freddie just blinked at me. "What?"

"Nothing," I said quickly, realizing I wasn't supposed to know any of this, but finding it very hard to keep my mouth shut when Niall was involved. "Never mind."

"Well, is there anything I can do?" Freddie asked, gesturing toward my dress. "I can pay for the dry cleaning?"

"Or." I tipped my head toward San Fransokyo, where I knew Ghirardelli's was. "Maybe you could get me an ice cream?"

Freddie nodded, his face relaxing into a smile. "Yeah. I could do that."

He threw out the Irn-Bru bottle, and we walked up the pier, our feet falling into step together. I wasn't sure why I was doing this, exactly—I knew that it couldn't lead to anything. But the truth was, I'd missed him. And even though I hadn't been able to stop the disaster that the Eton Mess performance became, the time when I'd been trying to had been some of the most fun I'd had—because of him. Because of the *us* we'd been able to become for just a few hours, when he was the one person who understood what I was going through.

But none of it *lasted*, I reminded myself even as I snuck looks over at him. Which was why he was looking at me with a small, polite smile—the way that you look at a stranger. Which was, of course, all that I was to him.

"I'm Freddie," he said, in that wonderful accent, giving me a nod.

I know, was on the tip of my tongue, but instead I just smiled at him. "I'm Cass. Cass Issac."

"You're here for Grad Nite?"

"I am. Um, are you?" I asked, hoping it didn't seem too obvious that I knew the answer to this.

"No, I'm in the band that's going to be performing later. Eton Mess?"

"Oh yeah, I saw some posters for that."

"You'll have to come see us," he said as we reached the ice-cream parlor. "It should be good. . . ." For just a second, I saw a flicker of worry on his face, and I knew in that moment he was thinking about the manager who was coming tonight, and his nervousness about pulling it off. Knowing all too well how this would turn out, I had to look away for a second as Freddie pulled the door to the ice-cream parlor open and we stepped inside.

Freddie got the rocky road, like I knew he would. And having already sampled the mint chip, I chose the strawberry this time. As we collected our ice cream, I glanced over at him. I knew I could do what I'd done so many times now—explain about *Excalibur!* Go through the mental list I'd made of all the things about him. Convince him that this was happening. But as I took my first bite of ice cream—cold and sweet and good—I realized I didn't want to. I just wanted to be a girl at Grad Nite, one who'd had a meet-cute with a British musician and was having ice cream with him.

We stepped out of the parlor into the cool California night, and I felt myself shiver.

"You okay?" Freddie asked.

"Just cold," I said, starting to reach for my jean jacket, then realizing I was hampered by my ice cream. I held my cup out him. "Would you mind . . ."

"Not at all," he said quickly, taking it from me. "And you don't have to worry about me eating any," he added with a laugh.

"I wasn't," I assured him as I pulled my jean jacket on over my dress.

"I have this allergy," he explained as I shouldered my bag and took the ice cream back from him. "I can't do any raw fruit or vegetables."

I raised an eyebrow at him, trying to look like I was hearing brand-new information. "And ice cream counts? The allergen doesn't get . . . frozen?"

Freddie laughed, and I smiled just hearing the sound of it. "I don't want to risk it. I have—an important performance tonight."

I felt the smile falter on my face. "Right." I took a bite of my ice cream so he wouldn't read anything on my face. Because even though I wanted to warn him about what would happen at the performance—I knew it wouldn't change anything. That there was nothing to be done.

We walked for a moment in silence, both of us just eating our ice cream. I looked over at him, then back down at my scoop. I wasn't sure if this was . . . over now? I didn't know where things went from here. For all the time we'd spent together, we'd never before been precisely here.

"How's the strawberry?"

I gave him a smile as I took another bite. "It's great." I knew now he'd probably tell me about the Sweet Emporium, back home in Croydon. But, not even knowing I was going to, I took a breath and kept speaking. "The best ice cream, though—that's at Sweet Lady Luck."

"Oh yeah? And where's that?"

"Las Vegas."

"Vegas?" His eyebrows shot up.

"Have you ever been?" I asked, even though I knew the answer.

"Never. Always wanted to go, though. My brother, Jack, is desperate to go. He's just trying to save enough money. . . ." Freddie's voice trailed off, and he shook his head. "How do you know about ice cream parlors in Vegas? Do you live there?"

"No, I live in Harbor Cove. Like, twenty minutes from here. More in traffic." Freddie nodded and took a bite of rocky road, and I knew I could have left it there. But I found, to my surprise, that I didn't want to. "But—I used to live there."

"You *did*? That's brilliant. I didn't know anyone actually lived in Vegas. I'll have to tell Jack."

I smiled at that. "Yeah. I was there for . . . four months, I guess." I made myself keep going, even though I was very aware that this was uncharted territory. "My dads renovate houses, so we move a lot. And I used to think that I was fine with it. I really did. But . . . a friend of mine told me that maybe I'm actually more upset about it than I've let myself feel. I'm still processing it, I guess."

Freddie nodded. He was listening to me, just like I knew he would. "That sounds like a smart friend."

"He really is." I smiled, feeling a little lighter just for having shared this.

"You have to say what's on your mind, right? Otherwise, the words weigh too heavy on your heart." Freddie blinked, an expression that I recognized coming over his face. "Sorry," he said. "That just could be a good—"

"Lyric?" I finished for him. He glanced at me in surprise and I shrugged. "It just sounded like one to me. And you told me you're a musician."

"I'm trying to write the perfect song," he said, digging in his messenger bag and coming out with his black Moleskine notebook.

"You are?" I asked, surprised—I hadn't heard this before.

"I mean, I think all songwriters are, right?" Even though he bent his head to scribble the line, I could see he'd started to blush faintly. "But I feel like it's a daunting thing. And if you chase it, you'll probably never find it. I think it kind of just has to . . . appear? But maybe that's just what I say to excuse the fact I haven't gotten there yet."

"I'm sure you will." I smiled at him, even as I felt a wave of guilt hit me. Freddie was so talented, but the fact was, it wouldn't matter—his big break was just an hour away from getting undone by forces outside of his control.

Freddie's phone beeped, and he pulled it out and looked at the time. "I should really get going. I have to get ready for the show."

"Good luck," I said, trying to look nothing but supportive and happy for him.

"Thank you. I . . . um . . ." He ran a hand through his curls. "Maybe I'll see you again, Cass?"

I nodded and smiled at him. "I'm sure of it."

Freddie gave me a grin, then headed in the direction of the theater, breaking into a half run as he got closer.

I took a bite of my ice cream, then started toward the entrance that would reset all of this. But I wasn't running or hurrying to get there—I was just enjoying the walk, and my strawberry scoop. Talking to Freddie had been calming, somehow. I knew it hadn't fixed or solved anything, but maybe that was okay.

And by the time I'd made it to the wooden doors, I'd finished my ice cream.

110

O h no!" Freddie gasped as he stared at my dress.

"It's fine," I said immediately, maneuvering him around the puddle of Scottish orange soda.

"It's not— Your dress—"

I smiled at him. "Tell you what—buy me an ice cream and all is forgiven."

"Are you sure? Your dress is ruined. . . ."

"It happens all the time," I assured him. "Shall we?"

This time, I got the cookie dough. Freddie got the rocky road as usual, and I smiled at his expression when he took his first bite. "Good?"

"Amazing," he said as he grabbed some extra napkins. "You should really try this."

"Next time," I assured him as we stepped outside. "I promise."

We started to walk side by side, our feet falling in sync. "Are you having a fun Grad Nite?" Freddie asked. I let out a short laugh at that, and his face fell. "You're not?"

"It's—had some real highs and lows," I said, after thinking about how I wanted to phrase this.

"I bet it's going pretty fast, though?"

I smiled at that and took a bite of my ice cream. "That is *not* how I'd characterize it." I turned to him. "But tell me about you. What is it that you love about playing music?"

Freddie shrugged and shifted his messenger bag to his other shoulder. "Who said I love it?"

"Well—don't you?"

He grinned at me. "More than anything." He raised an eyebrow. "How much time do you have?"

"I have," I assured him with a smile, "a lot of time."

120

I was working my way through all the flavors at the Ghirardelli ice cream parlor. I tried the vanilla bean, and the chocolate, and the salted caramel. I had the coffee, and the moose tracks, and something called San Francisco Fog.

Every time, Freddie had the rocky road. And in the window we had before his phone beeped and he had to go get ready for the show, we walked around, ate our ice cream, and talked.

I'd been getting to know him before, of course—filling in the list of facts about him. But now the list was getting longer and longer as we chatted. We weren't trying to figure out my time loop, or to rescue his band from disaster. I'd given up on attempting to change the outcome of this, since it was pretty clear to me that I wasn't going to be able to. So I was just getting to know more about Freddie Sharma, filling in the picture of him a little more with every cup of ice cream, every conversation.

I was adding these things to my Freddie list, but I honestly I wasn't sure I needed to. I knew I'd remember these stories and facts about him that he was sharing with me. These details were starting to feel like they were inscribed on my heart, unforgettable. The lyrics, though, were a different matter.

I'd been trying to keep track of them ever since our first conversation, when he'd come up with the first couplet. But unlike simply knowing what his favorite TV show had been when he was a kid (something called *Thunderbirds*?), the lyrics were precise and specific, and almost every time we talked, something reminded him of a new potential lyric. I did my best to record them, typing them into my phone when I couldn't find paper, even though I knew everything would disappear the second I walked back through the doors. But the act of writing it was helping me remember.

In addition to learning more about Freddie and making sure to keep track of his lyrics, I was also sharing more about myself. It had felt so good to tell him about my dads—the truth about how I felt—that I'd started doing it more and more, the two of us exchanging information and opinions and truths as we walked around with our dessert. I told him about my friends—about Bryony, of course. But also about the other friends I'd left behind, the ones I'd tried to forget about . . . but truly never had. About how I'd treated Bruce, and how much regret I had about it. Things I never normally shared with anyone, I somehow felt like I could tell to Freddie, and know that he would listen to me.

And I was aware that everything started over for him each time—that this was always all new for him. That he wouldn't remember any of this.

But I would.

125

Freddie
- Brother named Jack
- From Croydon
- Loves Excalibur!/poster above bed/Geraldine Bewley
school project
- Weird fruit and vegetable allergy
- Rocky road ice cream/Sweet Emporium
- Surf liner up to LA for meetings
- Manager coming tonight
- Mates with Niall from school days
- Lyrics in black notebook

- Tristram's real name is Doug/Alfie is Aussie
- Always losing phone
- Mum told him he'd lose his head if not attached to his neck
- Always wanted a dog. Was planning on naming it Dodger
- Favorite TV show growing up: Thunderbirds
- Thinks George Harrison is the most underrated Beatle
- Thinks Harry Styles is the most overrated former One Direction-er
- If he could travel anywhere, it would be Alaska
- Discovered the truth about Santa too young and then had to keep the secret from Jack and his parents
- Really misses home sometimes
- Wants to write the perfect song—isn't really even sure what that means. Will know it when he hears it
- Thinks Force Awakens is the best Star Wars movie (he is incorrect about this; it is obviously Last Jedi)
- If he could have a superpower, it would be a tie between flying and invisibility (he later amended this to invisible flying; was unmoved when I told him you can't combine two superpowers)

In addition to all the facts on the Freddie list—all these details and opinions and memories—there were things I wasn't writing down.

Like the way he looked when he took his first bite of ice cream, surprised and delighted. The way he always held the door for me, the way he was always so concerned about my dress after he spilled the Irn-Bru. There was the sound of his laugh and the way he pronounced *brilliant* and the way his eyes crinkled at the corners when he really smiled. There was the way he made me feel like I had his full attention, even though he was on the cusp of a very big night and walking around and eating ice cream with a stranger probably hadn't been in his plans. There was just *Freddie*—so good and so kind. And with every one of these walks we had, I could feel myself falling for him just a little bit more.

I knew it couldn't lead anywhere—that there was no such thing as a future with someone who can't remember that they've met you. But I was having so much fun just getting to be with him for an hour or so each night, that I couldn't quite bring myself to stop it.

Not yet, anyway.

130

S o?" Freddie asked, looking over at my cup. For the first time, I'd tried his rocky road. It wasn't my favorite ice-cream flavor, but Freddie was always so enthusiastic about it, I'd thought that the time had come to finally give it a shot.

I took a bite and considered it, then gave him a smile. "Not bad."

"Are you kidding?" he asked, his voice jokingly indignant. "It's marvelous. It's not as good as the Sweet Emporium in Croydon, of course."

"What is?"

He grinned. "Well, exactly. But this is *excellent* rocky road."

"It is good," I conceded as I took another bite. And it was—it just wasn't as good as a lot of the other flavors at the parlor, all of which I'd now sampled. But I didn't know how to tell Freddie that without freaking him out.

He grinned at me. "Told you."

"Want to walk over there?" I asked, nodding toward the pier. We didn't always walk this way—we sometimes meandered past the arcade, or swung by the Ferris wheel, or backtracked toward Grizzly Peak. But for whatever reason, tonight I wanted to walk over by the pier and see the light reflecting on the water. I wasn't sure if it was always the most romantic spot in the park, or if it just felt that way because I'd been there with him.

"Sure," he said, giving me an easy smile.

We walked in silence for a few moments, and I steered us to one of my favorite secret spots in the park—the walkway underneath the Silly Symphony Swings. It was quiet there, and almost always deserted. You had a perfect view of the water, and the neon lights of the Ferris wheel. "Here's a question," I said, as we walked up to the railing. "If you were living the same day over and over again—like a loop—what would you do with it?"

"You mean like *Groundhog Day*?"

"Sure. Or, I don't know, *Pettigrew's Loop*."

Freddie stared at me, and I took a bite of ice cream to hide my smile. "You know *Pettigrew's Loop*?" he asked, his voice going high in excitement.

"I mean, it's a classic," I said, striving for a nonchalant tone.

"Right? But hardly any Americans have heard of it, which is just such a tragedy."

I shook my head. "Some people just don't have any culture."

"So—you were asking what would I do?"

I nodded. "Yeah. If you were in a situation like Bernard Pettigrew. But, I don't know, let's say here. At California Adventure."

"Oh wow, okay," Freddie said, nodding. His eyebrows drew together, and I knew that he was thinking this over—the same way he always did when I asked him a question, taking it seriously. "Well, first, I'd probably ride all the rides, just over and over again."

"Obviously."

"And then I'd eat all the food . . . and buy all the souvenirs I wanted. . . ."

"This all checks out."

"And then . . ." His voice trailed off. He leaned his elbows on the railing, and looked out over the water. "Hmm. I'm not sure."

"Yeah," I said, coming to stand next to him, leaning on the railing as well. "That's where it gets tricky, right?"

He looked out at the water for a long moment, then said, "I guess—then, I'd help people."

I turned to look at him. "*Help* people?"

"Well, yeah," he said with a small laugh. "Because that's what those movies are about, right? You go through the same day over and over again, so you get to see things nobody else does. It's almost like a superpower. And you can help people have the best day ever, because you've seen all the versions of it. Right?"

"Right," I said slowly, nodding. The wheels had started to turn in my head. I had tried to help Eton Mess—and then, when that hadn't worked out, I'd just given up. But maybe I needed to think bigger.

Before I could say anything else, Freddie's phone beeped. "I have to get going," he said, his tone genuinely regretful. "But maybe I'll see you again, Cass?"

I nodded. "You can count on it."

Freddie gave me a smile and then jogged off toward the theater. I took another bite of the rocky road. My thoughts were spinning, with Freddie's

words echoing in my head. All at once, I remembered Tabitha Keith, sobbing in the bathroom. Maybe there was a chance I could do something to
help her?

I checked the time, and realized I could just make it. I tossed the rest
of my ice cream in the trash and hurried away.

I ran into the bathroom, my heart pounding, wondering if I'd gotten the
timing right. But then a second later, I heard a snuffly sob.

I tried to think what I'd done the last time. I couldn't tell Tabitha
I knew she was the one crying in the stall. After what happened with
DitesMoi and her presence here getting blown up, someone recognizing
her from her shoes was probably the last thing she wanted.

"Um . . . Amy?" I called, remembering this was what I'd said before.

A second later, the stall door swung open and Tabitha Keith stepped
out, her eyes puffy and bloodshot. "Who's Amy?"

"Just a friend," I said, waving it off. "Never mind. Sorry."

I saw Tabitha wince as she looked at herself in the mirror. "God," she
said, shaking her head. She splashed some cold water on her face, then
blotted it with a paper towel. "I look pretty bad, huh?"

"No," I lied, hoping I pulled it off this time. "Just like you've been
crying, maybe."

"Well, that's true," she said with a sigh as she shook her hair back from
her face.

"Are you okay?" I asked, taking a step closer to her. "Is there anything
I can do?"

"Not unless you can turn back time." She ran a hand over her eyes.
"Could tonight *get* any worse?"

"Is this because of the DitesMoi thing?"

Tabitha whipped around to stare at me, her blue eyes wide. "You know about that? It's already out there?"

"Oh," I said, trying to backtrack, willing my brain to go faster. "Maybe? I kind of heard something. . . ."

She dug through her designer bag until she pulled out her phone. "I just can't believe this," she said. "I really thought I could trust my friends, you know? I didn't think they'd sell a picture of me to a gossip site."

"And you're sure that's who did it?"

Tabitha sighed. "Yeah. The picture that got sold was one with me and my friends. Nobody else would have had it. Just me and Em and River. There's no other explanation. I just . . ." Her voice cracked. "I just wanted one night, you know? One night when I get to be a regular person and nobody treats me different or stares at me . . ."

"When did this happen?" I asked, wishing once again that I had the ability to write any of this down and take it with me. "Like, what time?"

"I mean—we took the pictures pretty soon after we got to the park? By the Mater in the graduation cap by Cars Land, did you see him? It's—"

"So what time *exactly*?"

"Uh—nine forty? I don't know," she said, sounding taken aback. "And then I got a call about thirty minutes ago—telling me this was about to break. So something must have happened in between, I guess."

"Okay," I said, nodding. "I'll try to help if I can. No promises, though!"

"What?" She stared at me and folded her arms across her chest. "What do you mean—*help*? It's already happened."

"I know. But that doesn't mean it can't be fixed."

"But—" Tabitha started. Just as she spoke, I heard the crackle of a speaker.

"Make your way over to the stage," the voice on the loudspeaker said. "Eton Mess will be going on in just a few minutes!"

"I should go," I said, heading for the door. The last thing I wanted to do was to see Eton Mess crash and burn once again. Unless . . .

All at once, I realized that I might be able to do something about that, too. Not right now, of course. Or even in the next loop. But a plan was starting to form in my head, threads coming together in unexpected ways.

"Wait," Tabitha said, sounding thoroughly baffled now. "I don't even know who you are."

"Don't worry about it," I called behind me as I pulled the door open. "You won't remember this!"

131

W ho's ready to have the best night ever?" Sheridan yelled.

I pulled Bryony out of the way preemptively, and then just started sprinting full-out, my bag banging against my hip as I ran. I could hear her yelling behind me, no doubt asking pertinent questions like *Where are you going?* But if I was going to get all the way over to Cars Land in time to see what was happening with Tabitha, I couldn't stop and explain. Not that any explanation would have made sense to Bryony. What could I say? *I'm stuck in a time loop, and a celebrity told me when exactly she's going to be betrayed by her friends, so I have to rush there to make sure it doesn't happen.* I knew I didn't even have time to give her an excuse or fake a medical issue—I just had to *go.*

Judging by the yells and people saying "Hey!" as I pushed past them, it was clear that nobody really appreciated someone running at top-speed through Disneyland on Grad Nite.

"Slow down there!" I heard a sharp voice yell. It sounded like an adult—probably a chaperone—and I raised my hand in acknowledgment. The last thing I needed right now was to be delayed even further by someone deciding I should get a lecture about this.

I skidded to a stop when I reached the entrance to Cars Land and looked around frantically, breathing hard. I needed to find Tabitha. . . . I needed to see what happened here if I was going to make it right. . . .

I turned in a circle, and that's when I saw it. Mater, from *Cars*, was parked by the entrance to Cars Land. And sure enough, he was in a robe and graduation cap. There was a long line of people queued up to get their pictures taken with him, and cast members keeping the line moving.

I spotted Tabitha and two people who I assumed were the friends she'd mentioned. I looked at them closely, wondering which one of them had been the one to leak the picture. Tabitha had said that only the people in the picture—or taking it—would have had access so that did narrow the suspects down a little bit. I walked a little closer, pretending to scroll on my phone, hoping that I seemed nonchalant. . . .

"Cass?"

I froze and whirled around. The Emmas were in front of me, all of them looking surprised to see me. "Uh—hi, guys," I said, giving them a smile, while also trying to keep an eye on Tabitha's group. They'd just moved forward to pose for the photo, all three of them smiling wide.

"Hey!" Emma R. said, and Emma J. and Emma Z. waved—they looked much more relaxed than they normally did when I encountered them.

"What's up?" I asked, as I tried to sidle up a little closer to Tabitha and her friends without looking like I was a stalker. They'd gotten their photo and stepped out of line. They were hunched over Tabitha's phone, laughing together.

"Where's Bryony?" Emma R. asked, looking around.

"Yeah, I thought you guys were on the later bus," Emma Z. said. "I didn't think you'd get here so fast."

"We— That's true," I said, giving her a nod before looking back over at Tabitha. But I was too far away to see what was happening or hear any of their conversation. "I just . . ."

"You okay?" Emma R. asked, her brow furrowed.

"Yeah," Emma Z. said, shaking her head. "You seem . . ." A second later her phone beeped, and she looked down at it, distracted.

I glanced over and saw that Tabitha and her friends were already walking away. They were all laughing together—whichever of her friends was going to betray her was giving no indication of it. Or maybe they hadn't thought about it yet. Was I going to need to follow them all night? I sighed and started to head back toward the entrance.

"Uh. Cass?" Emma R. called after me. "Where are you going?"

"To try again!" I yelled over my shoulder. "Be right back."

132

Who's ready to have the best night ever?"

This time, I didn't yank Bryony out of the way—I couldn't spare the time. I said a silent apology to her as I started running, taking my wallet out of my bag as I ran, heading straight for Johnny's merchandise kiosk.

If he was perturbed by the sight of a senior sprinting full-speed up to his kiosk, he didn't look it. But then, in all the times I'd had interactions with him, he really didn't seem bothered by much. "Hey," he said, raising his eyebrows. "How can I help?"

"A hat," I gasped, looking around for one that would shield me, at least for a few moments, from the Emmas' notice so that I could help Tabitha.

I grabbed the first one I saw—it had Baby Yoda embroidered on it—and tossed it down. "As quick as possible please."

"What's the rush? I thought Grad Nite just started."

"Not for me," I said, as I thrust my card in his direction. "I have to get to Cars Land."

"And what's in Cars Land?"

"I have to help someone," I said, tapping my card on the reader he held out to me and waving off the receipt, grabbing the hat and ripping off the tags.

Johnny nodded and gave me a smile. "You're on the right track, then."

I had started to head off, stuffing my hair into the cap as I went, but this made me pause. "What does that mean?"

"It means you're on the right track," he said, pointing. "Cars Land is that way."

"Oh, right," I said, nodding, starting to run again. "Thanks!"

I ran as fast as I could to Cars Land, but even so, by the time that I got there, Tabitha and her friends were already walking away from Mater, all of them clustered around Tabitha's phone, looking at the pictures. I sighed and turned to go back to the entrance and start this over again. But I honestly wasn't sure I was going to be able to run any faster—it felt like I was hitting the upper edge of my capacity.

"Cass?"

I turned around, to see all the Emmas walking toward me. "I thought it was you," Emma R. said, smiling wide at me. "Cute hat! We were just going to go get some merch, want to come?"

"Yeah," I said, realizing too late that I probably could have bought the Mickey graduation ears since running full-out was the one way, it seemed, that I could make it to Johnny's kiosk before the Emmas. I filed this away as useful information and took a step closer. "Sure. That sounds—"

Just then, like before, Emma Z.'s phone beeped. But this time I was close enough to see her screen. I saw Emma's eyes get wide as she looked at her phone. She tapped her screen, then turned it to Emma J. so she could see it. Emma J. reacted the same way Emma Z. had—with silent surprise. I shook my head, trying to figure this out. I knew what I'd seen—but I didn't understand what it meant. It just didn't make *sense*—

But then, all at once, like puzzle pieces fitting together, I saw the answer. It had been right in front of me this whole time. Tabitha had told me her friends' names, after all. It was just an accident—the same thing had happened to me, in fact. But it was an accident that would have real consequences and would lead to Tabitha sobbing in a bathroom ninety minutes from now.

"Cass?" I turned to see Emma R. looking at me with concern. "You okay?"

"Yeah," I said, shaking myself out of this reverie, and giving her a smile I didn't feel at all. The other Emmas didn't notice—they were preoccupied with Emma Z.'s phone, both of them clustered around it, whispering in low voices. At least I had solved this mystery. But there was nothing to be done about it now—that would have to wait for another loop. "I should go find Bryony."

"Okay," Emma R. said. She looked over with concern at her friends, then back to me. "But I'm sure we'll see you later, right?"

"Oh, you can count on it." This was mostly for the other Emmas' benefit, but they didn't seem to have heard me—they were still having an intense, whispered conversation. At least I finally knew what they were talking about. I waved at Emma R., then headed back the way I came, feeling like I had made a little progress. I hadn't fixed anything—yet. But I had an idea of how I might.

"Cass!" Bryony was sitting on the bench with Amy and Carlos, Ms. Mulaney hovering nearby. She jumped up when she saw me. "What the heck!"

"Sorry," I said quickly, shaking my head. "I . . ."

"Is everything okay?" She paused and looked at me, her head tilted to the side. "Did you buy a hat?"

"Oh," I said, pulling it off my head and looking at it. I'd forgotten I was wearing it. "Right. I . . . saw it and thought—who doesn't love Baby Yoda, right?"

"It's actually Grogu," Carlos pointed out. I saw Amy roll her eyes at that, and Carlos clocked it. "What?"

"Nothing," Amy said, though I could hear the irritation in her voice. "Did I say anything?"

"You didn't *have* to say anything—"

"Okay, then," Ms. Mulaney said, interrupting Amy and Carlos's bickering. "Well, glad you're back, Cass. And now I hope you kids can have fun tonight. If you need me, I'll just be in the chaperone area. . . ." She pointed toward it. And just like I'd known it would, her canvas bag tumbled off her shoulder, and its contents spilled out onto the ground.

Amy and Carlos were still arguing, but Bryony and I bent down to help gather things up. The second I saw the manuscript, I drew in a breath.

I wasn't sure I'd be able to help Ms. Mulaney—but I knew I had to try.

133

L uckily, it wasn't that hard to get Ms. Mulaney's manuscript. I'd gone through the usual routine—but instead of leaving when she got her phone call, I doubled back behind her. I lurked out of sight, a few paces behind Ms. Mulaney while she had her dream-shattering phone call. Which meant I was there to see her take the manuscript out of her bag, look at it for a long moment—then drop it in the trash can and walk away.

Once I was certain she was gone, I hurried over and scooped it up, glad that it was still bound with its rubber band and I wasn't having to chase down loose pages. And then, with the draft of *Hurricane Madison* in my hands, I just had to find a place to read it.

I started out at a table by Smokejumpers Grill. But for whatever reason, the area that had been really conducive to learning piano was distracting as

I was trying to read. I ordered a burger to go—it was getting close to the same time that I always got hungry—and then took the manuscript with me as I headed across the park. I was keeping an eye out to make sure I wouldn't run into anyone—by this point, it was pretty much second nature. I had a map in my head of where everyone was, and where they were going to be. After this much time, I knew everyone's loops by heart.

I ended at Radiator Springs Racers. Even with the shorter lines because of Grad Nite, there was still about a half an hour wait. Which was perfect—I could read, and then when I reached the front, I could go on my favorite ride, then do it all over again. And what did it matter if it looked strange that I was by myself and reading in line? None of these people would remember it.

I opened the manuscript and started to read.

135

finished the book in three loops, reading it in line at Radiator Springs Racers. Every time I made it to the front, I would be surprised that so much time had passed—I was totally immersed in the world of the story.

It was all about this woman, Madison, an English teacher at an Orange County high school. She was dealing with personal and professional issues at work and with her friends—all as a rare hurricane bears down on the California coast. But then the book just . . . ended, with the storm getting closer and Madison not having learned all that much. I turned over the last page as I stepped up in line, wondering if I'd missed something. But no—*The End* was there as clear as anything. If I was being honest, I could understand why the agent had passed. It was *really* good—but it was just unfinished.

"Ready? Single rider?" I looked up at the cast member, who was smiling at me.

"Oh wow," I said, putting the manuscript back in my bag. "Uh, sure. That was fast." I could have sworn I'd only been on line for a few minutes.

"It comes in waves," the cast member said, giving me a smile. "Enjoy your ride."

"Thanks," I said, noting the time—10:19 p.m. I gave them a smile as I stepped forward. "I always do."

145

The plan was coming together.

I was going into each loop now with a sense of purpose—a different goal I needed to accomplish each time. I'd even taken to buying a notebook from Johnny and a pen—the notebook had the Sleeping Beauty castle on it, the pen had Stitch—so I could write things down. My lists were turning into complicated timelines and graphs, and even though it would have been *really* nice to be able to take these with me, I was doing them often enough that they were getting burned in my brain. Just like the Freddie list, or his song lyrics—at this point, I could have recited both from memory.

But each night, I picked someone new. I parted from Bryony and the Emmas and then fanned out over the park, focused on that night's goal.

I did one loop where I trailed behind Reagan, Zach, and McKenna, making note of where they spent most of their time, and when they moved to different parts of the park. I had a pretty good idea of what I was going to do to make things right with Reagan, and I noted it on my list.

Greta and Nora were a bit trickier, if only because they were more observant, both of them spotting me a few times before I learned just when I needed to hang back, look away, keep flying under the radar. But once I figured that out, and I'd been able to get a handle on where they were going and when, I devised my plan for them, too.

Bruce was a little bit harder, because seeing him always made my heart clench a little. I no longer had a crush on him. But just watching him laughing with his friends, or getting snacks, or waiting on rides, was enough to remind me of what I'd done, and how I hadn't taken responsibility—yet.

I spent one loop dashing around the park, verifying that people were where they were supposed to be, making the final adjustments to the plan, confirming that the diagrams were all lining up. I was reminded of my dads, the way that they always got before a house was being shown, when they checked and double-checked everything that could possibly go wrong, and made contingency plans for every outcome.

Now, I flipped through my notebook one last time, even though I didn't need to—I knew these plans by heart. I dropped the notebook into my bag and walked toward Pixar Pier. I crossed the bridge, looking at the lights on the water—it had never, in all these loops, stopped being magical.

I knew that in the greenroom, Freddie was preparing to go on. In the bathroom, Tabitha was crying, having already been betrayed by someone she never would have suspected. I knew where Reagan was, and Greta and Nora. I knew where Bryony was. I knew about the Emmas, and Ms Mulaney. Even Amy and Carlos.

I'd spent so many nights here, it had all led to this.

To the next loop—when I would try and make things better for every-one. When I'd say what I had needed to say for a long time. When I would actually pay off what Sheridan had been saying this whole time—and attempt to give everyone the best night ever.

I knew that I might have missed something—and that maybe I wouldn't be able to pull it off.

But I was going to try.

Part Five

It is rare to ever play a perfect game. But if you manage it—if you've learned from all your attempts and mistakes and chances and tries—be proud of yourself. You've achieved something momentous.

—*Excalibur!* video game manual, page 43

146

W ho's ready to have the best night ever?" Sheridan yelled.

I smiled as I looked around. I was back, once again, at the moment it always began. I suddenly had a new appreciation for the way Sheridan started our night. It was so hopeful, after all. Maybe I should have been following his lead from the beginning—he was the one who'd had it right all along.

And so, for the first time, I took a step closer to him. "Me!" I called out. "Best night ever. Let's go!"

Sheridan smiled at me, surprised, and gave me a nod. "That's what we like to hear, Cass! Right on."

"Uh, me too," Manny said, sounding a little like his thunder had been stolen. He lifted his phone, like he was going to take a selfie, but then just shrugged and walked away. And to my surprise, the people who normally crashed into Bryony simply ran past—the collision never even coming close to happening in this version of things.

I shook my head as I watched them go. I wasn't sure if I was going to be able to pull this off, but just knowing that I was going to try was making me feel buoyant. I felt like I was seeing this world, which had become so familiar to me, with new eyes. I took a breath, then let it out.

Tonight.

It would all happen tonight.

I'd prepped as much as I could, even though I hadn't been able to bring any of my plans in with me. But that was okay. They were locked firmly inside my head, and as soon as I could buy a notebook, I'd be able to write them down. I just had to trust that things would work out, and that I'd be able to pull this off.

"So," Bryony said, smiling at me, "what should we do first?"

"Bryony!" I pulled her into a tight hug.

"Uh. Hi, Cass," she said, giving my back two pats. "You all right?"

I shook my head and stepped back. "No. I'm not." Knowing what I wanted to say—and that I should have said this a long time ago—didn't make the actual saying of it any easier. I took a breath. "I'm so sorry."

Bryony blinked at me. "What are you talking about? Sorry for what?"

"I— My dads are moving. To Oregon. Tomorrow. And I didn't tell you."

"Wait." Bryony shook her head, like she was trying to catch up. "*What?* You're . . . moving?"

"No!" I said enthusiastically, practically yelling it. "I'm not! Isn't that great?"

"But . . . you said . . ."

"I *was* going to be moving," I clarified. "And I know I never should have gone so far down that road without telling you. But I'm going to talk to my dads. I'm going to tell them that I can't go again—not when I'd be leaving so much behind. Because I want to stay. I want us to hang out all summer and work together at the Mermaid Café—if they'll have me. And I don't want us to lose touch when we go to college. You're my best friend. You're so important to me. We can make it work—I know we can. Because I'm done walking away from the things that matter the most."

"Wow, okay," Bryony said, looking shell-shocked. A group of laughing seniors ran past us, and we stepped to the side of the path. "Those are—some big revelations. This all just happened? Like, in the last few minutes?"

"Oh no," I said, shaking my head. "It's been a long time coming. Also, I've been stuck in a time loop. I've done this, like, a hundred and forty times. Give or take."

Bryony frowned, her forehead creasing in worry. "Cass, you're scaring me. Did you hit your head or something? Do you smell burning toast? How many fingers?"

She held up three, and I pushed them away, smiling at her. "I swear I'm fine. I'm *better* than fine. I just thought you should know."

"That you're . . . in a time loop."

"Exactly!" Bryony just stared at me, so I added, "You know, like *Groundhog Day*."

"I know what a time loop is," she said faintly. "I just don't know why you think you're in one."

"Because I am," I said patiently. "It's okay if you don't believe me."

"I think you need some water or something," Bryony said, backing away. "I'm going to get Ms. Mulaney. Just stay there!"

"Not going anywhere!" I called after her cheerfully. I walked over to the bench that had become so familiar to me and sat, giving it a fond pat. To my left, I could see Amy and Carlos arguing. I let out a small sigh as I looked at them. I was going to have to talk to Amy later.

After a few moments—like I knew they would—Ms. Mulaney and Bryony came running up, Bryony carrying a bottle of water, both looking worried. I waved at them. "Hi, Ms. Mulaney!"

"Hi," she said, coming to a stop in front of me. "What's going on? Bryony said you're experiencing a break with reality?" She shook her head. "Tonight's instructions *really* didn't cover that."

"I promise I'm fine," I said. Bryony handed me the water and I took a long drink. "You didn't need to rush over here. But! I did have some thoughts about your novel."

"Your what?" Bryony asked, turning to look at Ms. Mulaney, who was staring at me, open-mouthed.

"How— How did you know about my novel?" she asked, a faint blush creeping into her cheeks.

"Because I've read it," I explained. "*Hurricane Madison.* It's so good, but there's an issue with the ending."

"When did you read Ms. Mulaney's novel?" Bryony asked, sounding baffled. "How did you even know she was writing a novel?"

"Yeah," Ms. Mulaney said, pulling her bag a little closer. "Did you go into my computer or . . ."

"Of course not," I said. "Look, I know you have that call with the agent later. I'm sorry to tell you it's not going to go well."

"I . . . What?" she asked faintly, looking gobsmacked.

"I mean, if they can't see you're talented based on this, you don't want to sign with them anyway, right? But my suggestion is to tell the story in a *loop*. Right now it just kind of ends. But if you start with the hurricane, and then we come back around to it at the end . . ."

"I . . . just . . ." Ms. Mulaney looked like she was having trouble keeping up. "I mean—I could see how that would work. I guess I never thought about . . ." Her voice trailed off, and she shook her head, like she was trying to get herself to focus. "But I don't understand *how*—"

"Don't worry about it," I said, even though I knew this was probably easier for me to say than for her to do. "Because it would work, right? Don't you think?"

"It would," she said, blinking fast. "I think it would . . ." She dug in her canvas bag and took out a pen, the one that I usually stole from her. She took the manuscript out of her bag and started scribbling notes on it.

"Cass," Bryony said, pulling me a few feet away from our teacher. "What is happening?"

"I *told* you what's happening," I said, keeping my voice patient. I remembered how hard it had been for me come to terms with it, after all. Freddie had been on board faster—but then, I'd essentially had a cheat code for Freddie. I felt some nervous butterflies start to swoop in my stomach as I thought about Freddie and what was—hopefully—going to happen later. If I pulled this off.

"A . . . time loop." I noticed that Bryony didn't sound quite as dismissive as she had before. Now it sounded more like she was trying to get her head around the concept of it.

I smiled at her. "Exactly. Now, I have to go take care of some things, but the Emmas are going to be here any moment."

"The Emmas?"

"There they are!" I pointed as they came closer, Emma R. waving cheerfully, Emma J. and Emma Z. looking much more preoccupied.

"Hi, guys!" Emma R. said, joining us. She glanced over at Ms. Mulaney, who was still scribbling down notes and muttering under her breath. "Uh—hi, Ms. Mulaney."

I pointed to Emma's bag. "Can I see the ears you got?"

"Sure!" She pulled out the Mickey graduation ears and despite everything, I saw Bryony's eyes light up like usual. "How did you know I got ears, though?"

"Lucky guess," I said, giving Bryony a small smile.

"These are really cute," Bryony said, touching the mini graduation cap and its tassel. "I might need to get some."

"It might not be possible," I said with a sigh. "I really tried. I swear."

"I thought you guys just got here?" Emma R. asked, as she put on the Mickey ears. She turned to Bryony. "Are these straight?"

Bryony reached out to adjust them, and I walked over to Emma J. and Emma Z., who were both bent over Emma Z.'s phone.

"Hi, guys," I said cheerfully. "I just wanted to tell you that you probably shouldn't sell that picture of Tabitha Keith to DitesMoi."

Emma Z. fumbled her phone, catching it at the last second before it hit the pavement, and Emma J. stared at me in shock. "How did you . . . What . . ."

"Who told you that?" Emma Z. asked, her eyes narrowed. "I mean—what are you talking about?"

"I know what happened," I said patiently, even as I snuck a look at my watch. I needed them to get on the same page as me, and fast—there wasn't a ton of extra time. I was suddenly glad for the bottle of water Bryony gave me, even if she'd gotten it because she was worried I was losing my grip on reality. I had a feeling I was going to need it—there was going to be a *lot* of running around the park tonight.

"What do you know?" Emma Z. asked, crossing her arms. She was trying to sound tough, but she kept sneaking looks at Emma J., and I could see that they both looked rattled.

"Everything. I know you were over by Cars Land, by the people taking pictures with Mater. And I know that Emma Z. got AirDropped a picture of Tabitha Keith and her friends." They exchanged a glance, then turned back to me, both looking increasingly freaked out. "It was an accident," I explained, taking them through what I'd finally put together. "One of Tabitha's friends—the other girl in the picture—is named Em. It was just a matter of AirDropping to the wrong person—and your phone must have been close enough. It could happen to anyone. But selling the pictures to a gossip site is *not* an accident."

"We haven't done anything yet!" Emma J. protested, and Emma Z. shot her a sharp look, one that clearly said *shut up*.

"But you're thinking about it, right?" I asked, looking between the two of them. "I mean, I get it." I glanced at Emma Z., remembering her scholarship that had fallen through. "I'm sure you have your reasons, and maybe you've even convinced yourself it's okay."

I saw them exchange a quick, unsettled look. I took a breath and went on.

"If you do it, it's going to ruin Tabitha's night—and probably beyond tonight. She's going to think her friends betrayed her, when all they were guilty of was bad AirDropping. And I promise, it's not going to make you any happier. It'll ruin your night, too." I glanced down at my phone and realized I was already behind schedule. "Look," I said, taking a step away. "I can't make you do anything. I can only tell you that I know how this turns out, and it's bad—for everyone. So why do that, you know?"

I waited for a response, but they just stared at me, both still looking incredibly flustered. Which I could understand. If someone seemed to know everything about what I was doing—including what I was only *thinking* about doing—it would really freak me out, too. I waited one moment longer, and when it was clear nothing was forthcoming, I just nodded.

"Okay, good talk." I left them behind, hurrying over to where Bryony was standing with Emma R. "So here's the thing. I have to run. . . ."

"Run where?" Emma asked.

"I just have to . . . take care of some things."

"At Grad Nite?" Emma asked, sounding baffled. "What kind of things?"

"I can't really explain right now." I met Bryony's eye. It was one thing to tell my best friend that I was in a time-loop situation—but I wasn't sure I wanted to go around telling *everyone*. At the very least, I simply didn't have the time to keep explaining it.

"This is . . . super weird, Cass," Bryony said.

"I know. But like they say on *Cereal*—that's the way the crackle pops."

Bryony's eyebrows flew up. "Since when do you listen to *Cereal*?"

"I've listened to *all* of it. It's so good! You were right."

"I always am," she said automatically, giving me a smile.

I checked the time again. "I have to run, but can you meet me at Radiator Springs Racers at ten fifteen?" Even though Bryony still looked confused, she nodded, and I gave her a smile. "Okay, cool. See you then!"

I turned and started running, knowing I was a few minutes later than I'd wanted to be. I glanced behind me at the other two Emmas for just a moment before they were blocked from view by the crowds. I had no idea what they were going to do with the picture they'd accidentally been AirDropped, but I'd done everything I could to try to convince them to do the right thing. It was out of my hands now.

Ten minutes later, I'd stopped at one of the bigger souvenir stores—for what I required, Johnny's merch kiosk just wouldn't suffice. I'd picked up a notebook and a pen, too. I needed to write something that I should have written a long time ago. And then I wanted to write out the Freddie list, and his lyrics. If everything went according to plan—which I was very aware was a long shot—he would need them.

I checked the time and then hustled over to Cars Land. As I speed-walked, occasionally breaking into a short jog when I could do it without bumping into people, I reflected on how much better this was—not having to worry about running into anyone. Not hiding from my mistakes and the girl I'd been when I made them. But out in the open, head up, looking around, on my way to try and make things better.

I made it to the Cozy Cone, with its snack options, and was relieved to see that the one I needed wasn't too crowded yet. I got in line and started writing the Freddie list. At this point, I knew the list like the back of my hand. It was because I'd memorized him—because I *knew* him. It wasn't just a series of facts. They were the facets that added up to him—to Freddie Sharma.

I was almost done writing out the lyrics when the person in front of me placed their order, and I stepped up to the window. "Hi," I said, dropping the notebook back in my bag. "Could I have twelve churros, please?"

146

I knew just where I'd be able to find Reagan, Zach, and McKenna—and I had timed it so that when they walked through the entrance to Cars Land, I would be waiting there, peace offering in hand. As I saw them coming, I took a deep breath and told myself that it would be okay.

I'd been through every other permutation of this, after all. I'd done the wrong thing, taken the easy way out, so many times now. And I knew that trying to do the *right* thing—not just feinting at it or doing the bare minimum and expecting that to make a difference—was the only thing that was going to make things better. Or at least be a start.

"And then I want to go on the swings," I heard Reagan say as I stepped into their path.

"Hi, Reagan," I said, giving them a wave. "Hey, Zach. Hey, McKenna."

"Hello!" McKenna said cheerfully, waving back. Then she paused. Wait, have we met?"

"Cass?" Reagan asked. They looked at Zach, whose eyes were wide. Cass Issac?"

"It's me," I said, taking a small step closer. "I'm really happy to see you ere. I just wanted to apologize."

Reagan frowned and crossed their arms over their chest. "Apologize?"

"I should have never just left like that—and then not stayed in touch ith you. It was a really awful thing to do. I know it hurt you, and I'm orry."

"Oh." They blinked a few times, then looked at Zach, who seemed qually thrown by all this. McKenna, however, was watching with rapt tention, like it was a particularly interesting TV show she'd stumbled oon.

"Ooh, what did you do?" she asked eagerly.

Zach took a breath. "Well . . ." he started, but I jumped in.

"I was a bad friend," I said, feeling the truth of my words deep in my ut as I spoke them. I saw Reagan's face change, taking this in. "And you ere a really good friend." I shook my head. "I know there's no undoing e way I behaved. But I wanted to let you know how sincerely sorry I am."

"Well—okay," Reagan said slowly. "I . . . Thanks for saying that, Cass."

"And!" I held up the bag I'd gotten from the Cozy Cone. "I bought you l some churros. I'm really sorry I didn't bring them to your birthday party. hope this helps."

Reagan gave me a small smile as they took the bag from me. "It does."

"Can you have one with us?" Zach asked, as he eagerly opened the

bag. Even from a few feet away, I could smell the heavenly churro arom
wafting out.

I checked the time, then shook my head. "I have to get going."

"Take one for the road," Reagan said, holding the bag out to me.

"Really?"

They nodded, and I reached in and grabbed one. It was still warm, an
I took a bite of the sweet cinnamon goodness. "Thank you."

Reagan gave me a nod. "Maybe I'll see you around?"

I smiled. "I hope so." They smiled back, and we had a nice moment—
until I remembered I had to get all the way over to the Ferris wheel. "Bye
I called, as I hustled away.

"Who even *was* that?" I heard McKenna ask before I got out of earsho

I smiled as I started to run, eating my churro as I went. I couldn't he
thinking about the look on Reagan's face when they'd forgiven me—an
how good it felt. Like something heavy had just been lifted off my shou
ders. Something that had been there so long, I'd just gotten used to it—an
had forgotten that things could be any other way.

I walked up to the Ferris wheel and took a deep breath before I cho
the line for the swinging cars. I didn't want to go on this ride again—but
knew, deep in my bones, that I had to. There was a group of four ahead
me, all wearing purple sweatshirts from a school in La Jolla, and they we
tall enough to block me from view.

Of all the stops on my apology tour tonight, this one was the trickie
to time—mostly because I could aim to be in the right place at the rig
time, but there were still a lot of moving parts, including literal movin
parts. But if I could pull it off—and I was hoping that I could—I knew
would be the perfect way to try to make things up to Greta and Nora.

I also knew that we would be in line for ten minutes, which was ju the window I needed. I took out my notebook, drew in a deep breath, and then started to write. It wasn't easy—facing up to how you've let people down never is—but as I reached the end of the letter, and the line had moved up to the front, I knew I'd said what I needed to.

I dropped the notebook back in my bag and double-checked the plastic bag from the gift shop, making sure that what I'd bought there was still safe and sound. Then I peered around the La Jolla group, to see Greta and Nora in front of them. Just like I'd planned on.

The cast members were getting people settled in the swinging cars, and I moved forward automatically, keeping my eyes on my old quiz bowl teammates, who were laughing at something on Greta's phone. They stepped up to get on their car, and the cast member looked at the La Jolla group behind them. "How many?" she asked.

"Four," they chorused, which was my moment.

"I'm a single rider!" I said, raising my hand but not stepping out of line or letting myself be seen—not yet.

"Great," the cast member said with a smile. "Come on up. Any other single riders?"

"Me!" I heard a voice behind me say. I turned around and saw, to my shock, that I recognized him—it was Tristram/Doug.

He wasn't yet in his Eton Mess outfit, and I realized as I looked at him that I'd never seen him wear anything else. He was in jeans and a sweatshirt that read CHICAGO! above the city's skyline. I blinked at him for a moment, wondering how this was happening—how I could have missed him in my recon. But in fairness, I hadn't been spending a lot of time looking behind me. I had been more focused on figuring out how I could get myself in the right car.

"Excellent!" the cast member said. "Single riders, step on up!"

I looked around her and saw that Greta and Nora were already in the car. I walked forward—at the same time that Tristram/Doug did. We bumped shoulders, and he took a step back.

"Sorry, go ahead," he said, using his real American accent.

"Thanks, Doug," I said automatically. His eyes went wide, and I tried to backtrack. "I mean—Tristram?"

"Do we know each other?" He started off sounding American but veered toward what I was pretty sure was supposed to be a British accent at the end, like he wasn't sure who he was supposed to be.

"Single riders!" the cast member called again, and I hurried forward, feeling like we were holding up the line. I hadn't foreseen the Tristram/Doug part of all of this, but I tried to tell myself that it would be okay. That this development might even *help* with the last—and most complicated—part of tonight. The part that I couldn't even let myself think about, or I'd get too nervous I wasn't going to pull it off.

I just had to keep doing this in sections. One piece at a time, and not letting myself get overwhelmed by everything that needed to happen in a pretty short period of time. And my focus right now was Greta and Nora.

I got into the car before Tristram/Doug and sat down. He followed, sitting next to me, and I could see he still looked freaked out—like his cover had just been blown. "Have we met before?" he asked in a low voice. He was still alternating accents every few words, which had the effect of making him sound Australian.

"Kind of? It's— I'll explain later."

"Explain what?" he asked, as the cast member stuck their head in the door.

"All set? You know you're on the swinging cars?"

I nodded, resigned, wishing that someone had pointed this out to me ìe first time around. "All set," I echoed.

Greta and Nora looked over at me, and their eyes widened in shock. he ride jolted forward, rising up, and I gave them a smile. "Oh, hey, guys."

146

Cass?" Greta asked, her voice strangled. "Cass *Issac*? What are you doing here?"

"Seriously," Nora added.

"Wait, you know them, too?" Tristram/Doug asked, looking around. "Is this some kind of hidden camera show or something?"

"What?" Nora asked, sounding baffled.

"What's happening with your voice?" Greta asked him. "It kind of sounds like you're glitching."

"That's Doug," I said, feeling like the moment had arrived to take the situation in hand. "He's pretending to be British. But he's actually from Chicago."

"No I'm not," he said, in what was maybe his least convincing stab at the accent yet. "I'm from . . . Hertfordshire?"

Nora shook her head. "I really don't think you are."

"And it says *Chicago* on your shirt," Greta pointed out.

Tristram/Doug—or maybe just Doug now—looked down at himself and sighed. "Yeah, okay," he said, now sounding totally American and relieved about it. "Hey, I'm Doug."

We rose up, and the car plunged forward. I gripped the seat, reminding myself to breathe. Even though I still didn't like it, it felt a little easier this time. After all, I'd done it once before and had made it through. I knew I could do it again.

"Cass," Nora said. "I can't believe you're here—"

"I know." I was about to continue on, when we suddenly plunged backward, and I was not quite able to stop myself from yelling, "AGH!"

"You okay?" Doug asked. "It doesn't seem like you like this very much."

"I really don't," I said through clenched teeth.

"Then why are you here?"

"Because I need to make amends." The car stopped rising, and we swung back and forth for a moment, hanging in the air—and I felt the same way, too, like I was suspended between who I'd been and who I was trying to become.

And if I wanted to change, I just had to keep going.

I took a breath to begin, but it was Doug who leaned forward to talk to me. "You said we'd kind of met," he said, his brow furrowed. "What does that mean? And who told you about me being American? We'd worked so hard to keep it under wraps."

"Why aren't you allowed to be American?" Greta asked, sounding like she was curious almost against her will.

"Because I'm in a band," he said, sounding resigned. "And we're all supposed to be, like, from a British prep school?" He shrugged. "I'm kind of getting over it, actually."

"You are?" I asked. In all my time with the band, I hadn't heard this.

"Yeah. I mean, I'd prefer to play music I'd actually listen to. It's a good gig, but you can only pretend to be British for so long."

The car rose up again and we started swinging forward. I took in a big breath, then let it out slowly, reminding myself I could handle this.

"I just can't get over the fact that you're here, Cass," Greta said.

"We really didn't think we'd ever see you again," Nora said, folding her arms across her chest.

"I know." I took a deep breath and faced the girls who'd once been my good friends. "I'm so sorry," I said, looking at both of them. "I shouldn't have just left like that—and then not stayed in touch. And I should have let you know that I was leaving, and that I wouldn't be on the team the next year. I didn't understand that it messed up your bowl chances."

"Bowl chances?" Doug asked, his eyes wide. "Do you guys—play football?"

"Academic quiz bowl," Greta, Nora, and I all said at the same time.

"Oh," Doug said, nodding. "That makes more sense."

"I feel awful," I said. And I wasn't just referring to my stomach, which was swooping around as we descended, about to take another loop around. "I promise, the last thing I ever wanted to do was hurt either of you. Because that time in Arizona—it was one of the best years ever. And that was because of you two."

Greta and Nora exchanged a look, and I could see they were both taken aback. Whatever they'd expected from me—it wasn't this. "Well," Nora finally said, her voice coming out hesitant. "Thank you for saying that."

We rode in silence for a moment, Doug looking around at all of us like he was trying to figure out what was going on.

"It's not like it makes up for what you did though," Greta said. But she didn't sound furious, not like the first time we'd been on this ride together.

I let out a long, shaky breath. "I know that." It had been the hardest thing to accept about this loop. That I could have all the chances in the world to do things differently during this one night—but all the mistakes I'd made before it were unchangeable, etched in stone. And just pretending they didn't exist—leaving every new town and trying to move on, never looking back—had only led to pain, on all sides.

I couldn't go back. But I could do better, moving forward.

"Wait, I have a question," Doug said. He leaned back, which caused the car to swing wildly.

I closed my eyes, trying to get my stomach to settle.

"Don't do that," I heard Nora say. "I don't think Cass likes it."

I opened my eyes and looked over at her, surprised and touched. I couldn't help but think about the first time we'd been here—when she'd been deliberately trying to make the car rock.

"That's my bad," Doug said, chastened. "Sorry."

I looked across the car at Greta and Nora. "Even though I can't change anything, I just need you both to know how sorry I am. How I would do things differently if I could."

"You can't, though, right?" Doug said with a sigh. "The ride only goes one direction."

"Uh, sure." I met Greta's eye, and she gave me a small, tiny smile—letting me feel like, for the first time in a long time, we were on the same page. I reached into the plastic Disney bag and pulled out what I'd bought earlier. I held it out to them. "I know it won't make up for anything, but I wanted to give you this."

"Disney trivia!" Nora read off the box, looking delighted.

"I know it's not going to be as rigorous as our quiz bowl practices, but it's something."

"Well, that's probably a good thing," Greta said. "I bet you haven't been keeping up with your training. We'd wipe the floor with you."

I laughed at that. "I'm sure you would."

We sat there in silence for a moment. But it didn't feel charged, or angry—it just felt comfortable.

"So, wait, *what* exactly happened?" Doug asked, breaking the silence.

I laughed, but before I could go into specifics, we were heading down to the ground—and I knew this ride was almost over.

"Well, thanks," Greta said, looking at the box. "This is really nice of you."

"And if you're ever back in Phoenix, we could play it?" Nora said.

I nodded, knowing how to spot an olive branch—even one that I didn't think I deserved—when I saw one. "That would be great," I said, giving them a smile.

We came to a stop, back at the beginning, and the cast member opened the door. As I waited for everyone else to get out, I felt a kind of peace settle over me. Like the energy I'd spent worried about Greta and Nora—either trying to avoid them or avoid thinking about what I'd done—had just dissipated. And I felt calmer and happier now that it was gone.

We all walked out together, heading up the path. "I guess I'll see you around?" I pulled on my jean jacket—it had gotten to the point of the night where I always needed it.

"See you around," Greta agreed, and Nora nodded.

"Oh, and come and see Eton Mess," Doug said. "We're performing at midnight. Over by Pixar Pier." A second later, though, he frowned. "But if you do see me, call me Tristram, okay? And pretend that I'm from Hertfordshire."

"Maybe," Greta said. She gave him a nod but didn't sound fully convinced.

"No, you really should," I said. "It's going to be a really good performance."

"Oh, thank you," Doug said, looking touched. Then he paused. "Wait, how do you know that?"

"It's just what I hope," I clarified. "But I'll for sure see you later, Doug."

"You will?"

I checked the time, and realized I had to hurry—I was about five minutes behind. "Bye," I said to all of them, but mostly Greta and Nora, no offense to Doug. "Take care."

I turned and walked fast before breaking into a run. I knew he wouldn't be there forever, after all. And I had to talk to my former prom date.

146

Even though I knew I was running late to find Bruce, I called the Mermaid Café as I dashed across the park. I needed to multitask here—if I waited too long, the restaurant would be closed. And I wanted to be able to tell Bryony the truth about actually applying.

I didn't think that hearing the happy yells of the seniors behind me, or the music playing over the park's speakers, was really helping me put forward the best impression. But I made my pitch to the manager I'd been able to get on the phone anyway. I told him I'd email my application as soon as possible—but that I *really* wanted the job. I told him all about my knowledge of facts, which usually didn't have any practical application—but it really would if the Mermaid wanted to start a quiz night.

The manager seemed intrigued by that, which gave me the confidence to add that if I got the job, I would really love to have the same shifts as Bryony Tsai. He had sounded a little harried—it was a Friday night, after all—but promised that he'd do what he could. I hung up, feeling like it was one more thing I could cross off my list as I dashed toward the Hollywood Lounge.

In my perfect version of this—the one that I'd written out in my plans—I would have already been sitting down, cool and composed, when Bruce showed up. Instead, by the time I reached the dining area, I was sweaty and out of breath, and I could see Bruce starting to walk away.

"Bruce!" I yelled as loud as I could. He stopped, and everyone else who was passing also looked over at me. "Uh—sorry," I said as I hurried over to him.

Bruce was staring at me like he'd just seen a ghost. "Cass?" he asked faintly.

"Hi. I thought it was you." He was wearing his SNAP CRACKLE POP CULTURE T-shirt, and I smiled.

"You recognized me from the back?" he asked, turning to look where I'd come from. "In the dark? From . . . far away?"

"Sure did." I took a deep, shaky breath. This conversation was the hardest one—there was a reason I'd left it for last. What I'd done to Bruce had been the most personal, and the most hurtful, and it was the one I was most ashamed of. I knew that we'd probably never be friends again. Those were the consequences of my actions, and I'd have to live with them. Right now, though, I needed to do what I could to give us both some closure. I twisted my hands together and jumped in.

"I just wanted to say I'm sorry." I could see the skeptical expression starting to form on Bruce's face, so I took a breath and kept going. "I'm sorry for all of it. For standing you up on prom night. For not telling you I was moving. For ignoring your letter and not ever being in touch afterward . . ."

Saying it all out loud really brought it home—just how much I'd messed things up. I swallowed hard. "I know it's not an excuse. But I liked you so much, and I was afraid if we started something . . . and then I left . . ." I shook my head.

The things that had made so much sense to me no longer did. Looking back, it seemed like a stranger had made those choices. A stranger who hadn't been courageous enough to be honest with anyone—least of all herself. "I wasn't brave enough to tell you what I was really feeling. And I derailed any chance of something happening with us. But more than that—I lost a really good friend. And I just hope you can forgive me."

Bruce looked at me for a long moment, then walked over to an empty table and sat down, like he needed to be sitting to process this. "Wow," he finally said.

"I know. Sorry to throw all that on you at Grad Nite. Why are you even here, by the way?" I asked, hoping I was pulling this question off. Me not asking this had seemed to bump Bruce every time, so I wanted to make sure to address it. "It's a long way from Seattle."

"We won an academic award." He still looked like he was struggling to find his bearings.

"Oh wow," I said, trying to look like this was brand-new information. "That's cool. Congratulations."

"I—don't know what to say," he finally said, glancing over at me. "I mean—it's not every day someone from your past shows up and says just what you've been wanting to hear."

I shrugged. "Maybe anything is possible on Grad Nite."

"We are at the most magical place on earth, right?" he asked, then frowned. "Why doesn't that sound right?"

"Happiest," I amended. "Happiest place on earth."

"Right." He glanced over at me. "Thank you for saying all that, Cass. I think the hardest thing was I didn't understand what had happened. What I'd done . . ."

"Nothing," I said firmly. "It was all me. All my fault."

"Well, that was the conclusion I eventually came to," he said, and I laughed.

A comfortable silence fell between us. I took out my notebook and ripped out the letter I'd written while waiting in line. It was essentially everything I'd just told him—owning up to my actions, and apologizing. "This is for you. I'm sorry it took me so long to write you back."

Bruce looked down at the paper, then folded it up and tucked it into his pocket. "Thanks, Cass."

"Thank *you* for hearing me out. I know you didn't have to." I stood up and looked at my watch. "Uh, but if you wanted to go by Radiator Springs Racers, I've heard there's no line at ten twenty."

Bruce pulled out his phone and frowned at it. "But that's in fifteen minutes."

"I know," I said, already starting to head in that direction. "I was supposed to have been here earlier, but then Doug was in my Ferris wheel car, and he slowed everything down."

"I . . ." Bruce started, then shook his head. "Wait, what?"

I waved this away. "It's nothing. But maybe I'll see you there? Or not!" I didn't want it to seem like I really needed him to show up—the last thing I wanted was for him to suspect that I had any ulterior motive. "Bye!" I yelled as I hurried away. Bruce still looked like he wasn't sure which way was up, but I really hoped that he'd show.

I got to Cars Land with time to spare and slowed down a little as I walked through the Route 66 replica town. The DJ was still spinning, and I saw Sheridan in the crowd, dancing with his arms in the air. I caught his eye and he waved, and I waved back. While most of my friends and I had been going through emotional upheaval, Sheridan just seemed like he had an amazing night every time, and I was happy to see it.

I felt myself smiling as I looked around at the neon lights, shining brightly as ever in the dark of the California night. I took it all in—the joy that surrounded me, the music, my fellow seniors, all of us on the cusp of our next big adventure. The magic that seemed built right into this place.

I could have been stuck in a time loop anywhere. It could have been a random Wednesday in March. But I'd landed *here*—and now, as I looked around, really seeing it for maybe the first time, I was nothing but grateful.

Bryony was waiting for me by the line for Radiator Springs, and I smiled when I saw her. To my relief, she smiled back, even if it was a little tentative. Not that I blamed her—I'd dropped a *lot* of information on her and then had literally run away.

"Hey," I said as I reached her.

"Hey." She gestured to the line. "There's, like, nobody here."

"I know! That's why I said to come now. It's the best time for it."

Bryony shook her head. "I'm still wrapping my brain around this, you know."

"That's understandable. It took me a while, too."

"It's *so* weird."

"I know." I shrugged. "But like they say on *Cereal*, the second bowl is easier."

Bryony laughed, her eyes lighting up. "I love that you listened to it."

"I listened to *all* of it. It . . . took a while."

"I can't believe you did that."

"Well, it was important to you."

Something softened in her expression, and she gave me a smile. "Is this, like, the hundredth time we've had this conversation?"

"I've never told you before."

Bryony stared at me. "Really? Why now?"

I took in a breath and then let it out. I didn't want to jinx anything—I didn't even want to speak it out loud. But I was also done keeping things from my best friend. "I'm thinking tonight might be the last one," I said, and then crossed my fingers in my dress pocket.

"And if it's not?" she asked, her brow furrowed.

"Then I'll try again." This was the realization that I'd come to when I was making my plans. If there was no getting out of this—if I truly was in a *Groundhog Day* situation, and stuck here for decades, then so be it. I would just do whatever I could to give everyone else their best night ever, again and again. There were worse ways to spend eternity.

"So what have you been doing? Besides listening to the podcast, that is. Have you learned a new language or something?"

I smiled. "Something like that." I glanced over and saw Bruce, looking a little baffled as to what he was doing there, walking toward us. "Okay, we're back on schedule."

"What schedule?"

"Uh, hi, Cass," Bruce said, a question in his voice. I smiled when I saw that he hadn't put his sweatshirt on yet—his *Cereal* shirt was still visible. "What are you—" Bryony turned around to look at him, and Bruce stopped talking and just blinked at her.

"Bryony, this is Bruce," I said, and I noticed Bryony had immediately started playing with her bangs. "Bruce, Bryony. I thought as two super-fans of *Cereal*, you guys should meet."

Bryony shot me a look, and I gave her a small smile, knowing she'd know what I meant by it. "It's nice to meet you," Bryony said, looking up at Bruce.

"You too," he said, his voice sounding a little dazed—the same way he'd sounded every other time he'd encountered my best friend.

"How do you know each other?" Bryony asked. She widened her eyes at me in a way that I knew meant *Is this your ex? Did you date?* I gave her a tiny head shake, and she nodded, looking relieved.

"Bruce and I were neighbors in Seattle," I explained.

"A couple years ago," he added. "It was really crazy to run into Cass tonight. She recognized me right away and everything."

"And Bryony's my best friend," I said, feeling my throat tighten around the words. It was like it had taken nearly losing her for me to understand just what it meant to have a friend like her. "She's the greatest." I gave her a slightly quavery smile, and she smiled back. I cleared my throat and tried to focus. "Okay! I have to go do . . . things. But I just thought you guys might want to go on the best ride in the park. And there's no line right now! So . . ." I shrugged and gestured to it, and Bryony laughed.

"Real subtle, Cass."

"What?" I asked, but I was laughing, too.

Bruce shook his head at me, then turned to Bryony. "I'm game if you are."

"Sure," she said, playing with her bangs again. "Why not?"

"Have fun!" I called, as I started to leave.

"Wait, Cass," Bryony called. "Where will you be?"

"I'll be at the Eton Mess show," I said, choosing my words carefully. The last thing I wanted to do was lie to Bryony ever again. "I'll see you there? Midnight?"

"Sounds good." She gave me an eye-widen that I knew meant *we will be talking about this later,* and I gave her one back that meant *you know it.* Then she and Bruce headed toward the ride, Bryony saying something that made Bruce laugh.

I stayed there for just a moment, watching until they were out of sight. I had no idea if anything would happen here, if this would turn into anything more than just hanging out on a ride. But that wasn't up to me any longer—they could take it from here.

I checked the time, took a deep breath, and then headed the opposite direction.

I had a show to save.

146

Freddie was right where I knew he'd be.

He was by Grizzly Peak, walking and carrying the Irn-Bru for Niall. A man on a mission. I'd been tempted to see if I could have encountered him earlier—like when he stopped short after getting the email from the manager. But the more I worked out my plans, I realized I couldn't get there in time, not with everything else I'd had to do. And plus—I needed to make sure Niall knew about the manager. I was pretty sure he always did; if Freddie didn't tell him, like in the loops where I came into the picture later, Niall found out when he looked at Freddie's phone.

I watched him for just a moment, trying to get my timing right. Just once, I was hoping to do this without getting splattered with orange soda. I took a breath and stepped into his path.

We crashed into each other, like I knew we would, but I managed to jump back at the last moment, out of the splash zone.

"Oh, I'm so sorry," Freddie said, looking from me to the bottle of soda on the ground. Everyone around us was giving the ever-expanding puddle a wide berth, and Freddie chased the bottle down and tossed it in the nearest trash can. "Are you all right?"

"I am." I smiled at him. "Hey, Freddie."

"I . . . Hi?" His smile widened, even as it became more confused. "Have we met before?"

"We have. A lot, actually." I took a breath. *"Excalibur."*

146

We ended up outside Award Wieners—it was the final place at the park I hadn't eaten, so I wanted to be sure to try it. As I'd tried to explain to Freddie what was happening—and what was going to happen—we'd both decided that we needed some food, and had headed here and ordered. Freddie had gotten the bacon dog; I'd stuck with the regular hot dog for what I was hoping would be my last Grad Nite dinner.

"Okay," Freddie said, turning to me once we'd both ordered and paid. "Just to make sure I have this straight—you're in a *time loop*."

I nodded. On the walk here I'd given him the basic facts—Grad Nite, my best friend Bryony, the night repeating. But like usual, it was taking him a moment to get his head around it. "Like *Pettigrew's Loop*."

Freddie's face lit up. "I love that movie! I can't believe you've seen it—"

"I saw it because you told me to," I said with a laugh. "I'd never heard about it before."

He shook his head. "This is so cool. I always wanted something like this to happen—which you know, of course. But it's still *brilliant*. Jack and I always would talk about it . . ." He trailed off and looked at me, head tilted to the side. "But maybe you know that already?"

"I do," I assured him, as I pulled the list out of my bag. I handed it over and saw Freddie's eyes widen as he read it. "This is my dossier on Freddie Sharma."

"This is . . . I really told you all this?" he asked, reading it. He looked up at me in horror. "I told you about *Geraldine Bewley*?"

I laughed. "You did."

"But . . ." His eyes traveled over the paper again. "Why would you write this out? Wouldn't you have to do it every time? Nothing would be able to come with you when the loop reset."

"That's right," I said, impressed Freddie had gotten there before me and hadn't had to conduct experiments to make this clear. "I guess it all just seemed like stuff I wanted to make sure I remembered." His eyes met mine, and my heart started to beat a little faster. "It all seemed important."

He gave me a smile, his dimple flashing. "Well, I don't know about that." He tapped on the bottom of the page. "What's this?"

"Those are song lyrics."

"That's what I thought. But who wrote them?"

I smiled at him. "You did."

He looked up at me, his jaw dropping open in surprise. "Wait—what?" But before I could explain more, our number was called, and we collected our trays and headed over to the tables outside the restaurant—a little bit tucked away from the bustle of the crowds, so we could eat our hot dogs in peace.

I took a bite—really good, it would be a close call between this and Angry Dogs—and then looked across the table at him. "Every time we've hung out, something has inspired you. It's never the same thing twice. And you always write it down, usually in your black Moleskine notebook. But since I knew you weren't going to remember, I just wanted there to be some record of it all."

His eyes were wide as he looked back at the paper. "This is mental. I was just thinking these lyrics were great. I didn't realize I was the one who came up with them!"

I laughed and ate one of my french fries. "I mean, I suppose that's better than thinking they were terrible."

He nodded as he picked up his hot dog. "You make an excellent point." We ate in silence for a moment—I was hungrier than I normally was, but I *had* been running a lot more tonight than I usually did. "So," Freddie said, setting the hot dog down and wiping the corners of his mouth. "We must have . . . spent a lot of time together. For you to know all these things. For me to come up with all these lyrics."

I gave him a smile that I knew I wasn't quite keeping the sadness out of. "We did." I looked across the table at him, struck once again by the dichotomy of it. Freddie was someone I knew so well—and he didn't know me at all. "It was the best," I said simply. "In the beginning, I told you everything that was happening—like now. You were the only person I told actually. The one person who understood. But then, more recently, we just . . . bumped into each other. And walked around for a bit. We got ice cream and talked."

Freddie leaned across the table, his eyes finding mine. "And did we . . . Did we ever . . ."

I shook my head. "No. I mean, there were vibes—"

"Oh *were* there," he said with a grin, raising an eyebrow.

"But—no. Nothing happened." The word *yet* seemed to hang in the air between us for a moment. I looked away and finished the rest of my dinner quickly—I could feel that I was blushing.

Freddie tossed his napkin on the tray and looked at his phone. "I actually need to get going. Not that I want to leave—it's that we have the show tonight."

I took a breath. "Right. About that."

The smile slid off Freddie's face. "What?"

"It doesn't go well," I said, not able to stop myself from wincing.

Freddie stared at me in horror. "But there's a manager coming to the show tonight. . . ."

"Oh I know," I assured him.

"What happens?"

"Well, Alfie gets food poisoning. Onstage. He eats some—as you say—dodgy prawns."

"Alfie," Freddie groaned, running his hands over his face.

"And for a while I was thinking I could stop it. If I stopped him from eating them as soon as possible. But he ate some at the restaurant, too—there's really no stopping it. And then, when we stop him from playing, the whole thing just doesn't work without a guitar player."

"Oh my god," Freddie said. He'd turned very pale, like he was picturing it all in his mind.

"There's more," I said grimly.

"There's *more*?"

349

"It's Niall," I said, knowing that I had to work my way into this.

"What about Niall? Does he eat the prawns, too?"

"I wish," I wasn't quite able to stop myself from saying. "No, he—sabotages you."

"He what?"

"He puts something in your water. Something that gives you an allergic reaction. Because he knows about the manager coming and doesn't want it to go well for you. I know," I said quickly, trying to get in front of Freddie's denials—he was already shaking his head. "I know he's your best friend. But I've seen it happen, over and over. And once, you didn't drink the water he gave you and nothing happened. And then you drank it in front of me to prove it and . . ."

"Hives," Freddie said hollowly. He shook his head. "This is . . . a lot."

I nodded, suddenly wishing I hadn't eaten all my french fries. He looked like someone who could have used some carbs right around now. "I know it is. And I'm sorry—I just wanted you to know."

"No, of course," he said, then gave a short, unhappy laugh. "So—it's going to be a disaster. And there's nothing we can do."

"That's what I thought," I said. "But I've spent a lot of time trying to figure out how to fix things."

Freddie sat up straighter. "Really?"

"Yeah," I said, leaning across the table. "I think I have a plan."

"Have we tried this plan before? Does everything work out perfectly?" he asked hopefully.

"I'm afraid not. This would be the first time."

"Well then." Freddie gave me a smile and leaned forward. "It sounds like you better tell me what we're doing."

146

Freddie gave me a nod, then pulled open the door that would lead backstage. We started to walk down the hall, and I paused at the stagehand poker game that looked like it was on its last hand.

"He's bluffing, Violet," I said, as we passed. "Not a single face card."

"Who asked you?" Van said, his face turning slowly red.

"Wait, what?" Violet called after me. But I just gave her a quick smile as Freddie pulled the greenroom door open for me and I stepped inside.

Doug and Alfie were already dressed in their Eton Mess outfits, and both had clearly done something to their hair. Alfie's was styled in a swoop across his forehead, whereas Doug had gelled his up into tiny spikes. Alfie sipped a Dr Pepper, and he smiled cheerfully when Freddie came in the room. I still couldn't help but wince, thinking about what was going to befall him, and in pretty short order, too.

"Hi, guys, this is Cass," Freddie said, gesturing to me.

"I know," Doug said in his real accent. He grinned at me. "How's it going?"

"You know Doug?" Freddie asked, sounding surprised. "I mean, Tristram?"

"We met on the Ferris wheel," I said, giving Doug a nod.

"She knew I was from Chicago," Doug said, grabbing a small bag of chips from the craft services table. "It was really impressive."

Alfie shot him a look. "Was this when you were wearing your shirt that literally said Chicago on it? Think that might have tipped her off?" he said this in a British accent, then turned to me, his face brightening. "Wait, if you know Doug is really American, does that mean I can go back to being Australian?"

I smiled at him. "Go for it."

"Oh thank goodness," he said, relaxing into his accent, his vowels immediately getting more stretched out and relaxed. "That's better, isn't it?"

"So," I said, glancing at the wall clock, realizing just how much we had to figure out before showtime. "Alfie."

He gave me a smile. "Yeah?"

"You can't play tonight."

"I— What?" he looked from me to Freddie. "Naur. Are you having a laugh?"

"Nope," I said, shaking my head. "You're going to get food poisoning onstage. It's the prawns."

"But I feel fine."

"You're not going to be fine, mate," Freddie said grimly. "We're trying to save you from being turned into a meme."

"Am I going to get food poisoning, too?" Doug asked, looking panicked.

"Uh—I don't think so," I said, thrown by this. "Did you eat any of the shrimp?" Doug shook his head. "Then I think you're good."

"But how can you *know*—" Alfie said, just as the door flew open again and Niall swanned in.

Like the others, he was now in his full Eton Mess look, a messenger bag slung across his chest. His hair had been tousled, in a way that I was sure was supposed to look accidental, but that I had a feeling had taken a great amount of effort to achieve. "Well, hello," he said, giving me a wide smile that didn't come close to meeting his eyes. "I didn't know we had guests."

"That's Cass," Freddie said. But he wasn't looking at me—he was looking at Niall, like he was appraising him. And I just silently hoped that he'd believe—as painful as it might be—that this was not someone he should trust. "She's a friend of mine."

I saw Niall clock my Grad Nite wristband, and when he looked back at me, it was with his usual dismissiveness. "Well, isn't that nice," he said, as he dropped his messenger bag at his feet. "But we actually have to get ready to do our show. It's an important one, right?" He directed this at Freddie. It was meant to sound excited, but I heard the bite under it—and judging by Freddie's expression, he did too. "So—Cassie, right? Why don't you run along and go get a nice spot out front." He pushed the door open wider and looked at me expectantly.

Alfie cleared his throat. "Well—Cass said I actually can't play. That I'm going to get food poisoning?"

Niall frowned. "How can she know that?"

"I mean, he did eat shrimp from a strip mall," Doug said, with a shrug. "Maybe it's just logic."

"Of course you're going to play," Niall said, waving this off. "It'll be fine. Freddie, you've got to hurry, mate. You're not even dressed yet. Chop, chop."

Freddie met my eyes. And for a moment, I wasn't sure what he would do—which side he would choose. Would he just want to believe it wasn't true? After all, he'd known Niall for years—and I was just someone that he'd met an hour ago, showing up with a list and a crazy story.

"You're right," Freddie finally said to Niall, and I felt my heart constrict. After all that I'd done to try and fix this, it was going to fall apart, when we were almost to the finish line. "I should get ready."

I looked between him and Niall, not sure what to say. I'd told Freddie everything—and he just hadn't believed me. I could know everything that was going to happen—all the events of the night—but I couldn't know someone's heart.

"Really?" I asked Freddie, my voice strangled. "That's—what you want to do?"

"Well, he *does* have to get ready," Doug said. "It's really not that big a deal?"

Freddie turned away from me and looked at Niall. "I wanted to go over the chord change on 'Summer Term,'" he said. "I think we're taking it too slowly. Also, mind if I have this water?"

He was reaching into the messenger bag before Niall could stop him, pulling out a plastic bottle. I saw Niall's face pale. "No—that's—mine."

"There's more on the table," Freddie said, pointing to it.

"Exactly," Niall said with a laugh he wasn't quite pulling off. "So grab one of those. You don't want to drink too much before we go on, you know," he said, talking faster now. "Maybe just save that bottle and wait until it's closer to showtime. Drink it then."

Freddie nodded. "It's a good call." Then he met my eye and gave me the tiniest of smiles. "Here you go, Cass," he said, holding the water bottle out to me.

"What? No—" Niall started, but before he could intervene, I took the bottle from him, opened it up, and took a long drink.

"Mmm," I said, lowering the bottle, and giving Freddie a smile. "That's good. Refreshing. Kind of tastes like there's cucumber in it."

The drumsticks that Doug was holding clattered to the ground, and I heard Alfie draw in a shocked breath. "What?" Niall said, looking very pale now. "That wasn't— I don't know what she's on about. . . ."

"Cass said that you were going to try and wreck my night," Freddie said quietly, and I could hear the hurt running through his voice like a seam. "That you were going to put something in my water."

"How did you know that?" Niall exploded, turning to me. "There's no way that—" He stopped short, only seeming to realize a second later what he'd just said. "I mean," he said with a short laugh. "There wasn't . . . That was *my* water."

Alfie shook his head, looking appalled. "I always knew you were a jumped-up bogan. But this is too much, man. What's wrong with you?"

"Yeah, you're not playing with us tonight," Doug said, his eyebrows furrowed. "You were going to poison our bass player? Dude."

"He was going to leave!" Niall yelled, pointing at Freddie. His hair was falling across his forehead, and his face was turning red. He no longer looked like the cute guy on the posters, pouting at the camera. He looked ugly and small. "There's a manager coming to see him tonight, did he tell you that? And he's going to leave this band, and all of us, behind." Niall looked around at his bandmates, like he'd just thrown down a trump card. But both of them turned to Freddie, smiling.

"You did?" Alfie asked. "That's dardy, mate, congratulations."

"How are you getting *more* Australian?" Freddie asked, but he was smiling, too.

"Seriously, that's awesome," Doug agreed.

"You're not mad?" Niall sputtered. "That he's leaving us behind?"

"You *kidding*?" Doug asked. "I'm over this band—I've been over it for a while now. If Freddie can get out and do his own music—I mean, isn't that the point of this? Why would I want to hold him back?"

"Thanks, Doug," Freddie said quietly.

Niall looked around at them, and it was like I could practically feel his fury building. "Fine," he snapped. "Who needs you? I'm *done*." He paused and looked around, like he was waiting for someone to beg him to stay. When this didn't happen, his face got even redder and he let out a short, mean laugh. "You think you can perform without me?"

"I think they'll be fine," I said, trying to sound more confident than I felt.

Niall whirled around to face me, his eyes narrowed. "*You*. This is all your fault, isn't it? Messing with my band . . ."

"It's not your band." I made myself stand up straight, and looked him right in the eye. "And I've watched you make this same choice, over and over again. Always this path, the one where you hurt someone who thinks of you as a friend. I don't know if it's that you're scared, or jealous, or just cruel . . ." Niall shook his head and scoffed. "But our choices matter, you . . ." I looked over at Artie. "What did you call him?"

"A jumped-up bogan," he said. "Because he is."

"Right, that," I said. "If there's one thing I've learned, this is it—we are the choices we make. They're what define us. And sometimes—if we're lucky—we get a chance to make different ones. But you never did."

Niall just blinked at me for a moment, then shook his head. "Whatever," he scoffed. "I'm out. Good luck without me, losers!"

He pushed the door open hard as he walked out, and it banged against the wall with a sound that made us all jump.

"Okay, that was a lot," Alfie said, shaking his head. "Good riddance to bad rubbish."

"Totally," Doug agreed. "But . . . what are we going to do without a lead singer?"

"Freddie can do it," I said. "Right?"

Freddie gave me a smile, then looked around at his bandmates. "I mean, if you guys are okay with that . . ."

"Perfect," Doug said, picking up his drum sticks and twirling them. "And I know that you're not going to step on my downbeat like Niall always did."

"But wait," Alfie said. "If I can't go on, we're just going to have bass and drums. And I'm really not sure that's going to work."

I shook my head. "It's not. You really need a third instrument in there."

The remainder of Eton Mess looked at each other, and I saw Freddie's shoulders slump. "So that means—we need to find another musician? In an hour?" I could tell by his tone he thought this was impossible.

Silence fell in the greenroom. Then I took a breath and stepped forward. "Will I do?"

146

Y ou okay?" Freddie asked me.

We were standing backstage, and I could hear the sound of the crowd that had gathered. My palms were sweaty, and this did not seem ideal, especially since I needed them to play an instrument in front of lots of people for the first time ever.

The band had all been on board with me stepping in, even after I told them I hadn't been playing piano *that* long.

Once we'd decided that I was going on, we'd all jumped into action. Freddie took the lyric sheets of the band's songs and wrote in the piano parts for me—letting me know which chords to play when, giving me a cheat sheet. We'd been able to run through the songs quickly, with me working hard to catch up, and when I'd seen the impressed, musician-to-musician looks the rest of the band had exchanged, I couldn't help but feel a swell of pride.

When we'd gone through the set list twice, doing the songs at three times the speed, I'd cleared my throat. "I think there's one song missing," I said, meeting Freddie's eye. "A solo. Right?"

I saw understanding dawn in Freddie's eyes as he pulled out the *Freddie* dossier, staring down at the lyrics he'd written. "I mean . . ." he said, sounding more nervous than I'd yet heard him. "I do have a melody I've been playing around with. It might work. . . ."

I gave him a smile, wishing I could tell him for sure how his big moment would turn out. But in this loop, I was just like everyone else—with no idea how things were going to unfold. Just trying to be brave enough, and hopeful enough, to believe it would all work out. Freddie took the keyboard and the lyric sheet off into the corner to work on his song, and before I knew it, it was showtime.

And now, as I stood in the dark of the wings, I felt just how nervous I was getting. All at once, I was realizing that there was a big difference between *saying* I could step in and save the day, and actually doing it.

"Cass?" Freddie prompted, and I looked over, realizing he'd asked me a question.

I tucked my hair behind my ears, willing it to behave for the next hour. "I think I'm okay? Hopefully?"

"You'll be great." He reached over and took my hand. A jolt ran through me—the same one that I felt whenever we touched. Over all these nights, all these loops . . . it had never changed. "Thank you for doing all this," he said quietly.

"I haven't done anything yet."

"But you *have*." Even in the backstage darkness, his eyes found mine.

"You tried to fix this. You told me the truth about Niall—you saved all those lyrics. You must really . . . care about the band."

There was a question at the end of that sentence, and I squeezed his hand, the one that was still holding mine. "More like one member of the band," I said, not letting myself look away. "Don't tell Alfie."

"Tell me what?" Alfie asked as he passed by backstage.

"What are you doing here?" I asked, not able to keep the alarm out of my voice. I knew all too well what was about to happen, even if he didn't.

"It's okay," Alfie said, holding up a trash can. "I'm prepared for the worst. I just didn't want to miss the show." He slapped Freddie on the back. "Break a leg!"

I took a breath, then looked back at Freddie. "I just . . ." I began, as I heard the crackle of a speaker, and I knew the band was about to be announced.

"We'll talk after?" Freddie whispered.

"Absolutely."

"Disney Grad Nite seniors and chaperones!" the announcer intoned. "Please welcome—all the way from jolly olde England—Eton Mess!"

The lights started swirling. Freddie squeezed my hand one more time, then strode out onstage. I took a big, shaky breath and followed, trying to tell myself that it would be okay. That normally, this performance involved food poisoning and hives and very little music actually being played. So the bar was *low*.

I stepped out onto the stage, squinting a little against the bright lights. I couldn't see the crowd—it was just a blur, but a very *big* blur, and looking at it was enough to make me even more nervous. So I turned away and walked to where the keyboard had been set up, at the back, next to Doug and his drum kit. He shot me a grin as he settled himself behind it.

I spread out the sheet music, covered in the notations that Freddie had made for me. Toward the bottom of the first page, I saw he'd written, *You'll do great, Cass!* ⌣

"Hi, Grad Nite," Freddie said. He stepped up to the lead singer's microphone as if he'd been doing it forever, like it was the most natural thing in the world. "You guys having fun?"

The crowd roared back, and Freddie's smile widened. "I'm so glad. It's a special night. One that just comes around once, right?" He glanced over at me, giving me a tiny wink, and I smiled back at him. "Just wanted to clear something up. We are Eton Mess, but I'm actually the only one from England. Tonight we thought we'd show you who we really are. Doug there is from Chicago. And Alfie's normally part of the band—sadly, he's a little under the weather tonight. But he's from Australia."

"Yeah!" came a faint reply from backstage. From how weak it had sounded, I had a feeling that Alfie's food poisoning had shown up, right on schedule.

"And that's Cass," Freddie said, nodding to me. I smiled out at the crowd, and even though I couldn't see them, I was pretty sure I just heard a gasp of shock. Whether it was Bryony, or one of the Emmas, or any of the other people that I'd made amends with tonight, I had no idea. "She's not British, either. She's from California."

I leaned forward into the microphone. "Harbor Cove," I said, and I heard a loud *Woo!* from all the people from my school who probably hadn't expected to hear their town shouted out by what was supposed to be a British prep-school boy band. "I'm from Harbor Cove," I said again. "I've only been there for six months—but it's my home." As I said it, I realized that it was true. Harbor Cove was where I belonged—and I wasn't about to leave it before I had to.

There was another *woo*, a little quieter and more confused-sounding this time, and I smiled. It was okay that the audience didn't know what I meant. I did—and that was enough.

"Ready?" I looked over and saw Freddie leaning back from the microphone, asking me the question.

I nodded, and Doug counted out *one, two, three, four* on his drumsticks—and the show began.

146

The performance passed in a blur. I focused on keeping time with everyone else, playing the right chords, making sure I wasn't missing my cues. I had been concentrating so hard on playing, it wasn't until the show was nearly over that I finally looked around, and took it all in.

I was standing onstage, playing piano in a band.

That was a sentence that would have been incomprehensible to me when I'd first arrived here, but I was doing it. The crowd was cheering and singing along with the choruses, and from the looks I could see Freddie and Doug exchanging, they also thought things were going well. The adrenaline was coursing through me, and my heart was beating hard—but not in a panicked or scared way. It was *fun*. I wasn't sure I was going to run off and join a band, but for right now, it was fantastic.

I hit the last chord and Doug crashed his cymbal and the crowd cheered. This was normally when the show ended—but not tonight. I stepped back from the keyboard, and Violet hustled out. She moved the keyboard to center stage, just behind the mic. She gave me a grin as she melted back into the darkness of the wings—I had a feeling she was still grateful about her poker winnings.

Doug got up from his drum kit, and we both walked off, letting Freddie take center stage.

"Hey, everyone," Freddie said. He smiled at the crowd, and you could practically feel it—the power of his genuine charm, how he was holding the audience in his hand. I just hoped that the manager was noticing it, too. "So for the last song," he said, and I was pleased to hear some disappointed groans from the audience. It meant they'd liked it! "For the last song, I wanted to play you something new. Something that I . . . wrote," he said, not quite managing to keep the wonder out of his voice. "But I never would be able to share it with you without someone very special," he said, glancing back at me in the wings. "So thank you, Cass."

Doug shoved me good-naturedly, and I shoved him back, feeling my cheeks get hot.

There was a smattering of polite applause, and then Freddie leaned forward and started to sing. He was singing the song he'd written, even without knowing it. All those fractions of lyrics that I'd saved for him—he'd spun them into a beautiful song, elegiac and yearning. And even though he was singing it to the crowd—it also felt like he was singing it just to me.

He was a natural there at center stage, singing in his clear, gorgeous voice, smiling at the crowd, at ease. And I was so happy this was the version of him that the manager was seeing—Freddie in the spotlight, singing a song that was his alone.

The stage lights dimmed slightly, and suddenly, from the wings, I could see the crowd clearly. I could see Tabitha Keith and her friends, their arms draped around each other's shoulders, no bad blood between any of them, crisis averted.

I saw Reagan and Zach and McKenna all listening to the music, rapt. I saw Greta and Nora standing next to each other, Greta lifting her phone to take a selfie. There were the Emmas, all in a line, dancing together. The stress and strain that I was used to seeing on the two Emmas' faces was totally gone—they were just having fun at Grad Nite. I saw Ms. Mulaney, nodding her head in time to the music. My eyes roamed over the crowd until I found Bryony—next to Bruce! I couldn't help but notice how close they were standing, the way he leaned down to say something that made her laugh.

I smiled as I looked at them and felt something in my heart expand as I took it all in. No matter what happened later, I had made a difference. My friends were having fun, singing and dancing, with no idea that things could have been very different. Because of what I'd done—because of what I'd finally figured out.

Freddie played the last chord with a flourish, and the crowd broke into cheers and applause. Freddie took a bow, and then exited into the wings, the crowd still clapping.

"Great show!" Doug yelled, louder than I was expecting—but maybe that's what happened when you played drums for an hour.

"You too," Freddie said, and they exchanged a high-five-hug combo before Doug turned and headed down the hall, back to the greenroom.

"Cass," Freddie said.

I smiled at him. "That was amazing! It was—"

But I didn't get a chance to say anything else, because that's when he swept me into his arms and kissed me.

146

I kissed him back.

I didn't hesitate, didn't think twice.

This was what I'd wanted to do ever since that first time we hung out, when we stood close on the bridge together. It felt new and exciting—but also it felt like something was finally happening that I'd been thinking about, and dreaming of, for a very long time.

My arms were around his neck and his were around my waist, pulling me close—so close it was like I could feel his heart against mine, both beating in the same rhythm.

We broke apart. Freddie rested his forehead against mine, and I could tell he was breathing as hard as I was. He pulled back slightly so that he could look in my eyes as he smoothed a piece of hair away from my forehead.

"Is that okay?" he asked, his brows knitting together. "I'm sorry—I should have asked first. I know it's kind of fast. . . ."

"It's great," I said firmly, and he laughed. "And also, let me assure you, it's *not* fast. I've been thinking about that for a very long time."

Freddie laughed and rested his hand on my cheek. "Really?"

"Really!" I reached up and finally ran my hand through his glorious curls, and the lock that always fell over his forehead. "We've had, like, thirty first dates. This has been torture."

"Well, yeah—but I don't remember any of them." He laughed again and leaned down to kiss me. I kissed him back and tried to lose myself in the moment—but his words were rattling around in my head.

I was suddenly aware, in a way that seemed to matter more than ever before, that we were not on the same page. I knew Freddie—I'd spent a ton of time with him. And this Freddie, the one kissing me right now, had only known me for a little over two hours.

But it was fine.

Wasn't it?

Freddie broke away again and lifted my hand and kissed it. "I have to go try to find the manager," he said. "I hope she liked the show."

"Of course she did. How could she not? She's wearing all black, and standing to the left of the stage. You can't miss her."

He smiled at me, the dimple flashing in his cheek. "You're the best. Maybe I can meet you by the exit? Just outside the doors?"

My heart started beating hard, but not with yay-I'm-kissing-this-cute-guy excitement—with anxiety. *Would* I be able to meet him outside the doors? I had no idea. "Yes," I said, with more confidence than I currently felt. "I'll see you then. Good luck!"

Freddie leaned down to kiss me once more, and I kissed him back, lingering for just a moment, wanting to press it into my memory, like flowers between the pages of a book—trying to preserve it.

"See you soon," he said, stepping back and giving my hand a squeeze before he started half-jogging down the hall.

My heart pounding and my thoughts swirling, I headed back to the greenroom. Alfie was nowhere to be seen—I had a feeling that he was probably dealing with the effects of the prawns. Doug was on the phone, but he gave me a smile and a thumbs-up.

I grabbed a water off the snack table, then collected my bag and jean jacket. I pulled my phone out of my purse, and smiled when I saw a stream of text messages and missed calls on my screen—from Bryony, Amy, the Emmas. The gist of all the texts seemed to be *What are you doing onstage?!*

Before I could respond to any of them, the phone in my hand vibrated with a call from Bryony. I waved goodbye to Doug as I left the greenroom, then answered the call. "Hey."

"Hey?!" Bryony echoed, her voice going much higher than usual. "Okay, we have so much to talk about because suddenly you play piano? And you did so good! And also there were such vibes with you and the lead singer! What's going on there?"

"What's going on with *you?*" I asked as I pushed my way outside. The cool night air hit me, and I pulled on my jean jacket. "I saw you and Bruce standing all close. Vibe *city*, population you two."

"You did not just say that," Bryony said, laughing, and I laughed, too. I was giddy with happiness—that this had worked, that I'd kissed Freddie, that Bryony and I could laugh and joke like this. That our friendship wasn't ruined, that I'd told her the truth, that we were okay. "Listen, they're hustling us out of here. But I'll meet you by the exit?"

"Just inside the doors," I said quickly. "Right?"

"Yeah," Bryony replied, and what we weren't talking about hung, unsaid, between us—that it might not work. That I might just get thrown back to the beginning of the night, once again.

"Great," I said. We hung up and I looked around at the crowd that was starting to disperse. There was only half an hour left of Grad Nite, and it looked like people were either heading to the exits or were trying to make the most of the time they had. Hurrying to rides, or to merch kiosks, or to try and get one last character picture. But picking a meet-up spot had been a good call on Bryony's part—I never would have been able to find her in this crowd.

"Nice job!" a girl called as she passed.

It took me a minute to realize what she was talking about—my piano playing. With a *band*, onstage. It still seemed like a wild dream—something it was going to take a minute to get my head around.

I looked down at the phone in my hand. I thought about what I'd said onstage and how good it had felt to call Harbor Cove my home. And then, before I lost my nerve, I called my dads.

I knew it was safe to call Angelo's cell phone—he turned it off every night, so it wasn't like the call would wake him up. I smiled as I heard the recording of his voice—and then when the *beep* sounded, I took a deep breath.

"Hi, it's me. It's Cass. I'm at Grad Nite—everything is fine. I just need to talk to you guys about something." I started to walk toward the exit with the crowd. Somehow, it felt easier to do this while I was in motion. "I don't want to go to Oregon. I want to stay in Harbor Cove this summer.

I've moved around too much, and I don't want to leave this time. I want to spend the summer with my friends, get a job . . ."

I hesitated, then took a big breath and made myself say it. "I feel like we've never talked about this. But it's been really hard for me, moving around so much. And I know I didn't always handle it well—but I'm trying to change that now. So I wanted to tell you how I was feeling."

I started walking faster now, dodging my way through the crowd. "And I know it's going to be complicated. But I think we can figure something out. You guys are the experts at renovations, after all. So I'm hoping we can just retool the summer plan a little." I felt myself smile. "I really miss you both. Love you. Okay, talk soon."

My feet slowed, and I dropped my phone in my bag. I felt so much lighter—like the last weight that had been on my shoulders had been lifted, once and for all.

"Hey, Cass." I looked over and saw that I was in front of Johnny's merchandise kiosk. I glanced down at my bag and saw that the monogram was turned inward—there was no way he could have looked at it and read my name—which meant he'd already known it. I had a feeling he'd known a lot of things.

"Hey, Johnny," I said. I was too far away to have read his name tag, but he didn't seem surprised that I knew him. It was like we were finally on the same page.

"Did you have a good night?" he asked. He raised an eyebrow. "Did you do everything you wanted to?"

I nodded, thinking over the night. The way I'd been able to fix things. The truths I'd told. The way I'd finally taken accountability for my mistakes. And then playing with the band, kissing Freddie . . . I smiled. "It was a night to remember," I said simply. "It was pretty perfect."

Johnny gave me an appraising look. "I'm glad to hear it." He reached for something and held it out to me. "That reminds me—I put something aside for you."

I took a step closer, not quite able to believe what I was seeing. He was holding out the graduation Mickey ears—the ones that Bryony had wanted and that I'd never been able to find. "Finally," I said, smiling as I took them from him.

He shrugged. "I just found a pair in the back, that's all."

"Sure." I laughed as I handed him the money. "Well—thank you."

Johnny handed me back my change, giving me a nod. "I'm happy you had a great night, Cass. That's all we want for the seniors who participate in Grad Nite. A life-changing experience."

"Well, it was certainly that." I looked at him, my thoughts spinning. There was so much I wanted to ask him. How this worked, and why, and most importantly—was it over? Would I be able to walk through the doors and into the rest of my life?

"So . . . did you find what you were looking for?"

I turned over the ears in my hand, but I knew that wasn't what he was talking about. "I really did."

Johnny smiled at me, a twinkle in his eye. "I'm glad to hear it. Good luck, Cass."

I smiled back at him and knew that this wasn't the moment to pepper him with questions. "I'll see you around, Johnny." I put the ears in my bag, and then I turned and started walking toward the exit.

146

I was nearly to the exit when I saw my familiar bench—and Amy sitting on it, looking miserable. I stopped and detoured over to her. She gave me a watery smile as I sat down next to her. All around us, people were streaming toward the wooden exit doors. They were being corralled by their chaperones, and I could hear instructions being yelled about buses and locations. I knew we didn't have a ton of time—but we had a moment or two.

"Carlos and I broke up," Amy said, her voice cracking.

"I know," I said with a sigh.

Amy stared at me in surprise. "What do you mean, you *know*?"

"Just . . ." I thought about how to put this. "I'm really sorry, Amy. But I think some things are what they are. And you can't change them, even if you try." That was the conclusion I'd finally come to, watching Amy and Carlos over all these Grad Nites. They rarely fought about the same thing, but they always, *always* seemed to get into a fight. Like both of them were just done, and changing the circumstances didn't change that. "Maybe you guys have just run your course. And it doesn't mean that what you had wasn't great. But maybe it's time to be Amy. And Carlos. And not AmyandCarlos. You know?"

Amy swallowed hard and wiped her hand over her face. She gave me a watery smile. "When did you get so wise?"

I laughed at that as I stood up. "It's been a long night. You pick up on things." I nodded toward the doors. "Are you coming?"

"I'll be there in just a sec," she said, pulling her sweatshirt around her a little more tightly. "Just need a moment."

I nodded and started toward the exit. How many times had I walked through those doors? More than I could count—and only to be brought right back again. What would happen now? My feet slowed, then stopped, and I could feel my heart pounding in my ears.

"Cass!" I looked over to see Bryony walking toward me—*holding hands with Bruce*. Bruce gave me a small, embarrassed smile, but Bryony seemed thrilled. She was no longer nervously playing with her bangs—she just looked happy and smitten.

"Hi, *you two*," I said, raising my eyebrows at them.

"Okay, enough of that," Bryony said, even though she was smiling widely. She gestured between Bruce and me. "I believe you two have met?"

Bruce laughed at that, and I shook my head. "Funny."

"So we should go, right?" Bruce asked, as he started to walk toward the exit. "We don't want to miss the buses."

"Right," I said, even though my feet didn't move. I was just staring at the doors in front of me. I could feel the hope fluttering in my chest—would this be the moment? Or would all of this just be erased? Was I about to be looped back around, Sheridan yelling about having the best night ever?

"Uh—is everything okay, Cass?" Bruce asked.

"She's fine," Bryony said firmly. She dropped Bruce's hand and came over to stand next to me.

"I just . . ." I said quietly. "What if it doesn't work? What if I just go back to the beginning again?"

"It'll be okay," she said, her eyes meeting mine reassuringly.

When I spoke, my voice was barely a whisper, like I was afraid to even say it out loud. "But what if it's not?"

She took my hand and gave it a squeeze. "Then you'll tell me what's happening, and we'll figure it out together. Until we get it right."

I swallowed around the lump that had formed in my throat. "Promise?"

She smiled at me. "I promise."

I closed my eyes for just a moment, concentrating. *I understand now*, I thought as hard as I could. *I don't want to do things over—I just want to move forward. I don't want to run away anymore. I want things to stick, whatever the consequences might be. No more ghosting. No more clean slates. Even if I make mistakes, I want them to matter—with the chance to do better.* I let out a long, shaky breath and opened my eyes. "Okay," I finally said. I looked at the doors.

"Everything all right?" Bruce asked.

"Everything's great," Bryony said, her eyes steady on mine. "Ready?"

I nodded. "Ready." I gave her hand a squeeze, then dropped it.

And then I walked through the doors.

SATURDAY, JUNE 10TH

W ho had the best night ever?" Sheridan yelled.

I blinked as I looked around.

I was on the other side of the doors.

I whirled around to look behind me. I could see people walking past, I could see the park on the other side—but I was *out*. I was through.

Time was moving forward.

"Oh my god!" I yelled to Bryony, who rushed up to me.

"It worked!" she yelled, and I pulled her into a hug.

"It worked," I said. My heart was pounding hard, and relief flooded through me. I was now on the same page as everyone else. I wouldn't have the cheat codes. I wouldn't know how every situation would turn out. I'd have to go through life figuring things out—or not—the first time around, with no do-overs. But I could keep going. People would remember conversations we'd had, and Freddie . . .

My mind snagged on the thought. *Freddie.*

"What worked?" Bruce asked, sounding baffled. "We just . . . walked through the doors."

"It's a big deal," I promised him.

"Very," Bryony agreed.

"I think I missed something," he said to Bryony, who laughed.

"Bruce has to get his bus," she said to me, "so we were going to go say goodbye. I'll meet you on ours?"

I nodded, still getting my head around the fact that I no longer had a script for the night—that we were moving in real time now. And if I messed up, I'd only have one shot—just like everyone else.

Bruce waved goodbye and then they were off. I stood there for just a moment, my thoughts whirling.

"Hi, there." I looked over to see Freddie jogging up. He pulled me into a hug, and I hugged him back. We stood there together for just a moment, and I just let myself enjoy it—how right it felt. How natural. He stepped back, smiling wide. "You made it!" he said. "You're out!"

I smiled back at him. "I am. It finally worked."

"How are you feeling?"

"Good. A little overwhelmed."

"Well, that's understandable. How many loops did you do? You must have been there a while."

"Almost a hundred and fifty? I think?" Freddie's eyes widened.

"Wow. That—that is a lot."

"Wait," I said, remembering. "What happened with the manager?"

Freddie's face broke into an excited, hopeful smile. "It went really well.

She said she liked my stage presence—and especially the new song. She wants me to work on it. Nothing's official yet, but we're going to meet next week. It's looking good, I think?"

"Oh my gosh—that's amazing!" This was what I'd wanted for him, all those times I was trying to figure out how to prevent disaster—this happy ending.

"Yeah, it's really exciting," he said, shaking his head. "I can't thank you enough. Without you, none of this would be happening."

"You did it," I pointed out. "I just helped get rid of some of the obstacles, that's all."

"So I was thinking, maybe next weekend, if you're free, we could meet up? I'd love to take you on a proper date. Maybe dinner? Just not—"

"Pizza," I finished for him. "Because you had that disastrous first date at the Pizza Express. And ever since then, you've been superstitious about it."

"Uh, right." Freddie nodded, but he looked taken aback. "I guess . . . we talked about a lot, huh?"

"Yeah." I could feel the smile fading from my face. "We really did." I looked up at him—at the face that was so familiar to me—then glanced away again.

"So—something other than pizza," Freddie said, his voice sounding like he was trying to make it cheerful. "What do you think?"

"I think . . ." I said slowly. I took a breath. "I think that I meant it when I said that it felt like we'd had thirty first dates already. Because that's how it is for me. I've spent all this time with you, and you've told me all these stories. I know you really well. And for you—I'm someone you met three hours ago."

Freddie took a step closer to me, his forehead creasing in confusion. "I mean, technically that's true. But…what are you saying?"

I shook my head. "I'm saying that doesn't seem fair, you know? I literally have a list full of facts about you. It's like I have the cheat codes. And I don't know if we can . . . start anything with that kind of imbalance."

Freddie shook his head, even as I could tell he was processing this. "I don't . . . That's not . . ."

"I really like you," I said. "But that's because I *know* you. And you don't know me at all." I knew this was the truth the moment I said it—it hit me somewhere deep inside.

"I'm sure we can figure it out, right?" Freddie asked. But there wasn't a ton of conviction in his voice, and I could see that he'd come to the same realization that I had.

"I don't think so." I felt the weight of these words land as I spoke them.

"Cass, let's go!" I looked over and saw Ms. Mulaney walking past. She tapped her watch. "Bus is going to leave soon."

"Okay," I called back. "Be right there."

I looked at Freddie, and he gave me a sad smile. I stepped forward and gave him a hug. He hugged me back, and I let myself breathe him in for just a moment—the last time I'd get to do this.

Then I broke away and looked up at him. "Take care, okay?"

He nodded, his smile trying to mask the disappointment in his eyes. "You too, Cass."

I gave him one last look, then turned and hurried across the parking lot, ready to rejoin my class, and get on the bus—the one that would, at last, take me home.

Part Six

What is the purpose of having endless chances if you don't learn something from them? Don't get frustrated—just try and implement what you discovered. Learn from it. And try again.

—*Excalibur!* video game manual, page 55

WEDNESDAY, JULY 19TH

C ass, can you give me a hand?"

I looked up from counting my tip money to see Bryony heading toward me, tray full of drinks in hand.

"Of course," I said, tucking my cash into my turquoise apron, the one covered in tiny tridents. "What do you need?"

"Diet Coke," she said, nodding toward the soda station.

"Got it." I filled up a glass with ice and picked up the soda gun. I garnished it with a lemon wedge and a straw—this was all second nature by now.

Bryony and I had both gotten jobs at the Mermaid Café after all. And despite the fact that waitressing was *hard*—my feet had never hurt this much in my life, and I had a faint scar on my hand from when I'd had a collision with a fellow waiter and a plate of very hot fajitas—we were also having a blast.

The other servers were a lot of fun, and Bryony and I had been able to get most of our shifts together. Since we were still new to the restaurant, we didn't have any of the best ones yet; we weren't going to get a Friday or Saturday night shift unless someone called in sick. Those were the prime tipping times, and not for the newbies. So mostly, we had lunch shifts and brunch—I'd learned the hard way that nobody wanted brunch. But I didn't mind. I'd even started something called Brunch of Questions!—which was a quiz brunch that had a few dedicated followers who came every week. Greta and Nora had been instrumental in helping with the trivia.

The morning after Grad Nite, my dads and I had sat around the kitchen table in the house and had a big conversation—one that had been a long time coming. I explained how I wanted to stay in Harbor Cove, that I'd been moving too much, and I didn't want to do it again before college.

And after a lot of discussion, we'd worked out a system. The house still hadn't sold yet, so three nights a week, one of my dads came down and stayed with me—they alternated, while the other one stayed behind in Oregon, keeping that renovation on track. The other days, I usually stayed with Bryony. Her parents were fine with it, and we loved it—it felt like an extended sleepover, especially since we got to hang out at work, too. And because we would be going our separate ways in September, we were trying to soak up as much friend time as we could.

Bryony and Bruce were still going strong, despite the fact that they were long-distance. She was saving up her tip money to fly up to Seattle to see him, and they'd been overjoyed to find out that they would both be going to University of Washington in the fall. So, if it was a long-distance relationship now, that was only going to be a temporary condition.

As for me—it had taken me a while to get used to my non-loop life. Even though it was what I had wanted, being back in the world without a net had been an adjustment. I was now in touch regularly with Reagan and Zach, and Greta and Nora. I wasn't sure we would ever be close friends again, but every time one of them texted or popped up in my social media feeds, I was always happy to see them.

I had also stayed in touch with Alfie and Doug. It seemed that Niall hadn't taken kindly to how much better the band had been received with Freddie as lead singer. He'd thrown a tantrum for the ages and gotten fired from Eton Mess. Apparently, he was back in England. Alfie had gone back to Australia, and Doug had returned to Chicago. He was playing in a band called Hot Beef and assured me it was good, even though the name made me have my doubts.

I hadn't followed Freddie on social media, but I would occasionally look at his page—until it started hurting too much and I had to log off. But I was thrilled to see that things seemed to be working out for him. He'd left Eton Mess, signed a record deal, and was posting a lot of pictures in a recording studio in LA as he worked on his first album. It was everything he'd wanted, and the fact that his dream had come true—and that I'd been able to help it happen—made me beyond thrilled.

And sometimes, when I would look at these pictures of him, I would feel sharply just how much I missed him and remember just how magical our connection had felt. And that was usually when I forced myself to set my phone down.

Now I placed the Diet Coke on Bryony's tray. "Here you go."

"Thanks," she said, giving me a grateful smile. "You're done for the day?"

"Yeah, all my tables left. I'm just tipping out." I nodded toward the corner of the restaurant, where one of our favorite regulars was in her normal spot. "Is she doing okay?"

Bryony nodded. "She's great. She wants to talk to you about a problem she's having with the middle, though."

I grinned. "Happy to." Like she knew we were talking about her, Ms. Mulaney glanced over at us and waved, and both Bryony and I waved back. She'd revised her book, tweaked the ending, and had found an agent she really liked. They were working on her manuscript together, and hopes were high that she'd sell it in the fall. Ms. Mulaney had taken to coming into the café several times a week, always after the lunch rush, to work on the novel and drink a series of iced teas that she always over-tipped on.

"I'll see you back at home?" I asked, as I untied the apron from my waist. This was one of the days I was staying with Bryony—we'd already decided we were going to get sushi for dinner.

She pulled out her phone, smiled at something she saw there, and then nodded. "Sure," she said. "Sounds good. But before that, can you just go check on table nineteen?"

"Nineteen?" That table was on the patio and wasn't even in my section—it was in Bryony's.

"Yeah, can you just swing by, offer water and drop off a menu? It's just one guest, and I'm a little slammed."

"Of course," I said, giving her a nod. "No problem."

"Thanks," she called, heading back into the dining room. "Have fun!"

"Have *fun*?" I echoed, confused, but Bryony was already out of earshot. Shaking my head, I grabbed several menus and headed out to the patio.

It was a pretty perfect late-afternoon day. The sun was out but not shining in your eyes—it was breezy and warm but not too hot. I headed over to nineteen, already putting on my professional smile as I reached the table. "Hello, welcome to the Mermaid—" I started, then stopped short when I saw who was sitting there.

Freddie.

He looked a little bit different. He'd gotten a haircut, even though I was happy to see that the lock of hair was still falling over his forehead. And his clothes were a little sharper, as though he'd gone through the rising-star-wardrobe upgrade. But his expression was heartbreakingly familiar to me—excited and nervous and happy.

"Hi, Cass," he said, running a hand through his hair. "I was hoping we could talk?"

"But . . ." I looked over and saw Bryony standing in the doorway. She met my eye and gave me a smile. I shook my head, realizing that I'd been tricked—but finding it hard to be all that mad about it.

"So," I said, as I pulled out the chair across from Freddie and sat down. "You and Bryony arranged this?"

Freddie nodded, giving me a smile. "I hope you don't mind. We've been talking a bit."

I blinked at that, surprised. "About what?"

"About you." I took a breath to respond, but Freddie continued on. "I've really missed you, Cass. And I know what you said was true—that I only knew you for a few hours. But that's enough sometimes, don't you think? To know that you like someone? Every time something good happens, you're the first person I want to tell."

I looked down at the table to hide my smile—it felt like warmth was spreading through my chest. "Oh yeah?"

Freddie nodded. "Yeah. And I know that you had the whole list about me, and you told me how that wasn't fair. So." He reached down into the messenger bag at his feet and pulled out a piece of paper. I leaned forward and saw that *Cass* was written on the top of it.

"What is that?" I said, even as I felt like I knew.

"It's your list," he said, giving me a nervous smile. "I filled it in with what I knew. About how kind you were to me. And how brave. And how you worked so hard to help me." I looked down at the paper, then up at him. "I feel like what's on here is the real you—and that's the most important stuff. And all the rest of it is just details."

I could feel my eyes fill with tears—but the happy kind. The kind you get when something overwhelmingly good happens.

"And so—if you'd be interested—I'd love to know everything else about you."

I laughed at that, meeting Freddie's eye across the table. All at once, I could see another way forward for us. Not where I knew everything about him and he didn't know me, but a middle ground, where we could figure it out. Together.

"That sounds good," I said, and I saw the look of relief pass over Freddie's face.

"Really?" he asked, his eyes searching mine.

"Absolutely," I said. I smiled and leaned across the table toward him. "I've got nothing but time."

Acknowledgments

First and foremost, I must gratefully acknowledge my fantastic editor, Brittany Rubiano. This book turned out to be way more complicated than we'd anticipated (Time loops are *tricky*??? Who knew?) but you were so brilliant and patient and enthusiastic the whole way through. There's nobody I'd rather wander around Grad Nite with! In the course of research for this book, I was lucky enough to get to attend Disney Grad Nite (twice!). Thank you so much to Melina Mata for making it happen—I'm so appreciative.

Thank you to Emily Van Beek and Veronica Meliksetian of Folio; Corrine Aquino of Artists First; and Austin Denesuk, Ellen Jones, and Kelly Berger of CAA—I'm so lucky to be on this team.

Huge thanks to Isadora Zeferino for another adorable cover, and to Marci Senders for the fantastic cover design. Thank you to Cassandra Phan, Sara Liebling, Guy Cunningham, David Jaffe, Dan Kaufman, Holly Nagel, Danielle DiMartino, Dina Sherman, Bekka Mills, Maddie Hughes, Matt Schweitzer, Crystal McCoy, Monique Diman, Vicki Korlishin,

Meredith Lisbin, Jerry Gonzalez, Augusta Harris, and Holly Rice at Disney Hyperion for all your incredible work.

And thank you to my friends, family, and terrier—you are all (particularly Murphy, sorry but it's true) the best.